MONSTERS

MONSTERS BEHIND THE GATES

A DETECTIVE NOVEL

JAMES REID

JAVERY GROUP ™
PUBLISHING

Published by Javery Group Publishing 2017
P.O. Box 1685 | Frisco, Texas 75034 USA
javerygroup@gmail.com

Book design copyright © 2017 by James Reid. All rights reserved.

Published in the United States of America
ISBN: 978-0-9977893-1-7
1. Fiction / Mystery & Detective / Police Procedural

DEDICATION

I dedicate this to my mother and father, Rose and Henry.
I love you and wouldn't be here without you.

ACKNOWLEDGMENTS

First, to Rose and Henry; my sisters, Ashley and Kirstin; my aunts, Lorraine and Carolyn; and my cousins, Kristina and Peaches (I still can't believe you're gone, Peaches. I love and miss you). All of you encouraged me to finish this project even when writer's block hit me multiple times. You helped me stay on course.

To Detective Tyus, Major Lee, Desmond, and Kim Jones, for giving me insight into a world hidden from most. This would not have been possible without your help.

To Dimple, CJ, Keshia Lynn, Joe, Kathie, Becky, Norma, Benn, Jaselyn, and Evita, who were my early guinea pigs in reading, critiquing my material, and putting me in touch with resources.

To Rafaela, for introducing me to my copy editor, Trai Cartwright.

To Trai, for providing the guidance for turning this project into an actual story and for giving me constructive criticism.

To my fellow writers, Kathryn, Marsha, and Helen, for supporting me.

And of course, I must thank my beautiful wife Jewel. From Day One, you believed in me. Your support and optimism have never waned, not even when the inevitable moments of doubt and frustration hit me. I love you, and I'm blessed to have you beside me.

There aren't enough pages to list everyone who supported and encouraged me, so if I have not included you, please know it wasn't an oversight. I appreciate all of you.

Last, and certainly not least, I thank God for all of the blessings he has given me.

CHAPTER 1

SATURDAY, JULY 26TH, 2003

There was something different about the naked woman in front of me.

She wasn't the average homicide victim found on Atlanta's west side. Most of them were already in bad shape when they were alive, long before someone decided to get rid of them. They usually had the same telltale characteristics; scars, faded tattoos, or gaunt faces resulting from steady diets of crack or meth. They were also frequently malnourished. Most of their bodies looked as if God had draped leathery skin over their bones and left the rest unfinished. One could argue that they'd been euthanized instead of murdered.

Not this lady. She had the physique of a swimsuit model. The woman was a palette of earth colors, with light-tan skin, ruby red nails, and dark-brown hair tinged with wisps of bronze highlights. She lay on a soiled mattress with her legs spread apart. Her breasts were round and firm and complemented her slim waist and serpentine hips. She didn't have leathery skin with blurred, faded tattoos. No reed-thin legs or arms pocked with needle marks and sores. I studied her and thought of one thing.

Who'd you piss off, lady? Who killed you and threw you in this hellhole?

Someone had covered her face with an oily rag. Dried tendrils of reddish-black blood had trickled from under it and down her neck. Several thin marks about an inch long clustered a few inches below her navel. Stab wounds. The punctures were clean and precise slits.

I stood in a small field thirty yards east of Jones Street, a street snaking through a poor neighborhood a few miles west of downtown. Although it was two-thirty in the morning, I plodded in a broth of humid air. My sinuses made me feel as if I had damp cotton jammed in my nose. I tugged at my wet shirt to circulate air across my chest, cursing the heat wave smothering the city.

Jones Street was asphalt when it left the neighborhood but became a dirt path as it traveled along the field's edge. The road was littered with cigarette butts and broken wine bottles deposited by generations of bums and winos. To my right were towering pine trees that blocked the glow of the city lights to the east. The dirt path stretched a few hundred feet, winding away from the field before spilling into a second poor neighborhood and becoming a paved street again.

The area was strewn with moldy sofa cushions, rotting tires, diapers caked with fossilized shit, and other garbage. But it had its uses. It was dark and secluded. Local prostitutes, all of them finalists for the World's Ugliest Transvestite, picked up tricks in Midtown and brought them here to earn ten bucks a blow.

Years ago, I spent many nights here when I was on patrol with the Atlanta Police Department (APD). When boredom struck, my partner and I lurked nearby and waited for a pro and his trick to show up. Once a couple arrived and got down to business, we snuck behind them and scared the hell out of them by flashing our lights and screaming through the loudspeaker for them to exit the vehicle. Often, the tricks would fall on their hands and knees, clasping their hands together and begging for leniency. Many were married white men in their '40's who dreaded the thought of friends and family discovering their weakness for black transvestites. They blubbered like snotty toddlers, and I bit my lip as I tried not to laugh. Once we got our comedy fix, we let them off with warnings and howled with laughter as they peeled away in clouds of dust.

Ah, the good ol' days. I sighed and looked around. Yellow

police tape cordoned off a six-hundred-square-foot grid around me, and our lights penetrated the darkness. Crime scene technicians (CSTs) processed the area and searched in a tight radius around the body. The dead woman lay in a small clearing in the surrounding garbage, as if someone had reserved a special area for her.

Several uniforms wandered outside the scene with blank expressions. I introduced myself. "Jefferson Strickland, lead investigator." My co-workers called me Strick, and to my friends I was Jeff, but I always introduced myself formally. It made me feel like an Atlantan James Bond. "Any of you take this call?"

One of them stepped forward. "I did."

I pulled out my worn notepad, the start of the case file for the unfortunate woman at my feet, and wrote the uniform's name and number. Officer Donald Bagley. Tiny orange freckles clustered on his nose and cheeks and he looked around with wide eyes. "Alright, Donnie boy," I said. "Tell me what you saw and heard when you got here."

"I had just left a call about a half hour ago...it was a domestic. This lady stabbed her husband in the balls—I mean, groin—with a fork after she found a rubber in the trash—"

"Focus. Tell me about this." I pointed at the body.

"Yes. Well, after I left that call, dispatch called about a body, uh...a *decedent*...right here. It was an anonymous call."

Of course it was anonymous. No one wanted to explain to the police what he was doing out here at this hour to stumble across a dead woman. "Anyone here touch her? Or that cloth covering her face?"

"No, sir."

"Good. You handled your first homicide well."

"Is it that obvious?"

"You keep staring at her like she's going to grab you." I considered doing a prank with the body to scare him, but decided not to. He was so green that he might've quit on the spot. The city already struggled with finding enough officers to put on the streets. I suspected it had something to do with the dangerous work, long hours, and less-than-stellar pay. Whatever the reason, I didn't want the brass blaming me for making our constant staff shortage worse.

"So do you guys find a lot out here?" he asked.

I examined the mattress underneath the dead woman. "A lot of what?"

"Victims. They say we get a lot of homicides in this area. They're usually prostitutes, aren't they?"

"Some of them."

"Why do they come out here? Don't they know it's dangerous?"

"They've got bills to pay and habits to feed. And not all of them are helpless. Most of them are dudes. They even rob their own tricks sometimes."

He recoiled. "They're trannies? Do their tricks know that?"

"They'd have to. The only way you'd mistake one of those ugly-ass dudes for a woman is if you've never seen a woman before. Hey, see those apartments over there? Behind those trees? Get some guys together and find some witnesses for me."

Bagley glanced at his watch. "But it's quarter to three in the morning."

"It's summer. There'll be people outside, standing around, doing nothing. They may have seen or heard something." I didn't expect him to find any witnesses. I just wanted him and his questions elsewhere.

"Strick!" boomed a voice behind me. It was Austin Wills, another detective on my shift. "Where have you been?" he asked. The man had a heavy Georgia accent, smothered under a thick twang. It was a fusion of Deep-South trailer park and Barry White.

"I already told you," I replied. "I was working leads."

Wills ducked his 6'3" frame under the police tape. His

reddish-blonde hair glistened under the lights like fire. He had a hawk-like nose and a square, cinder block head. If it weren't for the police shield clipped on his waist, he'd look like a super-villain.

He looked down at the woman. "What's up with this one?"

"I don't know yet. I'm curious what we'll see under that rag. I feel a nasty surprise coming."

"Witnesses?"

"Please." I touched her neck.

She was cool, despite the muggy, sauna-like temperature. There were few insects on her despite the racket of crickets and other bugs singing in the night. The dependable blowfly was absent. The insects lay their eggs on bodies, and the larvae help investigators estimate times of death. Given her temperature and lack of insect activity, I guessed the killer had dumped her in the field shortly before Bagley responded to the call.

"Where's the ME?" I mumbled. The sooner the medical examiner or his assistants arrived to inspect the body, the sooner we could leave. My shirt clung to me like Saran Wrap. Slaps and curses filled the night as kamikaze mosquitoes fed on exposed skin.

Wills eyed me. "You weren't working when I called you earlier. You were fooling with Stephanie. Admit it."

"Wrong. That's over now."

"About time. You should've dropped her a while ago."

It was a lie. I was on the phone with her when Wills called to tell me there was a fresh murder on Jones Street and I was next in the rotation. Stephanie had just given me the "it's not you, it's me" speech, a rejection I brushed off with several shots of cheap tequila. If Wills hadn't called me repeatedly, I would've been unconscious on my floor by now. "She gave me the speech."

He clucked his teeth and shook his head. "Didn't you give her five hundred to fix her car last month?"

"Eight hundred."

"Dumb ass."

Stephanie, an attractive and affable thirty-seven-year-old, had snagged me at a nightclub several months ago. She told me my brown eyes lured her from across the room, and my navy shirt complemented my bronze skin. She also said I had unique features and a mysterious aura. After we had danced and talked, she invited me to her apartment that night.

My shield was an aphrodisiac for some women, but it was Stephanie's anger at her cheating husband that fueled her sexual aggression. I never questioned her motives. I had my demons to battle, namely, the haunting memories of my ex-wife Erica. It hurt remembering how she could freeze me with her dimpled smile and warm touch. I needed to forget my divorce, and Stephanie was the prescription. But what started as a pleasure-filled coping mechanism had backfired. She had snatched the last lifeboat and jumped ship, leaving me on a sinking *Titanic*.

"I'd get my money back if I were you," Wills advised, lathering his words in that snarky tone that only friends can use without inviting an ass-kicking. "I'd sue the hell out of her. See if she's got some unpaid tickets. Put a boot on that car you paid to fix. Her ass wouldn't be driving anywhere if it were up to me—"

"Shut up and help me sweep so we can get out of here." I slapped at a fat mosquito on my arm, leaving a smear of blood. We had to keep moving; standing still for even a second made us targets for unrelenting waves of nasty pests.

Most of the uniforms had gone to canvass for witnesses, so only two officers joined our sweep of the field. We fanned thirty feet outside the perimeter of the yellow tape and circled back toward the body, scanning for anything unusual.

Several yards inside the boundary, we found a shower curtain lying atop the brittle crabgrass. It was dense and transparent, with a band of gold cloth embroidered at the foot of the curtain and silver triangles and circles in the middle. Reddish-black droplets and smears, most likely blood, stained some of the symbols. The rest of the curtain appeared clean and didn't have the weathered look of the surrounding garbage. The CSTs secured it as we continued scouring the field.

My stomach clenched as I looked around. The chance of finding trace evidence in this mess was like finding a particular grain of sand in the desert. The shower curtain was an obvious find, but nothing else stood out. It was 360 degrees of filth. A couple of the less-tenured CSTs were probably reconsidering their career choices. There was no "CSI" glamor in crawling through trash, searching for things that may or may not be evidence. Dodging drug needles and sharp metal objects, or smelling the stench of brownish-green substances and rotten condoms? Yeah, they never showed that on TV. No Hollywood cameras caught us recoiling from rats or snakes slithering from crevices. And there was no promise we'd find the clues that would lead us to the killer and squeeze a confession in sixty minutes with commercial breaks.

Bureaucracy was another problem. The APD had no crime lab capable of performing complex forensic tests, so we relied on the Georgia Bureau of Investigation (GBI) in nearby Decatur to complete them. But every police department in the state had the same idea. Inundated with requests (mainly ours), the GBI had placed a limit on the number of items that each police department could submit for a case—twelve. That was all right if the crime scene was a locked bathroom without windows.

But a trash dump?

Anything had the potential to be evidence. If it wasn't something that was out of place or screamed for attention, like a knife coated in blood, it was hard to tell what was related to the crime. I glanced at the rusted washing machine behind me. There were sun-bleached, cracked rubber tires to my right and the rusted chassis of a Chevy Caprice to my left. It was possible the killer touched them as he left the field. But more than likely, if we were to find any fresh prints, they would probably belong to some local junk man who had examined them to see if the items were worth selling. We could spend a lot of time and money we didn't have testing these things, just to come up with nothing.

An investigator from the Fulton County Medical Examiners Center (FCMEC) arrived. A wispy man named Paul, his job was to make a preliminary examination, and if necessary, request the ME to come to the scene. I waved him over to the body.

"She's all yours," I said. "Feel free to hurry the hell up." The mosquitoes were tearing our skin apart; swatting didn't help. I wanted to get back to safety indoors. "By the way, I touched her neck."

He wagged his bony finger. "Who told you to mess with my body?"

"Relax. I saved the best for you."

Paul whipped out a digital recorder and began dictating. He studied the cloth covering the woman's head and the streams of dried blood that led from under it.

He removed the rag.

We saw why the killer covered her face.

CHAPTER 2

"Jesus Christ," Wills exclaimed.

Her head resembled a plastic doll with its face smashed. A messy stew of flesh, hair, dried blood, and bone. I'd seen severe beatings before, but nothing like this.

Typically, Wills and I made nicknames for our case victims. It was a low-tech stress-reliever that added levity to a job sorely in need of it. The pimp we found charred to a crisp and thrown in a dumpster behind a McDonald's on Cleveland Avenue last year? SuperFry. The man shot through the eye and stuffed in an oil drum for selling fake cocaine to the wrong man? Bum-in-a-Drum.

I didn't think of a nickname for this woman. Even in this heat, I felt a chill as I pictured the murderer's rage. Crushing her face meant he despised this woman. It also meant he knew her; few strangers are motivated to bludgeon someone to such a degree. The location was also revealing. We were in a secluded area, and with its twists, turns, and dirt paths, no one happened on it by accident. The killer knew both the area and the victim well.

Her right shoulder and arm were stiff from rigor mortis. Lividity, the discoloration that appears when blood settles in the lowermost parts of the body, had stained her back a dark purple. Despite the carnage to her face, there was little blood on the rest of her body or the piss-stained mattress underneath her. The field was just a dumping ground; the actual murder occurred elsewhere.

Her fingertips looked like burnt pieces of charcoal. A couple of her nails were torn, and her knuckles were cracked and blistered. Paul covered her hands with a paper bag.

Establishing an ID would be a challenge. She had no face.

No bodily marks or tattoos. Her charred fingers would probably reveal no good prints. It wouldn't surprise me if her killer pulled out her teeth to keep us from using her dental records. I didn't bother looking at what used to be her mouth.

One of the officers called me to a spot near the street. She pointed at a sparkling object at her feet. It was a silver tag bracelet with an engraved heart attached. I picked it up with tweezers. It was smudged with dirt and specks of blood, but the name was legible.

I couldn't breathe.

The ground started to spin, and my chest ached.

God, no, this can't be her.

CHAPTER 3

The memories of that summer day several years ago came rushing to me.

Before I could bring the rental van to a complete stop, ten-year-old Kanya Lanise Glover bailed out and challenged the other kids to race to the gates of Atlanta's Six Flags amusement park.

As the children dispersed from the vehicle, I shouted for Kanya to wait for everyone. Erica, my wife at the time, glanced at me and smiled. "I told you not to buy them ice cream before we got here."

Kanya slowed down to let the other six children catch up. When a boy named Larry got within five feet of her, she streaked to the gate and proclaimed herself the fastest. Arguments ensued, and the children shouted like traders at a stock exchange.

While Erica was amused to watch me struggle controlling seven children on sugar highs, I prayed for the strength to be Daddy Day Care. Growing up in Columbia, MD, a suburb nestled outside Baltimore, I was spared the poverty commonly found in the Atlanta neighborhoods where I spent most of my shifts. I had the silly idea of providing a small group of at-risk kids some exposure by taking them to museums and parks and showing them a life beyond the confines of the projects. Seeing those kids laugh gave me hope that some of them would one day escape their miserable environments. Or at least have fun for a few hours.

That was how I ended up refereeing a track dispute in the Six Flags parking lot.

Every summer, I took a handful of kids there. But Kanya was unlike the others. They were a motley crew of predominately black and Latino kids, but she was Eurasian, the daughter of a

Thai woman and a white American man. She lived in an upper-class community with soaring property values rather than an eyesore of project housing that the city wanted to condemn. Ever since I met her and her family, she had treated me like an uncle, practicing the Thai custom of "Wai," or bowing in respect when greeting me. So after hearing of my field trips for at-risk kids, she begged to come along. Although the other kids knew she was my favorite, they didn't resent her. She made friends easily, and her playfulness and warm smile drew them to her.

Except when they accused her of cheating.

"Mr. Strick, Kanya cheated," Larry bellowed. "She ain't even let me catch up before she started running!"

When I agreed, Kanya dropped her jaw at my betrayal. "You were back at the van! You couldn't even see us!"

"Okay, you see that over there?" I pointed to a lamppost fifty yards away. "You two go over there. When I say 'go,' you run back here, and whoever is first, wins. Okay?"

"I'ma beat you this time," Larry boasted. He was a year older than Kanya, but the girl was blessed with her father's genes, so she was lankier and two inches taller. The other kids watched with great interest, little spectators with front-row seats to the southwest Atlanta Olympic gold-medal race.

When the runners were ready, I gave the 'go' signal. It was no contest. Kanya whipped Larry, who came down with a sudden, mysterious injury after falling behind halfway through the race. The kids tore into him as he limped to the finish line.

"Ha ha," screeched a kid named Bill. "Man, you ain't hurt! Kanya beat your ass!"

"Shut up, punk," Larry snarled. "Before I punch you in your mouth!"

As the two eleven-year-olds cursed like drill sergeants, I shouted that the trip was over. I had a zero-tolerance policy for fighting or cursing—they could do that at home on their own time. The rest of the kids turned on the two with furious complaints, so they made peace with glares and mumbled threats. When we entered the park and gazed at the crests of roller coasters peaking over the trees, everyone forgot the near-altercation, and Larry's limp healed instantly.

Immediately, Kanya yanked me toward The Big Terror, the park's largest coaster. I didn't like the looks of the imposing metal monster. "Let's ride something else, Kanya."

"But you *never* want to get on them! I need a grown-up to ride with me! They won't let me ride by myself."

"What about the Comet?"

She stomped her foot and pouted. "That's a kiddie ride!"

"And you're a kid."

"I'm ten! I can ride the Big Terror if you go with me. I'm tall enough."

I groaned as I looked at the huge blue-gray tentacles of steel rails and pipes, stretching up, up, into the sky. Old nightmares came to me. More specifically, thoughts of Rhonda Janes, the prettiest girl in my twelfth-grade class. I had persuaded her to go with me to Kings Dominion amusement park in Virginia. My ego demanded we tackle the biggest ride there. Seconds after we strapped ourselves in, I discovered that sausage, cotton candy, and an unknown predisposition for motion sickness didn't mix—and I splattered the toxic mixture on her lap. My hope of losing my virginity that night vanished, as well as any chance I had with other cuties in school once they learned how I treated the ladies. Ever since then, roller coasters were dead to me.

But not if Kanya had anything to say about it. The children circled us to wait for my decision. "Mr. Strick's scared of The Big Terror," Kanya exclaimed.

"You're too young, Kanya."

"They won't know! The sign says I need to be this high!" She leveled her hand at her temple. "You're scared!"

"Keep it down," I said. People nearby chuckled, and Erica was no help.

"I married a big baby," my wife whispered in my ear, snickering. "Now I know why you insisted on having me join you. Scared of a kiddie ride. Where is the man I thought I married?"

I turned to Kanya. "Ms. Erica will ride with you."

Before Erica could dispute my diversionary attempt, Kanya shook her head. "*You* promised you'd go on a ride with me!"

My wife laughed. "You'd better not break your promise to her. You're supposed to be a role model."

The children conducted a symphony of pleading and teasing, trying to goad me on The Big Terror. Finally, two teenage girls in the line offered to let Kanya ride with them.

Naturally, I couldn't allow that, nor could I stomach Erica's teasing. I rode the monstrous coaster with Kanya, and thankfully, my lunch stayed in my stomach where it belonged. I never told Kanya how much fun I had that day.

Now, as I looked at the body lying at my feet, it hurt to realize that I would never have the chance to tell her.

CHAPTER 4

Wills tapped my shoulder. "What's wrong? You all right?"

Ten years. It had been ten quick years since that summer day when Kanya, Erica, and two teenage girls prodded me into breaking my boycott of roller coasters. Kanya, or Lil' Kay Kay as I sometimes called her, had clutched my arm and screamed with glee as we zipped and plummeted through space. I didn't have kids, but I enjoyed those fleeting moments and wondered if the tender, protective feelings I had for her were similar to the bonds fathers feel for their daughters.

Please don't let this be Kanya.

I pulled out my keys and looked at the scuffed wooden emblem of the lion attached to it. The trinket was a prize she had won at a game booth after we rode The Big Terror. She gave it to me in that innocent way children give gifts, attaching a great deal of significance and a warm selflessness to the simplest of things. I twiddled the emblem and looked at her splayed body at my feet. She was going to turn twenty in a few days; I had intended to send her a card. It felt as if I had swallowed hot coals and my eyes began to water.

I ran to join the officers canvassing the nearby apartments. Residents stood outside and leaned out of windows, curious about the sudden police invasion.

"Somebody got killed?" asked a skinny teen. "Who? One of them man-bitches or something? I ain't hear nothing."

"Some girl got killed?" a woman asked. "She white, ain't she? Y'all ain't out here like this when it's one of us."

"I ain't seen jack," exclaimed a man in a green jogging suit.

Hear no evil, see no evil, speak no evil. It was the same every time.

"Right," I growled. "I know you're out here every night. You saw something."

"Man, how you going to tell me what I saw? I ain't seen nothing. In fact, I thought I was blind all this time until I saw y'all come up. I'll be damned…I can see now!"

I flung him against a car. "Oh, you think you're Richard Pryor? Well, I've got something funny for you. Maybe I'll run your old ass through the computer to see if you got any warrants. You won't be thinking it's funny when I throw your hilarious ass in jail."

"Why you got to go there, man?" he protested. "I told you I don't know nothing!"

I jotted his name and shoved him away. I paced and questioned everyone, hoping to spot something. Someone avoiding eye contact. Someone looking too interested. Or too nervous. Instead, I got the standard shrug or blank stare. No one saw anything. No one knew shit. The code of "don't snitch" ruled these neighborhoods, and thugs enforced it with intimidation and bullets. I spotted two cooperative faces, but they vanished into the group as I approached them.

"I'm sick of this 'don't snitch' attitude!" I exploded. "You've got killers and dealers here, around your children, and you don't care! You don't cooperate, but then you want to complain about crime. Fine, I'll arrest all of your asses! I bet someone will talk!"

Wills rushed up beside me. "What the hell's wrong with you?" he whispered. "Have you lost it?"

I stormed away from the crowd, angry at their silence and myself. Outbursts like that usually didn't elicit cooperation. The group outnumbered us twenty to one. And we had no way of knowing if some nearby maniac was ready to claim legendary street status by shooting a police officer.

Wills caught up with me again. "What is it? Is it the woman? You know her?"

"Her name's Kanya." My voice cracked like rice paper.

I had to tell my friends that their daughter had been killed.

CHAPTER 5

A report of an abandoned vehicle came over the radio. The car was in flames and located on Sampson Road, three miles west of us. I sent word for the responding patrol to call me with the registration information after the fire department put out the blaze.

Meanwhile, Kanya's body was on its way to the FCMEC for the autopsy and forensic analysis. The ME was going to make the official identification, but the silver tag bracelet was enough proof for me. It read *Kanya "Gorgeous" Glover*.

I felt a warm ray of hope. What if someone had stolen Kanya's bracelet and lost it in this field? The victim might just resemble her. My Kanya could be at home safe and sound asleep.

Right?

I shook my head. I had worked in homicide long enough to know that clinging to what-ifs was a waste of time. The victim was Kanya, and there would be no relief coming from a mistaken ID. Her parents, Pete and Lorinda, had been concerned for her safety ever since she had moved out of their home, as most parents would be. Now, I had to tell them their worst fear had come true.

It was routine for me to give death notifications. And each time, I felt a bitter tang in my mouth as I uttered my words. Relatives—at least the innocent ones—wailed in disbelief as I gave the news, and I hated pressing them to answer my questions. But there was no time to let them grieve first. I needed information to find the suspects before they destroyed evidence, killed a witness, or fled the country.

I had no idea how I would react when telling Pete and Lorinda about Kanya. I didn't want to see their faces.

God, how could you let this happen?

Pete Rennell was Kanya's stepfather. He had started an employment law firm, and his passion was fundraising for charities to fight lupus, the disease that claimed his mother. Although he socialized with Atlanta's elite, a club which I had little chance of joining, he never acted as if he were better than me. He invited me to his parties, golf outings, and poker games with fellow attorneys, executives, and other movers and shakers. However, his hectic schedule had kept us from seeing each other much over the past few years. I hated that our first phone call in weeks was going to be about Kanya's murder.

Lorinda was just as welcoming to me. The Thai native, who had Kanya and another daughter from a previous marriage, was a perfect complement to her husband. While he was easygoing and economical with his words, she bounced around subjects and seemed to loathe staying on topic longer than five minutes. Her good looks and knack for weaving entertaining stories from even boring subjects softened the shells of most people. The charming, high-powered couple was a prominent fixture on Atlanta's VIP lists.

The golden touch they enjoyed professionally eluded them when it came to Kanya. As she made her way through middle and high school, she ceased being the playful girl I liked to remember. Once respectful to her elders, she covered her ears when adults admonished her. When Lorinda confined her to the house and prohibited her use of the phone or computer, Kanya was content to exile herself to her room, venturing out only for kitchen or bathroom breaks. When that failed to break her, Pete tried confiscating her car keys. She simply sweet-talked her admirers into chauffeuring her around the city. Her parents didn't believe in corporal punishment, so when they once tried to loosen the reins on her, hoping she'd display some long-dormant maturity, she repaid their trust by going to New Orleans for four days and skipping two days of school. And they learned to never, ever leave their purses or wallets lying around the house.

My cell rang, interrupting my thoughts. The voice on the other end proved my earlier hunch correct. The burning vehicle was a 1996 red Honda Civic registered to Kanya L. Glover. Struggling to keep my voice, I called the CSTs and asked them to meet me at the car to see if we could salvage any evidence. Apparently, someone was working hard to make sure we wouldn't find any.

Back in my office at APD headquarters, my throat ached as I typed Kanya's DOB in a homicide incident form.

July 28, 1983

Two days. Someone had killed Kanya just two days before her twentieth birthday.

I pictured her big eyes and the gap-toothed grin that braces would later transform into a beautiful smile. Her grin transported me to the night when I first met her and her family a decade ago.

I was a rookie on patrol and had responded to a burglary call at their home. They had just returned from Hawaii and found their sliding patio door open. I checked the house. In the master bedroom, Lorinda's jewelry case still contained her pearl necklace, diamond bracelets, and earrings, and nothing else appeared to be missing. It seemed they had returned in time to scare the burglar away before he could finish the job.

Nine-year-old Kanya kept tugging my sleeve and asking me to check her room.

"I already checked, sweetheart, but I'll look again, okay?" We went to her bedroom. "See? No one's here."

"What about under my bed?" she asked.

I got on my knees and shined my flashlight underneath it, revealing nothing but a lonely pink sneaker. "Nope. All safe."

"What about my closet?"

"Kanya, he checked in here already," Lorinda said. "I'm

sorry, officer. She's just a little scared. Like me."

"No problem." I went to the closet and opened the door. "See? Nothing—"

A man burst out and swung at me. I jumped back and felt the *whiff* from his knife slicing the air in half, inches from my neck. Lorinda shrieked and fell behind Pete as Kanya screamed.

The burglar reached to grab Kanya. Pete moved to stop him, and the man slashed him, opening an ugly gash on his left hand. I jumped on the intruder, knocking the knife from his grip. We slammed into furniture, toppled a nightstand, and shoved the bed across the room. I lost my footing on the pink sneaker, and the thief bolted downstairs. As he darted through the kitchen, I flung my metal flashlight at him and cracked him in the head.

He crashed his forehead into the countertop and dropped to the floor. I leaped and landed on his chest. I felt one of his ribs snap, but he didn't flinch. His dilated pupils showed he was too high to feel anything, even after I elbowed him in the face a few times.

The family came downstairs after I cuffed him. Kanya looked at me with wide eyes. "You got him!"

Her demeanor struck me. Pete was groaning and wrapping towels around his hand as his blood dripped along the floor. Lorinda was tending to her husband and staring at the cursing, snarling thief on the floor, undoubtedly pondering the "what-ifs." Kanya gazed up at me as if I had swooped in with a red cape. As I led the burglar to my car, she beamed at me, showing off that cute, gap-toothed smile.

Two weeks after that call, Lorinda tracked me down and invited me to Kanya's tenth birthday party. I declined, but she begged me to reconsider. The invitation was Kanya's idea, she said, and the girl was adamant I attend since I was her "hero" who saved her from the burglar.

Reluctantly, I joined the party but was pleasantly surprised when I saw them under different circumstances. Pete and I shared similar interests, and I loved Lorinda's quick wit. Likewise, they enjoyed hearing my cop stories. Sharing my experiences with civilians without offending or disgusting them meant sanitizing things to the point of killing the story, so it was nice to talk freely with them. Meanwhile, Kanya, the lady of the hour, ran back and forth all day to show me her presents and introduce her friends. Lorinda joked I was their daughter's first crush.

I sighed and stared at the homicide report on my screen, the blinking cursor prompting me to stop reminiscing and do something.

I rubbed my palms down my face and took a deep breath. I was too close to this. Protocol dictated that I step away. Someone else can investigate it.

Few people knew I was a friend of the Rennells. Wills was the only one in the APD who knew my "secret," and that was only because I told him that I knew Kanya. He wouldn't tell anyone, but if I stayed on the case, there was a chance someone would discover the friendship. And if it came to trial, a defense attorney would imply I bent the rules or violated a suspect's rights just to appease the victim's family. In a highly publicized case two years ago, events at the NBA All-Star festivities in Atlanta led the D.A. to charge a star player with murder. After the jury had acquitted him because of a shoddy investigation, chain-of-custody issues with the evidence, and a circus-like atmosphere in the courtroom, the city was determined to avoid any more negative publicity. I couldn't afford any mistakes that would kill the chances of a conviction.

Some of my peers had been working murders for nearly twenty years. Gresham was one of the best detectives, and he was next in the rotation. He loved working murders. The case would be in good hands.

But no one succeeded every time. If Gresham found no promising leads, he'd just transfer Kanya's case to the cold case archive and move on to his next murder.

That wasn't going to happen.

The bastard who killed Kanya would not get away. It didn't matter if it took me years to find him.

I wouldn't let it go.

He was going to pay for what he did.

CHAPTER 6

My shift had stretched past fourteen hours.

It was Saturday afternoon; it took most of the day to locate Kanya's dentist and have him forward her dental charts to the ME's office. Dental records were the only means of formally identifying her. Most of her jawbone was still intact and revealed a single marker; she had something called a supernumerary tooth, formed beneath a lower incisor under her gums and invisible to the naked eye. Luckily, the killer had not been able to alter it.

It was time to call Pete and Lorinda. I rehearsed my words, but nothing sounded right. A throbbing pain pulsed down my throat as I dialed Pete's cell. I hoped he didn't answer.

It rang once. Twice. A third and fourth time. Maybe he was busy. Maybe I could avoid this call; take some time to wrap my head around things so I would know what to say and how to say it.

He picked up after the fifth ring. "Hey, Jeff," he said. "Long time, no hear! What's going on with you, man?"

I sensed his smile over the phone. "Where are you?" I asked.

"In Charlotte for the weekend. Visiting Lorinda's sister, Gina. What's up?"

I spoke, but nothing came out. Whatever I planned to say didn't seem suitable. The "sorry about your loss" sentiments sounded appropriate and empathetic—as long as they weren't addressed to anyone close. Now, they sounded phony and unconvincing.

"Jeff?" Pete asked. "You there? I lose you?"

"No," I said. "When was the last time you saw or heard from Kanya?"

He sighed. "Jesus. Don't tell me. Is she with you again?"

"Not this time. When did you last see her?"

"Jeff, honestly, it was about three weeks ago. I hadn't talked to her at all since then."

"You still have no idea where she lived?"

"You know she never told us. She made it clear that since she's on her own, her business is her business." He paused. "Why did you say 'lived'? Why are you asking me this? What's up?"

"She was murdered last night."

Another pause. *"What?"*

I took a deep breath and swallowed hard. "We found her body last night. Out on the west side."

He made a strange, guttural sound. "No, no…w-wait! How do you know it was her?"

"We know."

"Maybe you made the wrong identification, maybe there's some mistake in—"

"We used her dentals."

"Her dentals? My God, what happened? What—"

"Pete, I need you and Lorinda to come back home. Now."

"Wait, tell me what happened!" he barked, his voice cracking.

I heard Lorinda say something, but Pete's reply was unintelligible. Suddenly, she was on the line. "Jeff? What is this? What happened? What happened to Kanya? Where is she?"

I took a deep breath, steeling myself to say the same thing. "She was murdered last night."

"What? No! Where's my baby?" Her voice trembled. "What happened to my baby?"

"You and Pete have to come back home. I've got to talk to you." My throat throbbed.

"What happened to my Kanya? No, no, no! My sweet Kanya…"

I heard her drop the phone. Lorinda bawled and the background filled with commotion and high-pitched exclamations from several relatives. I hung up, tears streaming down my face.

Kanya's address was listed as 10976 Cedar Ferry Drive,

her parents' home. There were no other addresses or names of accomplices. I needed Pete and Lorinda to tell me about Kanya's last whereabouts, but even if they knew, I wouldn't get anything from them now.

Needing to clear my head, I left HQ to get a cup of coffee. I saw Kanya everywhere. Every young, light-skinned woman walking along the streets sparked a naive hope that it was her. A few minutes later, I arrived at a Chevron station on Spring Street in Midtown, just north of downtown. The Chevron was my routine stop, where I grabbed a coffee, a donut, and Twizzlers at the beginning of my shifts. Nothing memorable ever happened—except for that one night, two years ago.

I had arrived at the gas station at 10:45 pm. A group of teens lounged in the parking lot and blasted Outkast from expensive car stereos in cheap cars; each 'thump' of the earthquake bass threatened to crumble the vehicles into spare parts. The boys played cool to try to worm their way into the girls' pants, and the girls played unconvincing games of hard-to-get. No one paid attention to me when I pulled up in front of the store.

When I entered the store, the kids were just noisy. When I came out, they were raining punches on each other. I ran over and flashed my shield. The younger kids scampered like rabbits, but the older ones stayed. At only six-feet-one and 196 pounds, I was dwarfed by two boys large enough to play tackle for the Atlanta Falcons.

"What's happening here?" I bellowed.

"Nothing."

"It doesn't look like 'nothing.' Who started this?"

"We were just playing around." Some of the older boys tried affecting the glares of hardened convicts and stared at me. The two linemen folded their meaty arms across their barrel chests as others formed a circle around me.

I looked in one of the cars while keeping the two giants in my periphery. "You kids better not have any alcohol in here." I spotted a familiar face, the only light-skinned face in the group. "Kanya? What are you doing out here? It's a school night." A burst of laughter erupted from the group.

Kanya was seventeen at the time but looked twenty-five. Her hair was short, and she had slapped on layers of lipstick and eye shadow.

"Heyyy," she slurred. "Mr. Strick! Hey, it's Five-O, y'all!"

"Kanya, what are you doing out here?"

"Me?" She pointed at herself. "I'm minding my own god-damn business! What are you doing?"

"Excuse me?"

She leaned forward with a stupid-looking grin. "Oh, you can't hear now. I'll say it slow... *I'm-minding-my-own-god-damn-business!*" A girl next to her poked her in the ribs. "Ow, bitch!" Kanya snapped, whirling around. "That hurt!" Her breath reeked of alcohol.

I ordered everyone out of the car. They filed out in an orderly fashion, but Kanya spilled out onto the asphalt. I suddenly felt old. It was evident my Lil' Kay Kay was no little girl. Her sleeveless shirt displayed perfect cleavage, and her shorts were so tight that they looked like tourniquets wrapped around her long legs. She had always worn oversized shirts and sweat pants, even in the summer. Her male acquaintances, busy groping her with their eyeballs, seemed thrilled she revealed her physique to the world that night.

"Who bought this?" I grabbed an empty bottle and a carton of Icehouse. There were also three unopened bottles of Cisco and Everclear. Cisco's alcohol content was so high that it was well known as 'Liquid Crack.'

"Are y'all trying to kill yourselves?" I asked. "Where'd you get this?"

Kanya hurled curses at me and accused me of trying to run her life like her parents. The teens chuckled and winced in mock pain at the unrelenting flow of F-bombs. When I asked her if her parents knew where she was, she erupted.

"Why? You're not my dad," she shouted, backing up to the store. "I'm tired of everyone telling me what the fu—"

She threw up on the sidewalk and splattered the glass doors of the store, hitting us with a terrible stench. I ordered everyone to leave; Kanya was staying with me until I got her parents to pick her up.

A tall young man stepped forward. "But she rode with me, man—"

"Get out of here," I snarled, standing over the sick girl. "I don't care who she rode with. You ain't getting none of that tonight. And the rest of you leave that alcohol. You're lucky I don't have time for this."

"Punk-ass cop," Kanya moaned, in between dry heaves that contorted her face. "I'm not staying with you. God, I feel so bad...I gotta pee..."

She tried to sit up but fell back on the sidewalk. "Oh God oh God oh God...I'm so messed up...please, Mr. Strick...help me..." she begged. "I didn't mean whatever I said."

"I'll call your dad to come get you."

Kanya closed her eyes and shook her head. "No, no. He's not my dad. I don't want to see him."

I glanced at the silver tag bracelet she wore, the same one we would find near her body years later on Jones Street. "Then I'll call your mom."

"I don't want to see her either. I don't want to go home. Take me to your place, Mr. Strick...let me stay with you. I'll give you some of this sweet ass..."

"What?" I drew back and frowned.

Kanya stroked her crotch with vomit-covered fingers. "Yeah, I'm not a little girl anymore. I'm a woman. I'm old enough for you now. I'll do you so good, you'll want to marry my ass...oh, God, I feel sick..."

I stood helpless as she peed in her shorts and a golden puddle spread from under her.

Twenty minutes later, Lorinda arrived and was horrified at the sight. "Jeff, I'm so sorry about this," she said, her Thai accent growing stronger by the second. "She told us she was at a classmate's slumber party."

The drunk girl attended a private school where the main measure of diversity was rich white kids on one side and super rich white kids on the other. It was a safe assumption that none of Kanya's friends were classmates. I helped load her into the back seat of her mother's BMW. Lorinda reached in the glove compartment, pulled out some napkins, and wiped her daughter's bodily fluids from the tan leather.

"Kanya," she moaned. "Why do you do this to us?"

Lorinda's face revealed everything she voiced to me—the disgust, the embarrassment, and the hopelessness; that no matter what she and Pete did, Kanya was going to make their lives hell.

CHAPTER 7

I ignored the speed limit and zipped down Mt. Vernon Highway before turning into the Peachtree Springs subdivision. Peachtree Springs was one of those neighborhoods that everyday people like me dreamed of calling home. My job could have me in rooms strewn with blood and bodily fluids, so it was refreshing to see colorful, immaculate landscaping and pruned dogwoods lining the streets like giant sentries. Every house rested at least a hundred feet from the road and was protected by moats of lush Bermuda grass and cobblestone driveways.

But this wasn't a sightseeing visit. I pulled up into the driveway of 10976 Cedar Ferry. Pete and Lorinda's brick home was one of the more modest houses in the subdivision even though it qualified for the cover of *Better Homes & Gardens*. Their yard was a soft carpet of grass, and foxglove and hosta plants lined the walkway to their door.

I knocked on the door, and Pete opened it. "Tell me this is a mistake," he blurted, his bottom lip quivering.

The 6'3" tanned attorney sported a head full of salt-and-pepper hair, more salt than pepper, and the confidence and polish he usually exuded made him better suited for a movie studio than pacing in a courtroom, explaining violations in labor laws. Tonight, however, his face was worn, and his eyes were bloodshot. His smooth baritone had given way to a hoarse and raspy tone.

"Pete," I said, "I'm going to find who did this. But I need to talk to you two now."

I followed him to the basement, where we had spent many Sundays watching football. It was a man's sanctuary, with a leather wrap-around sofa, pool table, and projector with a huge screen. In one corner sat a gym machine and a rack of free weights. In the opposite corner was a display full of military medals, a pistol collection, and faded photos of a young Pete with fellow grunts in Vietnam. Past this room was a hallway leading to his home office and two smaller rooms.

Lorinda lay prone on the couch. She sat up as tears ran from her bloodshot eyes. A 5'5" attractive woman with a dancer's body and a confident demeanor, Kanya's mother had understandably aged years in one night. "Jeff, please tell me this isn't true," she cried.

"I wish I could."

She collapsed into her husband's arms. After several years of homicides, I was about to cry for the first time. I gnashed my teeth, steeling myself to keep my emotions in check. Just hours earlier, they had been enjoying their weekend. Then I called to tell them someone killed their daughter. And it wasn't just a murder—it was something so brutal, with so much overkill, that only her dental records could identify her. The drive from Charlotte must have been an eternity to them. It was almost four hours, with every minute filled with agonizing thoughts and second-guesses. Several hours of asking the same questions all grieving parents asked: *How did this happen? Who did this? Why did this happen? Where did we mess up?*

The questions were plenty. The answers never came.

"I know this is hard for you," I said, "but I've got to ask you some questions."

Lorinda continued crying on her husband's shoulder but appeared indifferent to his presence. She tore herself away from him and jumped up from the couch. "I need to see her. I need to see if it's really her."

I shook my head. "That's not necessary."

"I want to see her!"

I needed them clear-headed enough to answer my questions. Letting them see Kanya's battered face would destroy what little remained of their composure. "That's not a good idea."

"She's *my* daughter," Lorinda shouted. "You have no right!" She raised her hand at me, but Pete restrained her, and she relented and sank into his arms. "Why won't he let me see her?" she cried, her sobs muffled by his chest. "I need to see if it's really her..."

Pete looked at me with pleading eyes, as if begging me to make this stop. I told myself I was doing the right thing, but it didn't ease the sick feeling in my gut. "Pete, on the phone, you said you hadn't seen Kanya in three weeks?"

"About that long. We wouldn't see her for days sometimes." He paused. "Where did we go wrong?"

"We loved her so much," Lorinda said. "Why didn't she love us back?"

"I'm sure Kanya loved you," I said. I felt like a parasitic reporter with my weak condolences, saying anything just to get the details to break a story. "Was she dating anyone?"

"We suspected she was," Pete replied. "But she never acknowledged it."

"Why do you think that?"

"When she'd visit on occasion, she'd be wearing expensive clothes and jewelry. When we asked about them, she just said one of her girlfriends let her borrow them. We didn't believe it, but it's not like we could verify it. She shielded her friends from us pretty well. We never really knew the people she associated with."

"Did it seem she was having problems with this 'friend'?"

"No."

"Did she have a fight recently?"

Lorinda lurched forward and looked at Pete. "It was DeVaughn. He did this!"

"Who's DeVaughn?"

"Her ex-boyfriend," she replied. "It was him! It has to be. They broke up a year ago. They were always fighting. I never liked him."

"You know his last name?"

"Copeland," Pete answered. "DeVaughn Copeland. A low-life. He was about thirty when they first met, and she was only seventeen. We told her not to see him, but she didn't listen. That's when she moved out."

"Lorinda, why didn't they get along?" I asked.

Her pink eyes glistened in the overhead lights. "I don't know. They just didn't. She called the police on him after they had a fight last year. He hit her several times. They arrested him, and he went to jail last summer. And he sent her some threatening letters when he was in there. They just released him a few weeks ago."

"What was he threatening to do?"

"He said he'd kill her."

"He used those words?"

Lorinda turned her watery eyes downward and curled her lip in disgust.

"No," Pete responded. "He never said anything incriminating. And as a lawyer, I looked for anything I could use to keep him locked up longer. He would just keep writing that he was sorry, that he missed her, and he looked forward to seeing her one day in person. But we read between the lines." The attorney frowned. "And if he did this, I swear…"

"Lorinda," I said, "was Kanya worried that he was getting released?"

"No. But I was."

"He hit her, he got arrested, he spent time in jail, and he wrote her messages that you believe were veiled threats. But she didn't seem concerned he was getting out?"

"She didn't show it."

"Was she having trouble with anyone else?"

Lorinda shrugged. "I—I don't know."

"She clashed with a lot of people," Pete said. "She became belligerent over the years. Remember when you called us from the gas station that night? We were actually relieved when you said she was drunk. We expected worse. And you weren't the only one to call us about her, either. You have no idea how much we paid people over the years to settle various situations and keep them quiet."

I had always tried to make sense of Kanya's shift from playful innocence to consistent antagonism, which seemed to have started after middle school. Such behavioral changes weren't uncommon with teens; family issues, drugs, and abuse were the usual culprits. Regarding abuse, a child's parents or relatives were typically the first suspects.

But there was no evidence Lorinda or Pete had ever mistreated Kanya. Lorinda was certain Pete had never done anything inappropriate to her. Despite his attempts to gain her affection, Kanya never warmed to him. He had replaced her birth father, Lorinda noted, bringing a change in the family dynamic that Kanya viewed with confusion and anger. To her young mind, Pete was an intruder trying to snap the bond she held for her real dad. As such, Lorinda reasoned, Kanya would've used any reason to force Pete out of the picture and would've told her if he had abused her. In fact, Kanya was so indifferent to them that Lorinda once feared she would falsely accuse her stepfather just to disgrace him and drive a stake through their marriage.

While Kanya never made such a claim against Pete, her parents *did* suspect someone had sexually assaulted her, making himself a possible culprit for her abrupt change in behavior.

"Pete, you haven't heard from Daryl Langley, have you?" I asked.

Pete sneered. "Langley? No."

Daryl Langley was the assistant gym teacher at Kanya's middle school and a chaperone for one of her sixth-grade class camping trips. Days after the class had returned from a week-long trip, one of Kanya's teachers called Lorinda to voice her concerns about the girl's behavior. Once a serial giggler and talker in class, Kanya had refused to speak. The teacher once found her sitting alone in a stairwell, crying. When she asked what was wrong, the girl shook her head and ran away.

Lorinda and Pete went to the school to talk to the teacher, Mrs. Harris, and learned about Daryl Langley. Whispers circulated about how the twenty-seven-year-old ogled the girls in his class a bit too much. To the faculty, he was a problem waiting to happen. To the students, he was known as Hannibal Langley, the weirdo who ate girls with a side of green beans and sweet tea. And he seemed to have eyes for little Kanya Glover.

Pete and Lorinda had asked Kanya if Langley had approached her during the camping trip. She denied it, but they didn't believe her. After all, she had transformed from a playful, talkative girl to a sullen one overnight, around the time of the camping trip. Lorinda was infuriated that the school allowed a man known for eyeballing little girls to chaperone a week-long camping trip. Lorinda called the principal and demanded he fire Langley. The principal refused. Unless there was proof that some alleged molestation happened, he legally could not—and would not—do anything.

Pete stormed to the school and confronted Langley. Both men issued threats, followed those up with punches, and bystanders had to pull them apart. After Langley had filed a restraining order against him, Pete hired an investigator to tear through Langley's life. They discovered that the assistant gym teacher was the principal's cousin, and that molestation was hard to prove without physical evidence or testimony. Even though Langley fixed his wolf-like eyes on little girls and had opportunities to force himself on Kanya, it wasn't enough to make any charges stick.

"It was years ago," I said, "but he did threaten you for ruining his reputation, remember? Have you heard from him lately?"

Pete smoldered like an ember in a fire pit. "Why would he hurt Kanya? I'm the one he blamed. Why wouldn't he come after me?"

"There's no better way to hurt you than through your family. But it's probably nothing. That Langley episode was ten years ago, after all. I was just asking—"

"Oh, we'll find out if he or DeVaughn did this," he said. "I promise you that."

"Let me handle this, Pete. You don't need to get in trouble for something that won't change what happened."

"What do you think I'll do?"

"It's natural to feel what you're feeling. You want to hurt someone. Just don't do it. You'll make things worse. I'm serious. Because it won't be self-defense. It'll be assault or murder."

He balled his fists and looked away.

"Pete, promise me you won't confront anyone at any point in this," I said.

He looked at his wife. "Jeff, I can't promise that right now."

That was probably the best I was going to get. I should have asked him in private; I imagined it was difficult for a man to hold back his protective instincts in front of a distraught wife and mother who wanted justice. "Tell me about her friends," I said. "You know any of them?"

"Only Cheryl," he said. "I don't know her last name. Kanya brought her here once. She seemed like a nice enough girl."

"You wouldn't happen to have her number?"

He shook his head.

"What about her co-workers? You know any of them?"

The attorney sighed. "She didn't talk about GNB."

Kanya's job at Georgia National Bank was a sore spot for Pete. He had earned much of his wealth from a class action suit he led against the bank. A few years ago, he had represented a group of former female employees who claimed sexual discrimination. He had also handled a separate lawsuit against a GNB executive alleged to have allowed the toxic, sexist workplace culture to thrive in his department. The settlements from both suits made Pete a multi-millionaire.

Last year, Kanya got a clerical job at GNB, sparking a nasty argument between her and Lorinda. She accused Kanya of embarrassing the family by working there, a place Pete had declared hostile to women.

"Pete, she ever say why she applied there?" I asked.

"She said she needed a job, but it was to get under our skin. People asked me how I could let her work at a company I accused of sexual discrimination. She was legally an adult. I couldn't make her quit. Even if I could, it wouldn't have looked good either way." He clasped his hands together. "It seems so stupid now, how we argued about it."

"Did she owe anyone money?"

Pete shrugged.

I looked at his wife for answers, but she had locked her eyes on the floor. "Was Kanya acting strangely recently?" I asked her. "Did she say or do anything out of the ordinary? Anything that was different from what she normally did?"

She thought for a few seconds before lifting her eyes and pointing down the hallway. "She broke into Pete's office. This past Wednesday."

"But you hadn't seen her in several weeks?"

"No," she replied. "She'll come by when we're not here. She'll help herself to things, like food or snacks. But she never bothered with his office before."

"And I always lock the door," Pete said. "I don't know why she broke in there."

"She take anything?"

"Some cash from my desk," he said. "About sixty bucks. She also figured out my online banking password and looked through my firm's accounts."

"How do you know?"

"When I came down here to do some work, I saw the account summary detail on the screen. I knew I hadn't been looking at it. I'm the only one with the password. It's like she wanted me to know she'd been there."

"How'd she get your password?"

"I store them in a folder on my computer. You know she had a knack for hacking into things like that. My password is like ten digits long. It's not something she'd have been able to guess."

"What would she want with that information? Did she transfer any money from those accounts? Make some purchases?"

"No. And I froze the accounts when I realized what happened."

"She's never done anything like that before?"

Pete shook his head. "Well, she took cash out of our wallets and purses until we started hiding them in the safe in our bedroom. You know that. That's why I started locking my office door. But she never went so far to break into my office and computer."

"Did she say why she did that? You said it was like she wanted you to know she was there."

"We both called her and put her on speaker," he said. "She lied and said she didn't know what we were talking about."

"But she did say that she had good news," Lorinda said, "and things were going to change for her this Monday, her birthday. It was going to be a big surprise."

"A surprise?" I asked. "Like what?"

"She wouldn't say," she replied. "She just said we would see for ourselves."

CHAPTER 8

A big surprise on Monday?

What did Kanya mean by that?

I asked to check her room, and Pete led me upstairs. The second story had the same inviting warmth as the rest of the house. A mahogany cabinet in the hallway flaunted handmade Thai crafts, while portraits of friends and family took up much of the wall space.

I stopped at a picture of Kanya. The seven-year-old was pulling a red wagon full of puppies. The picture was taken when she, her older sister, and Lorinda still lived in Michigan with Boyd, Kanya's father. She had found a stray dog and brought it home, where it birthed a litter in the garage. After three days, Boyd swore he wouldn't spend another night hearing the yips and yaps of a bunch of shitting machines, so he threatened to drown them in a bucket. He must have been a man to take seriously, because Kanya loaded the retriever-mix puppies in her wagon, wheeled them around the neighborhood, and asked neighbors to adopt them. At day's end, she had spared all of them from her father's wrath.

I turned away from the picture and went to her room. Clothes, CD and DVD cases, books, and papers were scattered everywhere and her bed suffocated under layers of blouses, skirts, jeans, and bras. Magazine cutouts of here-today-gone-tomorrow pop singers and scowling rappers covered the walls, along with penciled graffiti. A dresser to my left had its drawers pulled half-way out, and heaps of clothes spilled out of them.

I approached the dresser to inspect photographs ringing its mirror and nearly twisted my ankle on a shoe.

"Sorry," Pete said. "After Kanya moved out, Lorinda told the housekeepers to leave the room alone. We thought she'd come back and Lorinda said she could clean it herself."

"She left a year ago, didn't she? The housekeepers haven't been in here since?"

He nodded and rubbed his hands down his face. "I—I can't believe this has happened. I knew the company she kept, the drugs...I knew it was bad, but...I still can't believe this."

On the mirror was a picture of Kanya boasting a perfect smile, her gap-toothed grin long gone. She radiated a gleefulness that made the photo come alive. The young woman snuggled with a black man who looked to be in his early thirties. "Is this DeVaughn?" I asked.

"Yes."

He was somewhat handsome, with sheer eyebrows and goatee, a pronounced jaw line, and even-toned deep brown skin. He sneered at the camera, trying to look hard for no real reason. "When was this taken?"

"Maybe a couple of years back." Pete walked to the doorway. "I'm going to check on my wife."

I scanned the chaos. Inside the dresser drawers were more clothes, CDs, and a collection of videotapes and DVDs. All of the videotapes had handwritten labels: *"Mardi Gras", "Chillin' in Chicago", "Cheryl and the ladies",* and others. More VHS tapes with similar titles were heaped in boxes, on the nightstand, and under the bed. The walk-in closet was an obstacle course—a sea of sweaters, jeans, and blouses covered the floor, and more videotapes were scattered on top. The tapes were old and dusty, but there were fresh fingerprint smudges on them.

Pete reappeared in the doorway. "Lorinda doesn't want to come up here. Anything else you want to ask?"

"Who's been in here recently?"

"I don't know. Kanya, I guess. Or maybe Lorinda? I haven't been in here. Why?"

"Someone was looking for something."

"How can you tell?"

"This room has been ransacked."

"She kept it messy and cluttered. And the housekeepers leave this room alone."

I shook my head. This was more than clutter. Someone was looking for something. It may have been a mess, but it was *her* mess. In the same way people can find a document under piles of paper on their desks, Kanya should have known where most of her things were. She wouldn't yank out drawers and leave clothes, videos, and books strewn all over. Either she was in a hurry to find something or someone else had rifled through her room.

"And those," I said, pointing to several unlabeled tapes and DVDs. "Someone has been looking through them."

Pete came over to inspect them. "It was probably Kanya. Like I said, sometimes she came here when we weren't home."

"You know what's on them?"

"Probably movies of her and her friends."

"You mind if I look at them?" If she bounced around in the streets so much and liked filming her friends, perhaps I could get lucky and spot someone familiar with our rap sheets.

Pete hesitated. I sensed that like many fathers, he had dreaded discovering his daughter doing what many rudderless, wayward girls did—shaking ass in a strip joint or making degrading porn flicks. Most people became uneasy after finding unlabeled videotapes in a loved one's collection.

"I just want to see if I can recognize some familiar faces," I assured him. "Who knows? It might give me a lead."

He sighed and nodded. "Okay." His eyes reddened. "We messed up so bad."

"You can't blame yourselves for this."

"We were responsible for her. I didn't protect her. I didn't do my job. I can't even tell you who her friends are."

"No one can protect their kids forever. They grow up and make their own path."

"You don't have kids. You don't understand. You never stop worrying about them."

"Pete, I can't pretend to know what you and Lorinda are feeling right now. But someone else did this. And Kanya didn't live here. You couldn't watch over her twenty-four seven. And she wouldn't have wanted you to."

He slumped against the wall. "Just...just keep us in your prayers."

I figured God had already given up on things. What else explained the homicides, rapes, and assaults every day in our city? God must have been asleep at the wheel while the unruly children in the back seat did as they pleased. Some days, I didn't think he was in the car in the first place.

Not that the murder of someone's child was anything I wished on anyone, but the fact that this just happened to my friends angered me. Why them? They raised hundreds of thousands of dollars to help those suffering from a debilitating disease. Just three months ago, after hearing of Nicaraguan peasants who had to stare through glass shards to read, they led a drive that donated thousands of eyeglasses to the poor in that country.

They weren't perfect, but who was? They paid their dues. If God needed to punish someone with this misery, I could've given him some names; I knew several evil bastards more deserving of tragedy and pain.

"I will," I answered, embracing him.

"And pray that we find whoever did this," he replied. His voice was instantly lower. His red eyes were affixed and staring not at me but *through* me. I sensed he was imagining what he would do to Kanya's killer if he got the chance.

I needed to find DeVaughn before Pete did.

CHAPTER 9

After a background check of DeVaughn Stanley Copeland, it was evident why Pete and Lorinda didn't want him near their daughter.

Before he met Kanya, the thirty-one-year-old Detroit native had already been arrested for possession of marijuana and assault but served just seven months; overcrowding had turned the Fulton County Jail into a can of human sardines. For years, the jail, nicknamed the Fulton Inn, dumped its human overflow in prisons throughout Georgia but soon found their castoffs unwelcome. The rest of the state bristled at how the metro area fed on Georgia's tax revenue while leaving crumbs for small rural towns. Their attitude to Atlanta's jail problem: *It's your mess, you clean it up*. Since the jail needed to make space for its guests, it gave early releases to inmates convicted of non-violent crimes or those nearing completion of their sentences. DeVaughn was one of the lucky ones released ahead of schedule.

After his fight with Kanya last year, he was arrested again and reserved another stint at the Fulton Inn. And despite his repeat offenses, luck was with him again. Because of civil complaints of its horrid conditions, the jail was slapped with a federal court order to reduce its overpopulation. The rate of early releases accelerated, and more convicts were freed, including DeVaughn, who had served just one year of a forty-eight-month stretch.

After his release a month ago, he had moved into a rented house on the west side of town. When I saw the address, I knew I needed backup before picking him up.

***

"So y'all think Robbins is getting life?" Wills asked us.

"Not as long as she's a woman," I replied, concentrating on the poorly lit road. It was late Saturday night, and street lights on the west side tended to die at early ages, courtesy of vandals' bullets. Sparse city budgets resulted in overgrown tree branches and bushes that obscured street signs and sent motorists into rage as they missed turn after turn.

Jessica, a short Missouri blonde on our squad, leaned forward from the back seat. "What do you mean, 'Not as long as she's a woman'?"

"Oh, please," I said. "You know when a woman kills a guy they go easy on her. And don't let her be a young blonde. She could be a suicide bomber and they'll still let her go. Like the Windrow case, remember? Everyone knew she killed her ex, and the jury still acquitted her. Robbins will get off, too. Free and clear."

"Don't hate us blondes. And Windrow was acquitted because it was self-defense."

"Jess, she shot the shit out of him. Twelve times. From fifteen feet away. And he was unarmed. How does that qualify as self-defense?"

"She's five-three and 135 pounds! He was what, eight-foot-ten? What should she have done? Wait for him to get close? Hell, no. Besides, you know men can't handle it when a woman leaves 'em. Y'all go berserk and shoot everybody. If women kill someone, it's self-defense, and we only get the ones responsible. You don't see us climbing watch towers and picking off innocent people because some man left us."

"You know if Windrow were a man, she would've gotten a hundred years."

Jessica grinned. "Hey, don't hate the player, hate the prosecutor."

"I'll remember you said that when one of your cases goes belly-up in court."

"Okay, if it wasn't self-defense, tell me why she shot him."

I shrugged. "Wasn't my murder. Maybe she got tired of look-ing at him. Maybe he was getting some on the side. Maybe the sex was bad."

She smirked. "Then I should've shot my ex."

Wills turned to Jessica. "Speaking of which, Jess, when are you going to transfer out of Homicide for me?"

She shook her head. "Wills, your confidence is truly unfounded."

I chuckled and kept my eyes on the asphalt. It was the first time I had smiled in nearly twenty-four hours. This was the part of the job I needed most—the camaraderie and the banter, especially between Jessica and Wills. He wanted her to transfer because he wanted to date her without breaking fraternization guidelines. I enjoyed their exchanges. It was one of the two rea-sons I recruited them to come with me to meet DeVaughn. The diversion they brought was welcome.

" 'Unfounded?' " Wills said. "You'd fall in love with me if I really laid it on you."

"Nah. I've seen you in the gym."

"What does that mean?"

"Okay," she said, as if warning that the words coming next were his fault. "First, you're built like a refrigerator. You look like that SpongeBob thing. Second, I saw you coming out of the pool. And from what little I saw, I can only hope that it was freezing in there."

I erupted in a booming cackle. Jessica held her own in a male-dominated occupation and had decided not to react with righteous anger every time a peer tossed sexual innuendos. Instead, she resorted to biting insults that made it clear that sharing the same job did not mean sharing her bed. She endured snarky attitudes from old veterans who believed she had no busi-ness trying to "be police", yet she approached her job with the same vigor, toughness, and bluntness of all of them.

Wills whirled to me. "What are you laughing at?"

I shook my head. "Don't look at me because she's digging into your chest."

Jessica patted Wills on the head. "Come on, Willie. I like you and all, but you're applying for a job you're not qualified for. Desperation isn't a good look. Just be cool and take some lessons from Strick."

"Who, *Cool Whip* here?" Wills asked. "That's his new name because Stephanie got him whipped. He gave her a grand to fix her car, and she still dropped his ass like he was on fire."

I wondered how sharply I had to swerve to launch my 'buddy' through his open window and into the bushes.

"Shut up, Willie," snapped Jessica. "There's nothing wrong with a man taking care of his woman. Strick just hooked up with a bad one." She leaned forward. "Steph didn't deserve you, Strick. You talk to Erica recently?"

I was trying not to think of my ex-wife, much less speak to her. A pain hit the back of my throat as I realized that I would never again enjoy the scent of her lotion or glide my hands over her body for a bedroom massage. "No," I replied. "It's pretty much over."

"You miss her, don't you? Yeah, you lost a good one. Now you've got some self-inflicting punishment thing going on with these other ladies. We need the real Strick back. He'd never let himself get punked like that."

"Damn, Jess. You know how to comfort a guy."

"You know what you need?" she asked. "A woman like me."

Wills whipped around to face her. "What?"

Jessica rubbed her fingers down my neck. "I'd treat you like royalty, Strick. You believe me?"

"Hell, no."

"I'm serious. Why wouldn't I want a man who takes care of his woman? Have you seen the morons who approach me out here?"

"I'm a moron, now?" Wills asked.

"It's getting old, Strick," Jessica continued. "I'm getting tired of these idiots."

"It's like I'm not even here," Wills mumbled to himself.

Jess massaged the nape of my neck. "I'll make you happy, Strick. I'm serious. I'll transfer out of the squad, too. But first things first…can you buy me a new car? It's hard for a single mom, and I hope you're gullible enough—I mean, *generous* enough to help me out. I'll even let you play with my panties."

I brought our company Ford Taurus to a stop as Jessica and Wills laughed and compared me to a slot machine making a payout. "Playtime's over, assholes," I said. "We're here. 157 Sampson."

The house was a jumble of old wood planks with peeling white paint. Security bars adorned every window. They were a touching thought, but based on the number of B&E (breaking and entering) calls in the area, the steel bars were just signs telling junkies which houses had things worth stealing.

We were in a part of town called the Bluffs, three miles from the Jones Street field. A haven for heroin users, it was a third-world country within a country, with decrepit homes and trash-clogged sewers that created pools of stinking water. At night, only ballsy or reckless cops pulled over suspicious individuals while patrolling alone. Only serious crimes in progress warranted stops without backup, and as the level of poverty and violence grew in The Bluffs, what constituted a 'serious' crime became debatable.

A civilian has been shot and he needs help? Oh, he's in that abandoned warehouse off English Avenue? The same one where someone called in a disturbance last week and shot at the responding officer? Sorry, but whoever he is, his ass is going to have to wait.

This was the second reason I asked Wills and Jessica to join me. There was no such thing as too much backup.

The yard of the house was Georgia-red clay, mixed with a few patches of dying brown grass. Green beer bottles, half-buried in the dirt, dotted the yard. Piles of old and fresh dog droppings clumped at the side of the porch steps.

The rhythmic thudding of hip-hop emanated from inside. I banged on the front door. Inside, a dog roared, and a child peeked through crooked blinds in the porch window. No one came to the door. I banged harder on it, the splintering wood nearly buckling from the pressure. A few seconds later, someone opened it, releasing a powerful odor of barbecue and marijuana.

The porch light came on, and a twenty-something man stood in the doorway. A genetic cross between a man and a rat, he was skinny and had a thin nose, protruding front teeth, and dilated pupils. He was on a first-class flight through the stratosphere, courtesy of weed and extra sweet barbecue sauce.

The rat-mouthed man studied my shield hanging from my neck. "That real?" he slurred.

"We're looking for DeVaughn Copeland," I said. "Is he here?"

The young man swayed, twitched, and looked around as if he heard strange noises. In the background, a rap song extolled the virtues of marijuana, and Rat Mouth suddenly seemed to remember my question. He strolled back into the house.

"You did *what?*" shouted a raspy voice from within. Immediately, DeVaughn rushed outside and closed the door behind him. He still resembled the man in Kanya's picture, but his bald dome had given way to tight braids that dropped down his nape. Wiry, he stood about six feet and sported a bushel of a goatee that jutted an inch from his chin. Two large Band-Aids were on the left side of his neck, and I observed scratches on his right cheek.

"Can I help you?" he asked.

"We're with the Atlanta Police Department. I'm Detective Strickland, and these are Detectives Wills and Branson. We'd like you to come with us so we can ask you a few questions."

"Questions about what?"

"Kanya Glover."

"What about her?"

I took a deep breath. "She was murdered last night."

"I heard."

"How did you hear that?" No one had reported it yet.

"Her mother and father. They called me, asking if I knew about it. Assuming I did it. They threatened me."

I pointed to the Band-Aids on his neck. "What happened there?"

He backed away. "Just going to ignore that they threatened me, huh? I see how this is going to go. And I was playing with Knox."

"Who is Knox?"

"My dog."

"And the scratches on your cheek?"

"My Rottie's a big dog. He loves to play."

"Where were you last night?"

"At a club. New Experience."

"When were you there?"

"Most of the night. Didn't get home until about 4 or 5, I think."

"When did you get there?"

"I don't know. 9, 10, or something."

"Where were you before then?"

He shrugged. "Running errands, doing things. Stopping here and there. Maybe the grocery store."

"You have receipts?" I asked.

"No."

"I'm going to need you to come with us to give a statement."

"About Kanya? You think I had something to do with it?"

"I didn't say that."

"You didn't have to, officer," he said.

"I just want your statement."

"I can't give one here?"

"We'd rather you come with us."

"Am I under arrest?"

"You want to be?"

He sneered. "Look. I know you already checked me out. Her folks sent you over here. I feel bad for them and all, but I had nothing to do with it. Besides, I'm eating. So if I ain't under arrest, you can go and leave my ass alone." He retreated inside and began closing the door.

I jammed my foot between the door and its frame. "It won't take long."

He looked at me. "Bruh, I'm not stupid. I know what's happening. I'm the ex-boyfriend, so I'm the first one you look at. I'm saving you time by telling you I didn't do it."

"You don't seem too surprised or upset to hear your ex-girlfriend was murdered."

"That don't mean I did it. Sorry if I'm not responding the way you think I should. I'm just real. I didn't like her. Bitch lied and had me thrown in jail. And she pissed people off left and right, so I'm not surprised something bad happened. But again, for the hundredth time, I had nothing to do with it. I didn't do it; I don't know a damn thing."

He tried to block my view inside his house, but I glimpsed a blue plastic bucket, with holes in the top, on the kitchen table. Next to it were a couple of high-pressure bulbs.

I smirked and shook my head. "Then it's not a problem if you come with us."

He sneered. "You just want me down there so you can twist my words around and make a case on me. Y'all already railroaded me. I just got out, and you're trying to put me back in. Hell, no. I don't trust you. You want me down there, get a warrant."

I leaned close to him. "You think I can't get one? You're no model citizen. You're Kanya's ex, you spent a year in jail for assaulting her, and a few weeks after your release, she ends up dead. I'll have a warrant in five minutes. So you've got two options. One, you come with me. Or two, you piss me off and make me get a warrant, and not only will I come back and drag you downtown, but I'll also seize everything you got in there."

"And I'll sue. I know my rights."

"You do? You also know the law says I can seize whatever I want from you if I think you acquired it by criminal means? I'll come up with a hundred charges for things you've never even heard of. But I don't even have to get creative for you. You've got a hydro bucket in your kitchen, and we know what you're using it for. Growing *and* smoking? And I'll add 'intent to distribute', too? That's a serious felony right there, so now I have the right to go inside and take everything. And try to sue. I'll have your case tied up in court for the next thousand years. Meanwhile, everything I take will stay in our property room until the case is settled."

"Shady-ass goddamn cops. I got a witness."

Behind him, Rat Mouth was sprawled on a couch, studying the progress of a well-fed cockroach scurrying up the wall.

"Him?" I asked, half laughing. "What the hell is he witnessing? Look, you want to do this the easy way or the hard way? I can play this game a lot better than you."

He turned around and cursed Rat Mouth for answering the door in the first place, spewing epithets that might have provoked a response from him if he weren't mesmerized by brown water stains on the ceiling.

The ex-con stepped outside. "Fine. Let's hurry up and clear me. So you can find the one who really did this."

CHAPTER 10

We drove to the APD headquarters, located in City Hall East. City Hall East was a 77-year-old massive block of brick and mortar built by Sears in 1926. The place may have been top-notch during the Depression but was outdated today. After the retailer had abandoned it, the city bought the dilapidated structure on the cheap in 1990, saying it would be a great home for the police. The idea was to modernize it, but constant budget issues made that wishful thinking.

Frequently, Wills and I daydreamed about a disgruntled city employee blowing up the building after everyone went home. Or at least putting it out of commission for awhile. We got tired of getting stuck in elevators or exchanging worried glances when they squeaked over the weight of two people. Covered parking decks were prime real estate, and people arrived early to avoid parking on the top deck, where cars became blast furnaces under the summer sun. Inside, the HVAC system turned the sixth floor into a sauna in the winter and into a meat locker in the summer. Everyone yearned for the "Goldilocks days", the times in late spring or early fall when the temperature inside wasn't too hot or too cold, but just right.

The elevator moaned as we went to the sixth floor, the Homicide unit. I led DeVaughn to an interrogation room. There were two interrogation rooms, side by side. Each was eight by ten with see-through mirrors. We dubbed the rooms the "Ovens"— Ovens One and Two. We called them that because they were where we "put the heat" on suspects. Corny as hell, yes, but the names stuck.

Each Oven contained a padded chair for the detective, a hard chair for the suspect, and a wood desk used for banging fists, sliding, and other good cop/bad cop theatrics. Overhead were two adjustable ceiling lights. I set them to maximum intensity so I could roast suspects under their harsh glare. From their viewpoint, the perps hung in a black void, alone on a giant stage with thousands of eyes heaping judgment upon them.

I tossed DeVaughn in Oven Two and joined Wills in the video room to observe him through the glass. "How long?" Wills asked.

"Might let him marinate for an hour. I don't like him."

"You think he did it?"

"We'll see."

"Give him your stare."

Jessica once said I had piercing eyes, and when I fixed them on people, it was like watching food blister in a microwave. Most people are uncomfortable with long silences and feel compelled to talk to fill the void. When I questioned guilty perps, they denied everything at first, but staring at them usually got them to expand on their alibis. The standard tactic: let them keep talking until they trip themselves on a lie. They'll try covering that lie by creating new ones, sinking deeper in a quicksand of bullshit until there's no way out. But my stare only worked on the inexperienced or stupid ones. Something told me DeVaughn would not be so easy to peg.

I left and returned to the video room thirty minutes later. Kanya's ex sat quietly, staring at the window as if he could see me. I left again and returned in fifteen minutes; this time, he had relaxed in the padded chair—meant for the detective—with his arms folded behind his head.

One can usually spot an innocent suspect. Innocent men in custody sweat as if they had just finished marathons. Thoughts of being turned out in prison for a wrongful conviction turned them into nervous wrecks. Conversely, the calm men were usually guilty. Some were tired of running and ready to confess. Some were young gang members who welcomed prison because it was a prerequisite for claiming badass status.

Then there were those men who were relaxed because they knew the police had nothing on them.

At first, I considered DeVaughn an insecure punk who tried to look street-hard. Replace the braids and goatee with a haircut, shave, and suit, he'd look like an accountant. He reminded me of a guy named Nedrick who lived in the neighborhood where I grew up. Nedrick, born in a middle-class family, was strikingly handsome. Girls spread themselves before him like red carpets, but he didn't want sexual offerings. He wanted people to respect and fear him. The problem was that people usually weren't afraid of a guy from the suburbs with movie star looks. His solution? To be twisted and merciless, earning the name "Nasty Ned." His signature move was castrating enemies with hot butter knives before killing them, and at age twenty-six, received four concurrent life sentences for slaughtering a rival and his family. He even tossed their sixteen-year-old son from their 8th story window as they watched helplessly.

DeVaughn wasn't as handsome as Nasty Ned, probably explaining why none of his priors showed a need to overcompensate with similar barbaric behavior. But I believed he was more dangerous. Ned was a sociopath who acted without thinking. DeVaughn's demeanor signaled intensity and thoughtfulness, as if he were studying people for weaknesses and waiting for the opportune time to strike.

I walked in the Oven, and he sat up. "You said this wouldn't take long. It's been an hour."

"Get up," I said. "You're in my chair." I informed him that I was recording the session, but he wasn't required to answer my questions. It was standard policy language, but my tone made it clear I expected cooperation. "Mr. Copeland, let's start by telling me where you were last night."

"I already told you at my house."

"Tell me again. For the record."

"Can I have something to eat first?"

"You trying to be funny?"

"You wouldn't let me finish my dinner. Remember? And I've been sitting in here for an hour. I'm hungry. You said I'm not under arrest, right? Which means I can leave. I'm just here to get this over with. It's the least you could do."

"Fair enough." I left and returned with a pack of M&Ms and a Coke and slid them across the table. His face tightened in disgust.

"This isn't the Taj Mahal," I said. "Now tell me where you were last night."

He shook his head and mumbled something about poor southern hospitality. "*Like I said*, I was at New Experience. With Lamont. The fool at my house."

"New Experience. On Pharr Road in Buckhead, right?"

"Yeah."

"What's Lamont's last name?"

"Goines."

"How long were you there?"

"Until four this morning or something. When they closed."

"When did you arrive?"

"About 9:30."

"9:30?" I repeated. So far, his story and times hadn't changed.

"The ladies there are nice. I get there early because the fine shorties leave after midnight."

"Then you stayed almost seven hours. Why stay so long after the fine ones were gone?"

"I like the cuties, you know, but the ones who stay late, those are the ones who give it up without a lot of work."

"So you were inside the club the entire time?"

He nodded.

"And someone can vouch you were there all night?"

"Yeah. Lamont. He was with me."

I considered having Rat Mouth picked up for questioning but decided against it. The last time I saw him, he was admiring the stains on the ceiling as if it were the Sistine Chapel. His testimony wouldn't make sense, and even if it did, it probably would be ruled inadmissible, given his state of mind.

"Anybody other than him?" I asked. "What about all those women? A player like you can give me some names of some ladies who'll vouch for you. You were there all night."

"I wasn't on my game. I just chilled."

"So you didn't talk to or meet a single person? For seven hours? Other than your friend?"

He shrugged and jutted his chin forward. "Yeah, I talked to a few people, but I don't know 'em. I don't go around writing names and numbers of people just so they can tell the police where and when they saw me."

"Where'd you go after you left the club?"

"Home."

"You stop anywhere?"

"No."

"Was Lamont with you?"

He nodded. "He was too drunk to drive so I let him sleep on the couch."

It was hard to concentrate. I wanted to get him creating holes in his alibi, but my train of thought kept getting interrupted by images of this smug bastard hitting Kanya or killing her. I didn't feel I was asking the right questions or succeeding in cracking his demeanor—and I just couldn't stop seeing her splayed body in the field. "When did you meet Kanya?" I asked.

"Couple of years ago."

"She was seventeen? And you were—what? Thirty?"

"What's that got to do with anything?"

"Just wondering why you couldn't pull a woman your age. You almost ended up on our sex offender registry."

"She said she was twenty-two when we met. I didn't card her."

"You're not one of those guys who likes kids or something,

55

are you?"

"Why? Are you?"

"Tell me how the relationship ended."

DeVaughn shifted in his chair. "It ended when she had me locked up over that bullshit charge."

"Tell me about it."

"Y'all didn't care what I had to say before. Why do you care now?"

"Because Kanya's dead. And you had a hell of a motive."

"Look, she lied! I never hit her." For the first time, he showed emotion. "We had an argument one night. We're at my place, and I told her to get out. But she wouldn't. She kept getting in my face, pushing me, so I kept pushing her away. You ever see that movie with Martin Lawrence, where the woman beat herself and said he did it? Well, that's what Kanya did. Right in front of me, she put a bar of soap in one of her socks and starts hitting herself with it. Then she called the police and said I did it. Judge set my bail so high that even Jay-Z or somebody couldn't afford it. He tried to say it was because of my record, but whatever. It was because I was messing with Pete Rennell's daughter."

"Now why would Kanya do that?"

"Bitch was crazy, that's why."

"And you never hit her? At that time, or any time before?"

He shook his head. "I don't hit women."

"But spending a year in jail made you mad, didn't it?"

"Not mad enough to kill her. You're not putting that on me. I wanted nothing to do with her when I got out."

He explained that Kanya picked fights with men he preferred avoiding, compelling him to "throw down" and risk a beating or be labeled a punk. It was as if she were trying to manipulate someone into getting rid of him. There were plenty of reasons for the relationship to die, but the final straw was the assault charge that landed him in jail.

"No one investigated your claim that she set you up?" I

asked.

He smirked. "Come on, man. What country are we in? She's the daughter of a rich white man. She says I beat her and she's got 'bruises' to prove it. Now look at my black ass and tell me who you think they're going to believe. Just because we're in the ATL don't mean we're not in the South."

"Your priors don't exactly help your credibility."

DeVaughn folded his arms and looked away. "We done?"

"When was the last time you saw her?"

He sighed. "Couple of weeks ago. At Lenox."

"What'd you do?"

"Nothing."

"You said she had you thrown in jail over a lie. You were inside for a year. And when you got out, you saw her in the mall and you didn't say a word to her?"

"Went the other way."

I folded my arms over my head. "That's difficult to believe, man."

"It's the truth. I go near her, she screams rape this time or says I stalked and threatened her. Again, who are they going to believe? She already had me thrown in jail once. I wasn't about to let her do it again."

"Did you have any contact with her while you were inside?"

"No."

"No contact at all?"

"Um...might have written her a couple of letters. Told her I forgave her, but that was it."

"You didn't think about getting back with her?"

"Hell no. I told you I wanted nothing to do with her."

"Then why did you tell her you looked forward to seeing her when you got out? I got copies of your letters."

He shrugged. "I was trying to forgive and be the better person. But some people are just bad people. I decided to leave her alone. Wait, it's not illegal to write letters and change your mind, is it?"

It was becoming clear I wouldn't get anything from him without evidence. And he knew it. He had prepared for this. "You said she made enemies," I said. "Who?"

"I don't know them that well but you might want to check out this dude named Ronnie. He goes by 'Grip.' He'll be out there slinging to them Tech kids on Northside. Red caps and X."

"Why him?"

"Well, he hooked Kanya up a few times, but he got mad when she wouldn't break him off some. I mean, he ain't the best-looking dude. Guess that hurt his feelings."

"You're saying he might have killed her because she didn't give him any ass?"

"Man, I'm sure you've seen worse. People are crazy out here and that boy is certifiable. That's all I can say." He opened the Coke can and drained it.

"Trying to eliminate one of your competitors?"

He feigned shock. "Me? I'm not in the game anymore."

"I guess that bucket in your kitchen was for medicinal purposes. Tell me about Kanya's friends."

"Well, there's Shawna, Marina, Cheryl...but I can't tell you much about them."

Cheryl was the friend that Pete and Lorinda mentioned. "You know how I can contact Cheryl?"

He shook his head.

"Do you know her last name? Where she lives? Where she works?"

"No."

"You know how to reach any of the others?"

"I told you I don't know much about them."

"Do you know if Kanya was dating anyone?"

He leaned back and clasped his hands. "Wasn't my business. If she was, I wouldn't be surprised if he had something to do with this. She probably screwed him over, too."

"Would you be willing to take a polygraph?"

"No, I would not."

"Why?"

"You can't use it in court. So why ask me to take it?"

"I think you're hiding something. If you got something to tell me, now is the time to come clean. Because no one will believe you later."

"You don't believe me now. What's the difference?"

"The difference is that I'm not a jury. I'm not the one you need to convince. Passing a polygraph would be in your favor. I suggest you have a better story to tell than the one you just told me."

He looked around at the walls, the mirror, and the wooden desk. Everywhere but at me. "I'm not hiding anything," he replied. "And I'm not taking no polygraph. You might rig the machine or the results or something."

"We don't do that."

"I don't trust y'all. Especially you. Every brother ain't a brother."

I went to the video room again to observe him. His alibi was weak but not hollow enough to arrest him for murder. I began kicking myself; I should have invoked the RICO statute to justify searching his place when I had the chance. If he was careless enough to leave marijuana-growing tools in view, who knew what other clues he might have left lying around? But I needed evidence to press him further. If I went at him harder with no proof and he didn't break, he'd see right through me. It was better to keep him looking over his shoulder while I worked the case and obtained a search warrant.

I returned to the Oven and told DeVaughn he was free.

"I'm clear of this?" he asked.

"Yep." *For now.*

"How am I getting home?"

"I'll have someone take you back."

He shook his head. "I can't have people seeing me get out of a cop car. They'll think I'm snitching on somebody. Someone gets arrested later, and people will say it was because of me."

"The car's unmarked and they'll drop you off somewhere nearby. We know the deal." I handed him my card and asked him to call me if he heard anything.

DeVaughn shoved my card in his pocket without looking at it. He followed me to the elevator and stopped suddenly. He walked back to the Oven and grabbed his empty soda can. We passed three waste bins on the way to the lobby, but he ignored them.

"Trash is right there," I mumbled, nodding at a bin.

"I recycle," he said. He walked out of the building, still clutching his can, and into the unmarked car I had waiting for him.

I watched the car disappear into the city streets. The bastard was smart to keep his can, which had traces of his saliva and DNA. If he discarded anything with his genetic material on it, the law considered it trash and part of the public domain— which meant I could collect it without a warrant and use it to pull his genetic profile to compare to any evidence. That was my intent when I brought him the drink, but he wasn't as dumb as I hoped. Without the can and without placing him under arrest, I needed a court order to take his sample. And at the moment, I didn't have enough probable cause.

His move was smart, but it also created questions. Was he just being overly paranoid that the system was out to frame him?

Or was he guilty of murder and worried that his DNA would link him to the evidence I had yet to find?

CHAPTER 11

It was shortly after dusk on Sunday. I leaned back in my car and closed my eyes; my eyelids felt like lead slabs. I wanted to fall into a coma and forget everything that happened.

Like finding Kanya's body.

Or seeing Pete and Lorinda's anguish.

Or the realization that after a day of exploring multiple possibilities, I still had no strong leads.

Kanya's cell phone was missing. Having her phone was the only way to see her recent calls; calling her carrier wouldn't help because she used a burner, or a prepaid phone, which didn't provide billable call detail records.

Earlier, I had tracked down Grip, the man DeVaughn implied might have killed Kanya because she refused to sleep with him. Grip, whose real name was Ronald Graves, eliminated himself as a suspect by proving he'd been in New Jersey with relatives for the past two weeks.

The team had lifted a partial latent fingerprint from Kanya's tag bracelet, but it was too degraded for AFIS, the Automated Fingerprint Identification System, to return a high-probability match.

The blood smudges on the bracelet did match her blood type (B+), but it would be months before the GBI completed a DNA test. I doubted it would matter anyway, as the blood was probably hers instead of her killer's. The police gods were always in foul moods; letting the blood be that of a felon already in the FBI's DNA database was too easy. They would give me a break only when my efforts to navigate dead ends ceased to amuse them.

I had visited the New Experience nightclub to see if DeVaughn was there Friday night as he claimed. After seeing his photo, the club manager recognized him as a regular—but said she hadn't seen him once that night, despite working from eight p.m. to six a.m. Saturday morning. The club's security footage was a waste of money; none of the black-and-white images were bright enough to identify a person's face, and they only showed a mass of blurred bodies bobbing on the dance floor.

The DVDs and videos I had taken from Kanya's room were of no help. Scanning hours of footage of her and her friends presented just one familiar face to me, that of an idiot named Larry Threet, who was now serving a twenty-three-year stretch for robbing a QuikTrip two blocks from a police station.

Although her videos didn't reveal much, I noticed something odd about them. Kanya had recorded them, lending her voice to describe events and make jokes, but she didn't appear in any of the footage. When someone wanted to capture her on a recording, she refused, growing irritated and cursing those who persisted.

Her quirks or my lack of leads didn't concern me as much as the fact that her murder had been reported on the news hours earlier:

"Kanya Glover, the daughter of local attorney and philanthropist Peter Rennell, was found dead yesterday morning west of downtown..."

That sound bite and lead-in were on all of the local channels. Because of Kanya's parents, her murder was going to garner attention, a development that was a cursed blessing. Higher-profile murders generated more tips than ordinary ones, and the brass funneled more resources to those investigations. The downside was that most of the tips were garbage—devouring the precious man hours spent verifying them—and the pressure to make arrests was suffocating. Thanks to television, people expected cops to solve murders within forty-eight hours, or the killers would ride off into the sunset, free to kill again and again. It was true that the longer it took to solve a case, the lower the chance it would be cleared. But I wanted my cases to stand tall in front of even the most liberal juries—and building strong cases often took longer than forty-eight hours.

I was sure my superiors would press me for fast results, but that didn't concern me. It was the expected pressure from Pete and Lorinda that bothered me. They would demand answers. They would want a suspect in custody. And I didn't want to let them down.

After downing my twelfth cup of coffee since my shift started yesterday, I drove to a deserted strip mall near Hartsfield-Jackson Airport. I parked behind Nina's, a boarded-up Mexican restaurant at the end of the mall. The strip was a deserted wasteland. Eight pole lights stood around the shopping center, and seven of them were shot out. The lone working light didn't show much worth looking at, other than oil-stained asphalt and boarded-up doors covered with gang tags and graffiti.

It was a perfect spot to meet Cornell "C-Dub" Wallen, my confidential informant.

I looked out my window, and he emerged from the shadows. For a permanently recovering addict who treated his veins as express lanes for dope, he was unusually punctual. I unlocked the passenger door, and he scrunched his six-foot-two, 170-pound body in the seat. He stank of liquor and cigarettes.

"It's been awhile," I said, turning away from his stench. "I need some 411."

He held out his hand. His arm was pock-marked after years of being a pincushion for drug needles. "Good," he said, "because I need some scratch. I'm broke."

I took out my wallet but kept it closed. "Don't waste my time like you did last month."

"What're you talking about?"

"The Woods murder. The kid who got shot at the cleaners on

Fairburn. I drove all the way to Macon for that bullshit lead you gave me. In fact, you've been slipping lately. A lot."

"Man, I tell you what I hear."

"So have you heard anything about Kanya Glover? She's Pete Rennell's stepdaughter. She was murdered Friday night."

C-Dub shrugged and frowned. "Who the hell are those people?"

I should've known better. His world revolved around junkies and drifters, not high-profile attorneys or philanthropists. I handed him the picture of Kanya with DeVaughn.

He scratched his face as if he had fleas. "Never seen her." He peered closer at the photo. "But he looks familiar. Yeah, I've seen him before. He used to sling around Northside."

"What do you know about him?"

"That's all."

"You sure you haven't heard anything about this girl? She was with him for a year and she's been in the news. Come on, now. You're my secret weapon."

My informant folded his arms. "Then you should split your paycheck with me since I'm always at your damn service. I don't know about this girl. Is that all you need?"

"What the hell is your problem?"

"I don't have a problem."

"Yes, you do. And I don't know why. I look out for you, I slide money to you every now and then..."

"Yeah, I'm just a bitch on your payroll."

I glared at him and took slow, steady breaths. A former electrical engineer in Oakland, California, C-Dub had let fun heroin binges grow into an addiction that destroyed his career and dumped him across the country onto West Atlanta's dirty streets. We met years ago after I arrested him for trying to sell me dope. With jail looming over his head, he spewed information like water from a busted hydrant, snitching on everyone. The quality of his info was surprisingly good, so good that I "adopted" him despite his propensity for getting arrested for various nonviolent crimes. Since his info led to many of my murder clearances, I had indebted myself to others in the APD or the DA's office for helping me keep him free on the streets.

As such, I expected more gratitude. "C, whatever problem you've got with me, you'd better get over it real quick. I keep you out of jail. And who bought you that ticket to fly home for your mother's funeral after you shot up all your money? I did. Now you're going to flex like this? Okay. Next time you're in trouble, don't call me. Your ass is getting locked up. And you know there are people from everywhere in this city, so someone in County will find out who you are and let your friends in Oakland know where you are."

"Damn, man. Just having a bad day, is all. You don't need to go there." He forced a smile, revealing beige teeth.

"Well, don't make me go there." I handed him ten dollars. "I need you to find out what you can. Call me when you hear something. If it's good, you'll get more."

C-Dub snatched the money and vanished into the shadows.

CHAPTER 12

After waking up the following Monday, I found I had drenched my bedsheets with sweat. It had taken two days of case follow-up before I could enjoy more than a couple of hours of consecutive sleep, but anxiety about my progress on the case and nightmares of Kanya kept me tossing the sheets. I kept dreaming I was at her tenth birthday party, reliving warm memories of sweet yellow cake, pink balloons, and presents—only to see them repeatedly morph into close-ups of her brutalized face, like a horrible video playing on a loop.

Kanya would have turned twenty today. She told Lorinda that a big surprise was supposed to happen. I was sure this 'surprise' had something to do with her death.

I was so drowsy that I felt drunk, stumbling about as if someone had given me anesthesia. My eyes ached and my limbs throbbed. I showered, dressed, and shuffled to my car in a zombie-like cadence. Sleep was the sweetest relief I could imagine, but there was no time for rest. GNB's corporate headquarters were open now, and since Kanya's parents nor DeVaughn could tell me anything, I hoped her former co-workers could provide some leads.

I went to a gas station, drained a nasty black coffee, and fought through morning gridlock to GNB's headquarters on Johnson Ferry Road. It was a glass and steel seventeen-story building surrounded by a ring of Georgia's ubiquitous pine trees. In front of the entrance, a fountain shot water in arching columns. I walked by to let the mist hit my face for a wake-up. After visiting the receptionist, an employee ushered me to the sixteenth floor and asked me to wait outside the office of Kanya's boss, Company Controller Richard Oliver.

Already, something was off. How did a young woman with

no experience or degree end up reporting directly to a high-ranking executive? As in response to my thought, the controller stepped outside. A man of average size, clean-shaven with a beak of a nose and a receding hairline, Richard tilted forward as he walked, like a modern day Atlas supporting the world on his narrow shoulders.

He shook my hand and released it quickly. "How can I help you, Detective? I don't recall getting any tickets lately," he said, tittering.

"If you have a moment, I'd like to talk to you about Kanya Glover."

He narrowed his eyes. "Kanya? What's this about?"

"She was murdered this past weekend."

Rich gasped and jerked his head. "What?" He peppered me with questions about whether it was a mistake, how and when it happened, and if a suspect was in custody.

"No," I said. "I'm hoping you can help me determine her last whereabouts. When did you last see her?"

He slumped into a chair and mumbled his disbelief. "Last Wednesday," he replied. "It was her last day. She had resigned."

"Why did she quit?"

"She said she found another job."

"Where?"

"I can't recall. Someplace near Cumberland Mall, I believe."

"Did she do or say anything out of the ordinary that day? Something she normally didn't do?"

He shook his head. "I didn't notice anything."

"How long did she work here?"

"About a year. I hired her to assist my admin, Natalie."

"Where is Natalie?"

"She's out today."

"Is she in tomorrow? I'd like to talk to her, too."

"I don't think she'd be able to tell you any more than I could."

"I still would like to talk to her."

"I'm not sure if she's in tomorrow. Perhaps Thursday? Or Friday?"

"You don't know when your employee is coming back to work?"

"She's been, uh, sick, so it depends on how she feels," he replied. "She'll call and let me know."

"Did Kanya work with others besides you and Natalie?"

"No. She kept to herself. She didn't socialize with anyone here."

"Did you work side by side with her?"

Rich cocked his head. "No. As I said, she assisted Natalie. I'm in meetings all day."

"Did you ever see Kanya outside of work?"

He frowned. "No. Why would I see her outside of work?"

"If you're in meetings all day, didn't work with her, and didn't see her outside of work, then how are you so sure she didn't socialize with anyone here?"

He glanced at his watch. "I-I misspoke. I don't know for certain. I just never saw her talking to people or going to lunch with them, things like that. I don't know what she did after work."

"Did Natalie talk about Kanya to you?"

"No."

"After working here a year, she made no friends? And Natalie never talked about her? Ever?"

Rich pursed his lips. "I feel like you're—pressing me for some reason. Like you don't like the answers I'm giving you."

"That's not my intent. I just want you to think clearly about your answers, that's all. It's critical for my investigation."

He took a deep breath. "Natalie may have mentioned small things about her, but it was only about her work. Like how Kanya may have helped her with some software application or something, but that's all. If Natalie knew about Kanya's personal life, she never mentioned it to me."

I clenched my jaws. How could everyone be so ignorant

about Kanya's friends, lovers, or acquaintances?

"Can you show me where she worked?" I asked.

Rich pointed to two desks, one large and one small, across from his office. The large one had a nameplate on top: Natalie Theron. The smaller one was clean and bare. "That's Kanya's," he said.

I opened its drawer and found nothing but two paper clips. "Did she leave anything behind?"

He shook his head.

"Can you give me her address?"

He opened a file cabinet behind Natalie's desk, pulled out a folder, and copied the address on a post-it note. The address: 10976 Cedar Ferry.

"This is her parents' place," I said. "She didn't live here. I need her address. Where did you send her checks? Or what was listed on the direct deposits?"

"That's all we have on file." He looked at his watch again. "Is there anything else?"

"What was her pay?"

"$11.50 an hour, I think. She worked about twenty hours a week."

"I need to see her payroll records, stubs, whatever you have."

He searched the file cabinet. After a minute, he produced copies of her last paycheck and direct deposit information, which indicated the same Cedar Ferry address. The controller glanced at his watch a third time.

"Am I intruding on your schedule?" I asked.

"I do have an important meeting in a few minutes."

"Mr. Oliver, do you know who her parents are?"

"Why?"

"Her stepfather is Pete Rennell."

"I know."

"So you must also know that a few years ago, he filed a class-action against this bank over allegations of sexual harassment and discrimination. And an executive was named personally in a second suit."

"And?"

"I'm curious. How did you end up hiring his stepdaughter?"

"I didn't know they were related at the time. They do have different surnames."

"She didn't list her parents as contacts in her application?"

"No. I can show that to you, if you like. It's in the file. Not that I understand why that matters. Natalie needed help, Kanya applied, and we hired her. I only found out who her father was afterward, but I didn't see a reason to fire her because of him. That lawsuit is in the past, and I've—*we've*—moved on."

"Can you give me Natalie's number?"

"But she's sick."

"She's too sick to speak? If she's supposed to return to work in a couple of days, she can't be near death."

Rich scribbled Natalie's number on another post-it and thrust it to me. His Blackberry buzzed. "I'm sorry, but I have to leave," he said. "Is there anything else?"

I thanked him for his time, handed him my card, and asked him to call me if he heard anything. He nodded, grabbed a folder, and we walked to the elevator bank. As we waited for the next car, he glued his eyes to his folder and skimmed through its pages repeatedly. After the doors opened and we stepped inside, he said he forgot a printout, darted out before the doors closed, and left me alone inside.

My stomach fluttered. After a steady diet of dead ends, something about Richard Oliver didn't smell right, so I was going to dig further into him. Especially after his reluctance to share Natalie's contact information. That only made me want to talk to her more.

Something told me he knew more about Kanya's last days than he indicated.

CHAPTER 13

Despite my new interest in GNB executive Rich Oliver, I still had few leads and worried that I had missed an important clue somewhere. Did we overlook some critical piece of evidence from the Jones Street field? Did DeVaughn, Kanya's parents, or her boss say something that meant more than what it sounded? At this point, I was following up on every loose end, no matter how thin it seemed.

After leaving GNB, my next destination was a townhouse in a subdivision off Windy Hill Road. It was a small neighborhood with townhomes so narrow that I could almost see both sides of the house from the front. I stopped at unit twenty. A U-Haul truck was parked nearby, and a Ford Escort stuffed with boxes and clothes sat in the driveway.

I knocked on the door, and a tiny woman with stringy hair and freckles answered. After I introduced myself and asked to speak to Kanya's old assistant gym teacher Daryl Langley, her demeanor shifted from curiosity to disdain. "I wish you people would leave him alone," she said. "It's not right. It's been long enough, don't you think?"

"What are you referring to?"

The diminutive woman sneered and led me through the living room, kitchen, and stairwell. The area was full of storage boxes and packing tape. We approached the master bedroom, where Daryl stood packing a suitcase.

"Mr. Langley?" I asked. "I'm Detective Strickland. If you have a moment, I'd like to talk to you."

When he looked up, I saw why he was an urban legend at his school and made students uneasy. A short, thin man with dirty brown hair, a beer belly, and a skinny neck, his right eye was frozen to the side while his left eye fixed on me. Despite a severe case of crossed eyes, he shot a hateful glare at me that rivaled that of any convicted felon.

"Where are you headed?" I asked.

"What do you want?"

"I'd like to ask you about Kanya Glover."

He shot the woman a knowing look. "See? Didn't I tell you? I told you they'd do this. I knew it." He faced me. "As soon as I heard what happened, I knew you assholes would be here. This is goddamned harassment."

"Sir, I don't know what happened before this. I just want to ask a few questions."

"No. You want to know if I did it." He jammed items in his suitcase and slammed it shut, leaving shirtsleeves hanging out. "Well, I didn't."

"Why are you in a rush to leave?"

"Is this a crime, too? If you must know, I just got a new job in Orlando. Amy and I are starting a new life. And you're slowing us down. I want to get out of here and never come back."

"Why?"

Langley scowled and tossed the suitcase aside without looking, almost hitting Amy by the door. "Why are you here asking me about that damn girl?"

"Just routine questions, Mr. Langley."

"No, they're not. I'm still the suspect for her. Always have been. Admit it."

"You're not a suspect. But since you were investigated years ago—"

"*I—never—touched—her!* I've said that for years!"

"But you did threaten her family, did you not? Didn't they get a restraining order?"

"And I got one against her father, too! So what's your point? I didn't do anything to her. Then or now. Hell, her family probably killed her for insurance money or something. Rich people do shit like that. They ruined me. So let's just say that Karma is a bitch."

"Daryl!" Amy exclaimed.

"I know what I said," Langley barked. "And I meant it. They blamed me for their girl being a screw-up. Yet, all she did was stay in trouble…"

"What makes you say that?" I asked.

"Oh, please. Yeah, the Rennells are such perfect parents. So perfect that their little princess got expelled left and right and ran around in the streets. I worked in the school system. People talk. You think I wouldn't hear about it? The Rennells ruined my life. They put me on the black list around here. Every time I applied for a job, it came up. No one would hire me. They thought I was a pedophile who got away." Langley stepped around me and yanked more clothes from the closet.

"You haven't seen Kanya lately, have you?" I asked.

He stopped and turned to me. "Why the hell would I have seen her? I haven't seen her in years."

"So what did you do last Friday night?"

"I was in Orlando. All weekend. Signing lease papers for an apartment. You want the name of the place, too?"

"Sure, if you have it."

"Unbelievable." He stormed out of the room and returned with a red folder. "Here," he said. "Highland Vista Apartments. See the stamp on front? July 25th. Friday. Three days ago. Call the leasing office, and they'll tell you."

"Not necessary."

He grabbed a phone, called the office, and had the leasing consultant confirm that he and Amy were there Friday afternoon.

"But wait," the ex-gym teacher said. "I bet you think I could've flown back here Friday night, just in time to kill the little princess, and then flown back to Florida. Call my credit card company. You won't find a record of me flying back Friday because we rented a car and drove to Florida that morning, and we just got back yesterday. In fact, I'll show you the receipt that shows what time we turned it in. And the mileage."

As I read the rental agreement and confirmed his story, the couple stood stiffly, facing me. "Well, thank you for your time," I said. "Here's my card. If you hear anything, please call me." Neither of them reached for it, so I dropped it on the bed.

Langley smirked. "Tell the Rennells I wish them luck."

CHAPTER 14

After enjoying Daryl Langley's charm, my next stop was the Fulton County Medical Examiners Center. On the way, I tried preparing myself to review Kanya's autopsy. My career had desensitized me to blood, so it was nothing for me to scarf a cheeseburger while watching an examiner flare a victim's chest cavity open, use power saws to slice through bone, and grasp slippery organs and guts.

But I dreaded seeing Kanya. I didn't want her sliced-and-sewn-up body to be my last memory of her. I already couldn't get the picture of her smashed face out of my head. But I had to find out if the ME uncovered any forensic details that shed light on the case.

The FCMEC was clean and new, unlike the part of town it resided. South of downtown on Pryor Street near Turner Field, the Atlanta Braves ballpark, it looked like a small office building full of dentists and accountants rather than a human chop shop.

Mike Yates, one of three associate medical examiners at the facility, invited me into his office. In his fifties, he sported a crew cut of silver hair and was always in his office, the autopsy room, or his convertible BMW that he drove with the top down even when the temperature was near freezing. His office was full of books, medical diagrams, organ replicas, and binders organized with military precision. The exception: stacks of papers and folders piled high on his two office chairs, a sign of his attitude toward visitors.

"Jeez," Mike said. "Your eyes are red. You can stand in the street and stop traffic. And why are your hands shaking? Are you on something?"

"Sleep deprivation. I don't recommend it. What do you have on Kanya Glover?"

"I just finished the autopsy not too long ago. So let me start with the good news. One of the GBI guys owes me a favor, so he said he'd try expediting tests of the samples I sent. Tox screen and follow-up and DNA."

"Thanks. So I'll wait eight months instead of nine?"

"He said they had some process changes going on, so it could be as fast as three weeks."

"No way." A few weeks to complete forensic tests may have been normal elsewhere, but it was a biblical miracle in Georgia. Since every police department went to GBI for tests on bodily fluids, the agency was like a Walmart on Christmas Eve with one checkout lane open. The backlog of analysis requests stretched for miles. Qualified scientists were scarce, and when they gained enough experience at GBI, they bolted for higher pay in the private sector. A nine-month wait for a DNA test was typical in Georgia.

"That's what he said," Mike replied.

"He must owe you a huge favor. You save his life?"

"Bigger than that. I introduced his sister to one of my friends, and they're getting married. As a thank-you, he said he'll try rushing the tests. 'Try' being the operative word."

"Surprised you didn't check out his sister for yourself."

"Oh, no. I've got a burn victim back here who looks better than her."

"And you hooked her up with your buddy? Doesn't sound like a good friend. Neither do you, for that matter."

"He's my best friend, actually. But he's uglier than she is, so they're compatible. Hope they don't have kids."

"Jesus, Mike," I said, shaking my head. It was evident why he was a veteran of two divorces and racing toward his third.

We entered the autopsy room. It smelled of cleaning chemicals and lemon freshener. Anatomical diagrams hung on the walls, and shiny autopsy saws, blades, scalpels, shears, twig-pruners, and other horror-film props lay on two portable islands. Two large scales used to weigh organs hung from the ceiling.

We stopped at a stainless steel table. In a plastic slot on the front was a folder marked "K. Glover" with her identification number.

The air rushed from my chest, and I felt the urge to vomit. Despite the floodlights we had set up in the Jones Street field, the darkness of the early morning had softened the obliteration of her face. Now, in the autopsy room, the overhead lights showed her crushed skull and torn flesh in excruciating detail. The vivid image seared into my brain like a cattle brand. I turned away, stifling a gag reflex. I couldn't see my Kanya like that.

"This is one of the worst blunt traumas I've seen," Mike said. "And I've done thousands of these. It was hard making a clean cut to remove the brain."

"Guess I don't need to know the cause of death."

"Not so fast. It wasn't from the beating." The pathologist pointed to purple bruises across her neck. "You see? Fractured hyoid, hemorrhaging under the skin. She was strangled. Whoever did it was strong."

I took a deep breath, glancing at her neck before placing my gaze to her lower body, away from the facial carnage.

"So," Mike resumed, "the beating was postmortem, used with something blunt and heavy." He drew his index finger across an indentation of a small half-circle above her left eye socket. "Look right here. This is the imprint of the object. If you find it, it's possible I can match it—hey, are you all right?"

I tried to swallow the painful lump in my throat. "I'm good."

"Your eyes are wet. The job getting to you?"

"Hate seeing things happen to kids." It felt as if a grapefruit lodged itself in my windpipe.

"Kid? Not many kids developed like this, Strick. This is a grown woman."

"Is there evidence of sexual assault?"

"You sure this isn't getting to you?"

"Mike, I've got things to do."

"Well, excuuuse, me. No, I didn't find any vaginal tearing or abrasions. And no semen turned up on the swab."

I had seen naked women on these tables before and thought little of it; now, I felt the urge to cover Kanya's body and turn off the lights. Let her have her dignity for one last time. "What's up with her hands?" I asked.

"Her fingertips were almost entirely burned. Like the beating to her face, it was postmortem." Mike looked at Kanya and shook his head. "Someone was upset with you, lady. He spent some TLC on you."

Flesh and bone are difficult to burn, yet her fingers were almost ashen. There were no ligature marks on her wrists or ankles, another indication she was dead when the burning happened. If she had been alive, he would have been forced to restrain her, and she couldn't sit through such pain without rubbing her wrists and ankles raw. I wondered if the toxicology results would reveal she had been drugged unconscious. That was the only way I could see someone burning her extremities without creating signs of physical resistance.

"There was also some water in her lungs and stomach," Mike said. "Consistent with a drowning victim. Just on a smaller scale."

"You said she was strangled."

"She was. I'm guessing she was in a pool or tub, and she ingested water as she fought her killer."

"What about a creek? There's one south of where we found her."

"Possibly, but I'd expect to see more organic debris or microorganisms in that water. There was none."

I recalled the shower curtain we found in the field. A tub was more likely, meaning the original crime scene was a bathroom.

Mike flipped through his folder. "I estimate TOD was between six p.m. and midnight that Friday. Her temperature was lower than that of the environment—the temp out there was 94 degrees—so she was in a cool location before someone dumped her out there."

"Trace evidence?"

"Of course, but you saw where she was. Her body and pubic region were full of fibers, dirt, and trash. I'm sure you'll understand it's going to take time sifting through that. And none of it may be relevant."

"I know." The killer's actions were all over the place. There was no evidence he assaulted her sexually, but he beat her, strangled her, nearly drowned her, and burned her fingers to a crisp. She had been killed three times.

The fingers perplexed me. Why burn them? Was it to keep us from using her prints to identify her?

No, that didn't make sense. If he wanted to keep Kanya's identity secret, it would've been smarter to hide her where no one would find her body, at least not for years. Instead, he dropped her in a location where it was certain someone would find her. And her dental records made the identification simple enough.

He didn't burn her fingers to torture or inflict pain. She was already dead. And if he drugged her, what was the point of torturing the victim if she couldn't feel it?

"What are you thinking?" Mike asked.

"Wondering why he burned her fingers."

"Maybe a signature. You might have a serial nut on your hands."

"No. This wasn't an opportunity killing. He knew her and hated her." I paused. "She fought back. My girl fought him. I think he burned her fingers to destroy trace evidence under her nails."

Mike cocked his head and lifted an eyebrow. "You think he'd do all of that? That would take a lot of time."

"He was in no hurry. You said he kept her someplace before he took her to the field, right? Did you find anything under her nails?"

"Nothing usable. Look at them. They're extra crispy."

"Then he did what he intended. I can't think of another reason. He already set her car on fire, and we got nothing from that. He's destroying evidence."

"Why didn't he just put her inside the car if he's going to burn it anyway? Or why not cut off her fingers and flush them down the sewer or something? Why go through all that?"

"I'm too tired to justify the mindset of this disturbed bastard. After what we've seen over the years, you expect logical behavior? Maybe he's taunting us. Maybe he watches too much *Forensic Files*. Maybe he wants to show how smart he is." I thought of the Band-Aids on DeVaughn's neck and cheek. I didn't believe his bullshit about his dog causing the scratches. If he was the killer, Kanya had left her marks on him.

"Maybe," Mike acquiesced. "As you said, we've seen crazier things."

Most of the people I arrested for murder were stupid. They were men who committed their sins in such brazen fashion that it was unbelievable they thought they could get away with it. Kanya's killer was smarter. Placing her in a garbage dump, setting her car on fire, and burning her fingers were all attempts to prevent us from collecting evidence and targeting him.

Ironically, his actions pointed him out as someone close to the victim. A random killer wouldn't go through so much trouble. Only someone who hated her, someone who knew he'd be approached by the police, would make such an effort. The mutilation of her face was a clear signal. He wanted to destroy her identity and erase everything about her. He wanted to hurt her loved ones by making sure we could never look at her one last time. It was rare for a random killer to engage in such overkill and take such steps to hide.

"What are you thinking now?" Mike asked.

"The son of a bitch thinks he's smart. But he'll make a

mistake. They always do." I had enough and turned to walk out. "Send me the report. I'll read the rest later."

"Wait," Mike said. "She was also pregnant."

I stopped. "How far along?"

"About seven weeks. Look at these stab wounds. Surprised you didn't ask about them."

I had forgotten them but now noticed the wounds were in a tight grouping below her belly button. After seeing them, I wanted to kill the assailant myself. If he ever made it to Death Row, I'd volunteer to plunge the needle in his arm and spit in his face as he struggled for his last breath.

"He stabbed the fetus," Mike said. "Like the other stuff, it was postmortem. He was aiming for it; it's too coincidental for a tight cluster of wounds in that spot, given the treatment to the rest of her body. She isn't visibly pregnant, so he knew she was expecting." The pathologist bit his bottom lip. "Either that, or she told him she was pregnant in a last-ditch effort to spare her life and he didn't care. I'm guessing he didn't care too much for the baby, either. You find the father, I'd say you've probably got your killer."

CHAPTER 15

Sleep deprivation.

All homicide detectives endure it at some point, especially when high-profile murders occur and the department plows its resources into the investigations. In those cases, it's common to work shifts stretching eighteen hours or longer.

My shift had stretched for over two days, with little snippets of sleep here and there. I was doing eighty miles an hour on I-75 towards the APD headquarters when I received news that gave me an adrenaline jolt. One of Kanya's friends had just called our hotline and needed to speak to someone about her murder. I decided to meet this friend at her job, speeding down the interstate while mulling over what Mike had told me twenty minutes earlier.

Kanya was seven weeks pregnant.

Lorinda and Pete never mentioned this to me. They probably had no idea. They were candid in sharing Kanya's troubles, so I saw no reason for them to keep it a secret. Besides, the girl never even told them where she lived, so it was unlikely she told them they were going to be grandparents. Kanya may not have even known she was pregnant at that early stage. But if she knew, why didn't she tell her folks? Did she plan to tell them later? Or did she intend to abort it?

DeVaughn was my prime suspect, but a new player had thrust himself into the spotlight. DeVaughn was not the father. He was still in the Fulton Inn when Kanya became pregnant, and Georgia doesn't allow conjugal visits in its correctional facilities. I suspected the father was the unknown boyfriend Lorinda and Pete had mentioned, the man who showered Kanya with gifts and jewelry. And I had a good idea who he was.

South of the I-285 interchange in Cobb County, I-75 is

surrounded by lush trees on both sides of the highway, but as it veers beneath an underpass north of Midtown, it reveals a panoramic view of towering monuments of steel and glass. At night, the scene sparkled. Reds, greens, whites, and blues dot the sky, with its winding streams of brake lights and neon signs. Even after seeing it thousands of times, I still loved that view of downtown Atlanta and felt a surge of optimism, as if all of my dreams would come to life just around the bend of the highway.

And each time I made that curve, I snapped back to reality seconds later. While most visitors saw the ritzy, impressive sections of the city, I saw the other side, the homes and communities so decrepit that I wanted to shower and cleanse myself after walking in them. As I passed through downtown and headed west, the change happened in less than a minute. Swank hotels morphed into motels tagged with graffiti. Clean office architecture became derelict buildings in need of razing. White-collar employees relinquished the sidewalks to day laborers or homeless people looking to pass the time. All in the span of three miles.

Atlanta was a city of contrasts. It was full of sleepy Southern charm but alive with electricity. It was a transportation mecca, with the world's busiest airport and smoothly-paved interstates. It also confounded motorists with a thousand streets named Peachtree, changed street names on the same stretch of road with no warning, and was notorious for hellish rush hour traffic that flung commuters into rage or despair. The city was one of the epicenters of the Civil Rights movement, the birthplace of Martin Luther King, and is home to colleges and universities that pump out black engineers, doctors, and lawyers. The metro area is also the home of Stone Mountain Park, a site formerly used for Klan rallies but now a theme park celebrating the heritage of the Confederacy.

The city's biggest contrast was its long-time slogan, *The City Too Busy to Hate*. Attempting to shed its Jim Crow heritage, the city promoted its booming economy and implied its citizens were too busy to be hateful bigots.

The City too Busy to Hate?

Atlanta's murder rate had just set a record for July, and I had an office pool to see if August would set another record. If Georgia's largest city was too busy to hate, its murders proved otherwise. There were plenty of people who weren't busy enough and had too much time to hate and kill. Kanya's killer certainly fit in that category, especially when considering the time it took to do what he did to her body.

The City too Busy to Hate? Not based on our homicides.

I arrived at a Chick-Fil-A restaurant in the southwest part of the city to meet Kanya's friend, Marina Gardner. A petite young woman with mocha skin and pearly eyes, Marina stood behind a register and gave mechanical greetings to customers. A man who looked about eighty held up the line by telling her she looked like a Hershey bar and he had a sweet tooth. He proved chivalry wasn't dead by offering to buy her a chicken sandwich. Her manager rescued her by asking her to meet me in the dining area.

She approached me and kept her eyes on my police shield hanging from my chain necklace.

"I see the customers love you," I said.

"Bert? Oh, he does that with all of the girls here. You are...?"

I introduced myself. "You called us about Kanya. I'd like to talk to you for a moment."

She winced and drooped her shoulders. "I heard about what happened last night. Do you know who did it?"

"I'm hoping you can help me with that. You two were good friends?"

"Used to be. We've known each other since we were twelve, but she got too wild for me. She started getting high all the time. In high school, she'd put on makeup and go to college parties. I went with her once. My dad almost killed me when he found out. We didn't hang out much after that. I didn't care for all of the drinking. I don't have time for parties now. I'm full-time at Tech."

"Do you suspect anyone who would have done this?"

Marina sat down and wiped her eyes. "Yeah. A guy she worked for. She told me he got her pregnant and he wanted her to abort it."

"Richard Oliver, her boss at GNB?"

"I think so. She never said his full name."

He was the man I suspected was the father, so it felt good to get confirmation of a lead that sparked some movement on the case. But the good feeling was swallowed by a burning anger—it meant he was the one most likely to have killed her.

"I felt bad for her, you know?" she said. "Just when she was getting her life turned around."

No wonder Kanya never mentioned her "boyfriend" to her parents. Working for Richard Oliver, the man Pete had claimed discriminated against women, was bad enough. Dating and getting pregnant by him? Pete and Lorinda would have blown a fuse, and the local media would've been a circus. It was evident why he acted so strange around me. "What else did she say about him?"

"Not much. She was thinking of keeping the baby."

"When did she tell you this?"

"A couple of weeks ago."

"Was that the last time you two talked? Or saw each other?"

"Yes. I called her. We hadn't talked in a long time. That's when she told me everything. So when I saw the news, I thought her boss might've had something to do with it."

"Do you know DeVaughn?"

She rolled her eyes. "Yes. He tried to sleep with me. Even when he and Kanya were still together. And he *did* sleep with another friend of ours, Shawna. When Kanya found out, she whipped her ass. Next thing we knew, Shawna had moved up to

Virginia. I guess it's embarrassing to get beat up by a pretty girl."

"When did that happen?"

"Hmm. Maybe a year-and-a-half ago?"

"Is Shawna the get-even type?"

Marina glanced upward. "Yeah, but I don't think she had anything to do with this. We haven't heard from her since she moved."

"When was the last time you saw DeVaughn?"

"About the same time I talked to Kanya. Maybe a couple of days later. It was at a club."

"New Experience?"

"Yeah. I was out with my girls, and we bumped into him."

"He say anything to you?"

"He asked about Kanya and if I knew where she was staying. But I didn't. I just knew she had a place in Buckhead."

"What about her other friends?"

"I know Cheryl. They hung together a lot. I can give you her number. She's cool, but don't tell her anything you want kept secret. The whole city will know it in an hour."

"Any others besides Cheryl?"

"No. Kanya didn't get along with a lot of girls. She said she didn't care for the drama."

I asked her if she knew any of Kanya's male friends, but she shook her head. Apparently, Kanya was extremely selective in whom she let get close.

Marina traced circles in the table with her finger, a slight smile on her face. "She's why I chose computer science as my major," she said. "Kanya was a nerd. She liked computers and games. One time in high school, our chemistry teacher told us we had an exam the next day. We didn't know the material at all. We never paid attention in class. He was some foreign guy, so we couldn't understand a word he said; he'd pronounce the elements all wrong and stuff. Later that night, she hacked into the teacher's directory and got the answers."

"And you sold them to the class?"

"No, we used them ourselves! The teacher, he knew something was up. We weren't the best students, and yet, we both got As, so he wanted to retest us. Kanya wasn't having it. She caused a scene and accused him of discriminating against Asian and black women. 'You don't think we earned that score? You saying we cheated? My stepdad's a lawyer, and he'll sue you!' The teacher apologized like crazy, and Kanya gave me this wink… God, it was hard not to laugh." Her grin disappeared. "I guess it doesn't sound funny when I say it now. Anyway, she got expelled the following year for something, and we didn't hang out much after that."

"What was Kanya like as a friend?" I asked. "Did she get you into any bad situations with others?"

"Not at all. She acted hard, but she was a sweet person. She'd have your back. She was stubborn, though. And she did have problems with authority. Like a lot of people."

"You ever meet her folks?"

"Once. I saw her with them in the mall. We talked for a bit. They were nice." She stared ahead. "She teased me when I told her I was majoring in computer science. She was always saying that's where the money is and how more women should get in it. But with me, she was all like, 'How'd they let you in the building? You can't even program your cell phone!' But she was happy for me—"

She wiped her eyes.

"Marina, when you talked to her a couple of weeks ago, did she say anything about something happening today? Like a big change or surprise?"

The young woman looked at me with a bemused expression. "Today? No." She rubbed her hand over her face. "Oh…today's her birthday, isn't it?"

"You feel Richard Oliver might have had something to do with this. What about DeVaughn?"

Marina didn't have the same strong suspicion for the ex-boy-friend as she did for the ex-boss. She thought DeVaughn was too smart to take the risk. He would have known that he'd be the first—if not the only—suspect the police targeted. More importantly, Marina said DeVaughn told her it had crushed him to watch his ten-year-old son Eric screaming for him as the police led him to jail. He had vowed never to do anything that risked separating them again. She believed it was GNB's company controller who had killed her friend or arranged for it to happen.

I wasn't sold on her beneficent view of DeVaughn, a repeat criminal who hated Kanya, but her suspicion of Rich was valid. The man was married, had a promising career, earned a good salary—and allegedly impregnated his teenaged employee.

Richard Oliver was now my primary suspect.

CHAPTER 16

I stopped at a QuikTrip and drained a coffee that tasted days old. Grimacing from the bitterness, I decided to call Natalie Theron, Rich's admin. I didn't care how sick he said she was; if she wasn't in a coma, she was going to talk. After seeing Kanya and Rich every day, she had to know some things that I could use to put her boss behind bars.

Before I dialed her number, my cell rang. "This is Strick."

"Uh, are you the officer who's working on the—the murder—of Kanya Glover? I got transferred to you." It was a woman. By her voice, it sounded as if she had been crying.

"Yes. Who am I speaking to?"

"Cheryl Tory. I was Kanya's friend." My heart pounded at the prospect of another break. She had a southern accent, one with a deeper twang than the typical Georgia lilt. "I just spoke to Marina, and she gave me your number," she said, her voice cracking. "She told me she just talked to you about her boyfriend?"

"Which one?"

There was a pause. "Her boss. His name's Rich. I know she had a fight with him last week. They've been fooling around although he's married."

That was the funny thing about working in Homicide. One could follow leads, research every detail, track witnesses, and question suspects until the Last Days, only to get nowhere. Then, when one least expected it, a big break materialized. A wish granted from the Police Gods.

Despite his education and influential position in his company, Richard Oliver was not a prudent man. I thanked God for people like him. They made my job easier. "Have you told anyone else about this?" I asked.

"No."

Now I had two independent corroborations pointing to the same man.

"I'd like to meet you now, if possible," I said, hoping to get through an interview without collapsing of exhaustion. "Where are you?"

"You know the Conifer Homes apartments? Near the Georgia Dome? I'm in apartment fifteen."

"I'll be there in five."

When developers built housing projects, they used the word "homes" in the names to convince residents they weren't living in projects. The marketing tactic fooled no one. Crime and squalor still plagued the places, and Conifer Homes was no exception.

Conifer used to be known as the Oasis Motel, or rather, the Ho-asis, given the number of prostitutes that turned tricks in its dirty rooms. The city had warned its previous owners, an Afghan couple who preferred cash-paying tenants, about their clientele. After five separate drug-related murders in the motel in the summer of '97, the city forced them to sell. The winning investor slapped on a microscopic layer of paint, installed cheap appliances, and changed the name to unveil the Conifer Homes.

Sweat trickled down my back as I stepped out of the car. The sun beat on my head and waves of heat rose from the cracked asphalt. Old air conditioners leaked from windows, creating streams of rusty stains down the exterior walls. The community was shaped like an upside down 'U', with one entrance. A two-story row of apartments lay straight ahead with a row of units flanking each side. Cheryl's place was to my right, the end apartment.

She opened the door and invited me in before I knocked. A tanned, young white woman with curly blonde hair, she was top-heavy with smooth legs. Her eyes were weary and pink.

Her place was small with cheap furniture and an assortment of dolls and doll pieces piled in a corner. The air smelled like bacon and Pine-Sol. Someone had attempted to stabilize the dining table with folded paper towels jammed under the legs.

"Ms. Tory, what do you know about Kanya and her boss?"

"A lot."

Kanya had confided in her with juicy details regarding her time at GNB. From the day he hired her, Richard Oliver dished out compliments and small gifts to the young woman, who reveled in the attention. He often complained that his wife Diane had no interest in sex, so two months after hiring Kanya, they consummated their affair in a Macon hotel. He continued spoiling his mistress by spitting out cash as if he were a human ATM. To Kanya, every day was Christmas.

Last month, that Christmas spirit vanished when Rich's wife cornered him with an unexpected letter. A jewelry store had sent it to the house, thanking him for his purchase of a $1,200 diamond pendant necklace. Diane had opened the mail that day, and after reading it, wondered why that jewelry wasn't gracing her neck, especially since her birthday was six months away and it wasn't a holiday. She demanded to see the item, but he squirmed out of his predicament by swearing it was a retirement gift for a long-time employee. Whether she believed him was unclear.

What was clear was that Rich was begging for trouble. Having an affair was bad enough, but having it with the daughter of the man who sued his company for sexual harassment was mind-boggling. But it wasn't surprising. I had caught and arrested several fugitives because they slept around. After their ride-or-die chicks had discovered their infidelity, the ladies flooded our hotlines with GPS-quality directions on where to find their no-good men. And if men facing life sentences couldn't stop themselves from cheating on women with intimate knowledge of their crimes—the very people they *shouldn't* have betrayed—there was no reason to expect a married corporate executive would be any different. Some men just didn't like to think.

"What did he do after his wife confronted him?" I asked.

"He told Kanya that they had to stop seeing each other. But they didn't, because a few days ago, she told me she was pregnant. And it was his."

"Did Kanya tell him this?"

"Yeah. Last week."

"How'd he react?"

"He screamed at her. Called her a stupid bitch." Cheryl paused. "He accused her of trapping him and demanded she get an abortion. She said he had this faraway look in his eyes; he got quiet and told her he'd make sure no one would ever know about the baby. Then she promised to abort it. She just said what he wanted to hear so she could get away from him that night."

"What day did this happen?"

"Last Tuesday. After that argument, she came over here upset, crying and everything."

"Where did that discussion happen?"

"Her place."

"You know where she lived?"

"Of course. Buckhead Towers."

An image of a landlord frolicking in piles of cash came to mind. Full of high-rises, condominiums, office towers, and expensive homes, Buckhead is not only the wealthiest section of Atlanta but also one of the most affluent communities in the country. The Towers lived up to its posh namesake and carried steep rents, easily charging up to $3,000 a month for a one-bedroom.

"How could she afford that?" I asked. "On $11.50 an hour?"

"GNB paid the rent. Kanya told me they leased a couple of units there. After she took the job, she told Richard she was looking for a place, and one of the apartments was vacant, so he said she could stay there until she found something. It was furnished, too. She moved in, and he never said anything else about it. And she didn't bring it up. She stayed there for a year."

"For free?"

Cheryl nodded. "I guess they didn't need the place that much. She was lucky."

No, she was young, cute, and legal. In another stroke of genius, Richard Oliver used company resources to pamper his mistress. I didn't know which was more astounding: his recklessness in the affair or that it lasted as long as it did without it being blown open.

"They met there all the time," Cheryl continued. "But after that argument, she moved in with me for a few days."

"She never considered going back to her parents?"

She shook her head. "Kanya said they were always trying to run her life."

"Did you tell anyone she was staying here?"

"Just Marina, I think."

"When'd you last see Kanya?"

"Last Friday."

"The night she was killed."

Cheryl nodded. "We were supposed to go to a movie. But she said she had to go do a couple of things first." Her bottom lip quivered. "I never heard from her again. I wondered what happened, why she didn't call. I was calling her a million times, calling her parents' house, no one was answering. " She gulped. "Then I saw the news. And I keep thinking about Rich and what he said to her."

"Where did she go? Did she see him?"

"I don't know. She just said she had to run out."

"When did she leave?"

"About eight. Maybe a little earlier. She said she'd be back by 10."

"Did she seem worried? What was her mood?"

"She was in a good mood." She paused. "It was funny; she was real upset on Tuesday and Wednesday, because of Richard, but by Friday, everything seemed great. She said she wasn't worried about money anymore and was getting her own place at the Towers. I said, 'You can't afford that,' and she said, 'I will by Monday.' "

"Which is today. She told her parents something big was going to happen. Any idea what was she talking about?"

"She said the same thing to me. But she didn't give me details. Said it would surprise everyone. I think she was blackmailing Rich and she expected to come up big time."

"Did she acknowledge that?"

"No. I asked her, but she wouldn't say. Just said I'd see soon enough. But she didn't seem bothered about him anymore. She also said something about going to college and starting a shelter."

"College? And a shelter?"

Cheryl nodded. "She had all these big plans, so that's why I thought she was blackmailing him. He probably was going to pay her not to tell his wife. Or maybe it was to get an abortion." She sighed. "I warned her not to mess with him like that."

"Her folks have money. Couldn't they have been giving her some?"

"She didn't like asking them for money."

"You said you warned her not to mess with him. You think she trapped Rich?"

She looked at me as if I had screamed a profanity in a church. "No. Kanya wasn't like that. But even if she was, she could've done better if she was trying to trap someone. She could've had an athlete or someone really well off. She was tall, young, pretty. Besides, as you said, her folks have money. She'd go to them before she needed to trap anyone."

"You don't think she trapped him, but you think she blackmailed him," I said. "They're similar. Both are done for money."

Cheryl folded her arms. "She wouldn't trap him."

"But she would blackmail him?"

She took a deep breath. "Maybe it's not blackmail. Maybe it's just making things right. He got her pregnant, so it's not right he leaves her to raise a baby by herself. I'm a single mother. I know how hard this is. If he's going to leave her hanging like that, he should provide something. She didn't get pregnant by herself."

"Why were you concerned enough to warn her about making things right?"

"I thought he'd hurt her. Or worse." She blew her nose. "She was just a kid. She didn't have her first boyfriend until she was seventeen. And he was a bum. Then Rich comes along, gives her a job, wines and dines her, buys her things…she'd never been treated like that. She was naïve. Rich knew what he was doing with her. And he had a lot to lose."

"You know her ex-boyfriend?"

"DeVaughn? Yeah, we dated a few years ago, I hate to admit. He's how I met Kanya."

"He said he didn't know you."

"He also lies."

"I'm sure you know he served time, after a fight with Kanya. He claims he never hit her, that she did it to herself."

Cheryl dropped her eyes.

"Wait—he didn't hit her?" I asked. "Kanya lied?"

She took a deep breath. "He deserved to go to jail. He hit her before. Several times. He even broke her nose once. And she never reported it then."

"Why did she lie on him that time?"

"She got sick of him. He was threatening to hit her. Again. So right there, she started hitting herself and called the police on him."

Hell hath no fury. "Was he ever violent with you?"

"No way. My two brothers…they're kind of crazy. They didn't approve of me and DeVaughn in the first place. I don't see color, but they're different. If he hit me, he'd have some down-home Georgia boys to answer to."

"So you think Rich had something to do with this. What

about DeVaughn? You just confirmed that she had him thrown in jail. I'd imagine he'd be upset with that. Especially if he had been violent with her before."

She pondered my question. "Anything's possible. But he's a lot of talk. I'm not saying he's not capable of it. But I know Rich was just as angry with her, if not more. And he has way more to lose. DeVaughn's life probably was better inside jail, anyway."

"In my experience, men who've got nothing to lose are just as dangerous, if not more. You still speak to him?"

She shook her head. "Not in a few weeks. Not much to say." A child wailed from a bedroom in the back. "I'm sorry, my daughter's a little sick. Gotta check on her." She pointed to a corner of the living room. "Kanya's things are over there, that suitcase and that box. Her family might want them."

Kanya's last possessions consisted of a blue Samsonite suitcase and a cardboard box the size of a small television. The luggage was full of tops, blouses, pants, jeans, and hair accessories. No cell phone. No note or planner that listed a Friday night date with her killer.

The contents of the box:

- A lime-green spring jacket
- Three DVDs: *Bad Boys, The Princess Bride, My Big Fat Greek Wedding*
- A manila folder
- Four homemade DVDs: *Chi-Town, Caribana, ATL July 4th, DC*
- One empty VHS sleeve for *An Officer and a Gentleman*
- One makeup and hygiene kit
- One MP3 player

I flipped through the folder. Inside was a job application for a receptionist position at the Coca-Cola headquarters and an application to Georgia State University. There was also a

SunTrust bank statement that listed transfers from an account labeled *Employment Law – Disbursements* to another unnamed account. The transfers were in increments of $6,000 and recurred every two weeks for the past six months. The balance of the disbursement account was $3,347. There was no information showing the recipient account, other than its last four digits.

It must have been the bank information Kanya had reviewed and printed from Pete's computer. What was she doing with it? She told Cheryl that she didn't need to worry about money again, but this account wasn't enough to ease any financial concerns. The balance could barely cover the rent for a month in the Towers, much less college tuition and the establishment of a shelter. And where was the money going?

If she planned to use that account to pay her bills, it wasn't clear how she would access the money. The account numbers weren't in the statement. And figuring out passwords and downloading answers for chemistry exams was one thing; sidestepping a bank's layers of encryption was something else. If she were that good, there were more lucrative targets out there for her than this account. Not to mention that Pete froze all access to the account shortly after discovering what she did, so there was no reason to hold on to the account detail.

Making a note to revisit the bank detail later, I was examining the homemade DVDs from the box when Cheryl reappeared.

"Kanya loved making videos," she said. "She always wanted to show me places she went to."

"Is she in any of them?"

"I haven't watched all of them, but probably not. She said it made her look fat. Which I thought was ridiculous."

I rummaged through the box. "Is this everything she had here?"

"Yeah. Almost. I was going to watch one of her real movies, but I don't know where I put it. My daughter might have moved it somewhere." On cue, her daughter called loudly from her bedroom. "I'm sorry, I got to go take care of her."

Judging from how she sounded, the little girl was either near death or didn't like me monopolizing her mother's attention. I handed Cheryl my card and thanked her for her help.

It was time to put some heat on Richard Oliver.

CHAPTER 17

My stomach twisted itself into a knot as I drove down Ponce de Leon and turned into the APD headquarters. It wasn't the dull ambiance of City Hall East that churned my insides, but my boss, Sgt. Brice Lourne, who made me want to call in sick every day. He had been off over the past weekend but was back in the office. Because of the higher-than-normal interest surrounding Kanya's murder, I couldn't avoid him.

I went to my desk to update her homicide case file when I heard Lourne speaking to someone in his office. Before I could sneak away, he called me on my phone. "Tiger, don't you go anywhere," he said. "Come here for a sec."

I wondered if condemned men felt similar chest pains when prison guards dragged them to the electric chair. Lourne sat at his desk, hunched over a mass of reports and scrunching his pitch-black eyebrows into a V. A bearish, leather-skinned dark man in his late fifties, he sported a shiny dome and rolls of thick wrinkles on the back of his neck. His mustache looked like a black caterpillar resting on his lip, and his face was pitted like an orange peel.

I stepped inside his office and glanced at the big red "547" on the wall. His "Countdown Calendar" was impossible to miss. A spiral-ringed notebook with three cards side-by-side and numbered from zero to nine, the calendar represented the days left until his retirement. He updated it daily, longing for the day he could tell the world to kiss his ass. I tensed my shoulders and wished I could flip that calendar to "000" and watch him vanish like morning fog under the sun.

"Where are we with this Glover-Rennell?" he asked.

"Waiting on the toxic and a blood test. We've got two prime suspects. Well, one is prime, the other is a high possible."

He looked at my hands. "Are you shaking?"

"Caffeine overload. I've been running on this nonstop."

"Are we close to an arrest?" Unlike police sergeants depicted on television, he never yelled or raised his voice. He didn't have to. His low voice still felt like ground glass chewing up my eardrum. A phonetic hybrid of Gilbert Godfried and Chris Rock, he sounded as if he was hollering even when he whispered.

"I might be."

"Who's the prime?" He looked down at a previous case update I had sent him. "The ex-boyfriend? DeVaughn Copeland? Or this teacher here? Daryl Langley?"

"We can scratch Langley. DeVaughn and another individual are the key players. The victim was pregnant, and I believe the second man is the father. DeVaughn was in lockup when the baby was conceived."

"Well, who's the second guy?"

"Her boss. Guy named Richard Oliver, an executive with GNB."

"I want a detailed briefing on this every day. It's been made clear to me that the girl's parents are in good with a lot of people, including the mayor. She asked the Chief about this yesterday, and it got down to me. We've got to work this hard, which means I need those briefings so I can report it when they ask about the progress. Starting now."

"I already send you daily updates on all my cases. That detail is in the info I send you."

"This one's supplemental. It's a special case. Make it detailed but concise because it's going up the chain. Send it to me and copy Shipley."

"How do you make something detailed and concise? Besides, I thought the daily updates I prepared already went up the chain. I guess no one has been reading them?"

"That one is for all your cases. You'll do another one just for this case. And stop using those big words in your reports. Acting like you're still in college."

I knew he didn't have an issue with my arrest reports. Prosecutors loved them. The more well-written and clearer the report, the lower the chances of a defense attorney poking holes in the arrest. No, Lourne was just in a sour mood and wanted to share the misery in his life until the day he could tell everyone to plant their lips on his backside.

"You want the same update I give you every day, which the brass reviews, and you want me to give it to you again separately—so the brass can review it again?" I asked.

"Man, just follow directions. You can't handle that? With all of those degrees?"

"I'm just trying to understand—"

"You don't need to understand. I just told you what I want. I've got orders, and they flow downhill. Can you just try, Tiger? Can you?"

I sighed.

He rubbed his brow. "Why are you playing police? Do you really want to do this work?"

Gresham, another detective, was approaching Lourne's office when he heard the sergeant's question, caught my eyes, and retreated. He had no interest in walking in and catching the overflow of one of the sergeant's patented sessions.

Lourne could be courteous and supportive, reminding everyone that his door was open if they needed advice. He could also spew insults and berate decorated officers for minor oversights that only a veteran with his twenty-six years of experience could spot. It wasn't uncommon for him to give people props in front of their peers, only to shatter those positive feelings minutes later by finding fault with everything they had done in life. No one could predict which Lourne would show up for work.

A native Atlantan, the sergeant seemed frustrated that my features and bronze complexion prevented him from categorizing me easily. He always asked me 'What are you?' and labeled me the Tiger Woods of the APD. Most people thought I was black, while others assumed I was West Indian or even Middle Eastern. The truth was a mix of everything; I had African, Mattaponi Indian, and even a little Scottish blood running through my veins.

When he asked me that question, I always responded that I was just American. Not because I was ashamed of my heritage, but because he was so curious about my 'identity' and it was my way of pissing him off. I didn't understand the mindset. Growing up in Columbia, MD, a suburban melting pot, I had a diverse array of friends. But it was different in the South. Lourne claimed I never fit with the brothers because I wasn't 'black enough'—whatever that meant—and would never mix with the white boys, either. To him, I was in no man's land until I could "figure out" who I wanted to be.

When he didn't focus on my genetics, he reminded me he knew more than I ever would and that my college degrees were a waste. He repeatedly asked why I got an MBA just to end up working as a police officer. Any reasons I gave never satisfied him. Giving people grief was more fun than trying to understand them.

I looked at his calendar and focused, straining to conjure some hidden, mutant telepathic power to move that '547' to '000'. "I'll get that supplemental update for you," I said. Being in his office sucked the air from my lungs.

"Why, thank you so much for remembering the chain of command. And we might open this up."

That meant pulling in other detectives to assist in the investigation, a standard practice for high-profile murders.

Luckily, Lourne had to take a phone call. Freed from his spirit-sapping clutches, I went back to my desk and dug into Richard Lanham Oliver's life. In doing so, I recognized a script all too familiar for wealthy men and pretty, young women.

Rich had been married for twenty-three years. A nineteen-year veteran of the bank, he had pocketed options and bonuses, and his bank account flourished in the '80s and '90s. He lived in a huge home in East Cobb County and owned a three-bedroom condo in Pasadena, California, where his two daughters lived. Not bad for a company's chief accountant.

While I knew Pete's firm had slapped GNB with the $5 million class-action sexual harassment and discrimination suit years ago, I also discovered that the alleged grievances occurred only in Rich's department. There was the second component of Pete's class action, the lawsuit filed against an individual GNB executive. And to no surprise, Rich was the defendant cited in that separate lawsuit. He had personally settled for $107,000 to cover the separate suit while the bank settled the class action for several million.

Despite this, GNB's Board had still supported him. In a statement, they maintained there was no proof the company fostered a culture of inappropriate behavior and that there was no evidence Rich had done anything wrong. They claimed to have settled only to avoid the publicity that would stem from a legal battle against former employees.

This time, the story would end differently. The same GNB executive, already accused once of sexual discrimination, had allegedly impregnated a direct report who happened to be the daughter of the attorney who had sued the bank. Furthermore, that same employee may have tried to blackmail him before suddenly winding up dead. If this became public, there was no coming back from it. GNB's Board would toss him on the street. Not only would the scandal heap loads of bad publicity on the company after they had already vouched for him, but he would also be a murder suspect, highlighting their terrible judgment in keeping him employed.

Rich would have no job. No money. No wife. And no respect. People have killed for far less.

CHAPTER 18

I walked past the GNB lobby receptionist and hitched a ride with an employee to the sixteenth floor. This Tuesday morning, I wanted to surprise Rich and read his body language.

The surprise was seeing his administrative assistant, Natalie Theron, sitting at her desk, looking robust and healthy, just one day after Rich implied she might have contracted the next pandemic. I introduced myself and asked for her boss. She replied that he was in Charlotte for a conference and would return Thursday. "May I take a message?" she asked.

The man cheated me out of an opportunity to see him squirm, but talking to Natalie was a consolation prize. In her late forties, she had reddish brown hair and pale skin that looked like the sun hadn't touched it in years. Wrinkled creases framed the sides of her mouth; she probably smoked two cartons a day.

"No," I said, "but I'd like to ask you some questions about Kanya Glover."

She paused, looked around, and scooted back from her desk. "Not here." She asked me to go to the freight elevator on the opposite side of the building and take it down to the basement, where I met her at the loading docks.

"I didn't want to talk about this up there," she said. "Too many ears."

"What do you have to tell me?"

Natalie shook her head. "When I heard what happened, I couldn't sleep." The woman stared ahead at the glass and steel buildings across the street. "Richard's a suspect, isn't he?"

"Something tells me you think he should be."

She lit a cigarette and released a long stream of smoke from her nostrils. "Well, he and Kanya had their thing. I don't know if they thought anyone knew, but I surely did. It went on for months. Then she suddenly quits her job, and a few days later, she's gone?" She inhaled deeply.

"So you think he's complicit in it?"

"Before yesterday, I could never imagine him doing something like that. But now?"

"How'd you know about the affair?"

"How could I not? There were so many signals. For example, she worked here late on Fridays. You know any nineteen-year-old interns who work late on a Friday night? And when he went on some of his 'business trips,' she either called in sick or was on vacation on the same days. Trust me. There were lots of things."

"Did Kanya ever mention their relationship to you?"

"No. But I knew. She'd show up with expensive jewelry, and I knew he bought them. I even discovered he was letting her stay in one of our company apartments."

"Oh, you're aware of that?"

"Of course. I process the rent payments for it. We lease a couple of them as a courtesy for executives and vendors in town for business. Our real estate department normally handles it, but Richard lobbied to manage it himself because of cost controls. I found out about their arrangement because she slipped up one day and mentioned it."

"You never said anything about that arrangement?"

"Not my place." Natalie sighed. "I already got blackballed for speaking up once. I used to manage another bank, and I spoke up about something they shouldn't have been doing. Well, they shoved me out the door a few weeks later. In this town, everyone talks. I couldn't even get an interview for two years before Richard hired me. This is the best I could get. So when I saw him using company resources for his little fling, I kept my mouth shut. That's probably why he hired me. He knew I wouldn't rock any boats. And I need my medical benefits."

"When was the last time you saw or heard from Kanya?"

"Last Wednesday. She didn't show up for work, so when I

called her, she told me she had just quit. She sounded distraught. Rich acted funny that day, too. He barely said two words to me. And when I found out what happened over the weekend, I wondered about him."

"Did she come here the day before she quit?"

"Yes. Something was bothering her. She made mistakes all day. So I sent her home. She wouldn't say what was wrong."

"Did she mention something that was supposed to happen yesterday? A big surprise?"

"No."

The timeline was becoming clearer. According to Cheryl, Kanya and Rich had their argument last Tuesday night, on the 22nd. Afterward, the young woman packed her things, came to Cheryl's, and on the morning of the 23rd, called Natalie and told her she quit. The young lady was pregnant and uncertain about her future, so it was understandable she sounded vexed when Natalie spoke to her.

But on Friday, the night she died, Kanya was in great spirits. She expected a windfall and was thrilled at the prospect of getting her apartment, enrolling in college, and starting a shelter.

Whatever changed Kanya's outlook had occurred between Wednesday and Friday. She had stumbled on an opportunity she hadn't anticipated—but planned to exploit.

"What's Richard's schedule when he returns?"

She fumbled with her Blackberry. "He has meetings all day. But he goes to Graddy's for a weekly networking brunch at ten. Try catching him there. I won't tell him about our discussion."

Little did Richard Oliver know that his life was going to collapse shortly.

CHAPTER 19

When Pete opened his door, I was startled by his appearance.

Even though he had dressed impeccably, his hair was frizzled, and his five-o'clock shadow had gone past midnight. He had a faint, sour odor. I could almost see anguish seeping out of his pores.

It hurt to see him like this. An hour ago, I told him I was coming to ask him and Lorinda more questions and to see how they were coping. His appearance gave me the answer.

Pete rubbed his face; his fingernails were chewed raw. "Where are things?" he asked. He picked at his lip as we sat down at the elegant, hardwood dining table.

"Still waiting on some forensic tests."

"Tests of what?"

"Some fibers, hair samples we found. It takes a while to get those tests completed."

"What about Kanya's co-workers?" he asked. "Have you been able to talk to any of them? Do they know anything?"

"I talked to her boss."

"Who?"

I took a breath. "Richard."

"Richard who?" He grew tense. "Don't tell me Richard Oliver."

I nodded.

He sighed. "Not only was she working there, but she reported to directly to him? Jesus."

"Maybe she didn't know the full history between you two."

Pete pursed his lips. "She knew. Out of all the places to get a job, she went there on purpose, remember? And she ends up working for him."

Several years ago, teachers had struggled to pull apart Pete and Daryl Langley at Kanya's school, so I didn't dare mention that Rich may have gotten her pregnant and argued with her days before her death. Pete was a churchgoing man, but he had a breaking point, like everyone else. I didn't want to test it and send him off on a vengeful rampage.

"How's Lorinda feeling?" I asked.

"She's been spending time with Rita, one of her girlfriends. Rita lost her teenage son a few years back, so she's been through something like this. And Alyson, Lorinda's other daughter, just flew in today. She's out with her."

"And you?"

"I stay at the office to keep busy. I can't sleep. Lorinda and I just lay in the bed and stare at the ceiling all night."

"I'm so sorry, brother."

He exhaled. "We've been blessed in the past. I have a great wife, thriving business, good friends. All I can do is keep telling myself that God doesn't make mistakes. There's a reason for everything." He rubbed his eyes. "But I'd be lying if I said that's easy to believe right now."

He offered his hand across the table and lowered his head. At first, I didn't reach for it, but an upward glance of his eyes asked me to reconsider. I gripped his hand, and he began praying for himself and his family, as well as for me to renew my faith.

I figured he was grasping at any hope of erasing his pain. And while he was thoughtful to include me in his prayer, I didn't know why. My faith took a huge hit during a botched holdup at a KFC four years ago. The cashier prayed aloud and begged the meth-induced robber to release him. The criminal answered his prayers by placing a bullet through his eye. The victim was a college student and active church member, but it didn't save him. And Kanya? For years, her parents had prayed for her safety. Those prayers also went unanswered.

How Pete was able to maintain his faith was a mystery to me. I figured I could be angry with God on his behalf. After all, my friend never had to see what that killer had done to his daughter's face.

I dug into my pocket and pulled out the bank statement I took from Kanya's folder. "I believe this is yours."

Pete reached for it, his left hand bearing the five-inch scar slicing across it, compliments of the burglar's knife ten years ago. He frowned as he scanned the document. "Wait, this is one of my firm's accounts. Where did you get this?"

"Kanya had it with her, among her belongings."

"You found where she was living? Where?"

I didn't need him calling Cheryl and squeezing everything from her that she had already told me. At least not yet. Otherwise, he and his wife would march straight to GNB headquarters and raise hell. "A motel in Gwinnett for the past couple of days," I lied. "We got a tip. But we still don't know where she was before that."

"What motel?"

"Lilburn Suites. But please, don't tell anyone. We haven't made that detail public. In fact, don't even go there to see the place. We have people checking it out to spot any suspicious regulars, and if some reporter follows you and reports on it, it'll draw too much attention. There's nothing to see, anyway. We checked out the room she rented. No foul play, no leads." I glanced at the doorway, trying to avoid his eyes. I told myself the lie was better for the case.

"Is her stuff still there?" he asked.

"No, it's all in my car. It isn't much; just a lot of books, cosmetics. Girl stuff. A few tapes and DVDs."

"Did you watch them?"

"I skimmed through them. Most of it's the same stuff Kanya always recorded. Her and her friends clowning around. Why?"

He sighed. "Lorinda's been collecting memories of her. She's obsessed with finding footage of her so we can make a DVD. Can we have her things? Or do you need them for evidence?"

"No, I'll bring them inside. We've already cataloged everything. But she's not in any of the tapes, so if that's what you're looking for, you won't find it. Now that I think about it, do you remember when I told you someone had been searching her room? You said it might have been Kanya. Could it have been Lorinda?"

"Um...could it have been Lorinda searching for *what*, exactly?"

"I don't know. But someone was looking hard for something. You said Lorinda was obsessed with finding Kanya's movies. She would've been searching in Kanya's room, right?"

"Of course."

"Was Lorinda looking for more than just tapes?"

He squinted his eyes. "I don't know what she would be looking for. Why do you ask?"

"I'm trying to discern what Kanya would have in her room that was of such interest."

Pete gave a blank look before shaking his head. "I don't know. Why do you think Lorinda was looking for something else?"

"Because someone was looking for more than tapes."

"Lorinda mentioned nothing else to me, only the videos. And I wasn't in there. It's possible Kanya made that mess. She was disorganized."

"Wouldn't Kanya have known where her things were?" I asked.

"Maybe. Maybe not. She also didn't stay here anymore, remember? She could have forgotten where she kept some things."

"True, but her room was ransacked. Drawers pulled out, clothes were thrown out, everything. Someone else did that, and I don't think it was Kanya. If it was that important to her, she would have already had it with her. Not unless it was something she didn't realize was important until later."

"Makes sense. But I wasn't in her room. And I don't think it was Lorinda, either. She may have been looking for videos, but I don't know what else she'd look for. I'll ask her when she gets back."

Determining the identity of the unknown scavenger hunter would have to wait. It wasn't main the reason I came to visit Pete.

I went to the car and brought Kanya's box inside the house. Pete searched through it and placed the tapes and DVDs to the side, glancing at each one. "Is this everything?" he asked. "Is anything missing?"

"That's it. But you're wasting your time. I haven't seen her in any of her movies. Remember the ones already I took from her room? I watched all of them, and she refused to show herself even once. She thought she looked fat."

Pete poured a glass of bourbon and placed it in front of him. "Lorinda insists on watching every video. She's hoping Kanya might have broken her rule and appeared in at least one of them. She'll look through these."

"Did Kanya suffer from depression?" I asked.

Pete stared at the books and movies stacked on the table. I repeated my question.

He swirled the bourbon around in his glass but didn't drink it. "We tried counseling. It seemed to help at first. Then, it didn't. Her quirks, we couldn't understand them. She liked recording videos but never wanted to be in them. But photographs? No problem. Couldn't figure that out. She was a beautiful girl; I don't know why she felt the way she did." He shook his head, his thoughts seemingly taking him to a gloomy state.

I pointed to the bank printout. "I want to ask you about that. What do you think she wanted with that?"

"I have no idea, Jeff," he replied. "Did she have any more statements?"

"No." I had already contacted SunTrust about the transactions. Citing privacy concerns, they only confirmed that the transactions were deposits to a bank chartered in Springfield, Illinois. To get names and details, I needed a subpoena from a judge or written consent from the account holder. "Can you tell me what those amounts are for? Who or what is it going to?"

The attorney studied the numbers. "These look like transfers from one of our disbursement accounts, but for what, I can't tell. We have several of them. I'll ask accounting about it."

"It's a total of $70,000 over six months. To a bank in Illinois."

"Oh, I know. We're establishing a small branch office up in Evanston. The money's for marketing and client development."

"Why would Kanya be interested in this?"

"That's what I don't get. She couldn't withdraw money from this." He snapped forward. "Unless...unless Richard's behind this somehow."

"What could he do with this?"

Pete sighed and propped his cheek on his fist. "I don't know. This isn't even our largest account. The balance is nothing. If Kanya wanted it, we would've given more than this if she asked."

"Pete, other than Richard, do you have anyone you'd consider an enemy?"

"That could be everyone I ever sued. Certainly Richard. But again, I don't know what he could do with this. He has more cash than what's in this account. I should know; we reviewed his finances when I got him to settle that suit."

I had three things on my mind: Kanya's anticipation of financial freedom, the bank account information, and Richard Oliver, a man who hated Pete and had an affair with his daughter.

There had to be a connection.

CHAPTER 20

I looked up at the Wednesday afternoon sky. It was cobalt blue, unblemished by clouds, and looked like it had been washed clean. The heat wave that had tormented the southern states with triple-digit temperatures had wafted over the Atlantic, blessing us with cooler temperatures. A breeze carried the fragrance of lilies and roses.

It was a perfect day for a barbecue, or to watch kids zip around Six Flags with parents struggling to keep up. It was not a day I wanted to be at a funeral.

Kanya's funeral was at New Life Church, a non-denominational church famous for its beautiful stained-glass windows. A huge obelisk rose out of its bow like a beacon, carved with images of Jesus and the disciples. It cast its shadow over us and lent its respects to the young woman whose life ended so abruptly. Bouquets circled the funeral party of relatives, friends, and a sprinkling of business leaders and local politicians.

Cheryl and Marina stood in the back. I saw Kanya's biological father, Boyd Glover, for the first time. A towering white man with a scraggly face, he sat in the first row with his arm around a redhead who looked as if she'd spread makeup on her face with a trowel.

Pete and Boyd couldn't have been more different. Pete was usually suave, confident, and successful. Boyd looked as if life had kicked his ass steadily for the last twenty years. His scalp clung to a few strands of brown hair trying to break free, and dark bags hung under his eyes. It was hard to believe he fathered a woman as attractive as Kanya.

Lorinda sat two seats away from her ex-husband, crying on Pete's shoulder. Next to her was a young lady in a black dress, staring at the closed casket with tears streaming down her cheeks.

I stood in the rear and gazed at the enlarged photo of Kanya placed beside her coffin. The condition of her face required a closed casket. I felt terrible that Lorinda never had the opportunity to look at her daughter a final time. I just hoped that emotion didn't compel her to run up and flip open that coffin lid for a final look. I didn't want anyone else seeing the image I was cursed to remember.

The minister began his eulogy and spoke of acceptance and celebration. He said everyone should celebrate that Kanya was in a better place. Lorinda cried, and Pete stared ahead, laboring to keep a calm countenance.

As the service ended and attendees offered condolences to the family, I noted people and took down license plates. Guilty suspects commonly attended their victims' funerals to divert suspicion, usually by grieving or overacting. But there were no Oscar winners today, and neither DeVaughn nor Rich were bold enough to show up. As the crowd dissipated, Pete called me over to him.

"Jeff," he said, "This is Alyson, Kanya's older sister." He nodded to the young woman in the black dress who sat next to Lorinda.

I recalled seeing pictures of her in the family's house. None of them conveyed her looks in person. She was stunning. The sisters had similar features, but Alyson was darker and had the caramel shade of her mother's skin. She was a couple of inches shorter than Kanya, and her dark, black arched eyebrows, neither thick nor overpowering, suggested an intensity beneath the lovely surface. She wore no makeup, and sorrow filled her soft brown eyes.

"My condolences," I told her. "I've known Kanya since she was ten."

She sniffled. "Thank you." Her voice was surprising. It was smooth and sonorous—yet still sexy and feminine. "You look familiar," Alyson said. "I think I remember. You were at Kanya's birthday party years ago, weren't you?"

When she mentioned the party, I remembered seeing her; she was nineteen or twenty at the time, which made her about thirty now. "Yes, I was. Good memory."

"You're the family friend they tell me about. The detective."

"Let's keep that on the low. I shouldn't be involved in this because of that."

She nodded and began to cry. "Thank you." She hugged me. "What was that for?"

"They said you took Kanya to parks and things. I'm glad someone was able to do nice things for her."

Before I responded, I saw Lorinda making a beeline to the rear of the gathering. "Cheryl!" she cried.

Cheryl whirled around. "Mrs. Rennell! I want—to say that I'm sorry this happened."

"Were you in touch with Kanya?" Lorinda blurted. "When was the last time you saw her?"

"Uh...Friday, but I don't know—"

"You saw her last Friday? Where? What was she doing? Who was she seeing?"

Pete rushed over to his wife, and they peppered the young woman with questions. Cheryl appeared flustered and glanced at me. I broke up the interrogation and promised the couple I'd find out whatever I could. After whisking Cheryl away, she asked if Pete and Lorinda knew about Rich and Kanya.

"No," I said, "and let's keep it that way for now."

"What if they find out? And they find out I knew and didn't tell them?"

"Then blame me. I'll tell them I told you to keep that quiet."

The family had already made Daryl Langley's life miserable for something that was never proven. If they heard Rich had screwed and possibly killed their daughter, there was no telling how far they would go.

CHAPTER 21

While Graddy's was a trendy place, the appearance of the Buckhead restaurant didn't lend itself to its high-society clientele. Kudzu sprinted up the building's sides, and the parking lot, with its dips and craters, resembled the surface of a river frozen in action. That didn't dissuade the movers and shakers, though. I scanned the cars in the lot, and each one appeared to cost at least twice my salary.

I parked my company Taurus between a couple of BMWs and waited for Rich to arrive for his weekly brunch. He had seemed nervous when I last spoke to him, so I intended to make him more nervous. If he was guilty, I hoped psychological pressure would squeeze a confession from him, because the forensic evidence was coming up empty.

Kanya's burned car yielded no clues. Someone had set the fire with gasoline, an accelerant too common to trace. The heat had liquefied the plastic, devoured the upholstery, and exposed a skeleton of blackened metal and wires. No useful evidence survived.

At least we had answered one question: tests of the dark splotches on the shower curtain revealed them to be human blood. Further tests were needed to determine if it belonged to Kanya, but I was positive it did. The curtain manufacturer, the Delightful Design Company out of Minneapolis, sold its designer curtains to hotels and individual consumers through a catalog. The model we found had a retail price of $599, almost guaranteeing the crime scene was in a nice location far from the squalor of Jones Street.

I called the company for a purchase list of that specific curtain. They kept individual purchase records on file for twelve months and hotel purchase records for three years. In the past year, Delightful sold seventeen of the curtains and the closest buyer lived in Miami; a phone call confirmed her curtain was still alive and well in her bathroom. I turned to the hotel records. The company shipped 536 of the curtains in the last three years; thirty-eight were sent to six hotels in Georgia (five hotels in Atlanta and one in Savannah). I called each hotel, and none of them reported any missing curtains.

I thought I would catch a break when we searched Kanya's Buckhead apartment. Unfortunately, after she moved out, a couple of consultants had stayed overnight for the past few days. A housecleaning service also visited regularly, so we found multiple fingerprints, fibers, and hairs. We found no evidence of blood or foul play, and every print we lifted belonged to someone who had rented the apartment or had approved access to it. None of the security personnel on duty remembered seeing her on the night of her murder, and there was no record of her scanning her access card to enter. It didn't mean she hadn't been there, however. She could have walked in through the security gate with another resident.

Seeing Rich pull up in his black Mercedes snapped me out of my thoughts. I waited a few minutes before I followed him inside the restaurant. Unlike its exterior, Graddy's interior was inviting, and the aroma of pancakes and bacon tempted me. I spotted Rich at a table in the back, with a newspaper spread before him.

"Mind if I join you, Mr. Oliver?" I asked.

Rich did a double take, then narrowed his eyes. "Detective. If you don't mind, I'm expecting someone any minute."

"I won't be long. I'd like to ask you about Kanya again."

"I thought we discussed this already."

"We did, but something's been nagging me. I hear Kanya was dating someone."

"And?" he huffed.

"I also hear—from a reliable source—that the man she was

dating is married. And he got her pregnant. You know about that?"

The executive flinched. "Why are you asking me?"

"I was just hoping you knew the guy. I'd like to get his story. Because from the outside, it looks bad for him. He's married, gets a teenager pregnant, and someone kills her. A jury would easily believe he did it. Even if he didn't."

He crossed his arms.

"I think this guy is another victim in this," I said.

"Is that right? How so?"

I lowered my voice. "People don't see the things I see. There are a lot of gold diggers out here, and I see the damage they do. They're smart. They're predators. Sure, they act naïve and innocent, but that's all it is—an act. They prey on wealthier people. They make it seem like it's your idea, but they target you before you see them coming. They look for men whose wives don't do much and leave them unfulfilled."

Rich pursed his lips.

"I can already tell what happened with this guy," I said. "He works hard, but his wife complains all the time. She's never in the mood. Never satisfied. So here comes Kanya—young, attractive, looking for someone to spoil her. She sees this guy and knows he's not happy. She does everything the wife won't. You've got an overworked, unappreciated guy who needs some attention for a change—and what happens? He and Kanya cross a line."

Rich nodded slowly, seemingly unaware of his body language.

"I don't even blame him," I continued. "Women cheat all the time, but justify it by saying their husbands didn't give them enough affection. Right? Well, no one considers that men might look elsewhere for the same reasons. Everyone wants to be appreciated."

Rich stared into space.

"That's all this guy wanted," I said. "But things go too far. These women get pregnant on purpose. They play with fire and sometimes get burned. And the courts understand this. They know people are emotional. They're called crimes of passion for a reason. People can relate. Juries can empathize with a man who falls victim to these gold-digging schemes. Kanya's guy needs to know that. That's what I'd tell him. If I knew where to find him."

The executive looked down at the table. "Maybe this—guy you're talking about had nothing to do with what happened to Kanya."

"Maybe not. But he should come forward and say so. The longer he waits, the less likely people will believe him later."

The executive chewed his bottom lip.

"Let's cut the bullshit, Rich. We know we're talking about you, right? I know what happened between you two. So perhaps you'd better start telling me some truth. Because you've been lying plenty already."

"Well, look. I—" Before he finished his sentence, he let out a huge breath. I turned to see a well-dressed balding man approaching us.

"Detective," the bald man said, "I'm Harold Vincent. I'm Richard's friend. And attorney."

Before I said anything, Vincent sat down at the table. "Strickland, right?" he asked. "What crimes do you specialize in?"

"Whatever needs solving. What about you? What do you specialize in?"

"You're investigating the Kanya Glover murder," he replied. "Richard told me he already spoke to you. So what is this here?"

"I just came here to eat. I saw our mutual friend here, and we just started talking."

"And did your conversation have anything to do with the case?"

"We talked about women."

Vincent took off his glasses and wiped them. "Are there developments in the case that concern Richard?"

If I said there were no new developments, the conversation was over. If I said yes, I'd have to expound on those developments, giving Vincent opportunities to poke holes in them and strengthen his client's defense. Having his attorney around was like trying to make out with the girl next door while her father sat nearby with a shotgun and watched. Nothing was going to happen.

"I just wanted him to refresh my memory," I said.

"Consider it refreshed. So charge him or leave him alone."

I wanted to tell Vincent that Rich's evasive replies only made him a stronger suspect. I had only asked him about Kanya's job and her relationships with her co-workers, yet it compelled him to lawyer up?

Regardless, I wasn't going to bring circumstantial evidence and hearsay to a legal gunfight. I drifted to the other side of the restaurant, out of their sight, and nibbled on appetizers while waiting for them to leave. After half an hour, they finished their meals and stepped outside where they talked a few moments before going their separate ways.

As soon as they drove away, I dashed over to their table, where their waiter was scooping up his tip.

"Don't touch anything," I barked, flashing my shield. "You got a paper bag?"

He gave me a confused look before leaving and returning with one. Using a napkin, I took Rich's straw, crimped the bottom end of it, and placed it inside the bag.

The waiter, a twenty-something Latino man, watched me intently. "What is that? Evidence? What'd that guy do?"

"Research. The CDC said there's a strain of flu going around. One of the side effects is halitosis that makes your breath smell like ass."

He stared at me before breaking into a smirk. "Are you messing with me, man?"

I gave him my steely look as I held up the bag. "Dead

serious." I had learned that if you look serious and speak calmly, people will believe almost anything.

He opened his eyes wide. "No, you're not."

"I hope you didn't touch their utensils without your gloves." I rushed out of Graddy's, appreciating the mix of skepticism and worry on the waiter's face.

Rich had been on the verge of crumbling before his legal pit bull showed up. But the morning wasn't a total loss. If his DNA confirmed he was the father of Kanya's baby, I was going to move him another step closer to prison.

CHAPTER 22

I had a rare Saturday evening off but spending it at the Georgia World Congress Convention Center wasn't how I expected to enjoy it. A mile or two south of Hartsfield-Jackson Airport, the convention center hosted a variety of events. Usually, they were dry and stuffy; a gala for some organization here, a fundraiser there—none of them was worth sacrificing a Saturday night off. Tonight's event was different.

It was the annual Dorothy Rennell Cure for Lupus, the charity Pete founded in honor of his late mother. I had never attended their fundraiser before, but Lorinda had implored me to come. Her request wasn't an invitation as much as it was a plea; she wanted Pete's friends to provide him an emotional lift as he presided over the program.

After I had entered the cavernous lobby, I saw a familiar face coming toward me. "Strick!" the man exclaimed. "What's up with you?"

It was Wes Byers, a homicide detective who left the APD last year to start his private investigation practice. A gregarious man, he had embraced the old APD tradition of sporting fedoras, which we awarded to detectives after they lost their virginity by clearing their first murder. I had shadowed him when I first started in homicide. Although he was good at his job and friendly with his peers, he would also act like he never knew you if it meant currying favor with superiors.

"Bad-ass Byers in the flesh," I said. "How's that practice going?"

He sipped from a glass of red wine. "Life's good. After eighteen years in Homicide, I knew I could make more money outside. Plus I got my pension, too? I'm straighter than straight."

"What are you doing here?"

"Ah, just meeting with a client."

"Helping one of these rich folks find out if someone is screwing their spouse?"

He leaned in close. "Yeah, but don't laugh. They pay me hundreds, even thousands for that. Real money. Hey, you're saying that's all I'm good for?" He slapped me on the back. "What are *you* doing here? Shouldn't you be working a case now?"

"My day off."

"And you wanted to spend it here?"

"I'm feeling charitable."

"Well, if you want to join me and get paid, just holler. I bet Lourne is still an asshole, ain't he? He ain't changing. And he ain't going anywhere; I don't care what he says."

"I'll keep that in mind."

Wes pulled me to the side. "I heard you're on the Glover-Rennell murder. Is that right?"

I stared at him. "Don't play coy. You knew the answer before you asked. Especially after seeing me here at their fundraiser."

He smiled. "So how's it going? You checking someone out here?"

"Why?"

He drew back. "Well, damn. You don't need to play me like I'm a civilian or reporter. I showed you the ropes, remember?"

"And you told me not to tell everything, remember?"

Wes smiled. "It's like that, huh? Well, even though I left homicide, it doesn't mean I don't miss it. I was just curious, that's all."

"I've got some suspects I'm working on." I looked around. "So, you're here investigating a cheating spouse?"

"Yeah."

"Your client and spouse live in Atlanta?"

"Yeah. So?"

"You think they'd bring their mistress or boy-toy to this place? Where hundreds of people could see them together, and everyone is taking photos?"

"Never said they were smart." He flinched and flared his nostrils. "You ain't buying that, are you?"

"No. Who are you really here to see?"

Wes placed his drink on a bar table. "The same people you're here to see, Strick."

"The Rennells? For what?"

"The same reason you're here. To find out who killed their daughter. They reached out to me for my services."

I felt the need to spit.

"Don't look like that," he said. "We can work together on this. You help me clear this, and I'll split the fee with you. They don't need to know."

"Are you serious?"

"Why not? It doesn't matter who clears it. The family will see justice served, APD ups their clearance rate, we get paid. What's wrong with that?"

Wes apparently didn't know the depth of my relationship with Pete and Lorinda. If he did, he wouldn't have made such an offer. I put aside thoughts of dragging him across the lobby floor and contemplated my response. I didn't want to slip up and reveal my friendship with the family, nor did I want to cause a scene.

"It's not just a check to me," I replied. "And you know that's foul."

He sneered. "Whatever. Like you haven't done some things. Look, you let me know if you change your mind. Hell, maybe I'll clear it on my own." He turned to walk away.

"Don't interfere with my case, Wes. Stay out of my way."

"They've got money they're willing to pay, so I'm investigating it," he barked, without looking back. "I got my contacts and CIs, too. So you stay out of my way."

I felt a boiling heat in my gut. I started to follow him, but someone tapped my shoulder. It was Lorinda.

"There you are," she said. "I was looking for you. Where are we today? Anything new?"

It was the same question she and Pete called to ask every day. And I had the same answer. "Not yet," I said. "Still working it."

"What about DeVaughn?"

"We're looking at him. We just can't pin anything on him now."

She curled her lip in disgust. "So what have you been doing?"

"We've got some forensic tests we still need to complete. That may give us a clue."

"When will they be done?"

"Soon."

"What is 'soon'? How long do they typically take?"

"A few weeks."

"A few weeks?" she blurted. Her Thai accent grew more pronounced. "That's ridiculous! Who can we call to get them done faster?"

I knew saying 'weeks' would incite that reaction, but I didn't want to set unrealistic expectations. "I'll try calling in some favors to get them expedited."

Unless we were dealing with a celebrity or public figure, the GBI would not move any faster. Being promised an ETA of only a few weeks was already a blessing, thanks to Mike's unattractive friend finding a wife. I wanted to spare Lorinda having an overworked and underpaid analyst tell her that her last name meant nothing, and he'll complete the tests when he was good and ready.

"Are you two ready for this tonight?" I asked. "I think people would've understood if you rescheduled."

"You let me know who we need to call to get those tests done." She wiped the corners of her eyes. "And Pete and I talked about this and decided to do it as scheduled. Pete needs support from you and his friends while he's up there."

"Of course. Where is he?"

Almost in response to my question, I saw Pete squeezing through groups of attendees to reach us. We proceeded through the same spiel that I had just gone through with his wife.

"Pete," I said, "did you hire a private investigator?"

He stepped back. "Why? Something wrong?"

"They sometimes get in the way of an official investigation. Especially if it's fresh and active."

"How so?"

"I don't want any witnesses telling him something that I want kept from the public, only to have him blab about it to some civilian."

Pete shook his head. "He assured me that what he discovers will be confidential, and if it's pertinent, he'll share it with the authorities. Look, if someone tells him something that helps him find out who did it, I don't care."

"But this is still a fresh investigation. Usually, people hire these guys if our official investigation doesn't resolve anything or we can't convict anyone. We're nowhere close to ending this. I know this guy. He's going to get in the way because he loves the accolades. And I'm going to work harder than anyone else on this."

"I know you will, Jeff. And we love you for that. But another set of eyes can't hurt."

"We've already got several detectives looking at this."

"And no arrests yet."

I sighed. "I just don't want you wasting your money."

Pete stiffened and narrowed his eyes. "You think we care about money? If he can find who did this, I'll pay him ten times what he's asking. Why are you so concerned about it? You don't want someone else to solve it?"

"Come on, man. You know it's not like that."

"Wes said your pride would get in the way if I hired him. And I didn't believe him at first. Now, I'm not so sure."

"Wes doesn't know what he's talking about."

"He said he taught *you* everything. So if that's so, I should be in good hands with both of you working on this simultaneously, right? He knows how you guys operate and he said he won't impede the investigation. It can't hurt, can it?"

I wanted to tell them what I thought of that asshole Byers' and his extravagant claims of mentorship, but I would've sounded petty and proved Pete's point.

"You're right," I said. "It doesn't matter who finds the guy. We just want it done. I didn't mean to sound like I did. Just want to make sure nothing complicates this case."

The attorney rubbed his forehead. "Jeff, I'm sorry. Just—just forget what I said. I know you want to help. Look, I'm going to get ready. I'll see you later in the ballroom."

Lorinda watched him disappear in the crowd gathering by the ballroom doors. "Don't take it personally about that other investigator."

"I'm not. Just wish I hadn't brought that up before he goes up to speak."

She faced me. "Jeff, Pete's a strong man. Good man and husband. But there's something you don't realize you're doing. And you'd better not ever tell him I said this."

"What am I doing?"

"It's not your fault. But you make him feel insecure."

"What are you talking about? He said that?"

"Of course not. He'd never say that. I don't even think he realizes how he feels. But I see it."

"What? How? Since when?"

"Since the night we first met. You came in like a shining knight and caught the burglar. Kanya said *you* were her hero. Not her father. You."

"Come on, Lorinda. That's ridiculous. Pete risked his life trying to protect you. He has that nasty scar to show it."

"We know that. But you were the one Kanya idolized. From the beginning, she never accepted Pete. When we moved here, she still missed her father. She was too young to know what kind of man he was. But still, she missed him, no matter how nice Pete was to her. Pete was a real father. And he feels he was supposed to be the one to protect us, not you. You remember her birthday party, when she ran around introducing you as the family hero who saved us? How do you think that made him feel?"

"I'm a police officer. I was trained to deal with that. That's what you called us for. And it still scared the hell out of me."

"And those times when you came to pick her up for your little kid trips? I could never get her ready for school on time, but she was never late for you. Always on time and all she talked about was you. She never looked at Pete like that. Now he feels like he failed us again. Last night, he told me that he thinks I don't respect him, that I'll leave him. I would never do that. But that's what he's thinking. And then to have you end up on this case. Out of all the detectives, it was you. It's almost like you're always reminding him that you're the only one to save us."

I cleared my throat. "I had no idea he felt like that."

"I think that's why he talked to that investigator. I think he needs to feel like *he's* doing something to find the man who killed our daughter."

"Jeez, it's not a competition between us."

"How would you feel if Erica had called another man her hero? Instead of you?"

The mention of Erica sent a twinge through me. I never considered how my relationship with Kanya undermined any paternal reverence she may have had for Pete. Kids can be uncomplicated, honest, and in some ways, cruel. They say what they think. Kanya thought I was her hero, her Superman. It never occurred to me that I was probably her favorite man—not Pete, who had the unappreciated task of providing for her and disciplining her. I was fun Mr. Strick, the man who took her to amusement parks every once in awhile. Pete was the real hero.

But Kanya showered me with her admiration.

"Why did he let Kanya come with me if he felt that way?"

"He doesn't have anything against you. Otherwise, you think he'd trust you like he does and still be your friend after all this time? He let her join you because she wanted to go." She glanced at her watch. "I have to meet with a couple of sponsors. You're staying the whole evening, right?"

I nodded. "I'll be in the back."

"But we reserved a space for you at one of the tables in front. With the rest of Pete's friends."

Based on what I had just heard, I was probably the last person Pete wanted to look at while he was giving his speech. "It's better if I keep a low profile. I'm not supposed to be that chummy with you guys, remember? I certainly don't want Wes suspecting something. On a different note, let me ask you—that fight between Kanya and DeVaughn? The one that landed him in jail? Two of her girlfriends told me Kanya filed a false charge. You know anything about that?"

Lorinda pinched the bridge of her nose and took a deep breath. "He deserved it. He hit her before, and she never pressed charges. You never saw her come home with that broken nose. Or that black eye. I wanted her to press charges against him long before then, but she never did. But this time, she got fed up and wanted DeVaughn in jail, away from her."

"So Kanya lied about that incident. And you knew it."

She stiffened. "So what does that mean now?"

"Ancient history."

Relaxing slightly, she looked around. "I have to go. And by the way, Pete hasn't officially hired that guy. At least, not yet. They're just talking."

She disappeared among the guests.

***

129

The fundraiser had a higher turnout than expected. It was possible the news of Kanya's murder and the collective sympathy of the attendees contributed to the numbers. People muttered about Pete and Lorinda's strength in carrying on with the event. A guest speaker led a prayer for the couple and thanked them for continuing with the benefit in light of their tragic week.

The speakers on the agenda, a representative from this company, another from that, soon melted into a stream of bland speeches. I sat at an empty table in the far left corner of the vast room and buried myself in questions.

Where did Kanya go last Friday night after promising Cheryl she'd return in time to see a movie? Could I get Rich to implicate himself? Was DeVaughn involved in this? What was Erica doing? Was my ex-wife even thinking of me now? Where was Stephanie? Laid up with another guy or getting another fool to buy her more tires? How could I entice Lourne to forget his retirement countdown and quit tomorrow?

A hand on my back startled me. "Hi, Jefferson. Or do you prefer Jeff?"

I turned to see Alyson behind me. She wore a burnt-yellow dress that contoured her curves perfectly. The woman looked like a piece of butterscotch candy. I glanced at my watch; an hour and a half had passed since I sat down. We had reached a scheduled break, and people were networking around the ballroom.

"Jeff, or Strick, but Jefferson's fine." I loved the way she said my name. It sounded like she caressed my name as it rolled off her tongue.

"Why are you back here by yourself?" she asked. "Aren't you supposed to be up front?"

"I can't appear too close to your folks. Besides, it's easier to observe from here."

"What are you observing?"

"Not much. I'm surprised your folks went ahead with this. They seem to be holding up well."

"In public."

"How have you been doing?"

Alyson folded her hands across her and looked down at the table, remaining silent for several seconds. "I tried telling myself it never happened, but when I saw her picture next to her coffin, it hit me so hard. Now I just try to tell myself she's in a better place." She looked toward the stage. "What have you found out so far?"

"Looking at a couple of suspects. But nothing concrete, yet."

"What about DeVaughn? You've got to be looking at him."

I told her we were, but we had nothing on him. I didn't mention that magistrate court judge Alvin Hartmann had refused to authorize a search warrant for DeVaughn's rented house. Since DeVaughn and Kanya had no recent contact with each other, no evidence linked him to her murder, and there was no proof he threatened her, he found insufficient probable cause to justify a search.

Hartmann must have worn bulletproof underwear when he made his decision because it was a textbook example of covering one's ass. He had approved warrants with far less stringency in the past. I knew his newfound rigid legality was the result of the fallout of that NBA case two years ago. In front of the nation, the case fell apart, especially after the prosecution relied on a key witness's testimony that contradicted her initial statements to police. Atlanta's police and judicial system became a running joke across the country. The LA Times—representing a city that had little room to talk about contentious, flawed public trials conducted in a media circus—wrote that Atlanta's fumbling of the trial made the OJ case look as if it had been carried out with the wisdom of Solomon.

Even though I had nothing to do with the NBA case, Hartmann didn't want his name associated with another one that had the potential of blowing up. While Kanya's case was hardly as notable as the NBA one, eyes were still on it. I sensed nothing short of a confession or video of the murder would be good enough for Hartmann, even for just a search warrant.

"When was the last time you saw Kanya?" I asked.

Alyson sat next to me. "Last Christmas. But I talked to her last Wednesday."

"What did you talk about?"

"Nothing much. Just said hello, seeing how she was doing. I missed my little sis. I wanted her to visit me."

"Did she sound troubled?"

She shook her head. "She seemed fine."

"Do you know her friends?"

"No. I rarely saw her, much less her friends. Lorinda and Pete never talked much about them."

There was a moment of silence between us. "You call your mother by her first name?" I asked.

She flared her nostrils briefly before smiling. "Old habit. When Kanya was little, she was always saying 'Mom! Mom!' I had to say 'Lorinda' if I wanted her attention. And it just stuck. What will you remember most about Kanya?"

"Let me think," I replied, startled by the abrupt change in the subject. "She was little when I spent most of my time with her. I'd say her little gap-toothed smile. And the time I took her to Six Flags."

"You still saw more of her than I did," she mumbled. "I didn't see her much after they left."

I felt Alyson was not only dealing with her sister's death but also some unresolved guilt of not spending enough time with her.

"I remember how everyone liked her," I continued. "Kanya was different from the other kids I watched. They came from bad homes, saw things children shouldn't see. Compared to them, Kanya was sheltered and naïve. Seemed to have nothing in common with them, but even at that age, she could connect with anyone. No matter who they were or where they came from. That was my girl."

Alyson grinned and nodded. "She gets that from Lorinda. I look more like our mother, but Kanya got her personality from her." Her eyes suddenly brightened.

"What are you thinking about?" I asked.

"Something that happened when we were still together. Someone had given me some chocolates for Valentines, and Kanya was begging for some. I told her to wait, but she said if I didn't give her any, she'd tell our dad I came in late the night before. So I decided to teach her a lesson. I found some chocolate Ex-Lax and put them in the Valentine candy wrappers—"

"Evil ass." I chuckled. "Sounds like something I would do."

Alyson's smile grew. "Kanya practically inhaled them. Later, she was running back and forth to the bathroom all night. I was in my room laughing, and she's like 'Mom! Mom! It won't stop! Mom!' Lorinda was frantic until I admitted what I had done."

"You are diabolical. Never would've guessed."

Alyson laughed. The sound surprised me; she sounded like a female Woody Woodpecker. It was odd coming from an attractive woman with such an alluring voice. It made me laugh just by hearing it.

"I'm not evil," she exclaimed. "I was just a typical teenager. But I paid for it. Lorinda grounded me for two weeks, and Kanya got even with me."

"How?"

"I was getting ready for a date a couple of weeks later. I was running around my room barefoot, trying to get dressed, and I was late. I left my room to go to the bathroom—and then I screamed my head off."

"What happened?"

"My sweet little sister had planted a bunch of freaking pins and thumbtacks in the carpet, right outside my bedroom door."

I laughed.

"Yeah, that little devil," she said, beaming. Alyson had a

beautiful smile, with a radiance that warmed me. "I fell, looked at my feet, and five or six tacks were sticking out of it. I've got tears in my eyes, it hurt so bad. Then Kanya jumps out in the hallway, like 'Ha ha! I got you back, Allie!' I tried going after her, but I couldn't stand, so I crawled after her, and she ran straight to Lorinda. I told her what happened, and Lorinda said I deserved it because of my prank. Which I did. But my sweet little sister almost crippled me, and my mother okayed it."

I shook my head and chuckled. "You two."

Alyson's smile faded. Her eyes reddened, and she dug in her purse for a tissue. "What did she do to deserve this?" she mumbled. "We couldn't even see her at the funeral. I hate she kept getting in trouble. I thought she'd grow out of it. When Lorinda told me she moved out last year and wouldn't tell them where she lived, I knew things had gotten bad. Kanya wouldn't even give me her address. She thought I'd tell Lorinda, no matter how much I promised I wouldn't."

She wiped her eyes, opened her purse, and flipped through a series of photos. "She was so cute and innocent back then." She showed me the picture of Kanya cradling one of the puppies she had spared from her father's death sentence. A glance was all it got from me. My mind kept coming back to her ravaged body on the autopsy table.

"Lorinda doesn't talk much about their life before Pete," I said. "You all lived in Michigan, right?"

She nodded. "In Flint. Kanya and I were born there. Native Flint-stones. Our father's from there. He met Lorinda when he was stationed near Thailand. They got married, moved to Flint after he got out of the military, and the rest is history."

"And later, Lorinda met Pete. Was it love at first sight like they say it was?"

"I wasn't there to see it."

"Well, I know your mom and father were having troubles—wait, I'm sorry. I'm getting too personal."

"You are, but it's okay. I'm well over it." She took a sip of wine as she stared at Pete and Lorinda's table near the lectern. "Lorinda and my father, all they had were troubles. He drank a lot and couldn't keep a job. He wasn't ambitious. They fought all the time. Did I mention he loved to drink?"

"Sounds like my old man."

"One weekend over the holidays, Lorinda went to Detroit with some girlfriends and ran into Pete, who was there for some conference. And they hit it off. She later divorced my father and moved here with Pete, along with Kanya."

"Why didn't you come with them?"

Alyson swallowed hard and looked away. "I was in high school. I didn't want to leave my friends. I've regretted it for years, though. If I came down here, I could've looked out for her. Kept her out of trouble."

I wanted to rub her shoulders. "Why do you think she kept getting into trouble?"

She frowned. "A bunch of reasons. Drugs? Wrong friends?"

"Do you think she was abused or molested?"

She leaned back. "I used to wonder about that. We used to talk on the phone a lot when she was little. She was a sweet girl. Then she changed in middle and high school. Fighting, going out with older guys, drugs, getting expelled. It sounded like behavior they say happens when kids endure abuse or violence. I told her that if someone had done something to her or made her feel bad, she could tell me. But she said nothing happened, and she was tired of Lorinda and Pete asking her the same thing."

"You must be referring to that gym teacher, Daryl Langley."

"That was an ugly situation. They said nothing was proven, but it didn't matter. He shouldn't have been allowed anywhere near children, from what I heard. Is he one of your suspects?"

"He was in Florida when it happened, so no. You asked Kanya if anyone hurt her. Did you suspect anyone of molesting or abusing her?"

"Like who?

"I don't know. Someone close to her?"

Alyson paused. "Like Pete or someone?"

Perhaps I was doing a poor job of hiding my discomfort of asking the question. I didn't think Pete was capable of such a thing, but that was the thinking of Jeff, his friend. As Strick, the detective, I had seen homicides bubble up from pools of dark family secrets, so I had to broach the subject. "Not necessarily," I said. "I'm just asking what you may have thought. Or still think. This is confidential."

She rubbed her hand across her cheek. "It crossed my mind. Even one of my girlfriends asked me about Pete after I told her what happened to Kanya. It's funny how we look at stepparents like that. It's a cliché…the wicked stepmother or evil stepfather. I never met Pete until a few years after they moved here. I know you never really know people, but I don't believe he did anything like that.

"In fact," she continued, "I think he hurt her by trying to be too nice. He bent over backward for her. And Lorinda followed his lead, so they both spoiled her. And when they finally tried to discipline her for real, it was too late. She had already been hanging out in the streets and doing what she wanted. At least, that's how it seemed to me." She sighed, gave a slight frown, and looked away. A distant look fell on her face, as if she had been whisked away to some faraway memory.

"You know," I said, "Pete and Lorinda said they took Kanya to counseling—"

Her eyes suddenly spit fire. "Oh, don't get me started. Do you know how much money they spent on that? She saw several psychiatrists and every one of them had a different diagnosis—attention-deficit disorder, depression, social anxiety disorder. They wrote prescription after prescription. They had her so medicated; it was no wonder she tried illegal drugs. They just kept writing prescriptions for her, and we later found out she was selling the pills at school. I asked Lorinda if Kanya could stay with me, so she could get away and have different surroundings, but she said no—"

Alyson stopped and wiped her eyes. "I'm sorry. I just get upset when I think about that. I shouldn't have said those things. It's just been a rough time." She glanced at her watch and stood up. "Jefferson, it was nice talking to you, but I'm tired. If Lorinda or Pete comes back here, tell them I went back to the house. If you need to ask me anything else, call me anytime."

I admired her as she walked away. Given the subject of our discussion, I felt a little guilty about my lustful thoughts as I watched her.

But I couldn't stop thinking about her for the rest of the night.

CHAPTER 23

The one benefit of my long hours and lack of sleep over the past week was that I had little time to think about Erica. Now that things had slowed down while I waited on the GBI to complete forensic tests, the memories of her rushed back. Seeing Alyson and her sweet physique last night didn't help matters. Every time I pictured her, it turned into a crushing reminiscence of my ex-wife.

Erica had returned to her hometown of Cleveland and was staying with her parents. I called them and asked to speak to her; it had been weeks since we last talked, and that was for a tax question regarding our home we sold after our divorce. Even though there was little chance of us reuniting—at least, in the near future—I wanted to hear her voice.

Her mother, Vivian, was having none of it. She told me Erica was unavailable and too busy to talk.

"When will she be back?" I asked.

"Who said she was out? I said she was busy. Busy with Frank. Her new boyfriend. I'll tell her you called, though."

I knew Vivian would tell Erica nothing. It was evident she threw out "Frank" to get under my skin. There probably was no Frank. It was one of those generic names easy to conjure up on the spot. But her attempt to ruffle me still worked. I soon wondered if Frank was real. The thought of Erica falling in love with another man made it feel like my chest was caving in—but I had my solution for that.

I poured a shot of tequila to dull the visions of Erica moaning and screaming as Frank thrust himself into her. He was lucky to have that woman. Her chocolate skin, brown eyes, and sexy, hypnotic smile usually melted my resistance to anything. She was fiery, and we had our share of disagreements like all couples, but when she cast her adoring look on me, I forgot why we argued. Before Erica, I never paid much attention to a woman's eyes. Now I believed they were one of the most beautiful things about a woman. The saying was true; the eyes were the windows to the soul. They never lie. No matter what the mouth says.

Being single and alone in my house made images of her and Frank even more vivid. Stephanie, who was probably cruising on I-285 in the car I paid to fix, was no longer around to keep me occupied. But a second shot of tequila began melting away the thoughts of Erica and Stephanie. I knew I needed a healthier remedy to take the edge off, but it was better than narcotics and cheaper than counseling. Before I took a third shot, my phone rang.

It was Alyson. She asked if I wanted to meet for dinner. I didn't ask her why she wanted to meet, nor did I care. I assumed she wanted to drill me about the investigation or continue our conversation from last night. Whatever her reason, seeing her again was a better alternative than lying in a drunken stupor, pining for my ex-wife.

We agreed to meet at Blue River, a seafood restaurant in Sandy Springs, north of Atlanta. When I arrived and spotted her rummaging through her purse in the lobby, my eyes darted over the orange dress hugging her body and hovered over her cleavage for a split second. I darted my eyes away. *Control yourself, Strick.*

Alyson saw me and smiled. She told me that since she didn't know anyone in Atlanta, she wanted to enjoy a meal with someone other than Lorinda or Pete. I had no problem being an alternate choice.

After we had sat at our table, I peered over my menu at the woman across from me. Did I brush my hair neatly? Did a renegade hair flare in and out of my nose with each breath? Her lips moved. She had brushed them lightly with a reddish-pink gloss, like the glaze on a candied apple.

"Hellooo?" she asked.

"Yes?"

"Did you hear me?"

"Sorry. I was thinking of something I have to do later. What'd you say?"

"Is there anything else I can tell you? About Kanya?"

I shook my head. She didn't press the subject, and as we ate, the topic shifted to lighter fare. We discussed the social scene in her hometown of the Windy City, whether Atlanta or Chi-Town had the worst drivers, and our favorite cuisines. That deep, yet feminine and confident voice of hers was sweetness to my ears. It reminded me of Alicia Keys.

"So what do you do on your off days?" she asked.

"Besides working ungodly hours? I travel, do a little photography. And I dabble with my electric guitar."

"Oh? You're a musician? Do you write your music?"

"I'm not that talented. I just play around. I can do a decent impression of Ernie Isley, though. Well, it sounds decent to me, at least."

"You'll have to play for me one day. And you're a photographer. Can you take some pictures of me?"

"Nude or clothed?"

"Uh, clothed. I don't know you that well."

"It's a legitimate question in portraiture. It's for the best, anyway. I don't want you trying to seduce me in vain with your goods." Looking at her gave me sexual thoughts, but her relationship to Kanya and the family made her off limits. It was inappropriate and a no-no for police protocol. Getting too close to Alyson gave a defense attorney an opening to throw doubt into the jury's mind. It'd be hard to claim I conducted an objective investigation after fooling around with the victim's sister.

But if Alyson gave me an opening, I doubted I would put up a fight.

"I think you'll be safe," she said. "Few men are blessed enough to see me naked."

"So you're saying you have a lot of lonely nights."

She smirked. "If I tried to seduce you, Jeff, it wouldn't be in vain."

"What do you have that I haven't seen before? You're used to guys telling you how pretty you are all the time, aren't you?"

"You think you know me. You're no different from other men."

"Look, Alyson, if you want me to take nude pictures of you, fine. Go through your little seduction or hard-to-get routine if it makes you feel better. Just know that I'm saving myself for the right nude model. I don't do portraits anyway, so I'm sacrificing here."

"Why not?"

"I look at crime scenes and victims all the time, so I've seen enough of people. Landscapes and nature scenes are more relaxing than bodies dropped in the street. No misery. No grief."

"Okayyy. Look, I didn't mean to bring up your issues. All I asked for was a picture. A *clothed* one."

"Fine. I'll make an exception this time. Just keep your clothes on, please. I'm not that easy."

"Oh, I'm not taking them off. And you'd be very easy."

"Stop talking about getting naked. I just see us as friends."

"Yeah, sure." She smiled. "I caught you looking at me. I'm not blind."

"And?"

"So you admit it?"

"Of course. I'm single. And if I see an attractive woman, I look. That doesn't mean I'll let you have your way with me, under the guise of taking your picture. But it's natural to appreciate a woman. Something would be wrong if I didn't."

"I thought you were married."

I had a feeling she already knew my status. "You know I'm divorced."

"No, I didn't. How long were you married?"

"Seven years."

"Do you have a girlfriend? Or are you enjoying your freedoms?"

"I told you. I'm waiting for the right nude model."

"How long have you been divorced?"

"What's up with the questions?"

"Oh. You can interrogate people, but you can't take it?"

I smiled. "What do you plan to do with this information?"

"Nothing. I was just curious. So what did you do before you become a cop?"

"What makes you think I did anything before this?"

She raised her eyebrows. "Lorinda said they met you about ten years ago when you were a rookie. You're a handsome guy, but you don't look young enough to have been working for just ten years."

"Your backhanded compliments need work."

She grimaced. "Just being honest. But hey, you still look better than lots of younger guys."

"Fair enough. I worked in business before I joined the APD. I was in finance."

"Oh, Wall Street? Like a stockbroker?"

"Hardly. Finance Manager for an electronics company. Boring as hell and definitely less lucrative."

"I could tell you weren't a lifetime cop. I dated a cop once. You seem a little more well-versed. And you don't mind me saying 'cop.' "

"So cops aren't well-versed?"

"Uggh…stop! You know what I meant! I bet you left behind a nice salary to get more excitement in your life, right?"

"It was an okay salary. Not a nice one."

"Why did you quit?"

"Corporate America wasn't for me. I wanted to help people who needed it, not some arrogant executives pocketing millions while laying people off every time earnings came up short."

"So you decided to become a homicide detective? Doesn't it get to you?"

"It can, but things aren't like they are on TV. Most of my time is spent writing reports and talking to people. But I'd rather chase serial killers than go back to some of the companies I worked for. At least I partially understand what makes a serial killer tick. Can't say the same for some of the executives I worked for."

She chuckled. "Wow. Tell me where you worked, so I know where *not* to go."

"Did you know a lot of CEOs share similar narcissistic and pathological tendencies with serial killers? The drive for personal gratification. The lack of empathy for others. The belief that they are the only thing that matters. They have a bit in common. Other than the killing part."

"Who came up with that?"

"Me. I've done some thinking about it."

"So it's just your opinion."

"I'm sure there's a scientific study somewhere that says the same thing."

"And what if you were the CEO of your own company? How would you describe yourself then?"

"As the greatest leader ever."

"You're right; I see the narcissism building already."

I grinned. "That life works for others, just not for me. So I quit to figure out what I wanted to do with my life. I have an uncle who was a cop, and I later found out the city was recruiting more college grads for the APD. It was perfect timing. A few months later, I was a rookie policeman, I met your folks on that B&E call, and the rest is history. Did narcotics, vice, and been in homicide for four years."

"Four years. I don't think I could last four minutes."

"With those eyes? You'd be a great interrogator. You'll hypnotize perps into confessing."

A woman appeared suddenly at our table. "Excuse me," she said to Alyson. "This may sound crazy, but were you in a commercial? I swear you look familiar."

"Probably," Alyson replied, with a slight smile. "Nice to meet you."

"I knew it," the woman exclaimed. "I was just telling my husband I saw you on TV." Our guest finally noticed me. "Oh, I'm so sorry to interrupt," she said. "I just had to see. Thanks!" Just as quickly as she appeared, the woman vanished within the restaurant.

"Well," I marveled. "I had no idea I was dining with a celebrity."

"Oh, it's nothing like that. I just did a little acting on the side."

"So what commercial were you in that produced groupies as far away as Georgia?"

She shook her head. "You'll laugh."

"Come on."

"No."

"Please? With sugar on top."

"Begging won't help."

"Then tell me, dammit. Is that better?"

"Not really!"

"Just tell me."

"You'd better not laugh, Jeff."

"I won't."

"Okay. It was a commercial for—a herpes cream." After seeing my face, she repeated herself. "A herpes cream? You know, for…"

"Oh, I heard you," I said, clamping my lips together. "Enlighten me. What was so special about your herpes cream versus the competition?"

"Well, it's clinically proven to fight irritation—oh, God." She moaned and covered her face with her manicured hands. "I sounded like the script! You think you're funny, don't you?"

"I just hope you're not a client. Did they cast a boyfriend for you? Some dummy who stood behind you and grinned while you talked about how the cream stopped your outbreaks and nasty-ass discharges?"

"Stop it." She began laughing, producing that goofy sound. I still couldn't grasp how someone so fine could have that laugh, but I'd get over it.

"Please tell me they're still running that commercial," I said. "I want to see it."

"Hey, I made a thousand dollars for thirty minutes of work. I'd bet you'd take a thousand dollars for a half-hour commercial about penile enlargement!"

"I don't endorse products I don't need. So when you're not talking about herpes and vaginal issues, what else do you do for a living?"

"You are silly," she replied, shaking her head and smirking. "When I'm not promoting feminine hygiene, I work in real estate. Nothing special."

"What kind of real estate?"

"Commercial. I don't talk about my job that much. It's stressful and long hours. I try to forget it as much as possible when I'm away."

"Well, I bet it helped you find a good deal on your place, at least."

"I rent a place near the Mile."

"Nice." Chicago's Magnificent Mile was a large, swanky row of establishments that made parts of Buckhead look like a strip mall. I eyed her brilliant white-gold necklace and Girard-Perregaux watch decorating her wrist. Although I couldn't afford to buy luxury watch brands at full price, I claimed some from auctions of seized goods, so I was familiar with them. Hers appeared to cost about seven to ten grand.

She caught my eyes. "You like my watch?"

"What are you, royalty? Real Estate pays that well? A place on the Mile and that watch?"

She chuckled. "I'm nowhere near royalty. And I live near the Mile, not on it. My place is tiny, so it's not all that. As for this watch, it was a gift from a guy I dated."

"Hell of a gift. What did he do for a living?"

"Played baseball for the White Sox."

"Oh, and that's the best watch you could get? You don't know how to negotiate."

"What kind of woman do you think I am?"

"One used to getting her way."

"Oh, really? First, let me tell you that I never asked for this watch. It was a gift—a gift I found out he had given to two other women as well. And second, what makes you think you know me?"

"It's my job to make assessments of people. Are you spoiled, too?"

"This is how you talk to women? No wonder you're single."

"They say pretty women have no sense of humor."

"I laugh when I hear something funny."

"I was talking about pretty women. Not you."

Her mouth dropped in feigned disbelief. "Wow…you are just sweeping me off my feet."

I chuckled. "Is your ball player one of the chosen few who've seen you naked? Is he still around?"

"He cheated on me, so he's history. And since we're on the subject, let's talk about that Rolex you're wearing. I hear cops don't get paid all that much. So are you on the take, like in *Training Day* or something?"

"I shake down criminals on occasion. Easy money. What are they going to do, call the police?"

Alyson cocked her head and gave a sly smile. "I can't tell if you're joking."

I shrugged.

"So you like being unpredictable," she said. "You like not letting people know what you're up to."

"Maybe. Maybe not."

We bantered back and forth, and the conversation flowed. I couldn't help but feel awkward, however. We talked as if we were on a first date while her sister's murder and my investigation hung in the background. But Alyson seemed to grow more comfortable as the minutes stretched into hours, punctuating the conversation with her trademark laugh.

I suspected she was trying to move on from Kanya's murder too quickly. From my experience, many coped with such loss by acting as if nothing happened, only to collapse under crushing grief days later. I believed she hadn't confronted the harsh reality yet and her breakdown was still to come.

Not that my state of mind was clear. Getting to know her carried a steep risk. I was attracted to her, and my idea of "getting to know her" went beyond platonic. I felt lust swell inside me as I glanced at her smooth skin, toned legs, and lovely breasts; I wanted to pleasure her until she exploded. But it was more than a physical desire. After enjoying her wit and sense of humor, I craved her mind as well as her body.

After three hours, we said our good-byes and promised to speak again. We had barely discussed the case, and during our time together, I hardly thought about Erica or Stephanie.

Alyson Glover had aroused an excitement in me I hadn't felt in a long time.

CHAPTER 24

As I approached GNB's headquarters, I was in high spirits and sensed a breakthrough coming. Even the drudgery of Atlanta's rush hour traffic didn't faze me.

It was 7:30 in the morning. I doubted Richard Oliver would expect me to pop up this early on this hazy Monday morning. He was ready to break at Graddy's before his attorney swooped in to save him. If I could get him alone, he might spill his secrets. But before applying the heat, I called the district attorney's office to see if Karen Simms was available.

Karen was not your stereotypical DA. Instead of a somber man delivering dry sound bites on the evening news, she was a fifty-two-year-old black woman who floated seamlessly between closing arguments in court and downing drinks with prosecutors and cops in local watering holes. A former public defender, she escaped what she called the "dark side" and joined the Fulton County DA's office, clawing her way to the top spot two years ago after her predecessor resigned following the NBA fiasco.

I ran some cases by her office to strategize on them, and since I intended to grill Rich, I wanted her thoughts. Few things were more frustrating to a detective than pouring his life into an investigation, only to have the prosecutor drop the charges because she wasn't confident in getting a conviction.

I was lucky to catch her. It usually took leaving five or six messages before she returned a call.

"Strick," she said, "Your ears are burning. I just got off the phone with the mayor about Pete Rennell's daughter. She seems to be under the impression that a conviction is a foregone conclusion, as if I've already got someone indicted. So I hope you're calling to give me someone I can indict."

Great. Lourne must have been spit polishing my case reports and overpromising results before sending them up the ranks. "Possibly. His name's Richard Oliver, an executive with GNB. You remember a class-action sexual harassment suit on them a few years ago? He was a big part of the problem."

"What's his story?"

"First, Pete Rennell's firm handled that suit against GNB. He also filed a suit against Oliver himself; a female employee had a beef specifically with him. Now, from last year up until two weeks ago, Pete's daughter worked at GNB *for* Oliver. I've been told from several sources that they had an affair and her autopsy confirmed she was pregnant. And of course, he's been married for twenty years."

"These guys don't learn, do they? I take it he's the father of the child, and he didn't want people to know."

"I'll know for certain after I get my tests done."

"Did he volunteer a DNA sample?"

"Not exactly. I got it from a straw he used at a restaurant."

I sensed Karen smirking over the phone. "Should have known. When do you plan to arrest him?"

"I want to talk to him first."

She paused. "So you don't have enough to make a charge stick now?"

"It's all circumstantial so far. We recovered minimal forensic evidence from the dump site, and I haven't even found the original scene yet. We searched her apartment and found nothing tying him or anyone to the murder. But he did lie about the affair under questioning."

"Of course he did. If you don't have the paternity on him yet, what's your proof of the affair?"

"Kanya's girlfriends and Richard's admin all but swore to it."

"Are they willing to testify?"

"I can get one of the girlfriends to do it. Not the admin. She's worried about her job and retaliation."

"Is the girlfriend clean? What's her name?"

"Cheryl Tory. She's got a shoplifting charge from several years ago, but she's credible enough."

"So we've only proven he's a shitty husband, not a murderer."

"The man lied. He claimed he never had any social relationship with Kanya, much less slept with her. So I'm going to confirm his paternity and get him to incriminate himself. I may not even need the test. He's ready to break."

"What if he doesn't?"

"I'll search his home, too. With the paternity and his false testimony, I'll have enough to get a warrant. He's hiding something."

She sighed. "Hopefully, you'll find something. I need more than a gut feeling on this one."

Without substantial forensic evidence, I had little choice but to resort to psychological tactics. Jurors were more sophisticated than in years past. Gone were the days of parading circumstantial evidence and employing courtroom theatrics to wow a jury into returning a guilty verdict. Nowadays, jurors practically told prosecutors that without a confession, they had better show DNA results or conclusive evidence; otherwise, don't even bother coming to court.

"Keep me posted," Karen said. "We don't want to blow this. And we don't need the blame game going around."

It was a warning. I knew the NBA case was at the forefront of her mind. She wanted to make sure everyone followed procedures to the letter of the law, and like Judge Hartmann, she wanted to cover her ass. She had seen how the former DA had his hard-earned reputation shredded overnight by negative public perception. She may have been chummy with the police, but she was also a politician. She had no problem shoving me and the APD under the proverbial bus if it meant avoiding the heat of another screwed-up case.

I had to move carefully.

***

"Good morning, Natalie," I said. "Where's Richard?"

Natalie Theron looked up from her desk in surprise. "He's in a meeting now."

"Either you can get him or I can."

I followed her down the hall to a room with large closed doors. She stepped inside, and a few seconds later, she and her boss came out.

Rich scowled at me. "What are you doing here?"

I flashed a look to Natalie, and she walked back to her desk, leaving Rich and me alone.

"What are you doing here?" he snarled. "This is harassment!"

As he stood within inches of my face, I took a deep breath. The younger version of me would've spent the next several minutes extracting my size twelve shoe from his ass. Instead, the older and wiser Strick prevailed.

"You lied to me, Richie. We stood right there in your office, and you looked me in the eye and told me you never saw Kanya outside of work. But Cheryl tells me otherwise."

"Cheryl doesn't know anything!"

"And that's funny. You sound familiar with Cheryl, although you said you didn't know any of Kanya's friends."

"No, wait. I didn't—"

"I also pulled Kanya's phone logs," I lied. "You want to guess whose numbers came up often?"

The executive stiffened. "I think I should call my lawyer."

I shrugged. "If you want to ruin your career and marriage, go ahead."

"What are you talking about?"

"I just want to chat with you. But every time, you get defensive. And if you call your buddy, he's going to tell you not to talk to me. But you've got a problem. You're a prime suspect in Kanya's murder."

"I didn't kill her!"

"Of course not. So if you can explain some things to me, maybe I can cross you off my list. But I can't do that if you keep lying and refusing to talk to me."

The color drained from his face. "I'm telling you I'm innocent. My attorney will—"

"Your friend can't help you if I arrest you. Because if you don't willingly talk to me, the only way I can question you *is* by arresting you. And once that's done, it's a wrap."

"On what basis?" Rich's forehead glistened with acrid sweat. "Is this what counts for police work? Harassment? What is your problem with me?"

I pictured the bastard screaming obscenities at Kanya in the apartment that night, his hair frizzled, his eyes bulging, his breath angry and hot. I could see the fear in her face as he demanded an abortion and threatened to make sure no one would find out about the baby or affair.

"Mr. Oliver, you have two options. One, you come with me so we can have a nice little chat and clear the air. Or two, I arrest you, cuff you, and walk your ass right out through the lobby in front of everybody."

"But I didn't do it!"

"I get it. Maybe a privileged guy like you doesn't understand the ramifications of what can happen if you're arrested. So listen carefully. An arrest is a public record. Journalists look at those records every day. So imagine this sound bite leading the evening news—'Earlier today, local GNB executive Richard Oliver was arrested and charged with the first-degree murder of Kanya Glover.' Everyone will find out about your affair. And at that point, it won't even matter if you're innocent or not. Your reputation will be ruined. And your wife will leave you. She'll be spending your money while some young stud screws her brains out—in the house you'll be paying for. And GNB? They won't have your back like last time. They don't want that publicity."

He slumped forward, breathing heavily through his flared nostrils.

"But all of this can be avoided," I said. "The choice is yours. So make your decision. What's it going to be?"

He followed me downstairs to my car.

CHAPTER 25

I threw Rich in Oven Two to let him marinate in his thoughts while I observed him from the video room.

GNB's company controller fidgeted and rubbed his hands together. His hair was suddenly damp and stringy, and pools of perspiration seeped through his shirt. Afraid he'd drown in his sweat, I entered the room, explained the interview process, and informed him that he could leave at any time since he wasn't under arrest. But as I did with everyone, I implied that while he wasn't required to talk, his future would go better for him if he did.

I pulled my keys from my pocket and twiddled the lion trinket Kanya gave me after winning it at Six Flags years ago. Every time I thought of him with Kanya, I balled up my fists. Drawing in slow, steady breaths, I asked him to describe his relationship with her.

"Can you turn off the camera?" he asked. "I-I don't want anyone hearing about this. I thought this was supposed to be confidential."

"It's standard procedure to record all interviews."

"Perhaps I should call my attorney?"

"If you want to, but why? You're free to go now unless I place you under arrest. Which I can do, if you prefer. Because we're going to talk, one way or another. And I'll call the newspaper and news stations to tell them I arrested you." While I could play mind games with him, I had to listen carefully. If he went down a path toward confession, I had to stop him and read him his rights before he went further. I didn't want a judge throwing out any testimony as inadmissible.

Rich sneered at me. "You're enjoying this, aren't you?" He paused before answering my question, divulging that he and

Kanya had been intimate for several months. However, contradicting Cheryl's statement, he claimed it was Kanya who initiated the affair, not him.

"So you were a loyal husband before she came around to seduce you," I replied. "Even though women have accused you of engaging in inappropriate behavior. Especially with your female direct reports."

He shook his head as if he had a nervous tic. "I didn't force her to do anything. She manipulated me. Things just went kind of overboard. She was always flaunting herself."

If there is a bond between cops and convicts, it's a shared hatred of rapists and pedophiles. They blamed their victims for their deeds and never took responsibility for their crimes. We once arrested a man for raping a woman, and when we asked him why he did it, he replied "She knew she shouldn't have been showing all that ass. And why was she walking down the street that late by herself? If we didn't hook up, it would've been someone else." *Hook up.* The man spoke as if the rape was consensual.

Rich sounded like that same man, only wealthier and better educated. I leaned back, trying not to turn up my nose at him. "Why did you keep lying about Kanya? You could've admitted this in the first place."

"I—I just wanted it to go away. If I mentioned anything about our affair, you would've thought I was involved with her murder, which you do anyway...look, I'm telling you, I did not kill her! I had nothing to do with it. You've got to believe me."

"Then who did it?"

"I don't know!"

"You had no reason to hurt her?"

"No. Why would I?"

I planned to revisit that in a moment. I hadn't mentioned the baby, and as far as he knew, the knowledge of the pregnancy had died with Kanya. "How did the affair end?" I asked.

"I told her we had to stop. I didn't want Diane finding out."

"How did she take that?"

"She understood."

"Really? You sure?"

Rich squirmed. "Well, she didn't like it, but she said she understood."

I asked him if he slept with her to get revenge on Pete for suing him. While he denied the affair was a revenge tactic, he admitted hiring her for that reason. What better way to discredit the man who labeled him a sexual harasser than by hiring his stepdaughter? After all, how could Richard Oliver and GNB foster such a discriminatory culture when Pete Rennell's daughter wanted to work there?

"My feelings about him had nothing to do with what happened between Kanya and me," he said. "I never planned for it to happen. Things just went too far."

"Did she threaten to tell Diane?"

He shook his head. "Kanya understood it was just a fling. Look, I didn't use her. If anything, she was using me."

"She forced you to buy her jewelry and gifts?"

"Well, no, but I was just nice to her. I didn't want to upset her. I realized I had put myself in a bad spot and I needed to get out of it."

"Why were you afraid to upset her?"

"She was young. I didn't want her having a little hissy fit and saying anything to Diane. She might have resorted to using our affair to extort from me. So I...spoiled her."

"To keep her from being upset? Why would she be mad at a man who's spoiling her and buying her gifts? A man who *isn't* pursuing her or forcing a relationship, as you indicated?"

"I don't know. She might have wanted more than I can give."

"But you just said she understood it was a fling. You're spoiling the hell out of her. So why would she be upset? Was it possible she saw it as more than a 'fling'?"

"I don't know. I...was just concerned."

"When did you last see her?"

Rich paused. "Tuesday evening, about a couple of weeks ago."

"Where?"

"Umm...her place."

"Which is where?"

He crossed his arms, looked at the floor, and sighed. "Her apartment."

"The one in the Towers," I said. "Yes, I know all about that, too. What time was this?"

"About eight."

"What were you two doing?"

"Just talking."

"About what?"

"About how we could no longer see each other. She told me she thought it was best if she left the company. And she quit the next day."

"How long were you two at the apartment?"

"About an hour. I left and went home."

"Did you leave together?"

"No. She was still there when I left. She said she had to pack her things. She was moving out that night. The place was fully furnished, so it wouldn't have taken her long."

"Did she return the keys to you? Or the company?"

"No, I don't think so."

"So she still had access to that apartment a few nights later, when she was killed?"

He nodded. "Probably. We didn't change the locks until the following week."

"Did she say anything to you about getting her own apartment there in the Towers?"

"No."

"Where were you the night she was killed?"

"At home. My wife and I watched a couple of movies. I told

you that already."

I sighed. "Listen, Mr. Oliver. These are the facts a jury will hear. You're a married executive. You admit to having an affair with a young lady who reported to you, and you've been sued for sexual harassment before. This lady is the daughter of the attorney whose firm sued you. You and she have a fight and break things off. She quits her job and later tells her friends she's getting a luxury apartment and a lot of money on her birthday. Right before her birthday, someone kills her. So my question for you: how do you think the jury will assume she planned to get those things?"

"I—I don't understand."

"They'll assume she was trying to blackmail you. They'll boil that down to one word: *motive.*"

"She wasn't blackmailing me!"

"They won't believe that. Not unless you have another plausible explanation for why she expected a windfall."

"How can I answer that? Perhaps her parents were giving her money!"

"You fooled around with her for almost a year, so I'm sure you know she never asked them for that. And from what I found, no one in Georgia won the recent Mega Millions lottery. So..."

"I don't know anything about her telling her friends about some money. If she did, it had nothing to do with me. She never blackmailed me, never threatened me."

I kept thinking about those bank statements Kanya had taken from Pete's law firm account. I couldn't figure out what she intended to do with them. The balance was too small to cover what she had talked about, like an apartment and college tuition. The average account balance over the last month was less than $4,000.

But Richard Oliver had money. And with a bastard child on the way and a marriage to protect, he would be willing to shell out a lot more cash than whatever funneled through the law firm account. Maybe Kanya had ideas about getting money from Pete's account somehow but later decided that her former boss and lover would represent a nicer payday.

"You say Kanya never threatened you," I said, "but you were worried she'd tell Diane. You bought her gifts to keep her happy and quiet. You're a married guy with a lot to lose. And then she ends up dead. A jury will believe you had involvement in that."

"She wasn't blackmailing me! And *I* didn't kill her!"

I tapped my finger against the table. "Then who did? Are you protecting someone?"

"I don't know...I know I didn't do it," he mumbled.

"Perhaps not. You seem like the type who'd get someone else to do his dirty work. An accomplice. Someone who either hated her or didn't need much convincing to kill her."

He shook his head and looked away.

"Someone like DeVaughn Copeland?" I asked.

Rich shuddered. "Kanya's ex-boyfriend? I don't know him. I didn't talk to him."

"It's easy enough to pull your phone records."

"I'm telling you, I never talked to him. I don't know anything about him."

"If you're involved with this, Richard, you need to 'fess up now. I'll work with you if you come clean or give me a name. But tell me now, because no one's going to believe you had nothing to do with this. No one's going to believe you were one of the last people to see her alive, and the only thing you did was have a polite conversation with her. Not when I hear the conversation wasn't that polite."

The suspect writhed in his chair as if his ass was on fire. He opened his mouth but didn't say anything.

"I got Kanya pregnant," he finally blurted.

That wasn't what I wanted to hear.

He closed his eyes. "That's why I was at the apartment that night. We were discussing the pregnancy. But that's it. That's all

JAMES REID

we did."

"Just a discussion? I heard it was more lively than that."

"Well, we did raise our voices a bit, but that was to be expected. There was no domestic violence situation or anything."

"What came out of that discussion?"

"She told me she was thinking of keeping it. I didn't want her to, for obvious reasons."

"And what did you say to that?" I asked.

"I didn't like it—but I had to accept it. I offered her money, but she refused."

"You offered her money to get an abortion?"

"To pay expenses for the child growing up. With the understanding that the arrangement would be secret."

"And she said no?"

"Yes. She said if I didn't want to be a part of the child's life, she didn't want my money."

"You're telling me a single, pregnant, twenty-year-old woman with no degree and no job…turned down your offer of financial support for the child?"

"Yes."

"I don't buy it, Rich."

"I swear that's what she said."

"So you went from shouting and screaming to being so concerned that you offered child support for the next eighteen years?"

"I didn't want her becoming angry and vindictive, where she'd make trouble for me later. I figured if I offered her money and let her know I was there for her, she wouldn't be as resentful. She'd be more agreeable to keeping things a secret and enjoying her life on her own. But I didn't kill her."

"What about DeVaughn? Is he involved in this?"

"I keep telling you, I don't know anything about him."

I folded my arms. "Are you protecting him?"

He shook his head. "How many times do I have to tell you?

I don't know if he had anything to do with this. I'd tell you if I knew. He could have done it; I know he didn't like her."

"How do you know that?"

"She told me. She told me their history."

Rich had used Kanya and spat her out. My desire to avoid prison was the only reason I didn't march him up to the top of the building and fling him off the roof.

My plan to rip a confession from him wasn't going to work. At least, not tonight. I wanted to show him the circumstantial evidence piled against him, and I intended to bring up the pregnancy as a final push to break through his denials. I expected him to lie, and to finally break after seeing the evidence against him and realizing no one would believe his story.

His admission that he got her pregnant before I caught him in a lie short-circuited my plans. It weakened my leverage in cornering him and making him believe he had no way out of his predicament. But the interview wasn't a total loss. He had given me more than enough to convince the judge to authorize a search warrant for his premises. For now, however, I had to send him home.

"Mr. Oliver, I'm going to have them look into this pregnancy story. If that and your alibi for Friday night checks out, then I should have everything I need from you."

I felt like I was fishing in a catch-and-release stream, reeling in suspects, finding ones the perfect weight and size, and throwing them back on the street. I certainly couldn't tell Pete and Lorinda about this development. Not at this time, anyway.

Every day, they had requested a status update. That wasn't unusual; every family with a modicum of concern for the victim wanted to know every detail of an open investigation. The difference this time was that I knew the victim and did something I never do—I promised the family I'd find the killer. It was a foolish pledge, one made in the heat of grief, and after several days, I still had nothing definitive to tell them. I couldn't keep stalling by saying I was waiting for forensic tests. Sooner or later, I'd have to show results. And releasing a married man who had gotten their daughter pregnant shortly before her death wasn't a result they wanted to hear.

Rich looked up at me, blinking his eyes rapidly. He sat for a few seconds, like a caged animal suddenly staring at an open door, hesitant to test its newfound freedom. "I'm free to go?"

"Yes."

The color returned to his face. "I'd like a copy of this interview," he said. "I don't want this getting out. I want to make sure what I said isn't misconstrued."

"That's not happening."

"You'll hear about this. I'm filing a complaint. You can be sure of that." The man had finally found his long-lost testicles.

"You are free to do so. But keep in mind: you had an extramarital affair with the victim and got her pregnant. I'll also be able to prove you used company resources to provide lodging for your mistress, something I imagine GNB won't like. You think filing a formal complaint against me will keep this quiet? Those claims can become public. When I'm asked to provide my side of the story, what do you think I'm going to say?"

He glowered at me but said nothing. We went down to the lobby, where I had someone drive him back to his office.

My stomach roiled as I again had second thoughts about releasing him. Perhaps I should have arrested him, but on what charge? I simply didn't have enough forensic evidence at the moment. I comforted myself with the fact that while Richard Oliver was well-educated, he lacked common sense. With everything he had admitted to doing, even Judge Hartmann couldn't find an excuse to deny a search warrant. I just hoped to find something that tied him to the murder.

I didn't want to tell the family I failed to keep my promise.

CHAPTER 26

I repeated the question to myself as I cruised down Peachtree Street toward Style's nightclub:

Why did I keep tempting myself with Alyson?

Every day, she had hit me with questions about the investigation: *Are there any new leads? When do you think you're going to arrest someone?* And with Pete and Lorinda calling me just as frequently, I felt attacked in all directions.

Alyson was skeptical whenever I told her I had nothing conclusive. Perhaps it was because she had dated a cop and was familiar with our habit of withholding details, but she swore I knew more than I indicated. Earlier today, she had asked me about the case again, and I told her I was following up on a lead. I didn't mention names; the family didn't need to know that I requested a search warrant for Rich's property. She asked if I were keeping things from them. When I denied it, she got off the phone in a huff.

So it was a surprise when she called me minutes later to apologize for her persistent questioning. She said she needed to blow off steam from the past week and heard about a nightclub that had salsa nights on Mondays. As an apology, she invited me out for drinks and dancing.

I couldn't say no. She would keep my mind off Erica and the case. Going out with her would also let me enjoy some romantic fantasies, fantasies that I considered harmless indulgences since I couldn't act on them. But I had to admit that going out on a date with her might swing that pendulum from a harmless indulgence to playing with fire. And part of me hoped things got hot.

I turned onto a side street in the Buckhead district. In the middle of the area's upscale restaurants and shops were bars and nightclubs emanating a rowdy, spring-break-like decadence. Most were zoned into adjacent blocks, allowing people to roam and taste-test the vibes of different clubs. My destination was Style's, a plain white building with purple neon wrapped around it. A line of people snaked around its parking lot and down the street. It was probably a trick. Buckhead nightclubs were notorious for letting lines form outside to create the impression they were at full capacity and popular destinations. Half of the time, there was enough space inside on the dance floor to run a game of full-court.

I pulled up to a public lot on the opposite side of the street from the club. Two men in white tank tops and baggy shorts manned the lot and passed themselves as parking attendants. While Atlanta was home to scores of corporate headquarters, these men embodied the city's illicit entrepreneurial spirit. Along with the Greenbriar Mall flea markets hawking bootleg CDs and DVDs, "parking lot attendants" sprouted near nightclubs and concert venues, commandeering lots in off-hours and charging rates that fluctuated on a whim.

After they had stated the rate was $15, I flashed my shield, got the price dropped to free, and stood by the street to see if Alyson was in the Style's line. I spotted a woman in a black dress approaching the club. Several men turned their heads as she walked past them. I couldn't see her clearly, but venturing a guess, I called out Alyson's name.

She smiled and waved for me to join her.

Alyson Phawta Glover aroused the envy of the women in line, particularly the ones in ass-baring skirts who had enjoyed a monopoly of receiving the men's thirsty looks before her arrival. Her middle name was Thai and meant "pleasing to the eye", proving Lorinda had the gift of foresight when she named her oldest daughter. Alyson's black dress was open in the back and showed off a small tattoo of a green butterfly in the small of her back. Her legs and calves were like a dancer's, smooth and shapely. But it was her eyes that grabbed me as usual. She seemed to be a woman of depth greater than most would guess upon first seeing her. The intensity in her eyes could be a blessing—or a warning—to the man who dared to love her. When she fixed them on me, I imagined they were saying "If you want me, you'd better be sure you can handle it."

"Aww, we're a matching couple," she said, inspecting me in my gray silk shirt and black slacks. "You look handsome."

"And you look good enough to be with me. My reputation won't take a hit tonight. I also liked how you bumped against me by 'accident'. You just wanted to feel my ass."

She hit me playfully on my shoulder. I felt three inches taller and puffed my chest out ever so slightly as men ogled her like hungry wolves eyeing a succulent deer.

"Jeff," she said, "I'm sorry for sounding the way I did, questioning you. I know you're doing everything you can for us."

"And I keep telling you that you don't need to apologize for that."

She nodded. "Ready for some dancing?"

"Let's eat first. We can come back." I extended my hand. She drew her hand up my forearm and rubbed my bicep for a few seconds, sending a tingle through me. As we got in my car, I complimented her dress and asked where she got it. Her response may as well have been in Thai; I didn't care where she got it. I just wanted to look at her without appearing too lustful.

Alyson smiled. "So where'd I get this dress?"

"What is this, a quiz?"

"You didn't hear a word I said, did you?"

"You distracted me."

"Men. Typical."

"Oh, please. That's the reaction you wanted when you decided to wear that."

"I wore this because I like it."

"You wanted to impress me for our date. And it worked."

"Who said this was a date? I just needed to get out and clear my mind after everything that's happened."

"You don't have to admit it, sweetie. I know the truth."

Alyson shook her head and chuckled. "Your ego is out of control. So where are we going?"

"I know a place you'll like," I said. "They have awesome food." We drove to Nan's, a Thai restaurant in Midtown that enjoyed rave reviews.

She grinned as she saw the sign above the restaurant's doors. "So, since I'm half Thai, you just went ahead and assumed I'd like a Thai place. Even though I've eaten enough Thai food over a lifetime. Okay."

"Actually, I wasn't thinking about that. I was just thinking of one of my favorite places. But I apologize for being politically incorrect. We can always go to the Chevron up the street. They have a good selection of microwave meat products."

"Hmmm. I'll let it slide this time, Mister."

After we had ordered our food, she leaned back and stared out of a window facing downtown. Buildings, cars, and neon signs were a picturesque backdrop of light against the black night. The green light from a flower shop sign outside reflected in her eyes, giving them a teal shimmer.

"This is a cool little city," she said. "You can smell the excitement in the air down here."

"Go a few minutes west of here, and you'll smell something, all right. Backed-up sewers."

"That's right, Jeff, just kill the mood. I swear I'm going to find you another job one day."

After several minutes, the host returned with our meals. As I ate, I looked up to see Alyson staring at me.

"Tell me the truth," she said. "Do you think we'll ever find who's responsible for my sister?"

"It's not about finding the person. It's about proving he did it. It's not easy to convict someone for the crime he committed."

She frowned. "Why?"

"Due process," I said. "The letter of the law must be followed. For example, if a search warrant's involved, it's got to be exact. If something is listed incorrectly, the judge can rule all evidence related to that particular thing is inadmissible. For example, say the warrant only allows us to search someone's house. If I go to his job and search his car while he's at work, that won't count. I don't care if I got a tip that the murder weapon is in the glove compartment. The judge can throw it out if I don't get that warrant amended.

"Now, assuming the warrant's okay," I continued, "the DA needs to decide if there's enough evidence to go for an indictment. Usually, she can present what she wants to get a grand jury to go along with it, but she won't go for it at all if she doesn't think the case is strong enough. If that happens, the guy walks. Even if everything's perfect and the case goes to trial, she'll probably arrange a plea bargain anyway, which happens almost all of the time. And if they don't plea bargain and try the guy for the crime he committed, the jury can find him guilty on lesser charges. Or they can acquit him. Lots of things can happen."

"But if the evidence proves he did it?"

"Even that's no guarantee. You have to understand a jury's made up of regular people. Normal people can't comprehend the things people do to each other. Last year, I had a guy who stabbed his eighty-year-old mother in the throat because she wouldn't change the channel to the Braves game. He said he was asleep when some home invaders broke in and killed her. His prints were on the knife, and her blood was all over him. When we asked him to explain that, he said he had removed the knife from her in an attempt to resuscitate her. He was clean-shaven, spoke in a soft voice, and was goofy-looking. He looked kind of slow, but the jury fell for his simple demeanor. We knew he was lying, but he got off."

"How'd you know he was lying?"

"Home invasions are usually planned and scoped. No one breaks into a house and takes out the weaker threat first. This guy was 260, but she was old, frail, and weighed a hundred pounds. Who's going to spend his time on her while there's a bigger, significant threat in the next room? Unfortunately, his neighborhood was having a lot of break-ins, so it gave his lie some juice."

"He got off because of that?"

"He got off because the jury had an easier time believing his bullshit about a home invasion instead of believing this teddy bear of a man stabbed his mom seventeen times over a baseball game. They see this chubby guy and can't imagine him doing it. Everything pointed to him, but they couldn't fathom it. They believed the lie. It was easier. It didn't upset their reality. Plus, the prosecutor was a little overmatched. It was his first murder case."

Alyson looked down and toyed with her food. After a few moments of silence, I asked her how her folks were doing.

She sighed. "Lorinda's coping. Pete's drowning himself in work." She pushed her plate away. "I don't want to think about this anymore. You need to help me clear my mind."

CHAPTER 27

Alyson coaxed me back to Style's and, again, I reveled in the envious eyeballing from several men as we stood in line. Several gentlemen behind us flirted with my date in hushed voices and broken Spanish, sprinkling words like *mamasita* and *senorita* in streams of gibberish.

"Are they serious?" she whispered. "If they bothered to look at my face they can probably tell I'm not a Latina."

"Well, it *is* Salsa Mondays here, after all. Plus, they seem perfectly content with looking at your ass instead."

"And they don't see you standing right here?"

"Oh, this is probably going to be the highlight of their week. But I can find a reason to arrest them if you want."

She turned to the offenders, snuggled close to me, and smiled. "Excuse me. There are plenty of other ladies here who'd find you guys charming, but I'm not available."

A couple of the clowns shrugged, cleared their throats, and looked away, while the others turned red. They turned their attention to four women behind them, but the ladies made it loud and clear they weren't interested in being backups on the flirtation hierarchy.

I grinned at Alyson. "You should learn Spanish so you can rap with gentlemen like that."

"Story of my life."

"Guys staring at your rear and mumbling pickup lines?"

"No, silly. That I get mistaken for everything, or I get insulted. Men come up to me, speaking Spanish or saying something stupid like 'me-so-horny'. I mean, come on. One guy asked if my dad was a GI or something."

"Umm...but he *was*, wasn't he?"

"Yeah, but don't assume the stereotype and ask me that!" She chuckled. "Especially when we first meet. Keep it to yourself if you think it."

When we stepped inside Styles, heavy bass music reverberated through us. Alyson clutched my arm and pulled me through a sweaty maze of bodies to the dance floor. The DJ blasted rap and pop songs to get the crowd warmed up. Alyson mouthed the lyrics as she danced, the rhythms flowing through her.

"What are you looking at?" she asked.

"You." The dense crowd pressed us closer together.

"You like what you see?"

"Ehh, it's all right."

"Um-hum." She draped her arms around me and caressed the back of my neck. I felt goosebumps as heat shot through me.

She rubbed my shoulders as she swayed her hips. I didn't listen to much rap. I didn't need to hear lyrics about someone capping someone; I saw enough violence for a living. But I liked the song the DJ played. The lyrics were about a man struggling to resist the lure of a woman not meant for him.

It was a hell of a song choice. I fell further into Alyson's pull as she gazed into my eyes. That harmless indulgence I had wanted was now starting to heat up. The DJ began mixing in a slower reggae song, blending the different beats into a perfect, mellow rhythm, then followed it with a bachata song. The crowd started to fill the dance floor.

Bachata music called for us to join at the hips, and like well-oiled gears, she adjusted her movements and stayed in tune. I was a cobra under her snake charmer's spell.

There was a last-second twinge of guilt. *You're going too far, Strick.*

I tried backing away to put some space between us, but the throng of bodies behind me stopped my movement. Alyson cocked her head as if to say "Too late now." She swayed her hips like a pendulum and followed me, a beautiful lioness stalking her prey. There was no escape.

I looked around to see if anyone was watching us. Everyone was in their world, drowning in the Latin rhythm around us.

Alyson pressed against me and felt my excitement. She raised an eyebrow but didn't move away. Instead, she drew in closer, and her warm body contoured me.

"Relax," Alyson mouthed over the pulsating bass. "Let's just enjoy this."

The last strands of my guilt disappeared.

***

Two hours later, our legs and feet sore from dancing, I walked Alyson to her car, where we talked for several minutes.

"I had such a good time," she said. "Thank you."

She leaned toward me, and I moved in to kiss her. Part of me hoped she offered her cheek at the last second; sure, it would have crushed my ego knowing I was destined for the friend zone, but at least I wouldn't be risking further trouble. But she met me head on. Her soft lips shot heat through me as if the sun was balled up in my chest. The taste of her was intoxicating.

As I watched her drive off, I knew that kiss was going to plague me. I suddenly understood how people became dope fiends. Addicts always chased that first-time high, the rush that came when they first tasted a narcotic. Even a stream of orgasms couldn't surpass that high, and no matter how often they indulged, the subsequent highs were never as exquisite as that first one.

Like those highs, the sensation Alyson aroused in me was something I had to feel again. I wanted to taste the rest of her. Damn the consequences or police protocols.

The anticipation of exploring her was more potent than heroin.

CHAPTER 28

From the outside, Richard Oliver's house, tucked among the twists and turns in a Marietta subdivision named Atlanta Country Club, looked even nicer than Pete's home. I pressed the doorbell. When he opened the door, I handed my search warrant to him.

"This is for you," I said. "It gives us the authorization to search the premises and vehicles."

Rich dropped his jaw. "What is this? We already talked about this. You said I was clear!"

"No, I said you were free to go at the time. Never said you were in the clear." I directed the team inside over his protests.

His wife Diane scurried downstairs, still in her pajamas, and glanced around at the early-morning activity. "Rich, honey, what is this? Who are you people? What's going on?"

Rich's forehead glistened with sweat. He led his bemused wife to a guest bathroom and shut the door. A few seconds later, we heard what sounded like a slap. The door flung open, and she burst out like a thoroughbred shooting from the gates at the Kentucky Derby. Rich followed her, but she shouted and repelled him with a windmill of flailing arms. She grabbed her car keys, bolted to the garage, and slammed the door almost off its hinges. Seconds later, we heard tires screech as a car peeled out of the driveway.

One of the CSTs, a goateed guy named Tim, smirked. "Welp...he won't be getting any of that ass tonight."

As a couple of technicians chuckled, I gritted my teeth. Instead of Diane screaming at Rich, I saw Erica shouting at me. There was nothing hypnotic or loving in my wife's eyes on that cold night a couple of years ago. They were red, angry, and full of tears as she cried and yelled at me for sleeping with Michelle, a svelte nurse at Grady Memorial Hospital. She pummeled me with her fists, asking me repeatedly through a flood of tears why I had hurt her.

I hated myself for it. I knew why Michelle and I attracted each other, although it didn't excuse my actions. The nurse wallowed in the same muck of humanity as I did and saw a daily procession of victims rushed through her hospital's doors. Like me, she had embraced a dry and macabre sense of humor to keep her sanity. And as we were alike, our spouses were similar to each other. Erica was squeamish about hearing about my job when I vented about the twisted people I ran across. In her twelve years of marriage, Michelle's husband never asked her how her day went. As a result, she and I felt like kindred souls, teapots on a hot stove with too much emotion and stress welling up inside. One night in an empty office at the hospital was all it took to release the pressure. It was my worst mistake.

It was after I stood in front of Erica later, as she hit me with her fists, that I realized that she was my kindred soul. Seeing the pain I caused her left me with a throbbing guilt I deserved and couldn't erase. I hadn't talked to her in weeks, and her mother, Vivian, was the perfect gatekeeper. As far as my ex-mother-in-law was concerned, I was dead to Erica and the entire family. 'Frank' was the new man who had claimed my spot.

Tim continued playing the comedian and quipped about Rich's prospects for reuniting with his wife.

"Tim?" I said.

"Yeah?"

"Shut up and do your job."

Rich's house was one of the nicest possible crime scenes I had worked. The hardwood floors of the dining and family rooms gleamed, and the kitchen floor tiles were rust-colored ceramic stones. There was a slight smell of cinnamon. The furniture was antique and traditional, not used for sitting.

The house was comparable to Pete's home but with one

difference. Pete and Lorinda's place was livable and genuine. It seemed the only purpose of Rich's home was to promote the talents of his interior decorator. He and his wife probably wore gloves around the house. Every item was spotless. They were either obsessive-compulsive, or someone had done a deep-clean to cover up something.

It didn't matter. If blood had been shed, it was almost impossible to remove every trace of it, no matter how thoroughly one scrubbed and cleaned. We went throughout the house, took photographs, and used a UV wand and chemicals to sweep for bodily fluids.

After an hour, we had yet to find anything.

I dug into my pocket for my powdered aspirin. The house was shaping up to be another dead end.

"Strick?" said Tim.

"What is it?" I felt one of my headaches coming. I swallowed three powdered aspirin packets and cringed. Delicious as a mouthful of chalk dust.

"You want to see this," he said. He led me to Rich's Mercedes S600 in the garage, popped the trunk, and shone his flashlight inside the spare tire well.

My headache vanished.

CHAPTER 29

I dashed to the family room, where Rich had sat in silence as we conducted our search.

"Mr. Oliver, would you come to the garage, please?"

He pulled himself up from his seat without a word. I led him to his Mercedes and pointed in the trunk. "What is that?"

Wedged between the spare tire and the wheel well was a gray twenty-pound dumbbell. On each side of the handle were two hexagon shaped weights with straight edges. Strands of matted, dark brown hair and black splotches of what looked to be dried blood were on one of the weights.

Rich shook his head. "That's not mine. I've never seen that before!"

"Then why is it here?"

"I don't know! It's not mine! I didn't put it there."

"There are strands of hair on it. It also looks like blood."

"That's not mine!" He looked at me. "You guys put it there! You're framing me!"

"No, try again."

"I've never seen that before!"

"I guess it somehow got hair and blood on it, found your car, popped the trunk, and nestled in here all by itself."

Rich opened his mouth to say something but stopped. The man was either innocent or an incredible actor; he excelled in the role of the outraged and fearful innocent man.

I took his arm and guided him to the wall. "Place your hands behind you. You're under arrest."

"No!" He yanked his arm away.

"You'd better turn around and put your hands up against that goddamned wall," I growled.

"What's the charge?" he shrieked.

"Murder. What the hell do you think?"

I planned to use the DNA test from Rich's straw to confirm his paternity, but I couldn't afford to wait for the results, especially now that I needed to request *another* DNA test to confirm the blood on the dumbbell belonged to Kanya. The man had money and was a flight risk. Considering GBI's backlog, he could be living under a new name in Argentina by the time the agency got around to my request. It wasn't critical for the charge to stick immediately; I just wanted the judge to confiscate his passport. Keeping him grounded would give me the time to shore up loose ends.

As Tim secured the dumbbell, I imagined Kanya smiling down on me. The wheels of justice were squeaking to life, finally beginning to turn.

***

Most Atlantans had heard about the problems with the Fulton County Jail. It was overcrowded, short-staffed, and known for its horrid conditions and faulty plumbing that released the faint stench of human waste from time to time. And like most Atlantans, Richard Oliver thought little of it. He didn't have friends or relatives languishing inside its walls, so he probably didn't care that the jail's records were so inaccurate that it mistakenly kept inmates inside for months after their scheduled release date. It probably didn't bother him that cell door locks could be broken for months at a time, allowing predatory savages to roam and sodomize weaker inmates.

I bet he cared about the Fulton Inn's problems now. As I led him through the jail's entrance, he glanced around in jerky movements, an unmistakable panic in his eyes.

We went to the reception area. Donna Suarez, a forty-something clerk, sat in front of a computer screen and typed the executive's name, description, address, social security number, and criminal charges at light speed. She muttered a booking number and looked up at my arrestee. Seemingly unimpressed, the clerk turned back to her screen. "Time for your glamor shot," she said.

"Mr. Oliver," I said, "allow me to introduce you to Donna, the sweetest woman in the world. She'll be my wife one day."

"Oh, no, Strick," she said. "You have enough ladies."

I winked at Rich. "And none of them measure up to Donna. *Ella es muy bonita.*"

She snickered. *"Y tú eres un artista tan mierda. Pero suena bien."*

My command of Spanish was limited to only a handful of compliments for women. I didn't understand what Donna said, but I knew *mierda* was slang for 'shit', so it was easy to assume the rest. I led Rich to a walled enclosure with height markings taped on the wall. The executive, who had been too shell-shocked to speak ever since I loaded him into the police car, turned to me.

"Stop," he pleaded. "We don't have to do this."

"You'll be all right," I said. "You'll probably get bail for a high amount. But if you don't make it out of here fast enough, I'm sure the homies in there will make you feel welcomed."

"I know who put that dumbbell in my trunk. I've been set up."

"Yeah, you said I put it there. Stand still for your mug shot."

"No, no…I'll tell you everything if you just take this off my record."

I stared at him. "Did you think this was a joke? That I brought you here because I had nothing to do?"

"I swear, I'll tell you everything. It wasn't me, it was DeVaughn."

"By the way, when they tell you to bend over for the body search, make sure you spread 'em wide enough that they can see your future. Or they'll do it for you."

He slumped over. "This can't be happening," the executive exclaimed in a broken voice, his eyes watering.

"A word of advice? You might not want to let these guys see you acting like this."

He tried to straighten up. "Why are you doing this to me?"

"You did it to yourself."

***

After he had been processed, I had Rich brought to a small meeting room. I sat across from him, drumming my fingers. The room wasn't the Oven, but it was good enough. He picked at his lips, his skin glistening with sweat.

"By the look on your face, I assume you didn't like the cavity search," I said. "By the way, you can see your attorney now. But what's done is done."

"Can I go if I tell you what happened? Can I get this expunged?" He sounded like a ten-year-old stuck in after-school detention.

There was no harm in humoring him. "Tell me what you know."

"DeVaughn killed Kanya. He put that weight in my car."

I stood up. "Okay. Good luck with everything."

"Wait, where are you going?"

"Home. This jail is the last place I want to be."

"But I just told you who did it!"

"You've been lying all along. I can't believe anything you say."

"I'm telling you the truth."

"You have proof?"

"No, but if you get him, you might find something. You can search his place."

"So we should just drop the charges against you? Just like that? Boy, bye."

"Look, here is what happened. He called me, okay? He had called me before he killed her. He said he knew I had gotten her pregnant."

"How did he know that?"

Rich shifted in his chair. "I don't know. I don't know how he got my number, I don't know how he knew about the baby. Kanya told me she never talked to him. Anyway, he told me she was going to tell her father about us and go public about the baby."

"And how did he know she planned to do that?"

"He wouldn't tell me. But he said if I paid him five grand, he'd take care of the problem and stop her before she could do it."

"So he could have just been making up that part."

"That's what I thought. I told him I wasn't going to pay him for that." He paused. "I didn't believe he'd actually do it."

"You didn't pay him to kill her? It's a remarkable coincidence that she's gone."

"Well, I did pay him...but *not* to kill her."

"Explain that."

"I'm not a murderer. Okay? I told DeVaughn I wanted no part of that. He did it on his own. But after he killed her, he threatened to call the police and tell them *I* got her pregnant and killed her. He said you'd test my blood and find out I was the father, and if I wanted to keep that from happening—if I wanted to keep this from getting out—I needed to pay up. So I did."

"If you refused to pay him for killing Kanya, why'd you pay him this time?"

"Are you listening to me? I never thought he would kill her! I figured he was bluffing. But afterward, I knew it would be nothing for him to call the police and tell you about me."

"Why did that force your hand? If he called to tip us off, you would've pointed us back at him. Both of you had motives, but it would have been your word against his. And they would've believed you over him. In fact, why did you keep lying, over and over, telling me you knew nothing about him?"

He was silent for several seconds. "I was scared. I didn't know what he would do if he found out I talked. I didn't want anything to get out."

"You're not scared of him anymore?"

He looked around the walls of the room. "Look where I am. It's gone too far. I just want to go home. I wish this had never happened."

"How much did he squeeze you for?"

The executive sighed. "Fifteen grand. At first, it was five. But he kept coming back, threatening me over and over. He wanted another five thousand. And another. He said that since I was so good at making payments, I needed to keep doing it."

"So after refusing to pay five grand for murder, you paid fifteen to keep him quiet."

"I didn't want people knowing about us. Look, I didn't want Kanya dead, and I didn't ask DeVaughn to kill her." He lowered his head.

"But you knew of the history between them, right?"

"I just knew they didn't like each other. They're exes. That happens."

"Did he say how he did it?"

He shook his head. "I don't know any details. I never asked."

"Then how do you know he killed her?"

"He told me. He said I owed him."

I rubbed my chin. "So you think he put the weight in your trunk."

"It had to have been him. I've never seen that before. If I had killed her with that, do you think I would keep it in my car?"

"I'm trying to understand why he would put it there. You were paying him regularly. Why get rid of his golden goose?"

"Because I told him I wasn't paying him another dime."

"When was that?"

"A few days ago. He wanted another five thousand dollars. That would have been a total of twenty. I refused."

"So he set you up because the good times were stopping."

"Yes."

"How'd he get to your car? It didn't appear the trunk had been opened forcefully."

He threw up his hands. "I don't know; maybe I valet parked it someplace, he saw me...I don't know how he did it. I can't answer that."

I folded my arms. "There's just one problem with that story, Rich. When people frame someone and set them up for us, they make sure they bring it to our attention."

He tilted his head to the side. "What?"

"I'm going to assume that what we found in your trunk is something that was used in the murder. So why would DeVaughn hide it there and keep quiet about it all this time if he wanted to frame you? We didn't receive any anonymous tip that told us to search your car. We eventually ended up there on our own."

"Maybe he knew that! Or maybe he was waiting for the right time when I no longer proved useful."

"Yeah, but it would have been risky for him to wait this long before making a move. It's been weeks. What if you found it before we did? Or you took it in for service, and they checked the spare? Then his leverage is gone, and his plan to make you take the hit falls apart. He wouldn't have anything to keep you in line. But he just left it there. And he never said anything. Why?"

"I don't know! All I can tell you is the truth. He has his reasons, just like he had his reasons for killing Kanya."

It didn't make sense. If DeVaughn killed her, he had to have known that planting that dumbbell in Rich's trunk would've forced the executive's hand. Rich had no desire to bring attention to himself, but if he realized his "partner" was framing him, he'd return the favor by throwing the spotlight on DeVaughn. The ex-con wouldn't want the attention, either. And if DeVaughn wanted to frame Rich and make it stick, he would've been better off calling in an anonymous tip and then killing him afterward.

After all, dead men can't snitch. We would've had our forensic evidence tying Rich to the crime, and he wouldn't have been able to protest and point in another direction.

On the other hand, despite the stupid choices he had made with Kanya over the past year—and there were plenty—I just couldn't believe he was dumb enough to store an instrument used in her murder in his car trunk. He had plenty of time to dispose of it, especially after I made it apparent I suspected him days ago. He also didn't slip up and mention any details of the killing I had kept from the public.

It was possible that he was telling the truth and he had never before seen the object in his trunk.

However, his newfound commitment to honesty had come too late. He had a rap sheet now, and once news of his arrest hit the airwaves, his career and marriage were practically dead. It didn't matter if the charges stuck or not. It also didn't help him that he couldn't provide proof that DeVaughn killed her.

I couldn't help but think that DeVaughn's smug attitude in his interviews revealed he knew that all along.

CHAPTER 30

One good thing came from Rich's arrest. Based on his statements, I had been able to persuade the magistrate to finally approve a search warrant for DeVaughn's house and vehicle. Later that afternoon, the CST team and I parked across the street from his dilapidated house.

As I walked to the house, DeVaughn and his ten-year-old son exited the house through a side door and walked to his old black Lexus, its bumper fastened to the chassis by red elastic cords. He froze when he spotted me. "What do you want?" he asked.

"Need to rap with you a bit."

"About Kanya? I thought we were over that."

"You thought wrong."

Eric stood beside his father, scowling at me with the same contempt exhibited by his dad. Only ten, and he was well on his way to demonstrating the generational mistrust that many black people, particularly in communities like The Bluffs, felt for cops. It didn't matter that my skin was brown. To some, I was Mark Furman with a tan.

DeVaughn patted his son on the shoulder. "Go play with Knox," he told him. Eric opened the door, gave us a final look, and disappeared inside.

His father faced me. "How long will this take? I'm trying to go somewhere."

"I wanted to let you know I arrested someone for her murder."

"Congratulations. Who did it?"

"That's not important. What's important is what he said about you. He told me that you two discussed a contract killing. You wanted money to kill Kanya. And when he didn't pay up, you killed her anyway."

DeVaughn shrugged. "He's been telling some tall tales."

"A jury will decide that. Sometimes it's about believability. Your word against his."

"Whatever. You're trying to make a case that don't exist. You've got nothing on me."

"Didn't you say you were railroaded because everyone believed Kanya and her Oscar-winning bruises? They didn't need real evidence against you then, did they?"

"Rich is a lying bastard."

"At least now you admit to knowing him, so we don't have to waste time with that lie anymore. So you didn't offer to kill her for money?"

He clenched his teeth. "Man, *he* was the one who tried to pay *me*. I told him no. Like I said last time, I just got out of jail and I'm not trying to go back. It'd be stupid of me to kill her when I know I'm the first guy you're coming to."

"Why did he want you to kill her?"

"He knocked her up. And he didn't want anyone finding out."

"How'd you know she was pregnant and he was the father?"

"Overheard it."

"From who?"

"I don't remember. Just things you hear in the streets."

"How much did he offer you?"

"Five G's before, ten after."

I observed the ramshackle house, with its wood-rotted porch floorboards, and the decaying Lexus birthing oil stains in the small driveway. "Did you take the money?"

"No. Does it look like I have fifteen thousand dollars?"

"You didn't extort him for money by threatening him?"

"I didn't get a dime. If Kanya's dead, it's because he went and did it. It wasn't me."

"And why did you tell me you didn't know about him when I asked you last time?"

"I didn't want him knowing I talked to you."

"Why?"

"He knew what went down with me and Kanya, with that phony assault charge. He wanted to get rid of her, so he figured if he could get someone to do it for him, it'd be me. When I said no, he was like, 'They'll still suspect you, so you might as well do it and get paid.' "

"That doesn't answer my question."

"If it got back to him that I talked to you, he'll think I snitched. He'll lie on me to cover his ass—which it looks like he already did. Black man's always going to be a suspect. I didn't want to put my word against his because I knew how it'd turn out. That's why I said I didn't know him. Didn't want to deal with all that."

"When did he approach you about killing her?"

"He called me a few days before he killed her."

"How'd he get your number?"

He shrugged. "Kanya probably told him."

"Did she give you his number?"

"No. What do I want his number for? Had no reason to call him."

"Did you talk to him after you told him you wouldn't accept his offer?"

"No."

Either one of the men was lying, or both of them had collaborated to come up with the same script to confuse the investigation. Both knew the same woman. Both had motives for murder. And both had thrown out the same dollar amount. The question was which one was lying about paying or receiving the money.

"Can I see your cell phone?" I asked.

"Why?"

"If you've got nothing to hide, you've got nothing to worry about."

He smirked before reaching in his pocket and handing his cell phone to me. I expected more of a protest. I noted his phone and IMEI numbers before returning it to him. "So when I pull Richard's phone records, I won't see your number calling him several times?" I asked.

He tugged on his goatee hair and rocked back on his heels. "Do what you want. It's your time you're wasting, not mine."

"So you don't mind if we come inside and take a look around?"

"You don't mind showing me a warrant?"

I whipped out the document and thrust it to him. "Here you go." I waved for the team to come and get started.

DeVaughn snatched the warrant and scanned it. "This is some bullshit. You already arrested the man. So you've got your case. What are you here harassing me for?"

"Nothing personal. Just business. Now, if you and your son will stay out of the way, that would be appreciated."

He frowned before stepping back and letting the team inside.

As soon as we walked inside, I saw dried eggs and scattered french fries on the living room floor, indicating no one had thought of cleaning it up over the past day. Dirty underwear sat on top of the dining room table. The air smelled like a wet dog. Used microwave frozen food trays covered the kitchen floor.

Having seen how stash houses hid money and drugs behind secret compartments and false doors, I told the team to search the walls, behind and inside appliances, and his Lexus. When one of the CSTs started hammering a hole in the drywall in the pantry, DeVaughn shouted at us, the vein in his temple bulging.

"Y'all going to tear my place up?" he barked. "I just rent here! Who's going to pay for that?"

"The city will take care of it," I said. "Maybe the county."

I told the team to search everywhere. As one of the techs grasped the greasy stove and pulled it from the wall, a small explosion of cockroaches scurried around. I stepped away and moved to the side; I didn't want a roach hitching a ride in my clothes to start an infestation in my home.

We later found a collection of magazine and video porn, depicting women in bondage positions, stuffed in a garbage bag under the crawlspace. One of the magazine cover images showed a woman spread-eagled, with each limb tied to a bedpost—and a white cloth placed over her face.

The scene at the Jones Street field hit me hard. Kanya's body had been displayed in almost the exact position.

I spread out some of the magazines and DVDs on a table and placed the bondage magazine on top of the others. I had DeVaughn brought to me, and I showed him the collection.

"You slipped up," I said. "You know why?"

For a second, his eyes stopped on the magazine cover and ignored the rest of the material. He adjusted his shirt as if a sudden itch had struck him, and then he turned away.

"That ain't mine," he said. "That was there."

"So you knew this was sitting in your crawlspace?"

"Last owner must have left it."

"You decided to leave it there, too?"

"I never think about it. I was working on the house and saw it, looked at it, but I don't fool with it. I got a little boy staying here."

I expected a lie, but I got what I wanted. For the first time, I saw a hint of anxiety in his eyes; his smug demeanor had vanished for a split second before he regained his composure. Although I couldn't use it to prove anything, that magazine cover presented a circumstantial link that tied him to the Jones Street field. Otherwise, it was an extraordinary coincidence that he owned a magazine depicting the same pose that the killer had recreated for his ex-girlfriend.

A couple of hours later, my mood had plummeted. While it was filthy, the house was devoid of anything I could use to arrest him. There was no marijuana or drug stash. Even the blue hydro bucket was gone. There were no bundles of cash hidden in compartments.

More disappointingly, we found no long female hairs or traces of blood in the bathroom or the rest of the house. Admittedly, that was a long shot; Kanya wouldn't have come by herself to an angry ex-boyfriend's home, nor did I imagine he'd be foolish enough to murder her in his bathroom. I confiscated his kitchen knives to test them for human blood, in case he used them to place the stab wounds in Kanya's belly.

DeVaughn stood outside on the porch, picking lint off his shirt. After we had secured some of his clothing for testing, he watched us search and unearth boxes, storage items, and clothes.

He snorted. "You won't find anything. I didn't do it. That girl wasn't worth getting locked up for. You need to worry about your boy Rich. You know, the man you already arrested?"

I grabbed his hand and pulled him to me. "Sooner or later, I'll find out how you're involved."

He yanked his hand away. "Get off me. You don't know me, bitch."

I stepped toward him, inches from his face. "You want to try me?"

He raised his outstretched hands and moved back. "I don't want any more trouble. You just watch your back, Detective."

I balled my hands into fists. "Is that a threat?"

"No, sir. I don't make threats. I'm just saying. When people look in the wrong direction, they get hit from behind. You might find that out one day."

CHAPTER 31

I drove to Pete's and Lorinda's home to tell them the latest case news. Pete answered the door. Although his appearance was slightly better than the last time I saw him, his face was still gaunt, and gray bags hung under his eyes.

"I hope you have something to tell us," he said, directing me inside. "Because I thought about what you said at our fundraiser. I didn't hire that investigator. At least, not yet. Lorinda convinced me to give it some time."

I was glad to hear that. Not just because it reduced the risk of conflicting statements and efforts in the investigation, but it also meant that smug bastard Wes couldn't count on spending his fee, at least not anytime soon. Once I gathered Pete and Lorinda in the family room, I told the couple the news. "I arrested Richard Oliver today. Charged him with Kanya's murder."

Pete's mouth dropped open as Lorinda gasped.

"R-Richard?" Lorinda stammered. "Not DeVaughn?"

Pete pursed his lips and flared his nostrils. "Why did he do it? To get at me?"

"They had an affair while she worked for him. And he got her pregnant."

"What?" Lorinda blurted. "My—my baby was pregnant? And he killed her?"

"I believe that was his motive."

She clutched her chest, and her eyes swelled as if she were hearing about the murder for the first time again. Pete stood motionless, breathing through his nose like a bull ready to rampage.

"He killed her to keep her from having the baby," he said. "And to keep us from finding out what he was doing with her." His voice was low and measured, but I expected him to erupt at any second.

"That's what I believe," I replied. "But it's circumstantial at this point. We're still working on the hard evidence."

"What hard evidence?" Lorinda exclaimed. "You tell us you're waiting on some test every time. What are we waiting for now?"

"We're testing evidence recovered from his home and car."

"What did Richard say when you arrested him?" Pete asked.

"He denied killing her. He says DeVaughn did it. But *he* denied it and pointed it back at Rich. Unfortunately, we searched DeVaughn's premises and came up with nothing."

He stared into space, his eyes unblinking. "You really think Richard did it, Jeff?"

"Both of them had motives," I replied. "I believe they may have worked together. I just can't prove it. Pete, you're not thinking of doing something, are you?"

He bit his lip. "No, I'm fine." He said the right things but his body language communicated otherwise. I was sure thoughts of vigilantism simmered in his head.

"So is this case finished?" asked Lorinda.

"Not yet," I replied. "Things still need to be analyzed, and if it's conclusive, we'll get an indictment—"

"What do you mean, 'if it's conclusive'?" she snapped. "What happens if it isn't? Are the charges dropped? Why do you come here and get our hopes up and tell us it may not work?"

Pete exhaled. "Honey, he's doing what he can."

I mouthed a "thank you" to him.

"Don't thank me," he snapped. "If Richard did this, or if DeVaughn helped him, just make this stick. Please."

***

The police gods were not making my life easy. Just when I found an opening, they threw more roadblocks in my way.

There was some good news. Mike Yates had studied the fractures in Kanya's skull and compared them to the edges and patterns of the twenty-pound dumbbell. He concluded it was "highly probable" the dumbbell caused the cranial fractures. A simple test revealed the dark splotches to be blood and the strands of hair stuck in the stains were microscopically similar to Kanya's.

Unfortunately, while DNA testing of the blood would determine if it were hers, it would still take weeks for the results. There were also no fingerprints on the dumbbell, and the design was a model used by health clubs and sold in sporting good stores everywhere.

We found two sets of fingerprints in the Mercedes's wheel well and trunk. One set was determined to be Rich's, which meant little since we expected to find them. The second set of prints did not belong to DeVaughn and garnered no close matches in the AFIS database. This wasn't conclusive; the perp could have used gloves, so I couldn't discount the possibility that DeVaughn had planted the dumbbell.

Mike had finally received the results of the rushed DNA paternity test of Kanya's unborn child; unsurprisingly, Rich was the father. Mike also shared the GBI's presumptive toxicology screen on Kanya. It was negative for common narcotics or tranquilizers, strengthening my theory that the killer burned her fingers after her death to destroy evidence under her nails. The fluid found in her lungs was soap water. It confirmed Mike's assertion that Kanya had been in a bathtub when someone attacked her.

Based on the autopsy report and the implications of the shower curtain, I had already requested an analysis of samples from the bathrooms in Rich's home and the Tower apartment where Kanya had lived.

It was the cleanliness of the Tower apartment that bothered me. It had been cleaned multiple times since Kanya had left. I wasn't concerned that the cleaning crew had inadvertently erased

traces of bodily fluids—blood could still survive strenuous cleaning efforts—but the crew might have thrown away or destroyed
other vital clues.

I reviewed Rich's call detail records and didn't see DeVaughn's
cell number in the logs. Like Kanya, DeVaughn used burners and
prepaid calling cards, which had no billing records. The device
number and information I took from his phone indicated it had
been activated just two days ago. If he had communicated with
Rich before then, it was under a different number I couldn't
trace back to him. It probably explained why he didn't protest
when I asked to see his phone.

Finally, I reviewed Rich's bank statements. If Kanya had
anticipated a Monday morning windfall, I expected to see transactions indicating her former boss and lover was the source of
the money. But there were no significant withdrawals from the
identified accounts over the past two weeks.

Meanwhile, things were taking a turn for the worse for the
former GNB company controller. He may have determined that
honesty with me was the best policy, but his sudden commitment to truth wasn't enough to save him. News of his arrest had
become public. And despite his testimony about DeVaughn's
involvement, the spotlight of guilt remained on the executive.
He had just as compelling a motive for homicide, and it was in
his car that we found the evidence related to the crime.

GNB had supported him during the first lawsuit but decided
they had had enough of the same guy getting in more trouble for
the same reason—women. In a one-sentence release, the company had reported that Richard Oliver had "tendered his resig-
nation, effective immediately."

As the company threw him on the unemployment line,
Rich's attorney persuaded the circuit court judge to grant bail
of $200,000, an amount the disgraced executive posted in two
days. To ensure he stayed in town to think about the error of his
ways, the judge confiscated his passport.

Pete and Lorinda considered his arrest a mixed blessing. They were relieved someone was in custody but were incensed at the low bail amount. The couple also fretted after I warned them nothing was final without a conviction, but they grew more confident that justice was coming after hearing the evening news. I guess seeing the reports on television and in the papers made the arrest seem "official," as if there was no way Rich could hide from the scales of justice barreling his way.

As their confidence grew, so did my anxiety. We had the dumbbell, but I still couldn't prove beyond a reasonable doubt that Rich—or DeVaughn—had used it. It wasn't what killed her; it was the strangulation. At best, I could charge one of them with abuse of a corpse. If the case went to trial now, Rich's attorney would drive that doubt by questioning why I had focused on him when there was another man, a convicted felon who had served time for assaulting her, who had just as much a desire to see the victim dead. To keep that doubt out of a jury's mind, I needed to prove that not only was Rich the murderer but that it could *not* have been DeVaughn. Or I needed to show *both* were involved.

Karen Simms wasn't going to entertain such ambiguity. I needed to find something else to make sure Kanya's killer didn't remain free.

CHAPTER 32

I barely heard the knocking on my door over the notes of Ernie Isley's guitar soaring from my entertainment center. I turned the volume down, did a last-second cleanup by stuffing wayward socks and t-shirts in a closet, and opened the door.

Alyson was an alluring sight, wearing a black blouse, blue jeans, and sandals that showed off polished red nails. She held a bottle of Merlot. Over the past week, I had joined the rest of the human race by working first shift, but that shift slot was ending, so I capped it off by inviting her over for a Friday night, home-cooked dinner. In truth, I had an Alyson fix. She kept my mind off the case—and any holes springing in it.

"I love a punctual woman. Technically, you're five minutes late, but I won't sweat that."

She smiled. "I'll make it up to you somehow. Nice place."

I liked my home at 5818 Smyrna Place—but it wasn't my castle. My last house, a brick, 3,400-square-foot contemporary with a finished basement in Marietta, was my dream. With its four bedrooms and large backyard, it was also Erica's dream home, but we had sold it after the divorce. She moved back to Cleveland, leaving me to find another place in Atlanta fast. I couldn't go back to the days of overpriced apartments with thin walls and cheap appliances, so I rushed to purchase this three-bedroom ranch in Smyrna, a suburb northwest of Atlanta.

While I missed the house Erica and I built, my new home grew on me. It was tucked away from the main roads but still close to the interstate and twenty minutes from the airport. Giant maple trees blessed me with ample shade in the summer and cursed me with never-ending brown leaves in the fall. I placed warm-weather plants inside for a tropical vibe and installed updated fixtures and stainless-steel appliances. It wasn't as grand as Pete's and Lorinda's home, but Alyson still appeared impressed.

"Oh, let me introduce you to my roommate," I said.

"Roommate? I thought you lived alone."

I opened the door to the sunroom, and my German shepherd came bounding up to greet her.

"Hey, you," she exclaimed. Alyson's eyes lit up, and she beamed at him, petting him and rubbing his head. She bore an uncanny resemblance to the picture of her little sister, when she had smiled with glee and posed with her red wagon of puppies. "He stays out in the garage?" Alyson asked.

"Not always. He's young, so he still jumps on people when they come through the door. I let him calm down first after hearing new voices."

"I don't mind him being friendly. Isn't that right, boy?" she said, kneeling down to rub his coat. "And what's your name, boy?"

"Maximus," I answered.

She stopped and looked up at me before chuckling. "Such a guy. A cop with a German shepherd named Maximus. You probably watched Gladiator a hundred times."

"Maybe I went too far. I should have done something manlier, like get a poodle and carry her in a pink purse."

"I've got one you can use."

After I had given her a tour of my abode, she took off her sandals and relaxed in the living room. "It's quiet out here," she said. "I took you for someone who had to be in the city."

"I work in it every day. I want to get away from it when I come home. The city will pay some of our housing expenses if we agree to live in specific areas of town, but I choose to stay here."

"You turned down free money?"

"Those 'specific' areas are hellholes. Places where they think crime will drop if people see police living there. But I don't like stray bullets, either. Now, if they paid me to live where your folks live, that's a different story. Now you relax. I'm going to finish dinner."

"Need any help?"

"I've got this."

"Wait, let me hear you play your guitar first."

"Now?"

"You said you play. I think musicians are sexy."

"Okay, but I'm not responsible for how much you'll want me afterward."

I led her to the third bedroom, where I kept my musical equipment and new Gibson electric guitar. I played 'Summer Breeze' at low volume on the CD player, plugged my guitar into the amplifier, and started strumming and stroking the strings along with the notes in the song. In fact, I was more engrossed with Ernie Isley's guitar than what I was doing with my instrument. I started feeling the rhythm, flowing in a zone and impressing my guest.

When I finished, Alyson looked at me and bit her lip, contorting her mouth. "You ever take lessons?"

"What are you saying?"

"Uh, nothing. What are we having for dinner?"

I put down the guitar. "No dinner for you. Go home hungry."

She snorted and released an avalanche of laughter. "I'm sorry. I just expected that you could...play. Max didn't even follow us up here. He saw us heading in here and knew what was coming, didn't he?"

"Hey, I never said I was great at it. It's just a hobby."

"But your guitar looks new! You bought a new guitar and never took lessons?"

"I'll get around to it. Look, I'm going back downstairs to finish dinner."

"That's right! Go to the kitchen and fix my dinner. I like my men serving me."

"Keep it up. I will play my guitar again."

She inhaled in mock fright. "I'm sorry. Forgive me"

I feigned anger as she responded with her goofy laugh.

**

After a dinner of chicken marsala, wild rice, and sauteed broccoli with garlic, we retreated to the living room.

She rubbed her stomach and leaned back. "That was delicious. Much better than the guitar. I will have to return the favor one day."

I dimmed the lights, and we nestled into the couch to watch *City of God*. She leaned against my shoulder and watched the screen, whereas I watched her. My eyes slid down and back up to her body, moving from her pedicured feet, journeying up her thighs and hips, making a pit stop at her breasts, and continuing to her lips and eyes. If I hadn't seen the movie already, I would've missed half of it.

When the movie finished, it was an hour before midnight. Alyson sat up and looked at her watch. "Wow, didn't know it was this late. I should get going; I don't want to overstay my welcome. Thanks for a great evening."

I hoped my face didn't show my disappointment. She ambled to the door, stopping to study my Ancient Egyptian art on the walls before facing me. "I'm flying back home after next week. You should come visit."

"Done."

Alyson opened the door, kissed me, and stepped outside. "Thanks again." She sauntered to her mother's Mercedes and fumbled around in her purse. "Great. Can't find my keys..."

Strick, she's giving you an opportunity, dummy.

"Alyson, come here," I said. She came to me, and I pulled her inside and kissed her. I felt her body grow tense, so I stepped back.

She looked at me. "What's wrong?"

"You tell me."

She relaxed. "No, it's nothing," she whispered. "I'm sorry. I was just—surprised. I was wondering if you would..."

She wrapped her arms around me and kissed my neck. The wet, warm sensation of her tongue excited me. We stumbled back to my bedroom as we embraced each other. She lifted my shirt and rubbed my body while massaging my chest with her tongue.

I worked her blouse and bra off, tasting her neck. Her breathing grew faster and deeper. My mouth became moist. I savored her as if she were a luscious dessert, exploring every part of her. Her scented lotion tasted mildly sweet, and the filtered moonlight seeping through the blinds illuminated her smooth skin.

I moved to her navel, caressing and tasting her as I moved further down. Alyson moaned, and her breathing revved higher, like an engine warming up. She unzipped her jeans. I wanted to ravage this beautiful woman. I took a deep breath to keep my urges in check.

She slid her jeans off and unbuckled my belt. I threw my slacks off, and she pulled me down to her. But I wasn't ready for that yet. I kissed her thighs and stopped when I noticed small burn marks. She covered them with her hands.

"No," she said.

"What happened?"

"An accident. Don't look at them. They're ugly."

"Nothing about you is ugly." She resisted for a few seconds but relaxed as I continued kissing her thighs, calves, and feet.

Her breathing revved up again. She grabbed me and pulled me to her, licking my chest and sucking gently on my fingers. "I want you," she moaned in harried breaths. "Right now."

I smiled. *Not yet.* I reached down to massage between her legs while I focused my mouth on her neck and shoulders.

She started to gyrate and thrust her hips. "Come on," she snapped. "Now."

In a lightning move, I slid on some protection.

"Ohh, my God," she gasped, her eyes meeting mine as I entered her.

***

A few hours later, I stood beside the bedroom window, watching Alyson sleep naked on the sheets with her back to me. I knew that once our eyes had met, we crossed a boundary. My legs felt weak as I gazed at her; I felt like I loved her. It was too early to be pure love, perhaps a deeper degree of lust, but whatever it was, I didn't want her to leave Atlanta. I had only explored the surface. She was too sassy, too smart, too sexy to leave now. She should be mine.

I no longer cared about the impact this had on Kanya's case. It had been a long time since a woman had excited me as Alyson had done, and I had tried to thrust pleasure on her so hard and deeply that she'd never think of leaving me. She had responded to my dirty talk with some of her own, asking me how I liked it, telling me I was going to love her before the night was over. Perhaps her goal was to have me so caught up in her that I would follow *her* back home.

All she had to do was ask.

I went to the kitchen to get a glass of water. When I returned to the bedroom, Alyson was awake and staring at the wall.

"Are you okay?" I asked.

She nodded.

"What's wrong?"

"Nothing." She gave a faint smile. "Still tingling from that pounding. What are you made of? Look at this room. Sheets are all on the floor; it looks like an earthquake hit us."

"You don't need to pump my head up, babe. I know you love me for my mind."

"I'm serious. I haven't had it like that in a long time." Her grin faded as she looked up to the ceiling. "I think I should get going."

"Now? Why? It's early in the morning. Just stay here."

"Lorinda and Pete will have a ton of questions if I come home wearing the same clothes. They'll ask where I've been."

"Just tell them you were at a friend's. I assume you didn't tell them you were coming here."

"Of course not. But you know Lorinda. Old fashioned. I don't want to look disrespectful coming in late."

"I understand. If that is the real issue, Alyson."

She began putting on her clothes. "It's not you," she said.

"No man has heard that one before."

Her eyes watered. "I haven't felt like this before...I don't know...I think I should just go."

"What's wrong? What are you afraid of?"

She paused. "You."

Covering her eyes, she grabbed her keys and left.

CHAPTER 33

The following afternoon, I sat in my car and watched the entrance of Jo's Chick'n, a fried chicken joint near Fair Street, south of downtown. As a stream of hard luck cases, wanna-be thugs, and blue-collar workers paraded in and out of the place, I thought about Alyson and our night together.

Why did she leave so abruptly early this morning? Hell, I knew I was rusty, but I didn't think I was that bad. She hadn't returned my calls today. Was she afraid I'd break her heart?

I forced myself to focus on the case-related problems facing me. A Senior Assistant District Attorney in the DA's office had called earlier to discuss the arrest for Richard Oliver and was concerned about the lack of evidence. He gave me the script I had already suspected; we didn't have proof that pointed to Rich while also exculpating DeVaughn. Everything was too circumstantial, and there was doubt surrounding Rich's alleged guilt, particularly when DeVaughn had just as much of a motive and opportunity.

In fact, the Senior ADA said, since DeVaughn had already been arrested for assaulting Kanya, if I were going to target one of those men on a circumstantial play, it should've been DeVaughn. Despite the only piece of physical evidence being in Rich's possession, there was just enough doubt for jurors to consider DeVaughn could have planted it. In summary, Karen was mulling over dropping the charges for now—unless I came up with something.

Ever since I cuffed Rich Oliver and threw him in the back of my car, I knew it was possible that Karen wouldn't run with the charge. I had wanted to buy myself some time to build the case. I just didn't expect to search the premises and cars of both men and find nothing concrete.

That was why I sat in my car, observing customers entering and leaving Jo's. I needed to press C-Dub, my CI, to use his eyes and ears on the street and Jo's was one of his favorite spots. As long as he was sober, he never missed the Saturday $6.99 Chick'n N' shrimp meal. Unfortunately, he had been ignoring my calls for the past two days, forcing me to stake out the place in the hopes he'd show up.

Calling Jo's a restaurant was a stretch. It looked as if someone had taken a sharecropper's shack, added dining tables, and hung a wooden sign that read *Jo's Chick'n* in big red bubble letters. The tiny dining area was a fire hazard when seating more than fifteen people. The owner, Black Joe, a wrinkled man with a leathery, weathered face, was always seen lording over grease vats where he deep-fried food into submission.

About ninety minutes later, C-Dub strolled up the street toward Jo's while talking on his cell. A woman, whose hair looked like a bunch of spider webs, accompanied him. Her denim shorts screamed for mercy as they strained to contain her prodigious ass.

I rushed up behind my CI and spun him around.

"What the f—?" he exclaimed. "Strick! Why you rolling up on me like that?"

I snatched his phone. "You don't know how to use this? I've been calling you for the last 48 hours."

Spider-Woman slid between us and pointed a chubby finger in my face. "Who the hell are you?"

I shot C-Dub a look of warning.

"Bitch, let me handle this," he hissed. Heeding his sweet talk, she stared at me as she backed away.

He turned to me. "Man, why you got to front me like that when I'm with my girl?"

"I don't like being ignored, Cornell."

"I told you I don't like that name."

"I don't give a shit. I asked you to find out what you can

about Kanya Glover a while ago, and I never heard from you."

"I'm still asking around, you know?"

"No, I don't know. Because you don't return calls. When I call you, you call me back. You know the rules. Hell, I gave you the name of her ex-boyfriend. That should have helped you."

"My battery died and I—"

I prepared to drop his phone down a sewer grate. "I'll be damned if I'm going to keep paying for you to use this phone."

"Okay, okay! My bad, I just got busy. Damn, I told you I'd ask around. You know what? Go ahead and drop it. I don't care. It's your money. In fact, why don't you just forget about me?"

I gritted my teeth. Antagonizing a good informant was a career limiting move for a cop, a couple notches below bitch-slapping a captain. But C-Dub's value had diminished over the last few months. His increasingly weak, time-wasting leads and bad attitude were threatening to ruin my clearance rate, the one thing that kept Lourne from making my life even more miserable.

"Okay," I said, putting the phone in my pocket. "Next time your ass gets in trouble, don't you call me. You're going straight to jail. And sooner or later, your homies back in Cali will hear about it."

California was a sensitive subject for him. Four years ago, the former-architectural-engineer-turned-heroin-addict helped set up a small burglary crew in the East Bay area. They convinced eight Salvadoran women to pose as housecleaners. They outfitted the ladies with uniforms and business cards and sent them knocking on doors in beautiful neighborhoods. Most people found their low prices suspicious, but there was always someone looking for cheap labor. Once inside a home, the women cleaned it well—while also scoping the layouts, identifying items to steal, noting model numbers of alarm systems, and reporting the information back to the crew. A week later, the residents came home to find their houses cleaned a second time, this time of their valuables.

An Oakland detective arrested C-Dub after he tried to fence a stolen custom pearl necklace. After authorities had threatened him with prison, he proved he didn't embrace the "don't-snitch" movement by regurgitating names galore. He didn't spare a single one of his crew. To ensure immunity, he even threw in bonus information about a drug dealer who controlled several blocks of the city and was a target of the Oakland Police.

C-Dub wasn't Mensa material, but he was smart enough to know no one would appreciate his running mouth. After selling out his crew, he put California in his rearview mirror and escaped across the country to hide in the ATL, where I later arrested him for trying to sell me a dime bag. In exchange for his flow of timely, useful information, I had done my best to keep him out of jail ever since.

"I knew you'd bring that up," he said, rolling his eyes. "Always threatening me."

"I'm not threatening you. I'm telling you I won't save your ass anymore. You know how many favors I owe for keeping you out of jail? But when I need you, you can't call me back."

"I swear, man, I just got some cash problems—I had to re-up my minutes, man..."

"I bet if one of these skanks out here called you to break you off a piece, that phone would've been working. You'd better tell me something about Kanya the next time we talk. I don't care how you get the information."

I returned the phone to him, and he slunk off, bellowing at his Spider-Woman to shut her mouth the next time he had business to discuss.

My top-notch CI was becoming unreliable; the dark flesh under his eyes told me he was falling deeper into the clutches of his habit and he no longer thought about reclaiming his past professional life.

I hoped he had enough left to squeeze one last clearance out of him.

CHAPTER 34

Alyson grinned. "You like this?"

"Absolutely," I replied, as I snapped photos of the mountain range with my camera.

"You forgive me?"

I nodded. "I like the way you apologize. You take me to nice places."

She covered her face with her hands. "You must think I'm a nut case, with the way I left Friday night. Don't you?"

"It's okay."

"That means 'yes.' I'm sorry, I just got so scared. It's been a long time since I felt that way about someone...and I thought about how I'd be leaving soon, and I've been hurt before. But I'm fine. I'm okay. I just had to...work it out."

"Well, don't go back."

She raised her eyebrows. "And do what? And stay where? Here, with Lorinda and Pete? No way."

"With me." The words flew out before getting clearance from my brain. It was what I wanted, but a split second later, I knew such an offer would scare her off. I decided to make a joke of it. "I won't charge you a penny more than what you're paying in Chicago."

"You'd charge me rent?" she said, feigning shock.

"You've got to earn your keep. I'm not going to fulfill your dirty fantasies for free."

"I'll certainly pay you not to play your guitar." She placed her arms around me. "I thought you'd like this. You like landscapes, right? Maybe you can take portraits of me next time."

We stood on the deck of a large observation facility at the top of 4,000-foot Brasstown Bald, Georgia's tallest mountain. Brasstown rests at the foot of the Appalachian mountain range in the northeast corner of the state, three hours from Atlanta and a few miles south of Murphy, North Carolina, the town where Eric Rudolph, the terrorist bomber of the '96 Olympics, was caught. The weather was crisp and bright, and an expanse of rich blue sky surrounded us. From my vantage point, I could take in panoramic views of four states: Georgia, North Carolina, South Carolina, and Tennessee.

"Don't worry, baby," I said. "I already took several photos of you when you weren't looking."

"No, take them when I'm ready."

"Can't. My policy is to take photos of people with embarrassing expressions. Like when you were scratching your nose earlier, and it looked like you were picking it."

"You'd better delete that!"

"It's a blackmail photo. In case you become famous doing herpes commercials and forget about me."

Alyson reached for the camera, demanding I delete the photos. I laughed as she threatened to get even with me when I was sleeping. Even though she chuckled when she said it, I figured deleting the photos was best for my future. "See?" I said. "They're gone. But seriously, thanks for bringing me out here. I needed this. How'd you find this place?"

"From something called the internet."

"If we start hearing dueling banjos, we're out of here."

"Dueling banjos?"

"Yeah. This is Deliverance country."

Alyson cocked her head. "What's that?"

"Never mind." Sometimes I forgot about our twelve-year age difference.

As was becoming her habit, Alyson had surprised me earlier this Sunday morning by inviting me on a trip to the mountains. We had plenty of time to drive here and return home for my night shift; I could sleep during the drive if needed. It was her way of apologizing, she said.

The temperature was seventy-five degrees, twelve degrees cooler than in Atlanta and much less humid. The only sounds were from periodic gusts of wind. Although there were few of the conveniences and amenities of the city, the surrounding quiet, beauty, and fresh air made up for it.

Alyson looked at her watch. "Hey, we have to get going if we're going to make it to the waterfall before dark."

I placed a filter on my lens to highlight her face against the cobalt sky and snapped a picture. Her image was more beautiful than the landscape photos I had captured. I took her by the waist and pulled her to me. The scent of her hair filled my lungs.

"Hey, don't get something started here," she said. Playfully, she pulled away.

As she paused to read a marker noting the history of Brasstown Bald, I thought about what we had enjoyed over the last two weeks. Every day, she asked about the status of the case, but dwelled on it less and less; she seemed content to talk about other things and spend time with me. I knew I was falling for her because I wanted more than sex. I wanted to claim all facets of her, good and bad.

I had suspected I fell quickly for Alyson because I'd been lonely and the romance was a perfect coping mechanism for getting over my ex. Not that Alyson's personality, smarts, and looks had nothing to do with it; I would've fallen for her under most circumstances. In fact, I was now beginning to think it had nothing to do with me being lonely—I just really liked the woman.

But what was *she* feeling? She implied she was so into me that she was afraid I'd hurt her. Why did she feel so strongly? I wanted to believe it was my charm, but there was another reason that came to me.

The death of a loved one was a powerful emotional stressor. Many women dealing with such loss drew close to men in protective roles—men such as homicide detectives. The magnetic pull between those men and grieving women sometimes led to lust and hot sex. Many people didn't understand the erotic relationship between death and sex, but homicide detectives were familiar with it.

Especially detectives in Atlanta. Most murder victims were young black men in the usual problem areas of town. They were gang members or innocents who found themselves in the wrong place every time. Most people gave those deaths no more than passing thoughts, so the mothers, girlfriends, or sisters of the victims were the only ones crying for justice. Those women saw the detective as the only other person who cared about their men. He was their shining knight. He would find the perpetrators. He would bring justice. He was the protective, calming influence. As a result, some of the grieving ladies came to love him. If he was halfway decent-looking, they all but threw themselves at him.

I was sure there was a clinical term for this reaction where death produced intense erotic feelings, but we called it GP, short for *Grief Poon*. Not every grieving woman suffered from it and not every detective took advantage of it. But there were exceptions. Ryan and Bates, detectives in another squad, were professional, capable, intelligent investigators—and dirty, lowdown assholes. The two married men were sharks roaming Atlanta's seas, taking advantage of anguished women for sexual pleasure. They had no shame in their predatory tactics, swearing that *GP* was the best sex.

I felt a bitter tang in my mouth thinking about those two, but was I doing the same thing with Alyson? She was gorgeous, years younger, and lived hundreds of miles away, circumstances that wouldn't make us the most compatible of matches. She was coping with the death of her sister and was drawing closer to me. And I welcomed it. Was I much different from Ryan and Bates? Was Alyson my GP?

I grimaced; maybe there was some truth to it. Alyson told

me she loved me for supporting her family. She said I was her hope of finding her sister's killer and seeing justice served.

My phone buzzed. I didn't recognize the number, but it was an Atlanta area code. "Strick."

The voice was rushed, but garbled. "This—Kanya's—I found one of her—"

"I can't hear you. Who is this?"

"—Carol—it's—I saw her movie—Officer—and it had—you have to see—"

"Who is Carol? Or did you say Cheryl? Is this Cheryl?"

There were too many dead spots in our location. The Chattahoochee National Forest surrounded Brasstown, and there were few cell towers in Deliverance Country. It was surprising the signal reached my phone in the first place.

"I'm in a bad spot," I said. "I don't know if you can hear me. If this is Cheryl, I'll have to call you back."

There was another distorted response. The caller fired her words in a loud, cracking voice, followed by silence. I redialed, but the call refused to go through.

Alyson walked up behind me. "Ready to see the falls?"

I asked to use her cell, but she didn't have a signal, either. "Sorry, but I'll need a rain check on the Falls," I said. "I have to get to a landline."

I had a hunch I needed to get to Cheryl fast.

CHAPTER 35

We drove ten miles down Brasstown's winding two-lane road before finding a convenience store. I used their landline and dialed Cheryl several times. She didn't answer.

"I'm sorry, Alyson," I said. "I know you put a lot of effort into this. But I have to get back to the city."

She shrugged. "I understand. Things happen. Too late to get to the waterfall, anyway." She froze. "You would tell me if it's about Kanya's case, right?"

"Yes. This is a different investigation."

"But I thought I heard you say 'Cheryl.' Isn't that Kanya's friend?"

"Different Cheryl."

She eyed me before turning back to go to the car. I hated lying to her and knew I would have to atone for it later, but I didn't want a thousand questions about the case.

We didn't talk much on the way back; I was too deep in thought. It took another thirty minutes before I could pick up a strong phone signal. I called Cheryl several times. No answer.

"Jeff," Alyson asked, "are we still okay with the case against Rich? He is going to serve time for it, right?"

"That's the plan."

She pursed her lips and sighed.

An hour later, we were speeding on Interstate 85 through Duluth when my cell rang.

"Strick, I got a '48'," said the raspy voice on the other end. It was Ed Cleveland, a brusque nineteen-year veteran with a penchant for wearing trench coats, even during stifling summer months. Everyone called him the Black Dick Tracy. He was an avid collector of photos of himself published in newspaper articles and bragged that guys had no fashion sense like men in his day. "Need your take on something. Can you meet?"

"I'm kind of in the middle of something," I answered.

"You might want to see this."

"Where are you?"

"By Wood Road. Near the Dome."

I felt a knot in my throat.

After Alyson had dropped me off at my house to get my car, I sped through the city to meet Ed. I didn't need directions. I knew where he was calling from. As I neared Wood Road, flashing lights served as beacons leading me to the Conifer Homes apartment complex.

Several uniforms hustled outside Cheryl Tory's apartment. A lab truck was parked out front, but I didn't see any medics. That meant Cheryl was dead. No need to rush an ambulance if the victim had already checked out.

Neighbors spilled out of windows and doors and strained their necks to get a glimpse of the activity. Officers walked door-to-door, taking names, asking questions, and receiving the standard shrugs and head shakes.

I flashed my shield and stepped inside the apartment. The couch in the living room, which I remembered had been under the front window, was now in the center of the room. All of the seat cushions were on the floor. The glass coffee table had been shattered, and shards of glass littered the carpet.

To my left was poor Cheryl, lying on the kitchen floor with her blond hair splayed behind her. A thick pillow lay next to her. A few feet from her was a large man on his back, dressed in a red t-shirt and jeans. A hole was in his forehead, compliments of what I assumed to be a well-placed bullet. Blood and bits of flesh stuck to the wall behind him.

Ed, a tall, gaunt Kansas City native who could've passed as Lurch's black twin, emerged from the bedroom.

"Strick," he said, holding a bag of corn chips and tossing them in his mouth like a circus animal. He pointed at the bodies.

"It appears she was suffocated...and you see what happened to his ass. Her name's Cheryl Tory. She's a friend of your Glover victim, right?"

I nodded. "Who's the guy?" I asked, rubbing my hands over my face.

"His name's Marcus Washington. Lives four doors down. No priors. So...you have an idea who might've done this? Since you know this girl? I think they came here for her. As you can probably guess, we don't have a lot of witnesses."

I looked at the bodies on the floor and shook my head. "How do you know the perp wasn't after Marcus?"

"I don't know for sure. But they're in her place, not his. He checks out and doesn't have a record. And she's the one involved in your big case. I figure he's just a wrong-place-wrong-time kind of thing."

"Anyone hear anything?" I rubbed my temples. A stress headache was shooting stabbing waves through my skull.

"Neighbor said she thought she heard some shots."

I glanced at the crater in Marcus's head. "I'd say her hearing is accurate."

"You want to talk to her?"

I looked around and felt a slight chill. "Where's the child?"

"Safe. She was at a babysitter's. The woman brought her back here, thinking her mother forgot to pick her up. She walked in to see this."

I exhaled, a small measure of relief. The child was safe, but unfortunately, she would probably be traumatized for much of her life. "Forced entry?"

"No signs."

"You find the gun?"

"No. No shells, either. He used a revolver or took his casings with him."

"Maybe I should look around first," I said. "I might notice something I hadn't seen last time. You okay with that?"

"You looking for something in particular?"

"Not sure."

I replayed Cheryl's phone call in my head. What I heard was something about her watching one of Kanya's movies. What were the words?

Something about Kanya.

Movie.

Officer.

I closed my eyes to think. Cheryl had given me Kanya's belongings to give to her parents. She had several homemade and commercial movies in her box, along with the bank statement, clothing, and hygiene products.

Did I take everything or did I leave something behind?

I recalled my interview with Cheryl. She told me she had placed all of Kanya's belongings in the box.

But also said she had misplaced something. A movie.

That's it.

I remembered itemizing her belongings and noted a movie was missing—a VHS tape of *An Officer and a Gentleman*. It was conspicuous because it was the only VHS among a collection of DVDs. And only the movie sleeve was in the box; the VHS tape itself was missing.

It came rushing to me. When I took Kanya's things, Cheryl said she had intended to watch one of her movies but had misplaced it; a comment I didn't think much of at the time. The VHS tape had to be the one Cheryl had referred to. Apparently, she found it, finally gotten around to watching it, and saw something she never expected. Something so alarming that she called me.

I told Ed we needed to find the VHS tape.

"VHS? People still watch those?" he mumbled.

"Did you find Cheryl's cell phone?" I asked, looking in Cheryl's empty VCR.

"No. Marcus didn't have one on him, either."

"She got a landline?"

Ed nodded. "Pulling the BellSouth records now. I'll run them by you."

After ten minutes of searching, I decided there was no point in looking for the missing tape. If there were scenes on it that disturbed Cheryl enough for her to call me, and if she wound up dead hours later, then it was footage her killer didn't want anyone seeing. There was no way the murders of two girlfriends were coincidences. Kanya had kept that tape for some reason. And if that tape was the reason someone had killed Cheryl and Marcus, it was long gone.

"Don't bother looking for cell phones," I said. "He took them."

"So it's the same guy who did your Glover victim and these two here? Who the hell is he?"

"I don't know. I just know it's the same guy. Same M.O. of covering tracks. But I have my suspicions. We might want to talk to DeVaughn Copeland and Richard Oliver to see if one of them gives up something we can use. My money is on DeVaughn as the perp."

"Why him?"

"DeVaughn's from the hood. Rich is a suburban white dude. People tend to notice white folks wandering in these neighborhoods, and no way is Rich coming here himself. Now, he'll definitely pay someone to do this. And DeVaughn knows this place well."

"You think they're working together?"

"I can't prove it. And I don't know the motive for killing Cheryl. Maybe she had knowledge of something." I sighed. "Let's go see what the neighbor is talking about."

We banged on her door. A young, dark-skinned woman with disheveled hair opened it. Sweaty and unclothed, she hid behind the door while her naked lover stood behind her in the dim light. He didn't try to cover his swinging pole; rather, he paced side to side, looking irritated that someone had the nerve to die next door and bring the police knocking.

"Didn't I already talk to y'all?" she asked.

"Yes," I replied. "But if you'll humor us by answering a few more questions, we'll be on our way."

Annoyed, she looked at her man and turned back to us. "Fine, hurry up."

Ed smirked at her lack of empathy.

"You said you heard shots?" I asked.

"Yeah. But it sounded like just one shot."

"Wait," Ed said. "You said you heard *shots*, not one shot."

The woman shrugged. "Yeah? So?"

"Well, did you hear one shot? Or two? Or more?" Ed asked, his face tightening. "It's important."

"I don't know," she huffed. "Probably one. I think one. I couldn't tell. And then I heard some yelling. I thought it was somebody's TV. I didn't know it came from over there."

"You heard yelling before or after the shot?" I asked.

She looked up in thought, sweat dripping from her forehead. "After, I think. Again, I thought it was a TV."

"What time was that?" I asked.

"Around seven o'clock."

That was an hour after Cheryl called me. "What were you doing at the time?"

"We were watching TV."

"You see or hear anyone leave the apartment afterward?"

"No. We didn't look outside."

I looked at Ed to see if he had anything to add, but he shook his head. "Thanks for your time," I said. She slammed the door, locking the deadbolt.

I turned to Ed. "Maybe after she gets dicked down, she might clear her head and think of something else. Let me know if she calls you."

I left Cheryl's with a slew of questions.

215

CHAPTER 36

By late afternoon on the following Monday, Ed had interviewed several people in the Conifer Homes project. As usual, no one knew or saw much. Three residents said they heard shouting, but that was a common occurrence on summer evenings when the liquor flew. Ed never found the murder weapon or any casings. A check of BellSouth records showed Cheryl made only one call from her landline in the past three days, and that was to her mother in Waycross; she had used her missing prepaid cell phone for most of her calls. Marcus Washington owned a regular cell phone, meaning he received a bill afterward with detailed call logs, but none of those calls revealed any connection to the murders. It appeared the man had simply picked the wrong day to visit Cheryl.

Ed checked on both Rich and DeVaughn. The newly unemployed executive was at home when Cheryl was killed, an alibi verified by his wife, albeit reluctantly. DeVaughn's whereabouts were unknown. He had yet to return messages from the APD requesting him to call and provide a statement. The team found none of Rich's or DeVaughn's fingerprints at the scene. The only usable prints we found belonged to Cheryl, her daughter, and Marcus.

Later that afternoon, Pete called me. "Jeff, do we have enough for Richard's conviction?"

"We're building the case," I replied.

"That's not what I'm hearing. I just called the DA's office. Look, we know you're doing as much as you can. But we have to know the truth. Is his arrest going to hold?"

I sighed. "There's a chance it may not. I think Lorinda was right all along. I believe DeVaughn was responsible. The two may have even conspired together. I just can't prove it."

"So now you're saying DeVaughn did it?"

I dreaded this day of reckoning, the day when the hope and optimism I kept peddling to the family started to dry up. "I think he was working with Richard. They both had strong motives and felt teaming up might work."

"Why did you only arrest Richard?"

"I had more evidence leading to him. I played a hunch and thought I could get him to confess."

"But he didn't. And now you're telling me his arrest might not hold. And you have nothing on DeVaughn."

"I'll get the man who did this. I told you that. Nothing has changed." I had long regretted making that promise. Every door I pried open led to another one that slammed shut. I knew better than to guarantee to solve the crime, but I wanted to ease their pain, and at the time, all I could offer were reassuring words. Unfortunately for me, they held me to them.

Pete mumbled a weak "thanks" before hanging up.

The case was fraying my nerves. At the same time, I felt guilty for worrying about my feelings. Whatever I was feeling could not compare to what Pete and Lorinda were enduring.

Alyson called me an hour after Pete hung up. I suspected she was just following up on the family concerns—I was used to their tag-team reconnaissance—but she mentioned nothing about the case. Instead, she asked me if I wanted to meet her for a bite to eat while she ran errands for her mother.

She always seemed to know when I needed a distraction. We met at a deli in Alpharetta and talked for about an hour. The family still didn't know that Cheryl, their daughter's friend, had been killed yesterday. It was only a matter of time before they found out what happened. I felt shitty for not volunteering that information at the moment, but I didn't want her and the family bombarding me with a new wave of questions for which I had no answers. The only saving grace was that there was no offi-cial connection to Kanya's murder. While I knew otherwise, the double murder in Cheryl's apartment was technically an unrelated incident.

"Hey, you mind making a run with me?" she asked. "I have to do some quick shopping. I won't be long."

"Heard that one before."

We went to a home improvement store called LuxuryHome. Alyson had promised her mother she would help redecorate some rooms and wanted my opinion on some things.

"I'm not the best person to ask," I told her. "I've been here before, and these prices ran me out."

"I'm not asking you to buy them, silly. Just want your opinion. Lorinda gave me her credit card. I'm also going to help myself to a few things to ship back home."

My heart shrunk. I didn't want to face the fact she was leaving Atlanta soon. "That sounds like credit card theft."

"Please," she said. "She knows. I should get more than a few things, anyway. It's not like she'll miss it."

"Alyson, what's up with you and your mother?"

"What do you mean?"

"I sense some tension between you two."

She pursed her lips. "There's no tension."

"You know, I do interrogate people for a living."

"And maybe you're wrong. That ever cross your mind?"

I kept quiet as we went up and down several aisles. After a few minutes, she stopped and rubbed her eyes. "Sorry. I guess I still blame her and Pete for what happened."

"They're hurting just as much as you are, if not more. You can't blame them for what happened."

Alyson turned away and browsed through light fixtures and gazed at a collection of crystal chandeliers costing thousands. She dumped knickknacks into her cart without looking at the price tags, and her pleasant demeanor returned as it filled with items. After twenty minutes, we went to the checkout counter when she whipped the cart around.

"I forgot to pick up Lorinda's order," she said.

She found an employee and asked him to retrieve her mother's order. He sauntered to the back of the store and returned with a tightly folded package wrapped in brown paper.

"Ms. Rennell, you have fancy tastes," he said, looking at the price.

"It's my mother's, not mine."

"What is it?" I asked, looking at the tag. "490 dollars?"

"A bath drape," the employee volunteered.

"Five hundred bucks for something that'll get wet and dirty?" I exclaimed. "That's crazy."

"All of this will probably run a couple grand," Alyson said, digging through the cart. "But some of this is for me. You like?" She held up a floor mat with floral designs. "This will look great in my bathroom."

"How much is it?" I asked. "A thousand?"

"Only a hundred twenty."

"You could get that at Target for ten bucks."

"But you didn't feel it, El Cheapo. Feel that *quality*."

I shook my head as I scanned the overpriced items. Alyson asked the employee for scissors to remove the brown packing paper and ensure the correct model had been shipped. Satisfied, she dropped the folded drape, wrapped in clear plastic, into the overflowing cart.

Something caught my eye. I grabbed the scissors, cut the plastic wrapping, and unfolded the drape on the floor.

"What are you doing?" Alyson cried. "You're messing it up."

My throat tightened as I held the shower curtain and studied its gold shapes and symbols.

It was the same as the one we found near Kanya's body.

CHAPTER 37

"Jeff, what are you doing?" Alyson blurted.

I turned to the employee. "Is this a popular model?"

He shrugged. "Not really. It's five hundred bucks, man. I doubt a lot of people are buying it. Then again, you see that big chandelier at the front? A lady just paid fifty-six thousand for it a couple of hours ago."

Alyson scrunched her eyebrows. "Jeff, will you tell me what you're doing?"

"When did Lorinda order this?" I asked her.

"Why?"

The young man glanced at the receipt. "Last week."

"Alyson, how'd your mom pick this one?" I asked.

"I think they had the same one before, in the guest bathroom downstairs. Why?"

"They had the same one? What happened to it?"

She let out a loud sigh. "I don't know. Lorinda said Kanya probably took it to her apartment. Are you going to tell me what's going on?"

"Meet me at your folk's house. I'll be there in an hour."

***

I juggled a kit of forensic chemicals and camera equipment as Pete answered the door. I told him I had bumped into Alyson at the LuxuryHome, and after talking to her, I wanted to inspect their guest bathroom.

Pete looked at my kit. "What is that?"

"It's for crime scene analysis."

"Crime scene analysis?"

"Yes. You placed a special order for a shower curtain, correct?"

"I didn't," he said. "Maybe Lorinda did. Why?"

"Alyson said you had the same one before. What happened to it?"

"Oh, that fancy one Lorinda had in the bathroom down here? It just disappeared. We thought Kanya took it to her place."

"When did you notice it was missing?"

"I don't know, about a couple of weeks ago? Lorinda will know."

He brought his wife downstairs, and I repeated my explanation for my unplanned visit. I asked her when she noticed the curtain was missing.

"After we returned from Charlotte," she said. "What is this about?"

"How long did you have the old one?"

"Years. Maybe five or six years. Are you going to tell me what's going on?"

That explained why the family didn't show up in the individual purchase records. The manufacturer only kept that data for a year.

"That shower curtain is unique. We found your old one in the field near Kanya's body."

They looked at each other. "What are you saying?" Pete murmured.

"I think she was attacked here and transported in the curtain. I'll know for sure after I check the bathroom. I'll need some privacy."

I went into the bathroom and shut the door. It was immaculate, with its marble floor, black porcelain tub and toilet, and gleaming retro faucets. Over the tub was a cheap-looking red curtain, apparently serving as a replacement until the real thing arrived.

I attached a wide-angle lens to my camera, placed it on a tripod, plugged in a remote shutter, and took test photos with the lights on and off. Satisfied, I jammed towels at the foot of the door to block outside light. Next, I took a bottle of luminol, a chemical that made blood appear bright blue under UV light, and sprayed it on the walls, floor, and fixtures. I turned off the ceiling lights, throwing the bathroom into complete blackness. I turned on a portable light.

The room lit up like a skylight.

Everything turned light blue. Smears and splotches of cyan plastered the walls, the front of the tub, and the floor. A throbbing pain shot through my gut as I photographed the large swaths of blue. Kanya's murder had been a massacre.

Luminol did have its limitations. It reacted to metal and bleach in the same manner that it reacted to blood. It could destroy the very forensic evidence one was trying to detect, so I used it as a last resort. But since the crime had occurred weeks ago, and there were no visible signs of foul play, I had no choice but to use it—and my hunch was correct. Someone had slaughtered Kanya in her parent's home, and I was certain it was her blood, and nothing else, that induced the reaction.

The sink. Toilet. Tub. Door. Even the ceiling.

All of them were covered in stains, smears, and flecks, frozen in patterns that radiated from the tub. I pictured the killer's arm flinging back and forth as he wielded the dumbbell, sending blood spatter and streaks in all directions. Several bloody footprints, clustered around the toilet, faced the door. The shoe patterns were plain and undistinguished, making an analysis of the tread difficult.

On the floor was a spatter-free area surrounded by smears and stains. Kanya had lain in that spot. She was already dead as her killer bludgeoned her. Her head was between the toilet and the tub as he hammered her face, again and again.

I turned on the lights. The bathroom looked clean again, showing no signs of the butchery that had occurred. The strongest luminol reaction happened in the tile grout and the caulk of the tub and toilet. It made sense. Those areas were difficult to clean and easy to overlook. I scraped residue from them and placed it in small plastic bags. I was positive it contained traces of Kanya's blood but hoped it held the killer's as well. When victims fought their attackers, it was common to find the assailant's blood or hairs at the scene.

When I opened the door, the family was in my face. "What did you do?" Lorinda asked. "What did you find in there?"

I took a deep breath. "This is where she was murdered."

"In here?" Pete howled. "Our home?"

The couple brushed past me and stepped into the bathroom. "How?" Lorinda blurted. "How did this happen?"

"Not sure," I said. "Is this bathroom used often?"

"Just by guests," Pete said, in a cracking voice. "We haven't had any in a while. How do you know it happened in here?"

"From traces of blood. You can't see it. Lorinda, you said you last talked to her on Thursday, the day before you left for Charlotte, right?"

She nodded, darting her eyes around the bathroom.

"This," I said, "happened that Friday evening when you were in Carolina. None of you spoke to her on Friday?"

They shook their heads. Pete paced and frowned. "How? How did he do this? How did he get in here? Who was it? Rich? DeVaughn?"

"I don't know yet. I'm still trying to put the events together."

He was silent for a few seconds before throwing his gaze on me. "So who do you suspect now? Both of them? Or is there somebody else?"

Before I could respond, Lorinda took a deep breath. "Jeff, just tell me," she said, "do we have enough on Richard to lock him away? Or are we going to start over?"

I inhaled. To soothe their nerves, I had overstated the chances of a conviction. It was a gamble I had lost. "It depends on the jury, Lorinda. A lot of things can happen in a courtroom. But I'll make this case as strong as I can."

"What if Richard's acquitted? Or the DA drops the charges? Then what? You don't even have anything on DeVaughn. It's all been about Richard...and now, we don't even know if that will hold."

"Lorinda, that's not what I'm saying—"

"I just want the truth," she bellowed. "What are the chances?"

"Honey, he's been telling us what we wanted to hear," Pete said. "Or what we needed to hear."

"Is that right?" Lorinda asked. "You've been keeping things from us, stringing us along—"

"Why don't you two leave him alone?" Alyson shouted. "He's doing what he can! He's the only one who gives a damn about her!"

The words cracked the air like a whip.

Lorinda turned to her daughter like the demon-possessed girl in *The Exorcist*. "What did you say?"

"Oh, please," Alyson exclaimed. "Both of you were so concerned about being Mr. and Mrs. Popular down here that you neglected her. Just like you did me—"

"Shut up!" Lorinda yelled, her eyes glowing. "How dare you talk to us like that? You don't know what you're talking about! You don't know what we sacrificed for her! Or you!"

"Oh, please! None of you did anything for me and probably less for her! You just threw money and therapists at her problems, and all they did was get her hooked on prescriptions. No wonder she tried other things. You never listened to her. You didn't help anything—"

"Alyson, shut up!" Pete barked.

"Or what?" Alyson aimed her scalding glare at her stepfather. "You'll kick me out? For telling the truth? You know what? Fuck this, I'll leave."

Lorinda raised her hand to slap her daughter, but I grabbed her arm in mid-swing.

"All of you stop!" I barked. "This is hard for everyone. You're saying things you don't mean and can't take back. You love each other too much for this."

My words quieted them but didn't stop the volley of angry looks between the three of them. Alyson stood beside me. Lorinda stared at us with burning eyes, tremors rippling through her body. Pete sighed and slumped against the wall.

"So none of you spoke to Kanya that Friday?" I asked, trying to reclaim my questioning.

Pete shook his head. Lorinda glowered at her daughter.

"Lorinda?" I prodded.

"No!" she snapped. After a few moments, she continued. "I didn't talk to her. I called her that morning and left her a message."

"What did you say?"

"I told her we were going to Charlotte and we wished her a happy birthday in case we didn't see her. We left a present for her."

Alyson rolled her eyes. "'*In case you guys didn't see her,*'" she muttered. "For her twentieth birthday. Yeah, it's not like that comes around every day."

Lorinda flared her nostrils.

"Alyson, please," I said, holding my hand up. "That's not helping." I turned back to Lorinda and Pete. "How long did you two plan to stay in Carolina?"

"Just for the weekend," Pete said, stepping in for a still-flustered Lorinda. "We planned to return Sunday night."

"But her birthday was Monday. You said you left a message wishing her a happy birthday in case you didn't see her. If you were coming back Sunday, wouldn't you see her on the following day?" Judging from the smoldering expression on Lorinda's face, my question lit another fuse.

"Of course we wanted to see her," she retorted. "What do you two think, that we didn't want to celebrate her birthday? That we didn't care? We did! But she didn't always go along with what we wanted. We hadn't even seen her for two or three weeks. We wanted to see her more, but she never came by, and she never would tell us where she lived!"

"I didn't mean for it to come out like that," I said. "I'm just trying to understand the total picture."

Lorinda paused to collect her thoughts. "We wanted to celebrate her birthday with her, but we knew she probably didn't want us around. She never mentioned any party plans to us, and when we talked about throwing her a party, she said she didn't want us to do it."

"So that was all you said in your voice mail? What about the present? What was it?"

"I told her I left some cash for her in the kitchen because we knew we probably wouldn't see her."

"How much?"

"A thousand dollars."

Alyson rolled her eyes again. "Always money," she mumbled.

"So she had to come here for her present," I said.

"We didn't know where she lived, Jeff!" Lorinda blurted. "How else could I give it to her?" Her Thai accent grew more pronounced, a trait revealed when she became excited or angry. "I couldn't send her a card. We didn't even know when or if she would even come here. We just wanted her to know we were thinking of her—"

Lorinda suddenly covered her mouth and tears streamed down her cheeks. "My God, no. If we hadn't done that, she might not have come here, and she'd still be—"

"Don't do that," I said. "Don't blame yourself. We don't know what happened yet. Now, I assume the money you left for her was gone when you came back." The couple looked at each other and nodded.

"Did you notice anything strange when you got back?" I asked. "Pieces of broken glass? A notification that someone tripped your alarm?"

"No. Nothing," Pete replied.

"Did you set the alarm before you left?"

"Yes. But Kanya knew the code."

"Did you tell anyone you were leaving town?"

"We just let my sister know we were coming," Lorinda said.

"Your housekeepers," I said. "Do they have a key?"

"No," she replied. "And I'm always here when they come."

I sighed. "I may need to come back for more tests, so as of now, this bathroom is off-limits. Right now, I'd like your permission to look around elsewhere."

The bathroom proved an earlier theory; Kanya had been bathing when her killer attacked. It was a convenient location for her killer to wash away trace evidence pointing to him. It explained why her torso and limbs were virtually bloodless when compared to her head and shoulders.

The doors and windows on the first floor revealed no secrets. The front door had a double-cylinder deadbolt with no turn knob; a key was required to unlock it from either side. There were no scrapes or splinters consistent with a forced entry and no missing, loose, or torn window screens. Seeing no sign of a break-in, I went to the basement.

For years, the only time I had come to Pete's "man sanctuary" was to relax. The blue-felt pool table, the leather sectional that swallowed me in its bosom, and the home theater system had just one purpose—to let me and Pete's buddies lose ourselves in marathons of sports and guy flicks. Now, instead of relaxation, I sought evidence pointing to a murderer.

And this time, something caught my eye instantly.

The rack of free weights in the corner.

It had been in the same spot for years and consisted of a set of hexagon-shaped dumbbells. I scanned the rack and noticed one dumbbell was missing: a twenty-pounder, the same weight and model as the one in Rich's trunk.

The connection to that dumbbell had escaped me. It was

a universal design I had seen before, but I mistakenly recalled seeing it at a gym, not Pete's basement.

I continued down the hallway toward the three rooms. The first room was full of storage boxes, and the second room was Pete's office. Neither had windows. The third room was the largest, with two frosted windows high on the far wall. Cardboard boxes leaned against the wall, and plastic containers packed with toys, stuffed animals, and blankets were stacked to my right. To my left was a painted metal door of the stairwell leading to the patio in the back yard.

Lorinda and Pete came into the room behind me. "Is this door connected to the alarm system?" I asked them. When Pete nodded, I asked if there was a motion sensor as well.

"Only on the first floor," he said, looking around the room.

I studied the top of the metal door. I blew in the crack between the door and its frame and released a tiny dust cloud. At the bottom of the door were dense clusters of spider webs. I tried to open the door, but it didn't budge; a hard tug finally opened it with a sharp rip. Paint flecks and dust fell as the sound of crickets and nocturnal life rushed in from outside.

I examined the two frosted windows, each a square foot in diameter and seven feet high on the wall. From the outside, they were only eighteen inches above the ground. Both window panes were dirty and had been painted shut with white paint that had long since grayed.

No one had opened this door or these windows in some time. I went back inside. A film of dust coated the cardboard boxes below the windows. "I don't see any sign of forced entry," I told them. "Kanya either let him in, or he somehow forced her to."

Lorinda shook her head. "It was DeVaughn. I'm telling you."

"Did she ever bring him here?"

"Once," she replied.

If Kanya were already in the house, she wouldn't have opened the door for him or Rich that night. Especially if she were alone. So how did either man get inside? He didn't trip the alarm—it would've notified the police, Pete, and Lorinda if that happened—and unless she wore headphones, she would've heard broken glass or the splintering of a kicked-in door. She certainly wouldn't have stayed in the bathtub and waited for him.

Her killer also couldn't have forced her to let him inside. She wouldn't have made herself vulnerable by enjoying a bath around someone with bad intentions, and I doubted his plan required her to be in a tub before killing her. How did he know where to find her in the first place? No one knew her schedule or that she was staying with Cheryl. Kanya certainly wouldn't have shared her whereabouts with her two ex-lovers.

Was there a third suspect? Someone Kanya would allow in the house, someone she would never suspect of wanting her dead? I could only think of her family members, but they were in different states at the time of her death. Perhaps it was one of her friends or an acquaintance?

Whatever the scenario, the killer had spent a lot of time cleaning up the scene. He was confident he wouldn't be interrupted. He took the money, so why didn't he take anything else? He had the time to do so. Other than the missing shower curtain and the cash, the family didn't notice anything out of the ordinary when they returned from Charlotte.

I asked the family if I could look in their upstairs bedrooms and closets, and they agreed. However, I saw nothing that appeared out of the ordinary. No odd stains or out-of-place objects that didn't belong.

Daryl Langley had suggested that Pete and Lorinda might have done it for insurance money, but that was unlikely. Kanya was only insured for $200,000, and they had plenty of money. Killing her for that amount wasn't worth the risk of life sentences. The timing also made no sense. Pete and Lorinda had endured a lot with their daughter; the suspensions, fights, drug-induced school absences, late-nights in the streets, the embarrassing phone calls whenever she got in trouble. Lately, she had been living on her own and planned to start college soon. Why kill her when she was turning her life around?

Again, I thought of the bank statement printout that Kanya had. Was Pete or his firm involved somehow? After all, it was in his company's bank that Kanya had shown mysterious interest. Then again, there wasn't enough money in that account for what Kanya had planned to do, and there was no link to any other accounts.

No, it was the videos. They had to be the key.

I was sure someone had killed Cheryl over a missing tape. Someone had also rifled through the tapes in Kanya's room. That was no coincidence. It meant the killer—or someone else involved in the murders—was able to get into both Pete and Lorinda's house and Cheryl's apartment.

And DeVaughn was the only one who knew of both locations. He had been to the house, and he had dated Cheryl before he met Kanya.

I tried to imagine what was on that tape. A murder? A steamy affair?

Lorinda popped into my head. She had been searching for Kanya's videos. My mind went down another unpleasant path.

Lorinda had to have known that Kanya never appeared in her films, yet she continued to search through each one. Was *she* featured on the mysterious video? I couldn't help but remember that Lorinda regularly insisted the killer was DeVaughn, despite evidence pointing to Rich. Even after I had proven his strong motive for murder, she remained skeptical. It was as if she wanted to deflect attention from the former executive.

Were Lorinda and Rich doing something they shouldn't?

I shook my head, stopping my runaway train of thought. *Strick, you're stretching things.*

The killer could be someone I had yet to locate. Kanya loved filming people, and she liked hanging out in the streets. This exposed her to some shady individuals. Her social network and habit of observing people and capturing them on tape made for a potentially dangerous combination.

She might have recorded something she shouldn't have.

The more I dug into the case, the more the questions bubbled to the surface.

There was something I was missing.

CHAPTER 38

By the following Wednesday, I began to hate the case. After having Pete's and Lorinda's bathroom and weight rack dusted for prints, we found none belonging to either of my suspects.

Not that I expected any definitive prints. It had been weeks since the murder, and the housekeepers had cleaned the bathroom several times. There were two unknown sets of prints in the bathroom, but we later confirmed that they belonged to employees with the housekeeping company. We dusted the other dumbbells in the set, in case the killer had tried a couple of them before he found the right weight. But we found no prints at all, not even Pete's, who confirmed he hadn't lifted one in over two years. And given typical GBI timelines, it would be several weeks before a sample analysis of the bathroom residue would be completed.

Pete, who had tried being the spiritual rock of the family, had descended into a funk. I remembered my discussion with Lorinda at their fundraiser. She confided that Pete was undergoing a crisis of self-doubt regarding his role as the family protector. He already felt he failed to defend his family from the burglar. The man believed he allowed her to walk into the clutches of a child predator on a camping trip. And he blamed himself for their failure to keep Kanya off from the streets.

This latest discovery devastated him. Their home was supposed to be a sanctuary, the safeguard against a dangerous world. To have Kanya executed in it was a cruel irony.

Ever since her spat with Pete and Lorinda, Alyson spent as much time as possible away from the house. We met at a coffee shop that afternoon. Her face was long and stoic. I imagined that knowing someone had killed her sister—right in the house—wore just as heavily on her as it did her parents.

"Have you figured out how he got in the house?" she asked. "Whoever did it?"

I shook my head. Yesterday, I had questioned Rich, who had denied ever going to the family's house. DeVaughn, who had finally turned himself in for questioning in Cheryl's murder, claimed the same. He was also released from custody since Ed couldn't tie him to either Cheryl's or Marcus Washington's murder.

She sipped her latte. "I wish you hadn't seen my outburst the other night," she said. "I'm sorry. I shouldn't have said what I said."

"Well, this isn't an easy time. Some things are said in the heat of the moment."

"I meant what I said. I just shouldn't have said it like that." She looked down at the table. "I got my ticket to go back home to Chicago."

The words jolted me. I knew she couldn't stay in Atlanta forever, but I had avoided facing that fact. "You're leaving us, huh?"

"I have to. It's too toxic in that house. Lorinda and Pete won't say two words to me. Can't blame them, to be honest. I tried to apologize. But I said too much."

I sighed. "When are you leaving?"

"Sunday morning. I don't want to leave like this, but I can't stay there."

I wanted her to stay with me but refrained from making the offer. I reached into my pocket for my aspirin powders, but I was out of them. The coffee I had been drinking now tasted terrible.

She fiddled with her cell phone and put it in her purse. "Let's get some air," she said.

"Where?"

"Our spot. You know, the park."

Piedmont Park was a rolling, fifty-five-acre patch of greenery a few miles north of downtown. It was a popular destination, where people gathered to bike, jog, play, and relax. We walked down a bike path, lost in our thoughts as we ignored the occasional jogger or couple passing us. The early evening air was crisp. Fireflies made green flashes of light as kids chased and collected them in jars.

We sat down on "our" park bench, the one that overlooked Atlanta's Botanical Garden. Alyson rested her head on my shoulder.

"Your hair smells good," I said.

She was silent for a few seconds. "I like being with you. You're easy to talk to. I feel safe with you."

"I like being with you, too. You're a breath of fresh air."

She snickered. "Wow. That was a Hallmark moment. You came up with that yourself?"

"I try."

"I do have to be honest. I felt kind of sad for you when I first met you."

"Why?"

"Your job's got you so skeptical of people. And your divorce probably made things worse. That's why I took you to the mountains. I wanted you to see some beautiful things for a change."

I damn near was in love with her, but I still wondered if her sentiments for me were genuine feelings or the residual effects of GP.

"Let me ask you something," I said. "You ever wonder why you...why we...have taken to each other?"

"Huh? I just told you why I liked you."

"Sometimes I wonder."

She sat up. "Wonder about what? If I really like you? You think I'm lying to you?"

"I'm not saying that. I've just seen people respond to things like this in different ways. They feel things that aren't true. They end up with guys, and things don't work out for the best."

Alyson furrowed her eyebrows. "What are you saying, Jeff? I shouldn't be here?"

"No, that's not it." I kept thinking of Ryan and Bates and how they took advantage of grieving women.

She waved her hand. "That's what I'm talking about. You're so cynical. You believe the worst of everything. You think I don't know what I'm doing? You think I'm not in my right mind?"

"I'm not saying that—"

"That's what it sounds like you're saying." She paused. "Look, what happened to my sister did bring us together, but it's got nothing to do with this moment. I know where I am. I know what I'm doing and who I'm doing it with. You just said people handle it differently, right? Why can't you just accept something positive for once?"

"Okay." It made no sense to argue if the woman was telling me she wanted me.

We sat in silence for a minute as she rummaged in her purse. "This is why you scare me, Jeff," she said. "It's hard for me to open up. I'm trying to do that with you. I told you I hadn't felt this way about someone this fast. And you sound like you're looking for an excuse for things not to work."

"That's definitely not it. You have no idea how crazy I am about you."

She relaxed a little. "Really?"

"Don't show me that plane ticket. I'll rip it in half."

Alyson smiled slightly. "It's an e-ticket."

"You do know that what we're doing is risking the investigation, don't you?" I asked. "That doesn't bother you?"

"Why do you think I haven't mentioned anything to your friends, who are so mad at me right now?" She leaned in closer. "I'm not like you, worrying about everything bad that can happen. Why can't we just enjoy this? Whatever happens, happens. I can keep a secret."

"Okay," I said, grinning.

Her smile disappeared, and I felt her stiffen as she looked up at me. "Don't hurt me, Jeff."

"Why would I?"

"I'm just saying."

"That won't happen."

Her body softened, and she smiled again. "Then kiss me."

"What's in it for me?"

She sat on my lap and placed her arms around me. "Stop playing and kiss me," she said, looking into my eyes.

Her mouth was delicious. I wanted to freeze the moment so I could relive that high forever.

Little did I know that I was about to come crashing down.

CHAPTER 39

I had just started my Thursday night eleven P.M. shift when my phone rang.

It was Lourne. While he had worn my nerves thin at the beginning of the investigation, he had calmed down after I arrested Rich. I had also cleared another homicide last week, which had bumped up the squad's clearance rate for the month. Things had been tolerable with him, and for the past few days, he had been going home earlier than usual, so I wondered why he was working well past the end of his shift.

He told me to meet him in Lieutenant Shipley's office immediately.

Something was wrong. Both Lourne and Shipley were here this late? It was odd that Lourne was in Shipley's office in the first place. While I wished he would retire, I still respected the sergeant's knowledge and experience. Lourne harbored no such feelings for *his* boss. His deferential behavior in front of Shipley was compelled only by the chain of command.

The sergeant hated that Shipley was younger and on the fast track despite spending most of his career on the safe shores of the administrative staff. The lieutenant was a college graduate with friends in high places and blessed with a gift for remembering names and details. Lourne derided him as an ass-kisser, and he hated reporting to him. I liked Shipley. The enemy of my multiple-personality boss was my friend.

I walked into the lieutenant's office. Shipley, a wiry, bespectacled man, sat at his desk with Lourne standing beside him with his arms folded.

"Close the door, Strick," Shipley said. He pointed to a manila envelope on his desk. "Take a look."

Inside were three photographs of Alyson and me on the

bench in Piedmont Park. One picture showed our faces clearly, and another showed us glued at the lips.

My chest sank into my stomach.

Lourne shook his head. "The victim's sister? What were you thinking? You know we can't afford this shit."

"We received these from Richard Oliver's attorney," Shipley said. "It looks like he put a tail on you. He also sent these to the DA."

"Yeah, you don't want to know what Karen has to say about this," Lourne added.

"So naturally," Shipley continued, "Mr. Oliver wants all charges dropped. Now, from what I understand, we're waiting on some blood analysis of residue samples from the bathroom. We're trying to see if we can place him at the crime scene?"

My throat tightened; I felt an urge to vomit. "Yes. Or anyone else."

"And if that doesn't pan out, then what? We've run a lot of tests and still have nothing definitive. We know where and how she was killed, but not who did it. We have plenty of suspicions, but no real proof."

"Not yet," I said.

"Well, Karen's not going with that," Lourne replied. "I guarantee you she's dropping those charges. Especially since the other suspect, Copeland, is still running around."

"That," Shipley said, "is exactly what Oliver wants, the charges dropped. Plus a public apology, as well as a settlement for three million. He's given the city three days to pay, or he's sending these photos to the media to highlight our 'objective' work. We know the city won't agree to that, so he's going to share these. And that's a problem. He claims the investigation was compromised—and he has a valid complaint. We could've justified his arrest based on what you had, but *this* complicates things. It's going to be hard to convince people that his arrest wasn't personal, especially if you have another suspect, who, by all intents and purposes, looks like the more viable perp. People might even suspect racial bias on your part."

"What, I let DeVaughn go because he's black and arrested Oliver because he's white? I'm not supposed to arrest white guys anymore? Come on, you know that isn't it," I said. "Oliver was a serial sexual harasser. A cheater who got the victim pregnant and then threatened her. He had plenty of motive. He had physical evidence in his car. He lied constantly. He was begging to be arrested."

Shipley threw his hand up. "I know there's nothing racial about it, Strick. I'm talking about public perception. People will note how you arrested one guy and not the other one with just as strong a motive. A decent defense attorney will use any angle he can to create doubt. In fact, forget what I said. He won't need to focus on any racial angle. He'll imply you arrested him because you were in love with the victim's sister and wanted to placate her and her family."

"It'll never even get to trial," Lourne said, "unless we've got some indisputable evidence, which I haven't seen. Look at this. You're groping all over the girl." He paused. "She's fine, though. I'll give you that."

Shipley glared at Lourne. "I don't give a damn if she's Miss America," he exclaimed. "Strick, you two seem very comfortable. This is no first date. How long has this been going on?"

"Couple of weeks," I replied.

"I'm not going to ask if it ever occurred to you that you shouldn't have let this happen. I'm not going to ask if you were aware of the reason we have a recusal policy and that it's not just for judges. Because to ask that would insult your intelligence, as well as ours, because it would say we haven't trained our people in the most basic of procedures. No, I'm simply going to say you knew these things and chose not to care. My question is 'why.'"

I could have answered that the wounds from my divorce were still fresh, my love life was on life support, and frankly, Alyson was sexy as hell. But divorce fallout and lonely nights could be the case for anyone in the department at any given moment. I saw the dead end approaching, but my desire to experience the journey outweighed the inevitable consequences.

"I was stupid," I said. "I didn't think it would get this far."

"You thought wrong."

I wanted to punch myself. Not just for getting caught. Not for already having the premonition that my romance with Alyson would end badly. I was also angry that I was so deep into her that I never noticed anyone tailing us or taking photos. Based on the depth of field and resolution, someone had taken the pictures with a powerful zoom lens. They didn't have to get too close. A flurry of questions ran through my head: Who was it? How long had he been following me? Or us?

Shipley shook his head. "Strick, we can't afford any more scandals or ethical breaches. We can't give opportunities for someone to claim police misconduct. We can't have another NBA mishap. We just can't. We have to take steps to maintain what little public trust we have left. Do you understand where I'm going?"

Just as GNB had distanced itself from Richard Oliver, the APD was distancing itself from me.

Shipley turned to the sergeant. "I have to do some damage control before this blows up. Take care of this." He dismissed us.

"Come to my office," Lourne instructed me. "You made me look like a damn fool. I just recommended you the other day for a special joint task force that's coming up. And you go and do this."

"I screwed up. No excuse."

"Listen," he growled. "I got to take you off this. You're on admin leave as of now. I put Gresham on it. Get him up to speed and transfer your files to him."

I stared at his countdown calendar. Still over five hundred days left. It was beginning to look like I wouldn't be around to see it reach zero. "Do I need to find another job?"

Lourne closed the door and sat down. "Look, Strick. I know you've had problems handling your divorce. I know that's why you got caught up with this woman. You've got to be smarter than that."

I was shocked by his soft tone. I expected him to embark on one of his ass-chewing sessions.

He shook his head. "What, you think you're the only one who's been through it? Hell, that's how you know you're doing real police work. For the past year or so, I watched you try to hide it. You thought no one else saw your pain. Divorce hurts. Even that silly-ass Wills told me he was concerned about you, how you were drinking and wasting time on these women out here. I should've said something to you, but as long as you were clearing murders, I figured you'd work your way through it. But that's my fault. I should've had you talk to someone before you screwed things up, like using that girl as a crutch."

I felt exposed and foolish, as if I had been walking around naked, thinking I had clothes on. "As you said, everyone has problems," I replied. "I can't burden people with mine."

"Ain't no time for that macho crap these days. You should've gone to Chaplaincy. What do you think they're there for? I talked to them when I went through my second divorce. And we had three kids, which made my situation worse. My wife was sticking it to me, and I wasn't even cheating on that one. Bitch took everything. House, car, dog...the judge would've let her take my damn life if she asked for it. I hated everything and everybody. But I knew I needed help. So I talked to someone. I've seen too many guys around here try to handle it on their own. That never works. That's what's wrong with us men. We bottle things up. We end up killing ourselves over time."

I couldn't believe my ears. This brusque man, a man who hated his boss because he didn't spend enough time in the trenches getting shot at, sounded as if he cared.

He seemed to read my thoughts. "Strick, if I tried talking to you about this, you would've said you had it under control. But you're no different from other guys. You think you know everything, but you don't. You should listen to me. I didn't last this long by being a fool. In our jobs, our lives are stressful enough. That's why we have support options. So if I were you, I'd talk to someone. But *don't* talk to a counselor on our payroll. You don't want that on your record, trust me."

I let his words resonate. "So I'm just on admin leave?"

"For now. If you're lucky. You'll be reprimanded for sure. Demoted or fired, maybe. That's what Shipley's talking to the Major about. OPS will run their investigation, and you'll have a disciplinary review. Because of that celebrity case, they're going to go by the book with you."

OPS, the Office of Professional Standards, is the APD's version of Internal Affairs. OPS investigates police behavior regarding civilian complaints and other procedure violations. In the past, officers didn't fear their investigations. They knew the procedures and ways around them. The Civil Review Board (CRB), a group providing citizen oversight of police misconduct, had long complained that OPS green-lit questionable officer behavior and held them responsible for nothing. Recently, the chief of police had vowed to improve the perception of the APD, and OPS was one of his targets. He installed Major Pitts, a former Marine and twenty-two-year veteran, as the cleanup specialist.

Pitts seemed not to care that he ruffled feathers and made enemies. He promised to try to demote, reprimand, reassign, or fire every bad apple. Some officers branded him a sellout who'd feed his brothers to the lions, but Pitts just hated blatant arrogance. He loathed the audacity of habitual law-breakers more than the fact that they broke the law itself.

"So I just need to sit at home?" I asked.

"I don't care where you sit. As long as it's not here at HQ. I'll tell you when or if you can come back."

"When is my OPS review?"

"They'll let you know. Maybe if Gresham finds something that puts away Rich or DeVaughn, that might make it easier for you. I guess you'd better pray he finds something quick." He paused and looked me in the eye. "Do *not* work this case. That's now Gresham's job. Understand?"

I stared back at him.

"Strick, I'm serious. I know you probably want to please this girl, so you need to stay away. We can't have you associated with this case if it goes to trial."

"What if I don't?"

He lifted his bulky frame out of his chair. "Then I promise you that things won't work out for you here."

CHAPTER 40

Richard Oliver had given the city seventy-two hours to pay a multi-million dollar settlement to cover lost wages, rescinded stock options, and the damage to his reputation. If they didn't agree to his offer or paid the settlement even one minute late, Rich would share the photos and create another public relations nightmare for the APD.

Hours later on the following morning, a reporter, Brian Ricci with WSB-TV, called me for a comment on Richard Oliver's arrest for the murder of the Rennells' daughter. At that moment, he was staring at several pictures showing a member of Atlanta's Finest shoving his tongue down the victim's sister's throat, and was curious if my arrest was a proper one. I hung up, wondering how he got the photos and my number.

Apparently, Rich had lied or reconsidered his seventy-two-hour timeline. He distributed the photos to various media outlets only hours after delivering them to my department. Perhaps he was tired of the public ostracism and wanted to show his arrest was due to nothing but an overzealous detective. Or maybe his decision to broadcast the pictures was about money; a smear campaign capitalizing on the APD's conduct in the NBA case might induce the city to settle a lawsuit quickly. Whatever his reason, it was now the APD's turn to roast in the spotlight of public opinion.

I stayed at home to figure out my next step. The long morning was interrupted by calls from Wills, Jessica, and others asking what happened. While they verbalized support, condemnation dripped from their words as if they couldn't believe I put myself into this situation.

At least they tried hiding their true feelings. Karen Simms held back nothing when she called to blast me. She asked how I could be so stupid. The pictures weakened the case against Rich, which was already weak enough and loaded with circumstantial evidence. The prosecution's efforts hinged on the credibility of the investigation, which I had just destroyed. She feared a jury could be convinced to believe a conspiracy of a police setup. She was close to dropping the charges and didn't care I was waiting for test results of the residue and blood samples that could put Rich at the scene.

Feeling in need of an ass transplant after Karen's lashing, I called Alyson to explain what happened. The family was going to find out soon enough about the photos once the networks ran the story.

"Jesus! Are you serious?" she asked. "How did they get pictures of us?"

"That's what I'd like to know. Did you tell anyone we were going to the park?"

"What? No."

"Are you sure?"

"Yes, I'm sure! Who would I tell? My folks? I haven't told them about us for all of this time, so why would I tell them now? Neither one of us wanted them knowing about us. I haven't told anyone."

"Then someone followed us. And they caught me in the perfect situation. Why did you want to go to the park all of a sudden?"

"Wait, what? Are you implying I had something to do with this? Because I wanted to go to the park? A place we'd gone to several times already?"

I sighed. "I don't know what I'm saying."

"I didn't tell anyone! And I have no idea who would be following us."

My legs felt weak when I thought of the humiliating episode. Here I was, a detective who was supposed to possess an eye for detail, a man blessed with powers of observation, and I had allowed someone to tail and photograph us in a park without noticing it.

"So what happens now?" Alyson asked.

"I'm off the case."

"My God." She sighed. "I'm sorry, Jeff. I...I can't believe this is happening now. What happens to the case?"

"They might drop the charges."

"Jesus."

"Where are your folks?"

"Upstairs."

"I'll be there in a few to tell them what happened, if they hadn't heard about it already. This is going to be on the news."

"God, they're going to hate me," she moaned. "They're going to blame me. I just can't believe this."

"No, they're going to save their disgust for me."

***

Whatever Rich's reason for jumping the gun on his timeline, it turned out to be a mixed blessing.

Considering the money he had demanded and the APD's inclination to avoid yet another PR disaster, I feared the department would've sacrificed me before the three days had passed. Their game plan would've been to suspend, demote, or fire me before Rich went public. They would portray me as an officer consumed by personal issues, an overzealous detective who was removed to protect a suspect's civil rights and maintain the propriety of the investigation. It wouldn't eliminate all of the negative publicity, but it would be enough damage control to blunt Rich's plan to cash in. Removing me before Rich went public would give the department grounds to say they took civil rights seriously and weren't responsible for the actions of a rogue detective.

But in his rush to put the screws to the APD, Rich threw

me a lifeline. Without time to plan how to get rid of me, the department suddenly had to defend itself against implications of police misconduct and another embarrassing murder investigation. Sacrificing me afterward would make it seem that Rich's complaints were valid and they had bowed to his pressure.

Still, I wasn't in the best situation. It only delayed the inevitable. I had to clear this case—and my name—quickly.

But first, I had to deal with another bit of unpleasantness. I had to tell Pete and Lorinda the news.

He opened the door and smiled. It was a weak smile, one that people forced to convince others that they were okay.

"Alyson said you were coming by," he said. "I need to apologize for the other night. We shouldn't have said those things."

He gave me the man embrace, a firm handshake with a pat on the back. "Things need to change," he said. "This shouldn't be the only reason we see each other."

I nodded. "How are you feeling?"

He grunted. "I can't walk past the bathroom without thinking about what happened. Right in here."

He already blamed himself for many things. Now he had to walk past another reminder of his "failure" every day. That only made what I had to say more difficult.

"Did Alyson tell you why I was coming?" I asked.

"No." He wrung his hands. "What's wrong now?"

I explained about the pictures, my suspension, and Karen's assessment of the case. Richard Oliver's hope of redemption rested in discrediting the APD, and those photos were evocative enough to make that hope a reality.

Pete took a sharp breath. He leaned against the wall of the foyer and rubbed his eyes. "You have to be joking. You and Alyson were fooling around?" he asked. "When you were investigating this? Why?"

"I don't have an excuse. Things just happened." I cringed at my weak answer.

"So now there's a good chance that they're going to drop the charges against Rich, isn't it?"

"It's possible."

"Of course it's possible," he snorted. "Jesus Christ. And after all of those reminders from you not to tell anyone we know you? And you go and do this? You two do this, knowing what could happen? No wonder she couldn't look at me when she came home."

I wanted to slink away.

"Weren't you waiting on some toxicology or forensic tests or something?" he asked. "But that no longer matters, does it? Because of this, it might drop everything!"

"We still don't know that yet."

"Jeff, you just gave him a hell of an out. His team would have to be full of idiots not to use this." He paused. "Of all people, you should have known this was inappropriate!"

I had no answer. Even I couldn't fully comprehend why I let this happen.

Pete clenched his jaws. "If you weren't a cop, I'd knock you the hell out right now."

"I'd understand if you did. I'll leave."

"Oh, no you don't. You're going to tell Lorinda this. You're not leaving that up to me. You're going to tell her what you and Alyson did and that the charges against Richard might be dropped."

"We don't know if the charges will drop."

"You tell her that." He sneered and walked up the steps before stopping halfway. "I knew I should've listened to my instinct and hired Wes. But no, I trusted you. And look where it got us. I figured he could've helped you, maybe take advantage of different resources. But I never thought you'd be your own worst enemy. Or ours." He disappeared upstairs, leaving me standing in the foyer.

Moments later, Lorinda came down, and I told her the news.

It was a recap of my conversation with Pete, only louder and angrier.

"You promised me you'd find the man," she exclaimed. "And you and Alyson might let him get away. And you couldn't even find anything on DeVaughn, who I've been telling you was responsible all along. This is your fault!"

She told me to leave.

***

As I was driving home from Pete's and wondering how my day could get any worse, Alyson called and asked to come to my house.

"Babe, I don't think that's a good idea. I don't think you should be anywhere near me."

"Why? Do you blame me for this?"

"No. I just don't know who's watching us. I don't need any more pictures of us together. Besides, I need to be alone."

"Please. I—I just can't stay here with them anymore. Do you know what Lorinda said to me after you left?"

"You want to stay with me?"

"Just for a couple of days, until I fly home Sunday."

While I wanted her company, I was paranoid. I didn't want the front page showing pictures of her walking into my house with a suitcase. "That's a bad idea. Especially right now."

She sighed. "Okay. I'll just check in a hotel. I can take care of myself like I've always done. Just know you're not the only one who's hurting."

She hung up. I fought the urge to call her back.

CHAPTER 41

As expected, Karen decided to drop the charges against Richard Oliver.

Our department released a statement in response, explaining that we arrested Richard Oliver based on the available evidence, the investigation of the crime continued, and the publication of photos of the lead investigator with the victim's sister had nothing to do with the dropped charges.

Minutes after that press release, Lourne informed me that I was to appear before the OPS board on Monday, in two days.

The brass planned to make an example of me. A suspension? Demotion? Banishment to a desk? I believed an outright firing was unlikely; a dispute with the police union might bring more publicity the department didn't want. Instead, I figured they would make my job so miserable or tedious that I would do the dirty work for them and quit.

It hurt to think of how I embarrassed the APD, and I felt worse when I thought of how I disappointed my friends. They had believed justice was at hand, only to see me give Rich an escape. Lorinda was infuriated, Pete was disgusted, and Alyson got the arctic shoulder from both of them.

I received the same frosty treatment on my job. Other than Wills, Jessica, and Gresham, no one in the department called to check on me. Of course, I heard from Wes Byers, whose subdued gloating knew no bounds.

But no one gloated more than Rich Oliver. He called and left me a scathing voice mail at my work number and on my cell:

"It doesn't feel good, does it, detective? Everyone looking at you, criticizing you. Putting your life under a public microscope. Well, things come back around. I'm innocent of the crime you accused me

of. Your own people acknowledged it. So just as you delighted in ruining my life, I'm going to sit back and enjoy watching you suffer. Have a good day."

The weekend hours crept along, and I thought more and more of Alyson. I shouldn't have turned her away; we were both catching hell in this together. But she refused to return my calls. I didn't blame her; I had left her stranded in the cold when she tried to escape her mother's biting tongue.

I went to the kitchen to pour a shot of tequila and saw my reflection in the glass door of the microwave. It was the face of an exhausted and lonely man that stared back. The entire city laughed at him. He couldn't get things going. I wanted to put my fist through his face.

I hurled the tequila bottle across the kitchen, where it bounced against the wall and shattered. Then, I collapsed to the floor.

Max, alerted by the noise of breaking glass, came to investigate. He sniffed me for a few seconds and tried to lick my face. When that didn't work, he barked several times. I figured it was his way of telling me to get my sorry ass up.

Slowly, I wiped up the mess.

To hell with Lourne and his threats. I had two days to act. Two days to clear the case, some way, somehow, before I had to appear in front of OPS. Two days to do what I hadn't been able to do in more than two weeks. But I had to do something.

I was going to find my CI and put the fire to him one last time. Not only had he not provided me information, the son of a bitch hadn't even tried. If this was my last time to use him, I planned to juice him for everything he had.

It was Saturday, so I drove to his favorite spot, Jo's Chick'n. No one paid attention to me when I sat at the bar. I ordered a beer and left C-Dub a voicemail, but this time I tried a new approach. I told him that too much was happening for me—which it was—and that I needed something strong to take the pain away—something stronger than alcohol.

Those were magic words to him, because about forty-five minutes later, he strolled up to me with a sardonic smile, showing off his gray gums and brown, rotten teeth. "You're looking bad, man," he said. "What's wrong?"

"Life."

His smile grew wider. "Look at you. Bad-ass Strick! Yeah, you look like you need some sugar. Something to get you right. I got you. I know who we need to see. How much you got?" He wet his crusty lips with glee. The stench of his breath almost made me gag.

I knew he couldn't resist seeing me sink to his level but his eagerness surprised me. He didn't even seem concerned about talking to me in public—something that always made him leery—nor did he seem to consider that I could arrest him for selling me heroin or facilitating a deal.

"Sugar?" I said. "I don't think so."

"What you got a taste for?"

"Nothing."

"What?" C-Dub scowled. "What you call me out here for?"

I grabbed his shoulder. "I'm done playing with you. You're going to do some work for me. You know that DeVaughn guy, the one you saw on Northside Drive? You're going to find him— and watch him. And then I'm going to have you do—"

He rolled his eyes. "Man, I thought that was over."

"*I* decide when it's over."

He curled his ashy lips into a grin. "You're not fooling me. You're hurting. I can see it. You need a little something, but you're scared because you've got them virgin veins. You're scared to ask—"

"Well, well," came a familiar, raspy voice behind me. "Look who's here."

I turned around. DeVaughn stood with his son, Eric, along

with Rat-Mouth and a giant whale of a man. DeVaughn sat beside me at the bar while the others found an empty booth. "What are you doing here, Detective?" he asked. "Slumming?"

DeVaughn turned to my CI. "You his friend?" he asked him.

My CI shook his head. "Just met him, cuz."

"Then step off, cuz."

C-Dub obeyed and walked outside. DeVaughn turned to his friends. "Yo, this is Detective Stankland," he bellowed. "He was the one harassing me about Kanya. Look at him now."

"That's all they do, harass people," the fat man said. He was round and sloppy. His grubby orange T-shirt looked like a tarp covering his beach-ball gut.

"What do you want, DeVaughn?" I snarled.

"Just wanted to say I'm sorry."

"About what?"

"I heard they dropped the charges against Richard. You were getting your freak on with Alyson. I also hear you've got some free time now. They fire your ass?"

Our eyes met. "I know you killed Kanya," I said. "I don't know if you did it for Rich or for yourself, but I know you did it."

He held out his wrists. "Then arrest me."

"Your time will come."

"You're taking this way too personal, bruh. But I know why. I'm actually jealous. You're a lucky man to tap that ass. I should've fucked Alyson, too. Instead of fooling with her crazy sister."

"DeVaughn, I suggest you get away from me right now. I'm being polite for the moment."

He shrugged. "And this is the thanks I get."

"For what?"

"Those cute photos I took of you and Alyson. I didn't even charge you. You were all caught up, looking like a lovesick little bitch."

I stood up. "That was you?"

"I thought you'd like seeing yourself with a bitch that fine."

I grabbed his forearm. "Who put you up to that?"

A fury came into his eyes. I felt his muscles tighten and his hand ball into a fist. "Get your goddamn hands off me," he said.

I squeezed harder, wanting to crush the bones in his arm. "How'd you know I was at the park? Who put you up to it?"

"I did, bitch."

"You're lying," I snarled. "Tell me who."

"Get off me!" He wrenched his arm away, and his friends jumped to their feet.

"You should be nicer, detective," DeVaughn said. "I could've done more than shoot your picture, and you wouldn't have seen it coming. Besides, you're talking big time with no backup. You ain't even a damn cop right now. Your ass is null and void."

The background chatter in the restaurant had died. The only sound was the hum of a television in the kitchen. Several customers stopped eating to watch us. Other patrons, no doubt seasoned by random outbreaks of gunfire in that area of town, hustled to the exit.

DeVaughn smirked. "Yeah, I think I'll holler at Alyson after this. Do her right. Make her scream my name—"

I slapped him and knocked him into the counter. Before he recovered, I slapped him again. He didn't deserve the respect of a man's punch. Rat Mouth leaped out of the booth and charged me. I grabbed my beer bottle and smashed it across his head, sending him staggering back.

Young Eric stayed in his seat, mesmerized. As the fat man tried to extract his bulk from the booth, DeVaughn lunged for my legs. I sprawled back. He swiped an armful of air as I seized his neck and slammed his face to the floor. He growled threats and tried to get up. I spun around him, gripped his left arm, and held it tightly between my legs. I had locked him in an armbar, hyperextending his arm. All that was needed was a few pounds of pressure to break it. Although I had immobilized him, he

254

continued spitting curses and threatening me.

I yanked his arm down and thrust my hips forward. He howled as I felt the sharp snap of his elbow separating. The sound of it was sweet to me.

Despite his agony, he continued shouting a stream of expletives about Kanya and me. I pulled the bastard's arm down further; I wanted his snapped bone to pop out through his skin. He roared in pain.

The air suddenly rushed from my lungs. It felt like a truck had flattened me. The Fat Man had knocked me on my back and rolled onto me. As I squirmed from under his flab, I felt a painful blow. A bloodied Rat Mouth had kneed me in the side. DeVaughn, his left arm hanging at a hideous angle, began kicking me in the face. There were flashes of white light. I felt something cracking in my face and mouth, which suddenly felt wet and salty. I tried to reach for my backup gun under my pants leg, but it was pinned underneath the Fat Man's blubber.

The excruciating blows continued. I curled up like a baby. I pictured my ribs breaking and my muscles tearing. The flashes of white light became red, then dimmed to black. I felt sleepy.

The blows stopped. Black Joe, the owner, had burst from the kitchen and brandished his shotgun. "Hell, no," he blared. "Don't kill his ass up in here! Take him across the street to the fish place. You're messing up my business!"

DeVaughn kicked me again. "Pick him up," he ordered his friends.

They held me by my arms and dragged me outside to the parking lot. The men dropped me on the asphalt, and someone kicked me in my stomach. It felt as if someone had scraped out my insides with a screwdriver. I heard Fat Man say something...

"...can't kill him here," he said. "Too many witnesses."

"I don't care," DeVaughn spat.

More punches. More kicks. I curled up to protect myself. Everything went dark.

***

"Young blood," came a voice. "You all right?"

Someone was rustling me. It was Black Joe.

"Where am I?" I mumbled. My words sounded funny; my lips were swollen. I touched my mouth, and my hand turned red with tacky blood.

"In the middle of my parking lot," he answered. "You need a doctor. Or somebody. Want me to call an ambulance? Grady ain't too far."

I sat up. I felt bruises, welts, and bumps on my face and body. "I'll be fine."

"Suit yourself. But you need to get up. You laying in the middle of my parking lot. It ain't but so big, and customers can't park."

I stumbled. "Did anyone call the police?"

"Hah," he said dismissively. "Even if they did, you'd be dead long before they got here. I stopped them fools from killing you. What the hell's the matter with you anyway, fighting three grown-ass men? You think you're Bruce Lee? You'll get your ass killed. If I were you, I'd leave before they change their minds and come back."

CHAPTER 42

Going to Grady Memorial hospital was out of the question. Too many people knew me there. I didn't want leaks about the investigator of the Kanya Glover murder being assaulted and needing treatment for his injuries. Instead, I drove farther west to Cobb County, visiting an emergency room under a fictitious name.

Despite the beating I had taken hours earlier, I had only one thought: I wanted to see Alyson before she left town. Since I rejected her before, it took a Herculean effort to persuade her to visit me. When she rang the doorbell, I peered through the peephole and saw her flaring her nostrils, ready to unleash.

She recoiled when I opened the door.

"What happened to you?" she shrieked. A purple ring encircled my left eye, my jaws were swollen, and blue stitches looped through my lip and cheek as if I were a Frankenstein experiment. I winced from pulsating bruises in my abdomen and thighs.

"Bar fight. Things got out of hand."

"Who did this to you? Shouldn't you be in the hospital?"

"I'll be all right," I grunted. "I needed to see you before you left. I'm sorry for not being there when you needed me."

She shook her head. "Forget it. I understand. Look, I'm here for you, now." After staring at me with pity, she exhaled. "I heard they dropped the charges against Richard. What's going to happen now?"

"I'm putting my focus on DeVaughn. I should've listened to your mother. She believed it was him all along."

She raised her eyebrows. "I thought you couldn't work the case anymore."

"I'm going to work this until it's finished. I don't care what they do to me."

Alyson thanked and hugged me. "How did DeVaughn get in the house? How did he know she was home?"

"I don't know. Maybe he followed her. Like he followed us. He's the one who took those pictures of us."

"*He* did it? How did we not see him?"

I shrugged. "We were too preoccupied with each other. I wish you weren't going back home tomorrow. Not on such a bad note."

"I'm thinking of changing my flight. I think I'll stay another week."

I almost grinned, but it felt like my swollen lip was about to split in two. "What made you change your mind?"

"I thought we had the man who did this. Now we don't. I feel like I can't leave without seeing something resolved. I feel like I should be here to do something. Anything."

"What about your folks?"

"I'll get a hotel."

I was happy she was staying; just not under these circumstances. "Your job is okay with this? You've already been away for a few weeks."

"I've got enough vacation time. I can work remotely. And I made a nice commission a few weeks ago."

Her apartment was near Chicago's Magnificent Mile, and she wore shoes that had women interrupting our dates to compliment her and ask where she bought them.

"I'd love to see that commission when things are really going well," I said.

"The money's not all it's cracked up to be. The key is that I save and bargain-shop."

She sat close to me and caressed my shoulder as I contorted myself on the couch to where things hurt the least. The non-narcotic painkillers I had taken from the hospital seemed in no hurry to work.

"I'll make you a cup of hot tea," she said. "It should make

you feel better."

Alyson covered us in a blanket and snuggled next to me as she searched for a movie. I sipped the black tea and nestled into my couch, my pains and aches melting into a warm sleep.

Then a phone call from C-Dub jolted me awake.

CHAPTER 43

CHAPTER 43

C-Dub had interrupted my beauty sleep to tell me he had just come across some information I wanted to hear.

"What is it?" I asked.

"I'm at a pool hall now. Maxxies. On Jonesboro and Lakewood?"

"And?"

"One of them dudes you were fighting earlier? He's in here. He's with another guy, and they've been talking some shit. Sounds like they were talking about your girl, the one you've been asking me about."

I was alert now. "You see DeVaughn in there?"

"No, the other one. The skinny one, the one with the jacked-up grill."

Rat-Mouth. "He's there now? Who is he with?"

"I don't know the other guy."

"Is he the other man DeVaughn was with today? The fat one?"

"No, some other guy. Never seen him."

"Did Rat-Mouth recognize you?"

"Nah. He never came to the bar when we were at Jo's, so I don't think he noticed me. Besides, he's blazed right now, anyway."

"What did you hear them say?"

"The other dude was doing most of the talking. Man, I couldn't hear everything; it's loud in there. But it sounded like he might have had something to do with killing her."

"And they're both there now?"

"Looking right at them."

I stood up. "Stay there. I'm on my way."

"Well, wait a minute," he said. "I think we, uh, we need to

come to an agreement first."

I frowned. "An agreement about what?"

"I need some scratch. And not no ten or twenty bucks, neither. I want fifty. If you got it, I'll still be here."

He spat his words and sounded overly excited. I feared he was about to start going through the "shakes", or suffering withdrawal from whatever substance he had been shoving in his veins. If that happened, he'd disappear underground for days on one of his crack binges.

But something didn't smell right. I had threatened to let him rot in jail, and he still avoided my calls and showed no urgency in digging up information. Now, he had suddenly uncovered some crucial intelligence for me?

Maybe it was a set-up. For what, I didn't know. I was his get-out-of-jail card. As much as he had complained about me, I was always the first—and usually the *only*—person he called to bail him out of trouble or help him with some family issue. Harming me would only ensure he'd get into a dilemma from which he couldn't escape.

No, it smelled like another one of his new schemes, where he gave me a bullshit lead to get some cash to fund his habit for the day. C-Dub was an on-again, off-again junkie, more on than off. Like every other addict, he was irrational and greedy when he was using.

Whatever his motive was, I had to check it out; I had no other leads.

But it didn't mean I trusted him.

Alyson and I had dozed off while watching The Matrix. I nudged her to give a hasty excuse, promised to return soon, and sped to the pool hall.

I circled the block twice, looking to spot anything out of the ordinary. After I parked behind the establishment, C-Dub appeared from behind a dumpster. I unlocked the car door, and he slid in. I frisked him immediately.

"What's your problem?" he asked. "You're going to do me like this?" He shuddered upon seeing my face. "Damn, they messed you up."

"Thanks for having my back."

"You know I left before it happened. By the time I saw it, it was over. Besides, Joe saved you."

"They're still inside, right?"

"They left about five, six minutes ago."

I gave him the evil eye. "Damn it, man, why didn't you call to tell me they were leaving? Did you get their plates, at least?"

"Something better. The other guy's name."

"What is it?"

"Where's my money?"

I sighed. He had been an excellent informant, but no CI had a permanent shelf life. We had cleared plenty of cases, but he was now a liability. His attitude had darkened, and his information had become less and less reliable. If he wanted to be free of me in exchange for promising news regarding Kanya's murder, it was a welcome price to pay.

"Tell me what you have first."

C-Dub shook his head and rubbed his arms. "I want to see the money. A hundred dollars."

"You said fifty. Now you'll only get twenty. You're pissing me off. Don't play me, C."

"All right then, fifty." He darted his eyes back and forth.

"Get out," I growled. "You were probably sitting on this the whole time, you greedy bastard."

"No, just gimme fifty, man. I won't ask for nothing else again, but I think you want to hear this. I thought you cared about this case."

I was just as desperate as my conniving informant. "I'll give you fifty if what you tell me is good."

"Let me see it first."

I clenched my teeth as I pulled the cash from my wallet and

placed it on the dashboard. "Don't you touch it yet. Now talk."

"The other guy's name sounded like 'Lavell.' That's what the rat boy called him. I was shooting at the table next to them, and I heard him talking about how he did these two girls, right? I swear I heard him say Kanya."

"You sure?"

He shrugged. "That's what it sounded like. But I wasn't about to go up and ask him what name he said." He eyed the money on the dash.

"Back up. He was talking about two women. He said he killed both of them?"

"He ain't say 'kill.' He said he 'took care of their asses.' "

"And he said what sounded like 'Kanya'? Did he mention the other girl?"

"I think he said Sharon or Sherry or something. I couldn't tell."

He had to have been speaking of Cheryl Tory. "Did he say how he killed them?"

"I didn't get all that, man. It's not like I had a wire on me. They had been talking before I got there, but I didn't start paying attention until I heard Kanya's name. That's when I started listening. And when they were getting ready to leave, he said something about going back to that girl Sharon's place. Think he said he needed to find something he left back there."

I thought of the missing *An Officer and a Gentleman* movie. "Did he say what it was?"

C-Dub huffed. "I don't know, man. I didn't want to make it obvious I was all up in their business. I wasn't trying to get shot. Whatever it was, I guess it's something he don't want nobody finding."

"He say when he was going over there?"

"I don't know. I'm just telling you what I heard. He might be going there now. I don't know. Can I have my money, now?"

"They left about ten minutes ago?"

He exhaled. "Yeah. He might have said more, but I had to stop to call you." He clawed at his dirty chin as if he had fleas. "Are we good? I told you what I know. That's good, right?"

"If you're lying just for the money…"

"I'm not lying. I swear. Hell, I know you'll find me if I did. I know what you can do. I just don't want to do this anymore."

He kept his eyes pinned to the money. I snatched the cash and stuffed it in my pocket.

"Come on, man!" he roared. "You promised."

I pulled out into the street, heading to Cheryl's apartment. "We're taking a little trip first. If it works out, I won't bother you again."

"Where are we going? Aw, hell, no, man. I don't want to get involved in this! Just give me my money and let me go about my business."

"If you want it, you're coming with me. I'll know if you're lying or not."

"Why would I lie? I can't make this up!"

I sensed he was lying about something, but I couldn't prove it, a fact he pointed out with colorful fury. If this Lavell was real, he might have already decided to visit the apartment at another time. Or he may have already stopped there while I was talking to C-Dub. My CI swore he was telling the truth and that I was looking for an excuse not to pay up.

He had a point. I had never mentioned the murder of Cheryl to him. The fact that she and Kanya were friends was something I kept out of the papers. How would he know that the deaths of the two victims were related unless someone told him or he overheard it?

If he was telling the truth, and this Lavell intended to go there tonight, I wanted to be there to meet him. But in case something did go wrong, I wanted C-Dub there so I could wring his neck.

CHAPTER 44

On our way to the Conifer Homes apartments, I called Wills and asked him to check the computer to cross-reference a "Lavell" with Cheryl Tory, Marcus Washington, or Kanya Glover. After making Wills swear to keep my request a secret, I found that Lavell was indeed real.

Lavell Merson was the thirty-six-year-old father of Cheryl's daughter. Ed Cleveland had already questioned him about Cheryl's murder, but his alibi had checked out. I considered calling Ed with this latest hearsay but decided to see Lavell myself. It was my tattered reputation that was on the line, and only I was going to do something about it.

Lavell may have been real, but did he kill three people? I could visualize him popping up to see his ex-woman, finding her entertaining another man (Marcus), and jumping to conclusions. An argument could have started, things turned physical, and it ended in a double homicide.

But why would he have killed Kanya days before? How did he get inside the house?

Theories started running rampant. If Kanya and Cheryl were good friends, she would have known Lavell. Perhaps they knew each other more than people thought. Maybe he had made a sexual advance to the young woman, and she rebuffed him, something he couldn't let go unanswered.

"See, I told you I wasn't lying, man," C-Dub grumbled. "Why don't you just drop me off?"

"If I do, it won't be with the money."

"I don't care. Just drop me off."

"Now you don't want it?"

"I don't want to be involved in this! If something goes down, I don't want them seeing me with you. They'll remember I was at the pool hall and they'll know I said something. They get away and see me later, that's my ass. You won't be there to save me. That ain't worth fifty damn dollars."

When we pulled into the parking lot of the complex, the moon hid behind a mass of clouds and turned the sky into black velvet. The wind alternated between roaring crescendos and calming rustles as it whistled through the trees. It was a perfect night for a thief. It was dark, no one loitered outside, and when the wind got going, it was loud enough to swallow the sound of breaking glass and splintering doors.

I parked on the opposite side of the street from Cheryl's apartment and waited. C-Dub sunk low into his seat.

I didn't have a visual on Lavell. The description Wills gave me—a black male, 5'9", average build, dark complexion, with an unknown tattoo on his bicep—was the default description for half of the men in the area.

Thirty minutes passed. My butt was numb, and my sore muscles felt as if they were fossilizing. The painkillers were wearing off. Meanwhile, C-Dub complained about unjust treatment, fidgeting as if an army of ants were crawling over him.

Another twenty minutes went by. It was 1 a.m., and residents began turning off lights. The clouds began to break, and the faint moonlight started to give shapes to our surroundings. Maxxie's was twelve minutes away. It was possible that Lavell had come here when we were at the pool hall. I probably missed him by ten minutes.

We had been sitting in my car for almost an hour. It had been calm outside, and no one had walked near her apartment. If anything were going to happen, it would've happened by now. I glanced at my informant. His nonstop whining and musty odor were fraying my nerves.

"C, get out," I said. "If I have to listen to you whine or smell you any longer, I'm going to scream."

He sat up. "What about my money? How am I going to get

back to my girl's place? I don't want to walk all the way back—"

"Take the bus." When he got out, I crumpled up the cash in a tight ball and flung it at him. He scrambled to pick it up, jammed it in his pocket, and walked away, mumbling curses for good measure.

I sat in my car another twenty minutes, observing the area. A resident pulled up in front of his apartment, went inside, and soon turned out the lights. Other than that, there was no activity.

I got out of my car, deciding to take a look at Cheryl's apartment. If Lavell had been there, maybe he left a clue behind. Perhaps the absence of something I had seen inside the apartment earlier might spark a lead. It was a long shot.

The temperature was unseasonably comfortable—seventy-three degrees was a treat for an evening in late August. But no one loitered outside, an uncommon situation on summer nights. There was something eerie about the night, which had started with its schizophrenic wind, blustering furiously and exhaling as if a storm was debating whether to hit us. But in the past hour, it had grown quiet.

Cheryl's front door was locked and still sealed with police tape. I went to the rear of the apartment to the concrete patio and peered through the sliding glass door. It was jet black inside. I pressed my tactical flashlight against the glass and shone it in the kitchen and living room. No one was inside. I tugged at the patio door handle, but it didn't move.

I went back to the front door and jiggled the doorknob. Noticing the deadbolt lock was splintered and possibly broken, I took out a credit card, slid it between the latch and strike plate of the door, and jiggled it for a few seconds. The door clicked opened.

I pulled out my personal .45 caliber handgun and stepped inside. I stood motionless, trying to hear if anyone was inside. I then sprayed the room with a swath of light from my flashlight for a few seconds, turned it off, and moved to the side. I turned on my light again and repeated the action, making my way through the apartment. The idea was to make sure I wasn't a stationary target in case someone was watching me. I had no idea what I was looking for; the movie I was looking for was long gone. Nothing appeared different since I had last visited. If Lavell had killed Cheryl and Marcus, what was so important that he had to return for it days later?

I crouched in the darkness and thoughts flooded my mind.

Kanya.

My upcoming review with OPS.

Alyson.

Oh, no.

I remembered I left her on the couch at my house. C-Dub might have come through with a promising lead one last time, but without knowing when or if Lavell would come, it didn't help.

I opened the front door. Something zipped past my head, and I felt a sting on my ear. There was a sharp crack. Something flashed in front of me.

Crack! Crack!

I dove to the floor and scurried to the kitchen. Someone was shooting. Bullets tore through the apartment and glass shattered everywhere. Dust and plaster rained.

The only light came from my flashlight, which was rolling on the floor and illuminating the room. I didn't know if I had been hit. I was too scared to look.

I cowered by the refrigerator. The TV in the living room exploded under an assault of metal. Slugs riddled the couch and pieces of foam burst from the cushions like popcorn. I smelled burning plastic. Cracks and pings echoed as bullets tore through the stove and struck the refrigerator.

I heard two gun sounds but couldn't tell what the weapons were. One sounded like a semi-automatic rifle; I guessed the other was a nine-millimeter.

I reached for my cell in my pocket. My phone and leg were wet. I held my breath as I looked down, expecting to see blood gushing from an artery, but it was water—a pipe under the sink had ruptured. I tried dialing, but the phone was dead.

There was a brief lull before the shots started again.

I couldn't move. The sound of my heartbeat hurt my ears. Sparks popped like cheap fireworks. Wiring was exposed somewhere—and I was laying in a pool of water.

Why didn't I call my mom this week?

I smelled more burning. More bullets. It was deafening.

I don't know why I thought of my mother, Rayne. I loved her but never told her enough. Nor did I tell others how I felt. Tomorrow was never promised.

God, don't let me die. Not like this.

The commotion stopped. I crawled from behind the refrigerator, broken glass and shards of dishes crunching under my weight. I cursed the noise; it was giving away my position.

I heard the shooters reload. They were by the front door. My heart hammered as I tried forcing my eyes to adjust to the darkness.

"Go around the back," one of them said. The voice sounded familiar.

Someone approached the back yard and stopped several feet from the glass patio door. He swept the area with his flashlight. He came closer and stopped when his light illuminated red splatter on the kitchen floor, courtesy of a shattered bottle of ketchup. He leaned closer to inspect the red spill. "What the fu—"

I fired at his chest three times. He fell forward into the kitchen and dropped his handgun and flashlight, sending them scattering across the floor.

"You got him?" yelled his partner from the front. "You got him?"

When no one answered, the other shooter sent a hail of

bullets into the apartment. More metal tore through the wall, inches from my head.

The man I had just wounded shot at me. I sent three more hollow points into him, jerking his body with each hit.

The second shooter at the front stopped shooting. A few seconds later, I heard a car drive off. I crawled to the front of the apartment while keeping an eye on the wounded man behind me. The door looked like a wooden slab of Swiss cheese; I could see the parking lot clearly through its holes.

I reminded myself to breathe and looked at my watch. The episode, which seemed like hours, had been two or three minutes.

Shit.

I was supposed to be on admin leave, and I had just shot someone. My stomach began rumbling.

OPS conducted investigations whenever officers discharged their weapons. They grilled us with questions such as: *Did the suspect fire first? Did you give clear warning? What was your background?* Discharging a weapon was supposed to be a last resort. Everyone under investigation faced second-guessing, even after a shooting was deemed proper and lawful.

But I was a suspended officer, involved in a gun skirmish for a case I wasn't supposed to be working. Worst of all, the bullets meant for me could've killed someone nearby. I already had an OPS review to decide the fate of my career. This situation would certainly kill it.

I needed to be far away by the time a patrol car showed up. If the shooter in the kitchen died, I wasn't going to be around to answer questions. I had to find out who had just tried to kill me.

Outside, another car started up and drove off. I crept back to the kitchen, stepping over the wounded man. I bolted around the apartment and peered around the corner to the street. Was the other shooter still out there? My beating heart almost burst through my chest. Staying low, I dashed to my car.

When I reached my door, the driver-side window exploded.

I hit the asphalt. The second shooter sent another volley of bullets in my direction. I crawled behind another car and waited for everything to stop.

Don't let me die, God.

When I heard him eject his magazine, I sprinted back to Cheryl's backyard. His bullets struck the siding as they chased me back around the building. I dove into the shrubbery behind her patio. My lungs were burning. I kept forgetting to breathe.

The shooting stopped.

I looked toward the street and saw him. The shooter squatted beside an old Chevy Impala thirty yards away; a street light betrayed him when its light reflected off his gun. I had him in my sights—but my background was bad. A miss could kill an innocent in the apartments behind him.

My assailant had no such moral dilemmas. He had sprayed bullets as if he held a water gun. Suddenly, there was a sweet, beautiful sound that made me want to cry—the melody of distant police sirens.

The shooter fired a last burst of bullets in my direction. When I heard a vehicle accelerate out of the lot, I jumped up to run back to the apartment.

I needed answers.

271

CHAPTER 45

My head was going to explode.

I wanted to hurt somebody.

Two men had just tried to kill me. They made me beg and pray while cowering like a frightened rabbit. They made me revert to my childhood and wish for my mother. A flood of irrational, unrelated thoughts came over me. I couldn't stop thinking about how my mom used to make my favorite dish of crab cakes.

I had been petrified. I couldn't even remember my police training.

It made me furious.

I retrieved my flashlight from where I dropped it and shined the light over the slumped figure I had shot. He was still alive. Barely. A pool of dark blood was spreading from under him. His wheezing came in shallow bursts.

I kneeled over him. "You missed me."

He moaned something. When he opened his mouth, he revealed teeth impossible to forget. Rat Mouth.

"Why were you trying to kill me?" I asked.

"We—had you." He coughed, spraying blood and spittle from his lips.

Fearing hepatitis or HIV, I jumped back. I looked at his tattered red chest. "Tell me, or I'll let your ugly ass bleed to death. I don't know if you've noticed, but you need a doctor right now."

"Call...call the ambulance..."

"Why were you trying to kill me? Where's DeVaughn? I know he was with you."

Rat gazed at the ceiling with watery and bloodshot eyes.

I stood up. "Then die."

He mustered a gurgling shout. "It w-was DeVaughn...he

said…teach you a lesson. Call the…ambulance…"

Considering how I had turned his chest into a sponge, an ambulance couldn't do a thing for him. "How'd you know I was here?"

The dying man opened his eyes wide, and tears streamed down his temples. "D—Don't let me die, man…"

I saw that look before. Many of my homicides were street thugs, guys who boasted about taking out enemies and going out gloriously, like Scarface. But as they lay dying in dirty streets, all of them wore that same terrified expression. There wasn't much glory in that life. I guessed they were afraid of finding out if Hell was real.

After laboring to fight the inevitable, Rat stopped breathing. The sirens grew louder. I sprinted to my car and tore out of the complex seconds before a patrol car arrived. Heading north, I suffered a dizzying headache and pulled over to the shoulder of the highway.

In ten years with the APD, I had never killed anyone. It was only the second time I had fired my gun, and the first time was a warning shot. I kept hearing that gurgling sound Rat made as he breathed and seeing his eyes rolling back. I had wanted to kill him for trying to kill me—but then felt guilty after doing it.

I opened my door and vomited, releasing my seething rage, confusion, and remorse. But something still burned in me, something I would've never thought possible until tonight.

Even so, I didn't think he had the courage to do it.

C-Dub, you dirty bastard. You set me up.

CHAPTER 46

Even though I doubted he'd be there, I sped to DeVaughn's house. He had just tried to kill a cop. It didn't matter if the cop was active duty or suspended, Kanya's ex-boyfriend had just made himself a marked man. He also couldn't know if Rat Mouth was dead or snitching on him at the moment. He had to assume the worst case and believe his homeboy was giving him up. Going home was not the smart move.

But I had nothing to lose.

I called Wills and regurgitated the events of the last few minutes. "I need you to meet me at 157 Sampson," I blurted. "DeVaughn's place. Remember where it is?"

"Jesus, that was you, Strick? I heard the disturbance call go out. What the hell happened?" He couldn't believe I had gotten myself into a shootout for a case I wasn't supposed to be working. "I'm up in Marietta; I can't get there that fast. Don't go there yet."

"I can't let him get away." I hung up and raced through the city streets toward The Bluffs.

I wanted to wrap my hands around C-Dub's neck and squeeze. I knew he wanted to break free from me, and I even suspected something odd was going on, but I still never thought he would try to have me killed. I was so desperate to solve the case that I got stupid. The signs of his brewing betrayal were there. After the lies, bogus leads, ungrateful attitude, and unanswered calls, his new information was just too coincidental. He let me lead the way straight to an eventual ambush.

I still had unanswered questions about how he put it in motion, but I would deal with him later.

I parked a block north of DeVaughn's house. The only sound was the occasional thumping bass of a car stereo passing on an adjacent street. Using the shadows, I approached his house.

The lights were on, and someone was inside, running through the house before stopping in the master bedroom. The bedroom window was cracked open, and I heard DeVaughn yelling at someone on the phone, periodically barking orders at his son to finish packing.

"Look," DeVaughn bellowed, returning to his phone call. "You'd better have my money, or I'll do what she was going to do. I'm coming over right now."

The conversation stopped. He cursed to himself as he ran through the house. I crept onto the porch and peeked through the window.

I was lucky. DeVaughn had to come home to pick up his son and finish last minute business. But he was clearly on the move.

I decided to lay back and follow him; I wanted to know who was on the other end of that line. As I backed away from the door, DeVaughn burst through it holding a black gym bag, his left arm in a sling. He froze upon seeing me.

I aimed my .45 at his face. "Get on the ground."

He didn't comply. Eric appeared behind him, looking at us with large eyes.

"Get your ass on the ground," I shouted. "Both of you."

"My boy ain't got nothing to do with this." DeVaughn dropped the bag and stepped away from the doorway. He kneeled on the porch, and Eric followed his lead.

I kicked the man in the stomach, sending him doubling over. "I'm going to make this hurt."

He coughed and grimaced but stayed on one knee. I reared back to kick him again but heard a murderous growling. His Rottweiler was barreling down on me.

"Get him, Knox," DeVaughn shouted, reaching for his gym bag.

"Don't move!" He stopped but kept his hand stretched toward his bag.

Knox was too fast. I turned to shoot the animal in self-defense, but couldn't—Eric was standing behind the dog. The canine slammed into me and knocked me to the floorboards, sending my gun sliding behind me. The dog plunged his fangs in my left forearm.

It felt like searing hot nails had pierced my flesh.

Knox soon sought a better prize—my neck. He clamped his jaws on my shoulder and nudged his hot mouth upward, homing in on my jugular. All I could hear was loud, guttural snarling, and my arm and shoulder started going numb.

"Kill that bitch! Kill him," DeVaughn yelled as he got up and ran inside. "Hold him, Knox! I got something for him!"

The man had bluffed me. There was no weapon in his bag, but he was fixing that problem. I looked behind me for my gun, only to give Knox better access to my neck. I rammed my fist on his thick skull, but it was like whacking a bear with a flyswatter. Lying on my back, there was no leverage to swing.

I glimpsed my .45 behind me and squirmed to grab it, dragging the big dog with me. Trying to grasp the gun somewhere behind me, I swept my arm back and forth like a snow angel. DeVaughn bounded in my direction, his footsteps thudding through the floorboards. "Oh, I got something for you, baby! You ready?"

Lord, please help me...I feel it...

I hooked my finger into the trigger guard. Dragging it with my fingertip, I picked up the gun and sent a bullet into Knox's side. The canine yelped and leaped away before limping to the corner of the porch.

"You shot Knox!" DeVaughn stood over me, leveling his stainless steel revolver to my eyes. "Drop it, bitch."

I complied. My arm felt like it had been soaked in gasoline and set ablaze. Pain radiated from my shoulder to my back. Eric rushed to the family pet. "He shot Knox, dad! He shot Knox!"

"And he's gonna pay for that. And for this," his father said, glancing at his broken arm.

The boy looked on with surprised eyes. "Are you gonna shoot him?"

DeVaughn whirled around to face his son. "Boy, hurry up and get the rest of the stuff like I told you."

The shouting and growling had piqued the neighbors' interests. Several stood on their porches and watched us. The thug turned back to me. "Last time, I took your picture. This time, I'll take your life." He twirled his revolver. "Like I did with Cheryl's friend. You saw what happened to him."

I winced. Every inch of my body was on fire. "That was you? Why?"

"She had something that I wanted. She didn't want to give it up, so I took it. His ass, well, he was just in the wrong place."

"What did you take? A video?"

He tipped his head to the side. "How'd you know that?"

"What's on it?"

DeVaughn shook his head, a slight grin on his face.

"Did you kill Kanya?" I asked.

His grin disappeared. "Yeah, I did. You happy?"

"Why?"

"Because I didn't like the bitch. She had me thrown in jail."

"Did someone pay you? Richard paid you to kill her?"

He snorted. "That weak-ass punk. He couldn't—wow. If you could see your face. What, you loved that little bitch or something? Oh, yeah, I killed her. Everybody thought she was pretty, but she wasn't when I got done with her. I made sure she wouldn't have a real funeral."

I clenched my fists and shook my head.

"Awwww...you don't like that?" DeVaughn leaned closer. "I hurt her, man. I did her real good. She was begging me to stop. She kept trying to ask 'Why?' while I squeezed her throat harder and harder. And her eyes. They started turning red as I choked her. She's trying to fight me, looking all terrified and shit, like she can't believe she's really going to die. Bitch didn't have anything smart to say then."

I saw my little Kanya tugging at my sleeve to check her room. She was introducing me to her friends as the hero who saved her from the burglar. Then I pictured her flailing and struggling, praying for someone to save her, only to fall lifeless at the hands of this bastard. My throat hurt as I imagined her realization in those last seconds, her terrible awareness that her ex-boyfriend was killing her.

"Damn, bruh," he said, "You look like you're about to cry."

I needed to keep stalling him. "You were talking to Richard just now, weren't you?" I asked.

He drew back. "You were out here listening to me?" The felon smirked and shook his head. "Oh, by the way, your boy at Jo's? He sold you out for twenty damn dollars. All I had to do was just tell him what to say to get you out there."

My cell phone beeped twice. It was a coded message. My partner had arrived.

"Drop the weapon, now!" Wills was in a shooting stance at the side of the porch, his gun aimed at my suspect.

DeVaughn turned to him, and then whirled around and fired at me, striking the floorboard next to my head. Wills sent several rounds into him, hitting his upper back. DeVaughn's legs buckled, and he dropped to the floor.

I grabbed my gun, and both Wills and I screamed for the murderer to give up. Since he shot at us first, no warning was necessary, and I wanted to shoot a dozen holes in him for trying to kill me tonight. But I also wanted him to talk.

"I ought to kill you three times," I growled.

Grimacing as he propped himself up on his bad arm, DeVaughn lifted his gun to shoot me. In the deafening aftermath that followed, his body slumped onto the porch, his torso shredded by bullets. He had chosen his way out. Suicide by cop.

Eric ran onto the porch and screamed when he saw his father

fall. DeVaughn breathed in weak, gurgling hushes, as his buddy had done earlier tonight. He lifted his hand to touch his son. After he had cradled the boy's cheek in his bloody right hand, his arm dropped to the porch with the thud of dead weight.

The boy cried and begged his father to wake up. Wills led him away, and at first, the child acquiesced but then thrashed with the fury of an adult. We bound his wrists with flex-cuffs, but a group of onlookers protested that we were treating him too harshly. I didn't give a damn about their feelings. Eric was old enough to pick up his dad's gun and use it.

The boy strained against his restraints. "I hate you! I'll kill you!"

Wills eyed DeVaughn's body. "Now, how the hell are we going to explain this?" He turned to me. "Jesus, what kind of hell have you been through? You look terrible. Are you all right?"

I shook my head. The hot, throbbing ache branched out from my arm, up my shoulder, and through my neck. How many nerve endings could a man have?

"We've got to get you to a hospital," he said.

I wasn't keen on checking in to a hospital for the second time in one evening. Wills helped me up from the floor and looked at Knox whimpering in the corner. "Thought you liked dogs," he said.

"That's why I didn't kill him."

"Well," he said, pointing to the dead man, "You shot the shit out of him."

"I didn't like him." The floor spun like a pinwheel, and I grabbed his arm.

"Take it easy. I'm going to get some medical assistance out here and get you to a hospital."

"I'll take myself." I stood still until the floor stopped spinning.

"Man, you're bleeding all over the place. Don't be stupid. I'm calling them now, and then I'm calling to get Smith out here. He's on deck. He can close out this homicide."

I looked at Eric, who was screaming and wriggling with his cuffs like a fish caught in a net. "Don't call Smith. Call this in anonymously. I'm not supposed to be here, and neither are you. You've done enough. You saved my ass."

Wills looked at the carnage on the porch. "What are you saying?"

"We've got to roll. Now."

He shook his head. "I'm not leaving until I see you in an ambulance and Smith gets here. Jesus, you told me you already shot and killed one man earlier tonight, Strick! We've got to answer for that, too."

"We will, but not now. I'm in too deep as it is."

Wills frowned. "You should've thought of that before you ran over here without backup."

"What the hell did you want me to do? The bastard tried to kill me. Twice. If I didn't get here when I did, who knows where he would've run to? He was on the move."

"I can't afford to lose my job or get suspended. I've got child support up the ass. I don't have degrees like you where I can get something else that pays just as much, if not more. This is all I've got."

I had put him in a tight spot. If we didn't file a timely report of the shootings, it would look like a cover-up. And if someone discovered that, it would be a hundred times worse than pictures of a detective kissing the victim's sister.

"I'll call Smith," I said.

"And say what?"

"That all of this is on me. I called you for backup, and we shot in self-defense."

"When are you calling him?"

"Within twenty-four hours."

He shook his head and pointed to the people across the street watching us. "No way. They're going to say we were here, Strick. When they describe us, Smith will know it's us. We need to stay here and clear this up. They are cracking down on misconduct and our asses will—"

I pointed to DeVaughn's lifeless body. "That son of a bitch killed three people, including Kanya, and I don't have all of the answers. I need those answers. I need to clear my name. Time is of the essence. Gresham and Smith and anyone else will slow this down."

"I don't like this, brother."

"You know I'd help you. Remember the Millar case?"

"Asshole. I knew you were going to bring that up." He shook his head and sighed. "What about the kid, man? He's going to tell Smith we were here, too."

"No one knows our names. Unless these people are picking us out of a lineup, I can't worry about that now. We never identified ourselves. I just need until Monday, man. I'll tell Smith everything. I'll tell him that I had forced the situation and you only shot to save my life. I'll take the blame."

"You know that won't fly, Strick. You know that, don't you?"

"I'll tell them I lied to you to get you out here, that this situation was an exigent circumstance, and I had to act immediately to stop another crime in progress."

Wills exhaled. "I don't believe I'm agreeing to this. I'm going to get fired. After this, Strick? We're even. I don't want to hear about Millar again. Where are you going now?"

"I need to follow up on something and get to a hospital." I also needed time to plan a story that explained this night.

People seeped out of their homes and stood in front of the house, berating us. "How y'all going to shoot that man like that in front of his boy?" yelled one.

I removed my shirt gingerly and wrapped it around my forearm. "I'm going to Grady," I told Wills. It was easier to explain the dog bites and scratches rather than the ass-whipping I had taken earlier; I would just say I was walking down the street after visiting an informant when a dog attacked me. Fortunately,

I had been bitten rather than shot; hospitals reported gunshot and stab wounds to the police, and my co-workers were the last people I wanted to see.

Wills called 911, affecting the persona of a frantic neighbor who'd just witnessed a shooting. He warned me that the patrols were en route.

"What y'all going to do to that boy?" yelled a man.

"Goddamn crooked ass cops!" shouted another.

I picked up DeVaughn's gym bag. Inside it was his cell phone and bundles of cash. As soon as we stepped off the porch, several pissed-off-looking men blocked our path.

"Y'all just going to kill the man and leave his boy and run?" spat the ringleader, a skinny, older man.

I held my .45 in my right hand and DeVaughn's bag in my left. The simple act of clutching the bag nearly brought me to tears. Blood trickled down my left arm and collected under my palm and fingers, making the bag strap stick to my flesh.

"Where they think they're going?" the ringleader asked, emboldened by his support group. "We're tired of this shit! Y'all come in here, shoot us, do your dirty work and harass us—"

I took a bundle of cash from the bag and threw it in the air. The fluttering, crisp bills sparked a flurry; the men pushed and shoved each other, and others who had watched the episode from their porches joined in the free-for-all. Men, women, and children ran through the streets, snatching each bill they could find.

During the commotion, Wills and I ran to our cars. I knew he had questions about the money, but answers would come later. I threw the bag into the passenger seat and sped off, watching people in my rearview chase money floating down the street.

CHAPTER 47

It was a miracle I made it downtown to Grady Memorial Hospital without blacking out from the pain.

Grady wasn't a glamorous facility. The non-profit hospital faced persistent budget shortfalls, and many of its patients were poor, homeless, and had no insurance. But it was the best hospital in the metro area for treating severe trauma. Its doctors gained plenty of experience dealing with GSWs (gunshot wounds), stabbings, and beatings.

I thought I had my ruse figured out when I decided to visit Grady instead of going to a hospital farther away. But after checking in, I realized that once Smith arrived at DeVaughn's house, he would find the wounded Knox, hear testimony from Eric and others, and check nearby hospitals to see if they admitted anyone to treat a dog bite. The administrator at Grady helped me register under a different name, but that would only delay Smith's investigation. Sooner or later, I needed to come clean about those shootings before someone found out I was at the scene.

After I had got my arm cleaned, stitched, and bandaged, and took a series of shots and painkillers, I went to my car to inspect DeVaughn's gym bag. There were four wrapped bundles of cash. Three of them had labels that read "GNB–$50." Each of the three bundles totaled $5,000.

The fourth bundle, wrapped with a blue rubber band, totaled $10,000. The bundle I had tossed at the mob was also wrapped with the same blue band. If the stack I had thrown was the same amount, it meant DeVaughn was on the run with a total of $35,000.

Rich was truthful when he said he paid DeVaughn $15,000. The money with the GNB labels had to have come from him. It didn't mean he was honest about the reason he paid him, however. Was it an extortion payment or a fee for a contract killing? The additional $20,000 presented another question.

I reflected on DeVaughn's likely sources of income. It was common to arrest low-level drug dealers in roach-infested homes and find garbage bags filled with drugs and thousands of dollars. They couldn't use checking accounts and were too unsophisticated to launder much money, so they stashed cash in refrigerator components, in walls, or under floorboards. Those were the signs of a moderately successful low-level dealer.

DeVaughn didn't appear moderately successful at anything. His whip was a beat-up Lexus instead of a tricked-out ride or a luxury model with gleaming rims. He rented a dilapidated house in a crime-ridden neighborhood. Other than bars on the windows, he had none of the security systems high-earning dealers used, like reinforced doors or security cameras. There was no bling or fancy electronics. Furthermore, the money bundles in the bag were comprised of clean, crisp bills, not the dirty, musty, crumpled dollars that changed hands between addicts and dealers.

The $20,000 didn't come from slinging.

I took DeVaughn's cell phone and hit redial, trying to reach whoever he was speaking to earlier. No one answered. I wrote the number—678-124-1935—to try later.

I kept watching my bullets slam into DeVaughn's chest and seeing his son crumple beside him. I leaned back and took deep breaths. Years ago, I had talked to a veteran cop who killed a perp in self-defense. When I asked him what it felt like, he said "Strick, when you kill another man, you never forget it. It stays with you. Even if he deserved it."

The guilt of killing two men earlier tonight overwhelmed me. I was fatigued and wanted to sleep, right in my car in the hospital parking lot. My body had had enough—a vicious beating, betrayal, being shot at, and nearly being mauled to death.

I tossed the bag into the back seat and heard something rustle inside it. I checked the side pockets.

It was a videotape labeled *An Officer and a Gentleman*.

CHAPTER 48

I broke every speed limit back home.

Alyson was still asleep on the couch. I searched through boxes in the garage and found my old VCR. I went to my bedroom, hooked the machine up to the television, and shoved the tape inside.

I expected to see anything but the movie. To my disappointment, I watched Richard Gere join the Navy and Lou Gossett Jr. holler at officer candidates. I fast-forwarded the tape. Twenty minutes, thirty minutes, forty minutes passed. Every time I pressed play, it was nothing but the movie.

Someone must have switched the tape.

This movie couldn't be why Cheryl and Marcus were killed. It didn't make sense that Kanya would've deemed it important enough to keep among her final possessions, especially since it was an old VHS tape and not a DVD.

I thought of Lorinda. She was searching for Kanya's tapes—and this movie was the only one I knew of that hadn't been inventoried or given to the family. Why would she care about this one?

No, there had to be something here, something that was recorded over the middle of the movie or at the end. I fast forwarded to the credits. Still nothing. I rewound it to the middle of the film and saw nothing out of the ordinary. Fatigued and upset, I watched it until I drifted to sleep.

I awoke to a black screen. The TV and VCR were still on. I looked at the tape counter—an hour and thirty-seven minutes of the movie had passed. It was too soon for it to be over. There was a 'thump' on the tape, and a door and room suddenly appeared on the screen. The colors were faded. The camera zoomed in on a bed with a white sheet.

"Get on the bed, sweetie," came a distorted and tinny voice from behind the camera. It was a man speaking. He repeated this command in a pleasant but stern tone. A petite, naked white woman sat on the bed with her back to the camera. Some soft jazz played in the background.

"Turn around, sweetie," the man said.

The woman didn't move.

"Come on," he said. The tape's sound was infected with dead spots. The man stepped into view. He was naked, except for white briefs over his pale skin. The camera showed him from his waist to his calves.

When he pulled down his underwear and stood next to her, she jerked back.

"Now, now stop…I told you," he said. "We've got to do this."

The man caressed her shoulders. He did this for several seconds before seizing her head. He placed himself in her mouth and began moaning. The woman tried pulling away, but his hands were vice grips locking her in place.

The man told her to sit still, but she cried and pleaded for him to stop. This wasn't porn; this was sexual assault.

"Do you want to be a woman?" he snapped. "Do you?"

I felt my skin crawl. It wasn't a small woman. It was a girl. Disgusting child porn.

I thought of Richard. The married man had no qualms sleeping with and impregnating a young woman less than half his age, a woman who came with a hundred reasons to be off-limits. It wasn't a stretch to imagine he liked them even younger; pedophiles came in all sizes and socioeconomic statuses. If Kanya had come across a video of Richard pleasuring himself with an adolescent girl, it all made sense. The blackmail, the murders, DeVaughn killing Cheryl for the tape, everything.

I forced myself to watch. The voice was metallic and thin; the tape had lost some of its audio quality. But the man sounded like the disgraced GNB executive.

Rich paused his thrusting and told her she needed to swallow everything he gave her. All girls, he said, did such things if they wanted to grow up to be women, get married, and have babies. Otherwise, they would be flat-chested and ugly, and no one would like them. He was doing her a special favor.

My mouth tasted as if I'd been chewing tinfoil. His vile words echoed in my ears. He loomed over the girl and forced himself on her yet again. "It's for your own good. I'm doing this because I love you."

The sounds of his sexual assault sickened me. I wanted to look away, but I sat frozen to the bed. Rich kept his face off the screen. He released a loud grunt in exhilaration, finished with his heinous act. The girl doubled over, spitting and trying to wipe away every trace of him.

"Nothing will happen if you keep doing that," Rich warned. "You won't grow." He stepped out of view to change the camera angle.

Little Kanya stared at the screen, tears dripping down her contorted face.

"No" I blurted.

She looked to be about ten or eleven.

The scene went black, and another one appeared, this one showing Kanya on the bed and facing the camera this time. She looked instantly older, about twelve.

No.

This can't be.

As the man approached her, I saw a long scar on his hand, an old wound caused by the slash of a burglar's knife.

CHAPTER 49

My guts turned to ice.

Pete.

I rushed to the toilet to throw up. Nothing came out. My stomach dry heaved as I clutched the sides of the bowl.

Pete. You sick fuck.

I looked back at the TV. The second recording began as the first. He told her she was becoming a beautiful woman and that only special girls had this chance. She could see for herself that his 'magic juice' was working because her breasts were starting to grow. Only special girls were lucky enough to have this love—as long as they were good.

This time, Kanya didn't cry. She stared ahead with dull eyes and didn't resist. The girl barely moved. She sat on the bed like a mannequin, her body to be used at his will. Pete offered "reassuring" words, then warned her that she'd never see her mother or sister again if she told anyone their "special secret."

Alyson knocked on the door. "Jeff? Are you okay?"

I forgot she was sleeping in the living room. "Just a minute." I had to compose myself.

"Are you okay?" She grasped the doorknob.

"Don't open it!" I pulled myself from the floor and turned off the television. After cleaning myself up a bit, I opened the door.

"Are you okay?" she asked. "I heard you yell."

"Bad dream."

Alyson leaned in closer, apparently seeing the bites from Knox. "What happened to your arm? Where did you go?"

I didn't have the inclination to answer her questions. "Nothing to worry about. It's over." I was sure my cracked voice betrayed my emotional state.

She plopped down on my bed and sighed. We sat in silence for what seemed like a minute.

Alyson stood up. "Okay. I try to get you to open up, but I can't. I know how you get when you don't want to talk or be bothered. I guess I'll head back."

"No, why don't you stay here?" I was going to confront Pete. I wanted an explanation, an understanding of why he tortured and traumatized a sweet, defenseless little girl. I wanted to hurt him. Alyson didn't need to be there to hear the things her stepfather had done to her sister.

"I didn't bring my stuff with me."

"I'll go to the store and get what you need."

She cocked her head. "You're going to buy my feminine products for me? You must really want me to stay. How about I spend the night tomorrow? Unless you want to keep playing Fight Club and coming back with more bruises."

"Please stay here."

She eyed me warily. "What's going on? Where did you go tonight?"

"Please. I have to run out, but I'll be right back."

"You're leaving me again? Why should I stay if you won't be here?" She looked at her watch. "And it's almost three in the morning. Where are you going at this time? Look, I'm trying to go along, but I can't stand it when you keep things bottled up like this. What is it? Something about our case? It's the only time you act like this. Is it about Richard? DeVaughn?"

"DeVaughn's dead."

She widened her eyes. "What? When? How?"

"Tonight. Heard it on the radio. Drug dispute. Look, just stay here for me."

"Wait...you can't just say that DeVaughn is freaking dead and change the subject. Is that going to impact our case? Are you going to tell me what's happening?" she asked.

"I can't get into it right now, but I'll tell you everything soon.

I promise."

She crossed her arms. "Okay. I'm going home. It's hard being around you when you're like this. I guess I worry too much." She grabbed her purse and walked out.

I sat back on my bed and mulled over what I had just seen. *Pete. You sick fuck.*

You call yourself a Christian. And I called you my friend.

I was sure there were more incidences of sexual abuse he never filmed. No wonder Ruth Harris, Kanya's sixth-grade teacher, found her crying in a stairwell after school. Pete was always going to be home, ready to creep into her room at night when her mother was asleep. The girl couldn't escape. She couldn't tell anyone the things he forced her to do, or she'd never see her mother or sister again. Kanya was alone.

I cried as I thought of what she had endured. Pete had crushed me. I had looked up to him and believed in him. Now, I couldn't get my bearings straight. Nothing made sense anymore. Hindsight kicked my ass with the acknowledgment that I should have recused myself from the case. While I had seen the evil things people could do to another, Pete had left me shell-shocked. My relationship with the family exacerbated my revulsion.

No wonder Kanya had experimented with drugs, fought in school, stole, and faced expulsion multiple times. No wonder she disdained her parents. Her behavior reflected classic symptoms of abuse that, in hindsight, anyone should've seen.

But we did see it. We just threw our suspicion on the wrong guy. Based on the tape, I believed the abuse started around the time of Kanya's camping trip or soon after. It was fortunate timing that gave Pete a perfect opportunity to play the aggrieved father and divert suspicion by confronting Daryl Langley and launching the investigation that trashed his career. Langley's strange looks and demeanor made suspicions of inappropriate behavior stick to him as if he were flypaper. All of us believed

Langley had possibly sexually assaulted Kanya during that trip and the incident was the start of her problems. None of us wanted to consider the danger was closer to home, even though many statistics and our own arrest records showed otherwise. Pete was able to railroad and scapegoat Langley with precision.

The poor girl was robbed of her childhood and damaged by a self-indulgent monster masquerading as a protective, loving father.

I contemplated the tape's journey as it changed hands. Pete created it and kept it for years, obviously to enjoy in intimate moments with himself, but it ended up with DeVaughn. DeVaughn had taken it from Cheryl, who found it among Kanya's belongings.

Now it was evident what Cheryl tried to tell me when she called me. She had found the movie, watched it, and saw Pete forcing himself on Kanya. She probably intended to turn it over to me, but DeVaughn somehow learned that she had it.

Cheryl was known to run her mouth. I speculated she was so disgusted by what she saw that she had to tell someone about it. She chose DeVaughn; he was her ex-boyfriend, and they both knew of Kanya's parents, so he'd be able to relate to her disgust. Telling him what she saw ended up being the last mistake she'd ever make. DeVaughn, who had already killed Kanya—presumably for money—saw the video as another opportunity to get paid. It had to have been Pete he was screaming at on the phone; the ex-con was demanding money for the return of the tape.

But why was Kanya keeping this awful reminder of her childhood among her key possessions? How did she get it in the first place? Pete would've kept it under lock and key.

I remembered—it was in his home office. The one Kanya had broken into only days before someone strangled and bludgeoned her.

Pete had to be behind it all.

The video was why Kanya had been killed.

CHAPTER 50

My thoughts raced as I drove to Pete's. I should've turned the tape over to Gresham since he was the acting lead investigator. But I had been breaking protocol all along, so there was no reason to start following guidelines now, especially after seeing what Pete had done. I wanted to look him in his eyes and slap the cuffs on him—if I didn't find a reason to shoot him first.

Waiting at a red light, I pulled Kanya's picture from my wallet. She was so photogenic. I was no psychiatrist, but it didn't take much for me to understand why she refused to show herself on video. She could never forget her stepfather's strong hands clasped around her head and serving as his sexual toilet, over and over for years.

I thought of something that happened several years ago, on a warm Saturday in November. I went to Pete's to watch the Georgia vs. Auburn football game. Kanya, in the seventh grade at that time, had since stopped joining my field trips. I hadn't seen her in weeks, so when I saw her in the kitchen pouring a glass of fruit punch, I smiled and walked over to hug her.

She flinched as if I had electrocuted her. There was no 'wai' this time, no sweet, customary Thai greeting. She looked at me, then Pete, then back to me. "Hi," she muttered, before turning away.

I held my arms out. "No hug?"

"It's too hot." The temperature outside was in the high seventies, but she had bundled herself in sweatpants and an oversized gray sweatshirt. She sidestepped me, and instead of walking past us to go upstairs to her room, she gave us a wide berth by going through the dining room, living room, and foyer before ascending the steps.

I looked at Pete. "I say something wrong?"

"Puberty. Don't take it personally. You got the nice Kanya today. Usually, she doesn't say anything at all."

"I used to be her first crush. Guess I'm old news now."

"Happens to all of us, my friend."

After all of these years, I felt stupid for never seeing the reason for her behavior. If she had been anyone else, I would've picked up on it, or at least noticed something was off. But she was the daughter of my friends, and they were beyond reproach. At the time, I thought Kanya's choice of clothing at home was due to personal preference, that of a young girl feeling awkward about her physical changes. Instead, she probably cocooned herself to conceal her maturing body and douse her stepfather's perverse urges.

I rubbed my face as I turned into the Peachtree Springs gated community. Usually, I enjoyed driving through the vibrant entrance. But tonight, every section of ornate landscaping, every shrub pruned to perfection, every blade of grass reeked of hypocrisy. How could such a place suggest tranquility when a monster like Pete Rennell hid behind its gates?

When I saw Kanya in the kitchen that day, he had already been abusing her for years, based on the videos. He had trapped her in a loathsome routine, and there I was, standing with him, laughing and smiling. No wonder she wanted nothing to do with me that day. I remembered how she looked back and forth at us, calculating in her mind that she could no longer trust me. I was once her hero, but I had become her tormentor's friend. In her eyes, seeing me align with Pete was a betrayal. How could she trust anyone? She probably suspected I would do the same things Pete did to her if we were alone.

That notion sent a sharp pain through me.

Kanya, I never would've done that to you.

I know what happened. I'll make sure everyone knows the truth.

And I'll make sure Pete answers for it.

CHAPTER 51

I turned off my headlights as I eased through the subdivision. I parked two houses down from Pete's house and called Alyson on her cell to ask where her parents were. She said Pete was downstairs in the basement and Lorinda was asleep. I asked her to let me inside quietly.

"You're outside?" she asked. "Right now? Why?"

"I need to see Pete. I need some advice from him."

"This early in the morning?"

"We know he's a workaholic. He only needs a few hours of sleep."

A few seconds later, she came to the door in a nightgown. "You're acting mighty strange tonight. What is that?" She pointed to a plastic grocery bag I held.

"An old fight on tape."

"You came here—at this time in the morning—to watch boxing. And to ask for advice. Okay." She shook her head. "You're like a sphinx, with your secrets." She started leading me to the basement.

I stopped her. "I'll see him. You go back to sleep."

"Jeff, seriously. What the hell is going on?"

I wasn't going to wait to catch Pete when he was completely alone. This was going to happen now. "I just need to ask him something real quick," I replied. "You know how I get when I need to get a question answered."

Alyson threw her hands up. "I give up. Must be a guy thing. Good night." She retired upstairs.

I walked downstairs to the basement. The light in Pete's office was on. I heard typing on a keyboard.

The rack of free weights caught my eyes again; the empty twenty-pound slot triggered images of Kanya's battered face. I looked at Pete's display of war medals and wanted to burn them. Whatever honor he earned by serving his country had been wiped out by several minutes of tape.

The typing grew louder as I approached his office. I had longed for the day I found Kanya's killer. At times, I considered bringing the guilty man to a secluded spot to enact justice; I even debated inviting Pete to have the first crack at him. But here was the man responsible, barely ten feet from me. Part of me wanted to believe that he was the victim of a scheme using advanced video technology to disgrace him and create the ultimate scandal. I couldn't fathom that my friend brought us to this point.

I took a deep breath and stepped into his office.

"Jesus, Jeff," Pete exclaimed. "You scared me! How did you get in here? What are you doing here?"

"Alyson."

He studied my bruised body. "My God, what happened to you?"

"Come out to the bar, man. I need a drink." With a blank look, he followed me into the main room. I poured a shot of vodka and drained it. His face disgusted me. I couldn't shake seeing him hover over a frightened, helpless little Kanya, forcing himself upon her again and again.

"Jeff, what happened? What's wrong?"

I held up the plastic bag and pulled out the movie of *An Officer and a Gentleman*. "This version's a little different from the one I remember."

Pete narrowed his eyes.

I put the tape on the bar. "Nothing to say?"

He looked at me.

"Answer me."

"I don't have much to say, Jeff."

I wanted to knock his head off. "You sorry, sick piece of shit. You were behind it all, weren't you? Tell me how it happened."

The attorney glanced at the handguns in his display case.

I unholstered my .45. "Try it. Please. Let's see how fast you are."

Pete glowered at me. I'd never seen that look on his face. At that moment, I knew my old friend would kill me if he got the chance. "Tell me how you did it," I said.

He remained silent.

"Pete, I'm going to make this hurt if you don't answer me."

"You're an intelligent man, Jeff. What do you think? She was trying to ruin me, and I couldn't let that happen. I had no choice."

"How was she going to ruin you?"

"Take a guess. She wanted money for that tape. If I didn't give it to her, she would've gone public with it."

"She found it when she broke into your office that day, didn't she? How much did she want?"

"More than what I was willing to pay. She wouldn't have kept her word. She would have gone public with it regardless."

"So *you* were the windfall she expected on her birthday, not Richard. You were the one she was after. And you killed her."

"She was going to cross me regardless."

"Well, Pete, I couldn't blame her."

"Perhaps. But self-preservation is important to me."

I spit on the carpet, disgusted by how calmly he spoke. There was no shame. No remorse. "Tell me everything, you nasty son of a bitch. I mean everything."

He scowled. "You think you're better than me? You go around screwing and you chased away the one woman who loved you. Even Alyson wasn't safe from you. She doesn't know you like I do. You couldn't control yourself, you ruined your career, you involved Alyson in it—and you have the nerve to look down your nose at me?"

"Are you serious? You killed your own daughter, man."

"Stepdaughter, as she liked to say. And I didn't kill her.

DeVaughn killed her."

I opened my mouth but couldn't find the words. I had allowed this man to charm me over the years and be my friend. As a detective, I was supposed to be a keen judge of character, and yet, I failed to see this ugly side of him.

"Don't judge me," he said. "I have my vices, like everyone. But I loved Kanya. I don't care if you don't believe me. I raised her and kept a roof over her head. I gave her a life of opportunities. She and Lorinda would never have enjoyed this lifestyle if they stayed with her first husband. What have you done for anyone? How have you helped anyone? You destroyed your marriage. And for what? Dallying with a nurse? You used Alyson. You used her in a sad attempt to validate your pathetic life. You are no better."

The words hurt. "Get up," I said. "I'm taking you in."

"You're arresting me?"

"Yes," I growled. "You make a sudden move, and I'll blow a hole in your damn head."

"You can't arrest me!" he thundered.

"Raising your voice won't help."

I told him to head to my car; I had been so anxious to confront him that I left my flex-cuffs in my glove box. He walked up the steps, and I was a couple of paces behind him. When we emerged into the foyer, I felt a blow to my head.

CHAPTER 52

As the black haze lifted, my skull ached and throbbed. My sight returned; I was lying face-down on the basement carpet.

Alyson knelt over me. "Are you okay? Oh, my god, I'm sorry. You took a fall down the steps. I hope I didn't hurt you."

I tried to rub my head, but my hands were tied behind me. "Alyson, what are you doing?"

"I can't let you arrest Pete."

"He killed your sister!"

"I know. It was my idea."

My lungs froze; it felt as if a truck parked itself on my chest. My body grew weak and seemed to turn into jelly. "Jesus, Alyson," I mumbled. "Not you."

"I'm sorry."

I wanted to scream. Why did I care about Kanya so much? What was the point? Her own family wanted her dead. Despite saving me twice tonight, it seemed as if God had played a cruel joke by letting me live to see this moment. My strength seeped from me as I lay on the floor. Evil had won.

"Why, Alyson?" I asked.

She sighed and looked away from me.

Pete bounded down the steps. "Is he awake?" He turned to Alyson. "I told you to cover his mouth."

"He just woke up," she replied.

"Where's the duct tape?" he asked.

She tossed him a roll of silver tape. He held up my .45 to make sure I noticed it. "Good call," he told her. "You were right. He didn't know."

"This needs to be the end of it," she said. "Is Lorinda still asleep?"

"Don't worry. I slipped some of her Restoril in her tea, so she should be out all night. Didn't want her interrupting us tonight. But you ought to check on her anyway."

"You didn't kill her, did you?" she asked.

"No. That would be hard to explain to the authorities. Sorry to disappoint you. I do still love her, you know."

"Whatever." Alyson caught my eyes and turned away.

Pete watched her ascend the steps. "Yeah, she's easy to fall for, isn't she? But you knew that." He sat next to me. "I appreciate you taking Kanya's case so personally. You're a good friend. For that, I suppose I can address your earlier question."

He looked to see if Alyson was out of earshot. "Yes," he said, "Kanya found the tape and threatened to go public unless I paid her. She wanted a million. That wasn't going to work for me."

"When did this happen?"

"Like you guessed, the day she broke in my office. I was careless and left my safe cracked open. I had to run out and figured since I was alone in the house, locking the office was enough. But no. I was out for only about an hour, and she happened to drop by during that time.

"So the little bitch snooped around and found the tape," he continued. "She called me and demanded the money. I panicked. I needed time to figure it out. I told her it would take me a few weeks to get that much. But she said no, she wanted it by her birthday a few days later. I knew I had to get rid of her. Even if I paid her, I knew she wouldn't honor the deal. But I needed someone else to do it. She'd never come within a dozen miles of me."

"So you got DeVaughn to do your dirty work."

"It was easier than I thought. I knew how much he hated her. In hindsight, I wasted the twenty grand I paid him. He would've done it on general principle. The hard part was luring her here. I didn't know where she lived, where she hung out, anything. I had to find a way to get her here so that I could have DeVaughn waiting for her.

"So I suggested to Lorinda that we visit her sister Gina in Charlotte that weekend. She wanted to try to stay here for Kanya's birthday, but I talked her out of it. It's not like Kanya ever wanted us around, anyway. I told her to let Kanya know we'd be gone that weekend and to leave her a cash present for her birthday. But I had her tell Kanya that it came from *her*."

I looked up at the ceiling and shook my head.

"No, Lorinda didn't have a clue what I was doing," Pete said. "But Kanya couldn't suspect I was trying to lure her to the house. I needed Lorinda to sell it."

He explained that when Lorinda asked why she had to go along with the ruse, he said he was doing her a favor. Kanya had always accused her of taking his side in disputes. If she made the monetary gift seem like it was her decision, a decision made without consulting her husband, Kanya might warm up to her. Lorinda had wanted to soften her tense relationship with her daughter, so she agreed to play along. "After that, all I had to do was give DeVaughn the key and the security code before we left," he said. "He was here, ready and waiting for her."

Pete affected his relaxed baritone and stood with perfect posture, speaking with the confidence of a polished attorney who had just swung a momentous trial in his favor. He showed no remorse and seemed pleased that his murderous scheme had succeeded.

"What if she didn't come here when you wanted?" I asked. "Your genius plan would have failed."

"Then we wouldn't be speaking under these circumstances. But I was confident she would come. She was young and greedy and loved to party. Even though she thought she was getting much more in a couple of days, she still wanted that money for the weekend. It was a small enough amount to make Lorinda's story believable. And DeVaughn would've waited here all weekend for her. Yes, I admit I was lucky. It was a rushed, desperate plan that actually worked."

I clung to a sliver of hope that our friendship would be enough to let me escape the basement alive, but Pete's candid explanations indicated he had no such intention. After the past few hours, I had little strength left. I could only prolong things by keeping him talking and hoping an opportunity presented itself.

"How did you get DeVaughn to do it?" I asked. "You couldn't tell him about the tape."

"I told him she stole some financial data from me, which was true. I knew he'd look for it himself, but he couldn't do anything with a bank statement. Besides, he didn't need much convincing. The money I paid him was just to show I was serious. But he made the same mistake Kanya did. He got greedy. With Richard and with me."

"You involved Richard, too?"

"No. He was supposed to be the scapegoat. DeVaughn's job was simple: eliminate Kanya, frame Richard. That last part should've been easy, considering how stupid that man was. And DeVaughn was smart about it, at first. He placed the weight in his car; he stabbed her to make it look like Richard tried to abort his baby—but he got greedy and contacted Richard to extort money from him. Which was stupid. If DeVaughn had never contacted him, Richard wouldn't have been able to point you toward him. Unfortunately, that created too much doubt and ambiguity in your case. Without that, you might have put Richard away or pushed him to accept a plea."

"You knew Kanya was pregnant before I told you?"

"All along. DeVaughn found out from one of her mouthy girlfriends, and he told me."

"You knew about Kanya and Rich before I told you? You knew she was pregnant? And you still killed her? Like she was nothing? You sorry—"

"I didn't want to kill her. She forced me to."

I had never seen this man before. I was certain he was going to kill me, and this time, I had no backup. My decision to come here with no backup would end up being my last stupid decision. I clung to every second because I didn't know how many I had left.

"So you were the one looking for all of her tapes, not Lorinda," I said.

"No, she really was trying to make a DVD. But I used it as a way to deflect suspicion."

"By putting it on her." I shook my head. "How'd you expect to find your video if Kanya was gone? What if DeVaughn or someone else found it?"

"That was the thing that caused me heartburn. I was a nervous wreck. I could stop her, but finding the tape before anyone else did was a different matter. She had no reason to bring it to the house, so I doubted DeVaughn would find it when he killed her. But I didn't know where she lived, and I couldn't tell DeVaughn what I was looking for. All I could do was pray it was lost or somehow thrown away. And my prayers weren't answered—at least, not immediately. DeVaughn somehow found it and tried to blackmail me, just as Kanya tried to." Pete glanced at the tape and smiled. "But you brought it back to me. Now I'm going to burn it."

He looked up at the stairs and smirked. "You were in love with Alyson, weren't you?" he asked. "She said you were so smitten that she thought it made sense to get friendly with you to see how close you got to us. Everything you did and said, she relayed to me. By the way, I hear DeVaughn's dead. Since you have the tape now, I assume I have you to thank for that. One less thing for me to worry about."

"How is Alyson involved with this? Why did she want Kanya dead?"

"She had her reasons." He walked to the bar and took a deep breath. "I feel so much better after that confessional—a load off my chest. But too bad it comes to this, buddy. You shouldn't have come alone."

"Who says I did?" I strained at the cord that bound my wrists.

A look of panic appeared on his face before he dismissed the notion with a wave of his hand. "I know you, Jeff. You're a loner. Always have been. The fact that you came here instead of turning it over to your replacement proves that."

He picked up the video sleeve and slid out the blank unlabeled VHS tape that I had substituted with the real video back in my bedroom. The self-assured look on his face vanished.

"Where is it?" he asked.

"Safe."

"Where's the tape?"

Hate swelled in me. His face was on every sick pedophile I had arrested. "Anything happens to me," I said, "the real one will be sent to some reporters, judges, the police, every damn body in Atlanta. You can kiss all of this goodbye."

"It's in your car. Or at your house." He slammed the butt of my gun into my mouth. I tasted metallic pain and spat blood onto the beige carpet.

"Where's the tape?" he asked. He struck me again.

I spat blood again and used my shoulder to smear it into the carpet. He kicked my stomach and the bite wounds in my forearm. Agony spread from my limbs to my groin.

"Where is it, Jeff?"

"Now my blood's in your carpet," I said, catching my breath. "You messed up."

"I'll get a new carpet."

"In the next hour? My partner knows I'm here. You think they won't find this evidence? Give yourself up, and I'll keep you from getting a death sentence. Even though you deserve it."

Alyson came back downstairs to the basement. "Lorinda's knocked out—" She spotted my bloodstains on the carpet. "Pete, what are you doing? Why is he bleeding in the carpet?"

"Don't worry about it," he said.

She scowled. "What is wrong with you? What if Lorinda sees that? That's not going to come up."

Pete rolled me onto my back, tore off a piece of duct tape, and slapped it over my mouth. "I said don't worry about it. We'll take him to his car and worry about the blood later. Did he park in the driveway?"

"Couple of houses down. I'll go get it." She turned to head upstairs before Pete grabbed her arm.

"No, I'll get it and bring it into the garage." He pulled my keys from my pocket. "We'll put him in the trunk and then get rid of it."

"Where?"

"Somewhere far away and isolated." He handed her my gun. "Watch him. Make sure that cord doesn't come loose. I have something special planned for him."

CHAPTER 53

I turned to my side and looked at Alyson. She pointed my pistol at me with her forearm resting on her knee. With my hands behind me, I strained and shifted my wrists to loosen the cord. She looked away, but I sensed she felt my stare.

She kept her gaze on the stairs. "I bet you hate me now. Don't you?" she asked.

I didn't like her ass at the moment, but she was my only chance of survival. My old friend had no reservations about killing me, but perhaps she had a few strands of a conscience remaining. As I moved my throbbing mouth and jaw, the tape loosened.

"For what it's worth, I liked you," she said, refusing to look at me. "I really did. But I can't help you now."

I spat up blood, making it seep through the tape's edges to appear I was choking. She sat on a barstool and swung her legs back and forth. I continued coughing. The tape began to flop off my mouth.

"Jesus," she said. "Don't you die on me down here." She put my gun to my temple and pulled the tape off my lips. "If you scream..."

I swallowed gulps of air to catch my breath. "You wanted to kill your little sister?"

"No, I didn't. I hated that it came to that."

"What the hell did she do to you? My God, are Lorinda and I the only ones who gave a damn about her?"

Alyson sneered as she reached for the roll of tape. "My mother barely knew Kanya was alive in the first place. I loved Kanya."

"So much that you killed her?"

She tore off a new piece of tape.

"Don't do this," I said. "You don't want to go down for killing a cop in Georgia. Let me go, and I'll testify it was Pete and that you assisted me."

"Sure, why not? Will I go to jail?"

"I'll look out for you."

"So you'll let me walk away? No, I don't think so."

I felt the cords slacken around my wrists. "You loved your sister so much that you killed her. Or were you just following Pete's orders?"

She took a deep breath.

"Oh, I'm sorry," I said. "You just had the idea, that's all. You know, as much as everyone talked about how bad Kanya was, she wasn't as screwed up as you."

She glared at me, and her bottom lip quivered. "You don't know what you're talking about. I didn't want it like this."

"I'm trying to understand! Why did you kill her? You were the one who needed therapy, not Kanya." I continued straining to loosen the cord.

"Now I see why he shut you up." She reached forward to place the tape over my mouth, but I wriggled away from her.

"Spoiled bitch," I said. "You use people and justify it when you do something foul."

She stopped. "You don't know anything," she snarled. "Let me tell you something—"

"I've heard it all. Psycho, crazy bitch."

"Jeff, I swear I'll—"

"Now I see why your mother hates you."

"Shut up!" Her beautiful face morphed into an ugly mask, her eyes bulging and her nostrils flaring.

"Did I touch a nerve, you psycho bi—"

She jammed the pistol to my temple so hard it felt like the barrel pierced my skull.

"Were you there?" she growled. "Were you? Did your mother treat you like shit? Did she leave you with an alcoholic father who beat you when he got drunk? Who burned your legs with cigarettes because he didn't want you wearing shorts? I was sixteen and had to sleep outside in a shed to keep his drunk buddies off of me while he's passed out. In the winter in Michigan. You know what that's like?"

My plan to rattle her had worked a little too well. It was easier to overpower someone who was angry and not thinking clearly, but the plan seemed to be a bad idea at the moment.

"Answer me," she demanded.

"No, I don't."

"Then you don't know shit!" She held my head to the floor and pressed the gun barrel to my temple. I prayed her trigger finger didn't slip. I saw her baring her teeth as she held the barrel to my head.

"I had to run away," she said. "Had to work in a strip club and have dirty men putting their nasty hands on me. Had to do things if I wanted to eat and keep a roof over my head. But Kanya? Lorinda loved her and gave her everything. I got nothing. She didn't want to bring me along when she moved here. She said she wanted me to finish high school—which was bullshit. My mother didn't like that I thought for myself and I saw who she really was. She was jealous. She hated that men noticed me before her. It was embarrassing, seeing her tell people she was my older sister. All she wanted was a sugar daddy, and when she found Pete, she thought things would be better for her if I weren't around. But the joke's on her. I'm milking her sugar daddy, right under her nose."

After a few seconds, she lifted the gun from my temple. "I loved Kanya," she said. "I don't care what you think. But I got sick of her wasting opportunities I never had."

"You and Pete have an affair?"

"An arrangement."

"He gives you money. And you take care of him in return."

"Doesn't cost me anything."

"You fooled me. I was crazy about you. I thought you felt something for me."

"I did. But we had to know how close you were in the case, and when you found out she was killed upstairs, you got too close. We knew you wouldn't give up, so we needed you off the case. I had DeVaughn follow us and take pictures. He wanted to kill you, but I just wanted you off the case. Pete and I underestimated your persistence."

I wanted to spit out the taste of her, the taste of that amazing body I had enjoyed and those kisses that once sent ripples through me. "You wanted her dead because of a sibling rivalry?"

"Kanya was miserable, and she wanted me to be miserable with her." She drew a breath. "Look, my life is finally comfortable. Every other week, Pete sends me money regularly. I don't have to worry about things. But Kanya found out about it and wanted to ruin it for me."

Finally, an explanation of the SunTrust bank statements Kanya had stolen. The recipient account in Illinois receiving regular deposits was Alyson's account, not a branch office as Pete claimed. There probably was no branch office. Just another lie. When Kanya broke into Pete's office and snooped around, she must have discovered Alyson and Pete's financial arrangement as well as the video.

"You don't even work in real estate, do you?" I asked. "Do you even have a job?"

"Humoring Pete is enough work. But it's better than my previous life. Too bad Kanya wouldn't let me enjoy it. Pete told me she was going to tell Lorinda about us unless he paid her a million. I had had enough. What Pete and I did was none of her business. She had everything, and she squandered it. Now she wants to ruin my life? No way."

"That's what Pete told you? Did Kanya ever tell you that?"

"No, but she called me and said my "free ride" with Pete would end soon."

"That's it? Nothing about telling Lorinda?"

"What she said was enough. She wanted to ruin my life out of spite. I'm never going back to how things were. So when Pete asked me what I thought we should do, I told him to do what was necessary. I saw it as putting her out of her misery, anyway. You saw her life. You knew how she was."

The lies and deception of this family astounded me. "You have no idea about his video, do you?"

"What video?"

"He played you, Alyson. And after he's done with me, he's going to kill you."

CHAPTER 54

I heard the garage door rumble as Pete pulled my car into it.

"What are you talking about?" Alyson asked me.

Pete came downstairs and grimaced at her. "What are you doing?" he asked her. "Don't talk to him!"

"Alyson," I said, "ask him why he wanted Kanya dead. It had nothing to do with you."

Pete snatched the plastic grocery bag off the minibar and tried to throw it over my head. I kicked at him and used my legs to keep him at bay.

"What's the matter, Pete?" I asked. "You don't want her to know the truth?"

Pete pulled the bag over my eyes. Lying on my back, I continued fighting with my legs. He dropped his weight on my chest and pinned me to the floor. I whipped my head from side to side, biting at him, trying to sever his fingers or anything that got in the way.

"Pete!" Alyson said. "Stop it. Not here."

"He lied to you, Alyson," I exclaimed, fighting and feeling Pete nudge the bag down over my face, inch by inch, covering my nose and mouth. "You're...next..."

"Don't just stand there," Pete told her. "Help me. Grab his legs."

I felt her clutch my left leg as Pete tightened the bag around my neck. The plastic suddenly sucked itself into my mouth. No more air. I felt a jolt of terror and bucked and thrashed, sending him lurching forward. Feeling he was off-balance, I shot my knee up to where I thought his balls were. He yelped but maintained his position. I kneed him again, trying to send his balls into his throat. He squealed and fell to the side.

I whipped my head around frantically until the bag slipped

off my chin, giving me a snippet of fresh air. "He played you, Alyson," I said, gasping. "He doesn't want you to know the truth."

Pete straddled me and wrapped his hands around my neck.

"Pete, stop," said Alyson. "Not here."

The crushing pressure around my throat threw me into agony. I couldn't breathe or see. My head and throat were going to burst.

"Stop, dammit!" she shouted. "Get off him. Take that bag off. Now."

Things started to darken…and then I felt Pete release his grip. He removed the bag, and I sucked in gulps of air.

"What the hell are you doing?" he asked her. "Have you forgotten whose side you're on?"

"Depends on your answer," she replied, pointing my pistol in our direction. "What is he talking about?"

"He's lying, Alyson," he said. "He's trying to distract us, to get us against each other. Come on, think!"

"Of course he is," she said. "But I didn't expect you'd suddenly forget our plan and be in a rush to do him right now. Down here, where you've already left evidence—his blood—all over the floor. Makes me wonder if there's something to what he's saying."

The attorney poured on his syrupy voice. "Listen to me, honey. He is lying. Okay? Please, put the gun down."

"Alyson," I said, "he was going to kill Kanya anyway. He just wanted you to think it was your idea so you'd go along with it. Tell her about the video, Pete. The real reason you wanted Kanya dead."

He turned to his stepdaughter with pleading eyes. "Honey, he's making up lies. Let's—"

"Why do you think he insisted on getting my car?" I asked her. "He thought I had his video in there. But he didn't find it. I hid it under the spare tire."

Instinctively, Pete turned toward the stairs.

Alyson noted the reflexive action. "Oh," Alyson said. "What was that?" She stepped toward him. "Is this video real? Were you about to go to his car?"

"He wants that video," I instigated. "You should see what's on it, Alyson. Especially since you think Kanya had it so easy."

"Shut up, Jeff," Pete ordered, his voice beginning to crack. He got up and reached for the duct tape.

Alyson shook her head and aimed the gun at him, motioning him away from the tape. "No, leave it there," she ordered. "What's on this mysterious video."

"He's too modest," I replied. "But I'll tell you. They're homemade porn movies of him and your sister."

Alyson stared at her stepfather with cold, flat eyes. "You were sleeping with both of us at the same time? You sorry asshole."

"Don't be jealous," I said. "It wasn't consensual, like with you two. This was sexual assault and rape of a child. She was only nine or ten when it started—and he did it for years. He told her she'd never see you or Lorinda again if she told anyone."

Alyson's mouth dropped as she stared at Pete.

"Oh, that's nothing," I said. "You should see what he did to her. Forcing her to blow him. Peeing on her. Telling her she had to swallow if she wanted to grow breasts and become pretty like her big sister. He told her all girls do this to become women. And when that didn't work, he threatened her."

The two lovebirds stood a few feet apart. Pete shook his head, pleading with her not to listen. She kept her eyes on him, scowling at what she was hearing.

I made sure she heard more of it.

"Now you know why she hated being on video," I said. "It reminded her of what this bastard used to do to her. And you thought you had it bad. Kanya probably wished she had a tool shed to escape to. It never occurred to you that she had to deal with her own hell. *All* of us missed things we should have noticed. We just didn't want to believe her problems were closer to home."

Alyson stood glued to the spot, eyeballing Pete. She clutched my .45 at her side and fiddled with it.

"Kanya had no one to turn to," I said, sensing she was about to erupt. "Everybody wondered what happened to that sweet girl. It wasn't drugs. It wasn't some gym teacher. It wasn't the streets. It was your pedophile boyfriend here, that's what happened. He killed that little girl years ago. You know, the little girl with the puppies in that picture you carry around?"

"He's…he's not my boyfriend," she muttered.

"Own up to it. You chose him over Kanya. Her life wasn't as great as you thought it was. But she found her chance to get even when she found his video. She was going to use it to get payback on him. That's why he killed her. And you let him."

Alyson's eyes became watery. "She called me. She was…she was going to stop it…" Her voice trailed off.

"She was giving you a heads up. She was after him, not you. That's why he killed her. This asshole just told you what he knew would work on you. And you helped him."

Alyson shook her head as her chin quivered. I could see the storm of emotions roiling inside her.

"Did you know she was also pregnant?" I asked her. "You were about to be auntie Alyson. Pete knew it but didn't give a damn. He had both of them killed. Kanya wanted to give the baby a safe environment, not like the one you two had. But you let him play you—"

"Shut up!" she screamed while glowering at Pete. Her eyes were like smoldering embers. "You son of a bitch," she hissed. "Is that true? Did you really do that?"

"Stop, Alyson," he said, backing up with his hands in the air. "We're losing sight of the picture here. He's lying. And you're falling for it."

"I am? Maybe we should get this video he's talking about.

We'll see who's lying."

"It turns out you were more alike than you thought," I told her. "Both of you had the same guy here. But she had no choice."

Alyson spun around to me. "You shut up or I'll—"

Pete lunged forward to slap my gun out of her hand. His timing was awful. At the last second, she stepped back, leaving him swiping at air. "What are you doing?" she asked.

"N-n-no," he stammered. He had the look of a boy caught with his hand in his mother's purse. "I'm just trying to get that away from you. You're too upset to handle it now."

"Oh, you know what's best for me, now? Jeff's telling the truth, isn't he? He said you planned to get rid of me. Is that true, too?"

Pete moved back. "That's a lie! Why would I hurt you?"

"Oh, I don't know. Maybe because I know everything and you don't want me knowing the truth. How did you plan to kill me?"

Pete retreated as Alyson stepped toward him. He implored her to stop and denied everything. Alyson followed him and aimed my gun at his forehead. She cursed him and kept asking him how he planned to eliminate her. They drifted down the hallway, and as they passed the edge of the wall, they were out of eyesight.

I rolled to my knees and stumbled to the minibar. Behind it was a decorative mirror on the wall. I turned around to see the yellow cord securing my wrists. Pete had bound me sloppily; apparently, he had intended to kill me quickly. Rather than tying the rope securely, he merely looped it around my wrists and tucked the end underneath itself.

I wriggled my hands until I got the loose end of the cord up through the folds and it unraveled to the floor.

"He's loose!" exclaimed Pete.

Alyson turned around to see me. Pete smashed his fist into her jaw, dropping her and my gun to the floor. It landed at his feet, and as he grabbed it, I dashed to the stairwell. He shot at me. The deafening blast reverberated in the basement.

The stairwell consisted of two flights of steps, parallel to each other. As I ran up the stairs, his thumping steps followed close behind. I entered the foyer, slammed the basement door shut, and turned off the lights in the hallway. I sprinted to the front door.

Oh, shit.

After letting me inside earlier, Alyson had locked the front door. It was a double-cylinder deadbolt, requiring a key to unlock it from both inside and out.

The basement door swung open. "Jeff?" Pete said. "Where are you, buddy?"

I hid in the den. He walked to the front door and stopped. I crept through the den and into the dining room. I thought the sound of my hammering heartbeat would give away my position.

"Come on, Jeff," he said. "You can't get out. I've got your phone and your gun. I know there's no help coming. So let's talk. I won't shoot you. You might even make some money from this." He moved toward the kitchen. "Your career is at a crossroads. Don't you deserve more than what they pay you for risking your life? I always told you that you never maximized your earning potential. Here's your chance."

After Pete had fired my gun, I feared Lorinda would rush downstairs to investigate and find herself in the middle of a situation where someone would end up dead. But there was no movement upstairs. Pete had given her a potent dosage, one that either killed his wife accidentally or allowed her to sleep through gunfire and shouting.

My back was to the wall of the dining room. On the other side of the dining room wall were the hallway and foyer. When entering the home, one faced the foyer and hallway to the right, and the stairs leading to the second floor on the left. The path through the den, dining room, kitchen, and hallway formed a square, which meant I could backtrack and circle right behind Pete.

He could also do the same to me.

"Jeff, you can't hide," he said. He had entered the kitchen, but instead of turning right, where we would have crossed paths, he turned left to search in the family room. "Just give me the tape, and we can put this behind us."

Alyson groaned from down in the basement. "Pete? Pete?" she shouted. He didn't answer.

"Pete?" she asked again. She made her way up the stairs. "Jeff?" While Pete was in the family room, I darted through the den to the foyer. I decided to head upstairs; perhaps I could escape through a window.

Before I reached the halfway point up the stairs, the basement door squeaked opened. "Pete?" Alyson said. "Where are you?" Fear dripped from her voice.

"Alyson, stay there," Pete ordered, from somewhere in the kitchen. "Jeff's out here somewhere. We need to work together."

She remained inside the doorway leading to the basement, refusing to step into the hallway. I positioned myself directly above her as I knelt on the steps. I leaned close to the stair railing and whispered her name.

She gasped.

"Shhh," I whispered. "We need to stop him. He has my gun."

She didn't answer.

"Trust me, Alyson. He can't afford to leave us alive." I moved down the steps slowly, careful not to appear in Pete's line of sight in case he was now in the hallway. With the faint light from a lamppost filtering through the frosted glass panels of the front door, my head would have made a perfect silhouetted target.

She stood still. "Why should I trust you?" she whispered.

"It's him or me. And you know what he's capable of."

A few seconds later, she asked, "How do we do it?"

Pete turned on the lights, blinding me. When my eyes

adjusted, I saw him standing in the hallway, aiming my gun at me. "You two won't do anything," he said. "Alyson, come out."

She obeyed. There was an ugly red bruise under her eye from where he had struck her.

"Now," he said, "both of you, to the garage."

Alyson turned to him. "Pete, look. I—"

"No," he said. "I stood right there and heard you. You chose his side. Now I consider both of you loose ends. Move. And Jeff, if you make a sudden move, I'll shoot *you* in the head."

We passed through the kitchen toward the garage. Alyson walked in front while Pete trailed me. She stopped and turned to us.

"Pete, don't do this," she pleaded with him. "I was just stalling him so you could—"

"Keep walking," he said. "Go to his car. You're driving. I have something special planned for you, too—"

Distracted, he stepped into me. In one movement, I shifted to my right, spun around, and grabbed his gun-carrying hand with my right hand. I grasped his arm and the barrel of the gun, putting him in a wrist lock. With an upward yank, I felt something snap inside his wrist.

He howled but didn't let go of my gun. He grabbed my left forearm and jabbed his fingers deep in my bite wounds. My eyes ran as I clutched the gun barrel. Neither of us wanted to release our grip—the first one to let go was dead.

My left arm grew limp, and I lost my footing; my body finally gave out from everything I had put it through in the past few hours. I fell to one knee, and my grip on him faded. He snatched his arm away and placed my gun in his other hand.

"You broke my wrist," Pete said. "I'm going to—"

He gave out a primal shriek as his eyes jolted upward.

Alyson had plunged an eight-inch kitchen knife between his shoulder blades. He dropped my gun and fell to his knees. She stabbed him again. Gagging, he reached behind him to pull the knife out. She shut her eyes and clutched the knife handle like a joystick, gluing herself to him as he thrashed about. Blood gushed down his back and onto the floor, creating a slippery red pool. My old friend stumbled around the kitchen like a drunken man, grasping for anything, as Alyson held on to him and the knife handle.

He opened his mouth but couldn't say anything. His eyes had that unmistakable panic I had seen in men taking their last breaths. That same look DeVaughn said Kanya had when he was strangling her. I hoped Pete experienced the same terror that his stepdaughter felt.

"That was for Kanya," Alyson murmured, tears flooding her face.

I grabbed my gun and aimed it at Pete, but there was no need. The tip of the blade had pierced the front of his throat. He collapsed on his stomach and stopped moving. A pool of crimson spread from him like a bright sunflower as he took his last breath.

Alyson sat in the corner by the dishwasher, shuddering and whispering to herself. As I looked down at Pete, I felt a mix of sorrow, anger, and disgust.

Sorry that my friend had destroyed the life of a wonderful young woman, practically killing her twice.

Angry that he had tried to kill me.

And disgusted that he had fooled me for all of these years.

I took a long, deep breath. It was a blessing that with all I endured over the last few hours, I was still alive.

Pete's heinous crimes, his betrayal of the religious beliefs he espoused, his calculating coldness—they were too much for me to deal with at the moment. It felt as if I floated outside my body and watched myself, for the third time tonight, kneeling over another dead man.

CHAPTER 55

Alyson stared at the knife handle sticking out from Pete's back. The floor, cabinets, stove, and dishwasher were smeared with streaks and droplets of blood.

"Jeff, what happens now?" she mumbled.

I called Wills, gave a brief explanation of what had just happened, and asked him to come to the house immediately. After finishing the call, I answered her question. "You have to answer for what you did to Kanya."

"I didn't kill her!"

"But you conspired to. It was your idea, remember? That's a felony, either way you look at it."

She shook her head. "I can't go to jail."

"We can't always get what we want."

"But I saved your life! He was going to kill you!"

"We saved each other. He would have killed both of us. So I owe you nothing."

"No, we can go away, Jeff! I have access to some of his accounts. We'll have enough to go wherever we want. We can pin everything on him. Who'll know?"

"I will."

"Please," she said, clasping her hands together. "Don't you want something different out of life? We can change that. Just you and me."

"We just disappear and travel the world, huh?" I looked around the blood-stained kitchen. "Is your mother really sleeping? Or did you guys kill her, too?"

"No!" she exclaimed. "She's just sleeping. We didn't hurt her. Only Pete is dead, and he got what he deserved."

"Oh, we'll see if your mother's alive all right, because I don't know how she could sleep through this. Besides, what will she say when she wakes up and learns her husband is dead and we disappeared with his money? You have a plan that answers that?"

She shook her head and frowned, evidently not wanting to ponder that question. "Jeff, I know you love me! We can go anywhere! Don't you want to be happy? Don't you deserve to be happy?"

It was telling that she didn't say that she loved me. "You make it sound so great."

"You love me, and I love you. That's why I helped you. We can go anywhere we want, baby. I can get his money now."

"Let's take a romantic trip to the Fulton County Jail. Turn around and put your hands behind you."

"Please, no," she whimpered.

As I approached her, she snatched a frying pan from the sink and swung it at me. Luckily, it wasn't as sharp as the butcher knife Pete had the misfortune of meeting. She threw the pan at me, but I ducked. She ran to the garage, where I grabbed her and forced her to the floor. She writhed on the ground, crying and shrieking for me to let her go.

"Alyson, it's over."

The words seemed to have a magical effect. She ceased struggling and went limp, her body convulsing in silent sobs.

When Wills arrived, I had him read her her rights.

CHAPTER 56

The next two days were hectic.

Alyson's tearful confession, the ballistic evidence linking DeVaughn's revolver to the murder of Marcus Washington, and Pete's videotape fueled a whirlwind of police reports and media coverage. All of the sordid details of Kanya's life were laid bare. The conclusion that her stepfather, sister, and ex-boyfriend colluded to kill her had generated immense interest. Every news pundit had something to say about the diabolical plan and commented on dark family secrets and society's tendency to ignore our children's cries for help.

And poor Lorinda. After Wills and the other first responders had arrived at the house, we awakened her to a terrible scene; her dead husband lying on the kitchen floor, killed by her daughter, who we led away in cuffs. And discovering the reason behind her husband's death, and the events leading up to it, sent her into a tailspin of depression.

At least I could finally clear the case, even if it caused some political heartburn. Since Mayor Dorsey had voiced support for the Rennells during the investigation, reporters sought her statement. Probably horrified that the man she vouched for was a murdering pedophile, she released a statement condemning Pete's acts and praising the APD's investigation. She also called for stronger state laws against sexual predators. Mrs. Dorsey spoke softly and never looked up from her lectern while she delivered her thoughts.

Richard Oliver also seized an opportunity to share his views with the media. In an interview from his doorstep, he protested how the APD had treated him and that he intended to file a mega-lawsuit against the city for destroying his career, reputation, and marriage. After reporters had asked him if his affair with Kanya was more responsible for his failed marriage, he kicked the reporters off of his property.

I saw neither the mayor's or Rich's interview; Wills informed me of them. From the moment of Alyson's arrest, I refused to watch the news or read the paper. I was too preoccupied with my OPS investigation and wondered how I was to be made an example of, despite the case clearance. I had to explain my involvement with three homicides: Rat Mouth, DeVaughn, and Pete.

I told Wills I was going to take responsibility for everything that happened at DeVaughn's and prepped him on what I intended to say to OPS. All he needed to do was stick to the story when—or if—he was called to answer questions. I also called Smith (who caught the homicides of both Rat and DeVaughn) and told him what happened. He was all right with it; those deaths were deemed to be shootings in self-defense and not unlawful homicides at the moment, so he wasn't stuck with open murders.

It remained to be seen if OPS would be as accepting of my story.

***

My OPS review, which had been moved to Tuesday, August 26, because of the heavy activity related to the case, was held in a windowless room. I employed the same psychological tactic of using dreary, dimly lit rooms to interrogate people. It made OPS's use of the practice no less effective on me. I was isolated, and the world didn't know or care what happened to me.

Three investigators sat before me behind a long desk, a la the Last Supper, with Lourne a couple of seats away from them at the end of the table. He looked at me with an unspoken message—*Don't say anything stupid.* I sat across from them, feeling like a target at a gun range. While it was a small reprieve that Major Pitts wasn't present, his three investigators, Officers Mates, Cowney, and Brandon, gave me dour looks that signaled they weren't going to be pushovers like other investigators in past OPS hearings.

It was hard to tell which one of them would play bad cop. I knew it was coming because the routine worked well, even against other cops. Mates, a fat man usually seen feeding quarters to the snack machine on the fifth floor, began the discussion. He explained the process, how and why it was going to be different from a typical investigation, and that they sought only to clarify my conduct and details of the Kanya Glover homicide case.

I knew the game. I did the same thing in my interrogations. Reassure them first, let them talk and dig holes for themselves, and ratchet up the pressure. Pull at any loose threads to unravel the lies.

"Let's start here," Mates said. "Since this was the cause of all of this." He held up the photo of Alyson and me locking lips in the park. "As you know, Detective, copies of these were sent to several parties. The whole city has seen them by now. They show you and the victim's sister on intimate terms and they clearly imply that you were emotionally compromised during this investigation. With your arrestee Richard Oliver threatening legal action against the city, these will be the key piece of his argument. This can cause citizens to lose faith in this department and perceive that we can neither effectively or fairly police our communities. So take this opportunity to explain what happened here."

I cleared my throat. "First, I assure you it wasn't misconduct—"

"Perhaps a blatant disregard for department policy?" interrupted Cowney.

Well, there was the bad cop. That mystery was solved. Cowney wasted no time in ripping my first response.

"I understand how it may look," I replied. "But it's not reality.

I suspected the family was complicit in the murder. Naturally, they weren't forthcoming with details or helpful answers. If you reviewed my case notes, you'd see that they wouldn't tell me much about their daughter, the victim. Not where she lived, her friends, anything. They were a well-known, influential couple who wanted to avoid any hint of scandal. Particularly Mr. Rennell. I had reason to think he knew more than he indicated, so it was necessary to get closer to the family to prove my suspicions. Alyson seemed the best bet. She was estranged from the family, so I believe she wouldn't be as concerned about protecting their reputation above all else. I started a friendship with her. I needed to display romantic intentions to get her to trust me."

Lourne put his head down. I couldn't tell if he was mortified at my response or trying not to burst into laughter.

The three investigators looked at me. "Are you taking this seriously, Detective?" Cowney asked.

"I don't consider this a laughing matter," I replied.

"You expect us to believe that?"

"It's the truth. As you know, the Rennells have strong connections, including our Mayor. Mr. Rennell didn't want to share details about their daughter's lifestyle because of their status. They had a lot to lose, in terms of their public profile."

I hated to discredit the family with a lie like that, if only for Lorinda's sake. Pete and Alyson lied and threw up roadblocks, but at least Lorinda had shared what she knew.

Cowney held up the photograph. "You're telling us that all of this was on purpose?"

"Well, I didn't plan for someone to take a photo and distribute it, but I did plan the semblance of a friendship with Alyson, developing her as a semi-informant. It was necessary to gain her trust, and getting close to her helped clear the case."

Cowney stared at me. He was a tall man with thick, brown eyebrows and tanned, reddish skin befitting that of a weathered cowboy on the plains. "Fine," he said. "So this was an

unapproved 'undercover' operation, which you didn't commu-
nicate to anyone."

"No, it was not an official operation, but I wouldn't call it
undercover, either. I didn't use an alternate identity. And that
photo showed a time where we both feigned romantic interest.
Keep in mind that she was responsible for those pictures because
she was trying to use me as well. She arranged for someone to
take them because they felt I was getting too close. They sent
them to Richard, who they knew would use them to get me off
the case. While I was getting close to her, she was trying to use
me to glean information on the case."

"So," Cowney said, "it's possible that *she* played *you.*"

"Not at all. Not if my suspicions about the family were correct and we have someone in custody who confirmed and confessed to the entire thing."

"So did you plan this 'operation' before or after you arrested
Richard Oliver? For the murder you now say you believed the
victim's family had committed all along?"

"After. In Richard's case, I went where the evidence took me
at first."

"As I understand it, Jefferson," Cowney said, "You've had
a divorce recently. I know that's a trying experience, one our
profession is well-acquainted with, unfortunately. One may seek
companionship, sometimes inappropriately, to cope. So when
I see these pictures, I think you went where your feelings took
you."

He had scowled and let out exasperated sighs whenever I
spoke, and now, he was shoving my divorce in my face.

"I understand your concern," I told him, "but that implica-
tion is not correct. If my objectivity were compromised, as you
indicate, I would've never been able to suspect or comprehend
that the family was guilty of murder."

Cowney frowned. "What does that mean? That doesn't mean

anything."

Brandon, a swarthy middle-aged man with a perfect head of hair and a New York accent, finally showed a pulse. "Detective, how did you come to arrest Mr. Oliver and later shift your focus to the Rennells?"

"All of this has been documented in my daily case logs and updates. Mr. Oliver had an affair with the victim—and his employee—and got her pregnant. He was sued for sexual harassment a few years ago, so if his affair became public, it would be devastating for him. He didn't want the child, and they had an argument a few nights before she died. He lied multiple times about his relationship with her. I later discovered he paid fifteen thousand dollars to the victim's ex-boyfriend, DeVaughn Copeland, the man who committed the murder. He also had an item from the crime scene in his trunk. I had reasonable cause to arrest him."

"So with all of that, you suspected the Rennell family?" Mates asked.

"Not initially. But I later came to believe that Mr. Oliver was merely a victim of extortion by Mr. Copeland, not a conspirator. DeVaughn demanded money from him on multiple occasions, not for killing her, but for keeping silent about the affair. I came to suspect the Rennells after I had determined the victim had been murdered in their home. If you saw the video of Mr. Rennell sexually assaulting the victim as a child, you would see his motive. She planned to make the video public to ruin his reputation. Mr. Rennell was the one who paid DeVaughn to kill her."

"Was this money recovered?"

"No."

"When did you shift to investigating Mr. Rennell?" Mates asked.

"Two weeks ago." Of course, it was a lie. I didn't suspect my old buddy until I saw his infamous movie three days ago.

Cowney frowned. "Why didn't you ever arrest the victim's ex-boyfriend?"

"Even though he had a strong motive as well, there was no evidence tying him to the murder at the time."

"Well, Detective," Mates said, "we have read your case updates. And I don't recall seeing any mention of your suspicions of the Rennell family in any of them. Why?"

"And if you planned this," Cowney said, "why didn't you inform anyone when you were placed on admin leave? You accepted it with no questions asked."

"I told him not to include it in his updates," Lourne said. "We needed to keep his suspension appearing legitimate."

All of us turned to him.

"Why?" asked Cowney.

"Look, we know the reason this case has gotten so much attention was because of Peter Rennell," the sergeant said. "The mayor and other city leaders have him on speed dial. We were pressed for multiple updates, and in the past, with cases like these, critical information sometimes got leaked to people not involved with the investigation. If we included information indicating he and his family might have been involved in killing their own daughter, that probably would've leaked too. Either to the family or the media."

"Sergeant," Mates said, "you don't think your superiors are to be trusted? You made your own decision to withhold information? Is that what you're saying?"

"I'm not saying that," Lourne said. "What I'm talking about is human nature. People talk. They slip up and say things they shouldn't, even when they don't intend to. I've been here longer than you. I was here for the Child Murders in the seventies. Things leak. It may be something big; it may be small. It may not hurt the case at all. But something will leak unless you control the information. And I decided we shouldn't risk it with this one, especially with the family being so close to it."

"That wasn't your call, Sergeant," Mates said.

Lourne shrugged slightly, displaying the comfort of a man close to retirement. "I was under the impression the department entrusts us to make good decisions. If not, then why are we here? Besides, we cleared the case."

I resisted pumping my fist in the air. This was Good Lourne, coming through to back me up in a big way.

"Well, that brings up other points that need clarification, sergeant," Mates replied. "Since you have the answers, can you explain why your detective confronted and fatally shot two men, Mr. Copeland and Mr. Goines, in the same night? When he was on administrative leave?"

"I'll answer for myself," I said. "First, I didn't confront anyone. I fired in self-defense. I had received a tip from my CI that someone he knew may have been implicated in a separate murder, that of Ms. Cheryl Tory. She was a close friend of the victim. As coincidence had it, my CI was in Ms. Tory's apartment complex, and he called me and said he noticed someone standing outside her apartment door, which was still sealed. I was nearby and drove there to meet him, to see if it was something worthy of passing on to Gresham."

"Is this CI registered?" Cowney asked, writing notes.

"Yes."

"And why didn't you inform Officer Gresham of this, since he was the acting lead investigator?"

"I wasn't sure it was one hundred percent reliable. I didn't want to add to the number of unpromising tips."

"You question the reliability of your own informant?"

"The quality of his information had suffered a bit lately, but no CI has tips that are one-hundred percent accurate."

"But you believed his word this time?"

"I took a chance. And when I arrived, I immediately observed a subject pacing in front of the apartment. He was attempting to force his way inside. I went to observe and found myself under fire. I was forced to shoot in self-defense. The ballistic evidence will corroborate that."

"You went to observe," repeated Cowney. "And under your 'observation,' you discharged your weapon and killed one man at one apartment complex and somehow ended up at the house of Mr. Copeland, where you and Officer Wills discharged your weapons and shot him fatally. Is this what normally happens when you go to observe people?"

This time, I told the truth and explained that Rat had indicated that DeVaughn was behind the botched hit. Knowing that he wouldn't stick around after trying to kill a cop, I had to detain him before he could flee the city.

"If time was of the essence, why did you call Officer Wills for assistance instead of Officer Gresham? In fact, why not call for any patrol officer for backup?"

"Wills was already close to the location and was familiar with it since we had interviewed Mr. Copeland there earlier. I didn't have time to walk Gresham through it and wait for him. Mr. Copeland opened fire on us first. We were forced to return fire in self-defense only."

"What was your background?" Brandon asked.

"The wall of the house. No bystanders or residents were in danger."

Brandon scrunched his brows together. "Not even the little boy who was inside the house?"

"No." I lifted my arm to show my stitches and bruises. "This happened when their dog attacked me. I couldn't fire in self-defense because the boy was standing nearby at the time. I knew my background and when it was safe to discharge. We positioned ourselves to ensure safety for others. The boy was unharmed, wasn't he?"

Cowney released a stream of questions regarding my judgment. He shook his head at my answers, saying they were well-rehearsed, and accused me of treating the inquiry as a joke.

"This is ridiculous," Lourne snapped. "I know we're concerned about our image and rightfully so, but I've seen you guys go easier on officers for more egregious bullshit. Guy got caught selling MJ from his cruiser trunk a couple of years back, and he only got rehab treatment and four weeks suspension. But you're screwing Strick here for something that didn't violate anyone's civil rights or even get the Civil Review Board upset. We cleared the case. The mayor gave us props publicly for the work."

Cowney, the bad cop, was not impressed. "Sergeant, I'm sure you can appreciate that she is also concerned about the professionalism of the police department," he said. "I also do not care what happened in past inquiries. This is a new day. And we don't have any CRB uproar *yet*. We have two African-American men shot by the police, and some civil rights group may demand an investigation—"

"DeVaughn Copeland was a sorry bastard," I interrupted. "He killed three young people. He sold drugs and had enemies everywhere. He and his associate both tried to kill me. No one going to hold a rally for them."

"We'll come back to that," Mates said. "I'd like to know why you confronted Mr. Rennell on your own instead of alerting Gresham of your suspicions. Or are you going to say you went to his home to observe him as well?"

Cowney snorted. "It looks like it, since he's dead, too."

"No," I said. "After I recovered DeVaughn's gym bag and the tape, I was curious and decided to watch it. When I saw what was on it, I was then certain Pete Rennell was behind the murder. I considered calling Gresham with the evidence and telling him to bring in Mr. Rennell for questioning, but I believed my suspect was a possible suicide risk."

"A suicide risk?" Mates asked, sneering. "How did you come to that conclusion? And why did that make you try to apprehend him yourself when you weren't supposed to?"

"The man was an influencer in our city. He couldn't afford

to let his secret out. He couldn't live with that. There was also a possible hostage situation. His wife and stepdaughter were inside with him, and I believed if an officer came to question him, especially about the tape, he would know that the game was up. He might have acted rashly, using either woman as leverage to try to flee."

Cowney crossed his arms and forced a laugh. "Wait. So you're telling us," he began, "that if you called Gresham or another officer, as you should have done, and if they had gone to apprehend Mr. Rennell, he would have killed himself? Or he would have panicked and killed his accomplice in an unfortunate hostage situation? Is that what you're telling us?"

"I know it sounds crazy—"

"You're right," interrupted Cowney.

"Look, I just told you about a tape where he sexually abused his young stepdaughter and later killed her over it. It wasn't hard to believe he would kill his other stepdaughter if he thought it was his only chance to escape. I didn't know Alyson was an accomplice at that time."

"So what happened, Detective Strickland?" Mates asked. "Did you go to his home to save this damsel in distress?"

"Yes, I went there to alert Alyson first. I wanted her and Lorinda out of there before he knew we were closing in on him."

"Why didn't you just call her?"

"I didn't want to tell her the truth of something like that over the phone. Afterward, I discovered that she was his accomplice, but she didn't know about the video nor did she realize she had been manipulated. They got into an argument, and she killed him in self-defense. Afterward, she surrendered and confessed."

Cowney facepalmed and shook his head. "This is a load of crap. Here's what I think. I believe you confronted Mr. Rennell on your own because you wanted to redeem yourself. You were suspended for legitimate reasons, and you continued to work the case in violation of orders. I don't care what you guys say.

I don't believe you planned this at all. You're piecing together justifications after the fact."

"Not correct," I replied.

"So this is your official stance? These are your statements you want on record?"

"It's the truth, so it should be on the record. You keep asking me the same questions and I keep giving you the same answers."

"Who's complaining?" Lourne blurted. "Other than Richard Oliver?"

"We're taking a proactive stance in the event of his lawsuit," Brandon said. "Among other investigations that might come up."

Lourne smirked. "That man is just wolfing to take the heat off his ass. He should've cooperated from the beginning and told the truth. If he had, none of this would have happened. He cheated on his wife with his nineteen-year-old employee, got her pregnant, and tried covering it up. From your line of questions, you're not really concerned about him. You're only worried about department regulations, which in this case, didn't hurt anybody."

"We're concerned about what our citizens think as well," Mates said, "not just Richard Oliver. We're concerned about the multiple procedural violations Officer Strickland made during the investigation—both before and after he was officially suspended. We're concerned about how you both withheld information when you were required to pass it on."

Lourne turned his seat to face the panel. "Look at it this way. Our heavily minority city saw that instead of putting the screws to young black men, we focused our investigation on two wealthy white guys. We got an arrest and a clearance instead of letting their money protect them. So we just showed that we're an equal-opportunity police force, which will help gain trust in the communities in which we police. Besides, it won't look right, having the mayor praise us before you punish the investigating officer. You might make her look foolish if you throw the book at Strick now. A reporter gets wind of it, and there'll be a bunch of questions."

"What do you mean by that?" asked Brandon.

"The mayor galvanized our efforts to support the Rennell family and practically implored the public to come forward with information. Problem is, her friend turned out to be a child-loving murderer. You know she's gotta be embarrassed that she vouched for him. Now, after she said, 'Good job police,' you want to say, 'No, mayor, he screwed up' and make an example of him. You'll embarrass her twice.

"And," he continued, "think about past complaints where we went easy on our officers after we investigated them. Brutality, civil rights violations—and people barely got two weeks' suspension. That's if you even acknowledged they violated rights in the first place. So go ahead and stick it to this man after he cleared the case. You'll have some reporter questioning why you came down hard on him when you overlooked things far worse. Like the guy selling weed out of his patrol vehicle."

"And as I said, this is a new day with our department," Cowney said.

"The public won't make that distinction or even care," the sergeant replied. "It's the Atlanta Police Department, regardless. You want to open us up to more scrutiny?"

The panel looked at Lourne and back at each other for several seconds.

Uneasy silence passed between us. The OPS men looked at me, but I knew that trick. I would not babble like some idiot perp compelled to talk because of unbroken silence. I would keep my mouth shut for days, if need be.

Mates sighed. "We're finished for today."

CHAPTER 57

People think that those who live in warm climates are used to the heat, but residing in Atlanta conditioned me to hate hot summers. The stifling heat and oppressive humidity contributed to short tempers and itchy trigger fingers—which, I guess, was a good thing since it kept me employed. This late August evening, however, was a treat of Indian Summer. Wills, Jessica, and I enjoyed a cool breeze in the Varsity's parking lot in Midtown as we chowed on chili dogs and orange sodas.

The Varsity was an Atlanta icon despite serving average food that left tourists wondering about the reason for its hype. On summer nights, the place was packed but not because of the food. It was the proximity to downtown, as well as the Georgia Tech coeds, that drew folks to hang out and people-watch. Young adults congregated in its parking lot, and the infamous Chevron, the scene of Kanya's drunken episode, was only a block away.

We isolated ourselves in a far corner, away from the youth hovering around the restaurant. There, I gave my co-workers a recap of my OPS review.

"Wait," Wills exclaimed, his mouth full, "You said you had a romance with Alyson as part of your cover?"

"You've got to be kidding, Strick," Jessica said, laughing and almost spitting out her food. "They believed that? Damn, baby. You lie so good."

"They didn't believe me. But proving I was lying is a different story, especially since the people who can dispute me aren't around anymore. OPS is on a mission to set an example with me, but I won't make it easy. They can call me a liar but not an idiot. Besides, they can't argue with the result—a clearance. And Gresham won't complain since it goes under him."

"Well, *I* know you were lying," Jessica said. "You were hot for that girl. She was gorgeous. She almost gave *me* dirty thoughts, and I don't even roll like that."

Wills rolled his eyes and gave me a look that said *I told you to leave that girl alone.* "So there's no problem?" he asked me. "Even though you went rogue when you were supposed to be on the bench?"

"OPS had a problem with everything, but the mayor's praise of the department worked in my favor. And I have to admit… Lourne came through for me. He made them look stupid. He nearly went Samuel L. on them."

Jessica whistled. "The man has a soul after all. So what happens now?"

"They recommended a letter of reprimand and four weeks' suspension—without pay."

"Four weeks without pay?" Wills said. "They've had guys do worse and they didn't get suspended at all. Guess they didn't like seeing you in the papers."

"Look at you," Jessica added. "You've got stitches in your lip, bruises all over you, you wince every time you move…yeah, you embarrassed yourself, but they couldn't cut you some slack?"

"I'm the sacrificial lamb for the new OPS," I replied. "Can't blame anyone but myself. I was stupid. But I'm appealing. The union will kill me if I don't, though. What helps is that no one made a civil rights complaint and Richard Oliver just dropped his lawsuit today—his lawyer must have told him that dragging this out will only let more skeletons pop out of his closet. And some of the brass are worried that we'll look bad if they drag me through the dirt after the mayor commended us on the case."

"You know they have other ways of making you miserable," Wills warned.

"Then I'll find something else."

"You're thinking of bailing?"

"I'm doing some soul-searching now."

"What about Alyson?" he asked. "She could mess up your

B.S."

My friendship with the family was something I never shared at the hearing. "She's got her own issues she needs to work through," I replied.

Alyson had believed Kanya was an unappreciative brat looking to spoil her meal ticket, and for that, she had to die. She justified the murder by saying she was putting her sister out of her misery, as if she were an old family dog that the vet needed to put to sleep.

But things changed after she realized Pete had manipulated her. I remembered watching Gresham interrogate her as she confessed in soft tones. Her eyes were blank, and she stared at the desk the entire time. Tears dripped down her face, but she never wiped them. She didn't mention my prior history with the family; I guessed she figured there was no need to make trouble for me. I never asked her why she kept quiet about it. I had nothing to say to her.

"You don't seem too worried," Jessica said.

"Too tired to worry." Between the betrayals of informants, friends, and lovers, and attempts to kill me, my emotional reservoir was dry.

Jessica smirked. "Lourne's getting soft, saving you like that."

Wills snorted. "He's ready for retirement. He doesn't care if they get mad at him. He wants to piss them off, anyway."

She leaned toward me. "Strick, you loved her, didn't you?"

I sipped my drink. "Wouldn't have worked."

"Why not?"

"She tried to kill me. Hard to trust someone after that."

Wills scooted a few feet from me. "Yeah, you've had people try to kill you three times in one night. If someone else wants to kill you, I don't want to catch a bullet meant for you."

Jessica chuckled. "I'm sure it was just a misunderstanding between you two, Strick. You going to visit her in prison?"

"Hell, no."

"Aw, give her a chance," she pleaded. "You'll never find anyone if you keep being so picky."

Her cell phone rang, rescuing me from another of her probing interrogations. She got out of the car for privacy, and Wills turned to me. "What happened to your CI? Didn't you say he set you up that night?"

"Yeah."

"So what are you going to do about it?"

"Nothing."

"You're going to let him get away with that?"

"It actually helped me. It's how I found the video that pieced everything together."

"So as a 'thank you', you're letting him go? You might as well send him some flowers."

"Flowers? No. But I heard he reconnected with some old friends."

"What do you mean?"

"He showed up here years ago after snitching on some buddies and high rollers in Cali. Now, I heard a rumor that someone made some calls recently to the Bay area and let them know where to find their old friend. He probably won't be seen around anymore."

"Hmm...I see. That 'somebody' wouldn't be you, would it?"

I shrugged. "Guess I'm in the market for another snitch."

"Damn," he said. "If I ever piss you off, give me a chance to make it right first. Let me ask you something else. Where's that money you took from DeVaughn? And don't tell me you don't have it. I saw you take that bag and make it rain for that mob."

"I don't have it."

"You do, too! No wonder you're so calm about everything. You don't care about the job; you're set."

"Wills, thousands of dollars doesn't qualify as being set."

"How much was it?"

"$35,000, but I don't have it."

"Well, you didn't turn it in! So what did you do with it? You'd better share the love, considering I saved your ass—"

"Wills, you won't believe me if I told you."

"Try me."

"I used some to get me another used car after DeVaughn shot the hell out of mine—and I had to pay extra to make the paperwork right. Then I used some to set up a college fund for DeVaughn's boy, and I gave the rest to a shelter for Women and Children in Kanya's name. It was what she planned to do."

Will shook his head as if he had a nervous tic. "You are the lying-est piece of s—"

"I told you that you wouldn't believe me."

"A college fund? That boy is going to hate cops when he grows up. He watched us shoot his father. You shot his damn dog. He's going to remember that forever. He might even come looking for us one day."

"Maybe a college education will send him down a different path."

"Yeah, let's make him a lawyer. Let's give him the tools to find ways to screw us royally one day, as part of his revenge tour." Wills rolled his eyes so hard that I thought they would pop out of his head. "A college fund. You sound like an after-school special. At least make your lies believable. And this woman's shelter? Please. You expect me to believe you didn't keep the rest after getting another ride? And why didn't you get insurance to cover your ride anyway?"

"I'm telling you, Wills, I didn't keep the money. There was a lot I could do with it, but I have an addictive personality. I start snatching dirty money and keeping it for myself, I won't stop. It'll get good to me. I got rid of that money before I found reasons to keep it. Besides, the cash was for the murder of a little girl I loved. I couldn't look at myself in the mirror if I kept it like that."

"You didn't think of giving me any? What the hell, man?"

"Sorry, bro. But it's not like I came out ahead. I'm right where I was before this happened. I might have upgraded my car with leather seats, but that's it."

Wills frowned. "Lourne is right. You don't fit in anywhere. You could've given me a couple grand, man."

I smiled. "You could've picked up some cash like everybody else when I made it rain. No one told you to run for your life."

He thrust his middle finger at me. "I would've at least gone to Hawaii for a couple of weeks. You're going to feel real stupid if you're suspended for a month without pay."

I wasn't that stupid. I kept enough to pay my mortgage for three months in case my appeal of the suspension was unsuccessful.

Jessica came back into the car. "Okay, Strick, where were we? You won't visit your girlfriend in prison, huh? You two made a cute couple."

"She was using me, Jess."

She shook her head. "From what you told me, I don't think so. After you gave her some Strick, she runs out of your house like a thief in the night? I think she fell for you and didn't know what to do. She sounds like one of those insecure, pretty-but-lonely types. Never learned how to have a relationship. She probably hadn't felt that way about a man before."

"Are you serious?" I asked.

She laughed. "Nah. She was just a crazy-ass, manipulative, nutcase."

For a second, I felt a hollow ache as I wondered what could have happened between Alyson and me under different circumstances. "I'm not thinking about her. You know who I feel sorry for? Her mother."

Jessica reared back. "Why?"

"What do you mean, 'why'? She lost her family, that's why. Her youngest daughter and her husband are dead, and her other daughter will be in prison for a long time. Don't you think that's a lot for someone to handle?"

"Oh, please," she spat.

"Woman, what is wrong with you?"

Jessica studied my face. "She's just as bad as her husband was. You can't see it because you got too close to them. You know I was in Sex Crimes before I came to Homicide. I saw hundreds of abuse cases. And if there is one thing I found out, it's this— when abuse like *that* goes on for that long, mothers know."

I shook my head, not liking the thought.

"Look," she said, "almost all of these sex crimes go on for years. But nothing happens in a vacuum. Every case I worked, there was someone who could've stopped it sooner if they stepped up. But they rarely do. They're screwed up, greedy, or afraid. They sweep it under the rug and hope no one notices. And some women can be awful. They don't want to ruin the family image. Some are so scared of being alone or giving up a lifestyle that they'll turn the other way when their kids suffer. You know this. And this Lorinda, she knew what was happening. Or she had a pretty damn good idea. Moms always know."

"How could a mother allow that?" I mumbled, trying not to admit that Jessica was speaking the truth.

"No one wants to believe her husband is a sick shit. She makes it personal and thinks it's a reflection on her. She asks herself *'If I love this man, what does it make me? What kind of person am I?'* No one wants to deal with that. It's easier not to acknowledge the truth. Or she may have just enjoyed the lifestyle that came with Pete. Let me ask—who was she married to before she met Pete? What did she do for a living?"

I didn't want to think about what Jessica was saying.

"Come on," she said. "Tell me."

"She was a housewife. Married to an ex-military guy."

"And what did he do?"

"He worked in a factory."

"Stop. I've seen this a hundred times. She's sick of the routine life. She finds Pete, a suave, ambitious guy who's going places. They hook up, and her life is so much better. But there's a problem. Her man likes screwing her little girl. That woman knew something was happening to her girl. No child is the same after something like that. She might not have known the details, but she should've sensed it. Mothers, we always have our antennas up. We worry even when nothing is wrong. Don't tell me she didn't notice something. I just think she didn't want to rock the boat. Hell, didn't you say she left Alyson behind in Michigan when she moved here? Why would she do that, unless she felt her relationship with Pete was more important? That tells you what was most important to her. Herself."

My last chili dog, which tasted okay a minute ago, suddenly turned nasty. My appetite had vanished after hearing Jessica's words.

I knew they were true.

CHAPTER 58

The next day, I stood in front of the oak door of Pete and Lorinda's house and took a deep breath.

Jessica's words burned a hole in my ears. Her implications echoed, repeating in my head:

Mothers know.

She didn't want to rock the boat.

She knew.

Alyson's relationship with her mother made me give credence to what Jessica said. Alyson did a poor job of hiding her disdain for Lorinda, which became more prevalent as I spent more time with her. Her recollection of her father's alcoholism and cigarette-burning abuse made it clear she blamed Lorinda for her plight, and watching her mother and Pete live in a luxurious home while spoiling Kanya intensified her feelings of abandonment. If Lorinda could overlook what Pete was doing to Kanya in their home, it was nothing for her to ignore what her ex-husband, Boyd, was subjecting Alyson to hundreds of miles away.

I touched the doorbell but didn't press it. A wave of second thoughts came to me. After a few seconds, I finally committed.

Lorinda answered the door. She appeared as if she hadn't slept for days, and her hair was tussled. "What do you want?"

"I came to see how you're doing."

"How *could* I be doing, Jeff?" she said abruptly. I sensed strong resentment from her. Kanya was gone. Her husband was dead. Alyson had sunk a butcher knife into his back and was scheduled for a long vacation in prison. I suspected that seeing my face refreshed her memory of those tragic events.

There was a tug-of-war inside me, one side tactfully trying to ask the burning question in my mind, the other seeking to go straight for the jugular.

I looked her in her eyes. "You knew about it, didn't you?"

"I knew about what?"

"What Pete was doing to Kanya. You knew. You may not have the known the details, but you knew something was up."

Lorinda shuddered, almost imperceptibly. She flared her nostrils, and her eyes became red. "How dare you ask me that!"

"How could you not do something?"

"W-w-what are you talking about?" she blurted, angling away from me. Her face was a mix of disgust and anguish.

"You couldn't help but notice something was wrong. We all overlooked it, but you shouldn't have. You did nothing to stop it. Why? Were you afraid? Or you just cared about your lifestyle more than your daughters?"

"Get out of here! How dare you?" Lorinda swung at me, but I sidestepped her. She shoved me off her doorstep and slammed the door behind me.

"You should visit your other daughter in prison and reconnect with her," I shouted at the door. "Maybe you can try giving a damn about your girls for once."

Did I go overboard?

I didn't care. It needed to be said. For Kanya and Alyson.

Ignoring the muffled sounds of Lorinda slumping against the door and sobbing, I turned and went to my car.

CHAPTER 59

It was a Wednesday evening and I sat in my car in the parking lot of the Life Metropolitan Church in Marietta. I had attended their night service, which had ended an hour ago, but I remained to savor some quiet time before my night shift started. It was surreal, me being within shouting distance of a church, but surviving three murder attempts in one night does wonders in making someone catch religion.

The events of the past week compelled me to step inside a church for the first time in years. But not just any church. Life Metropolitan was Pete's church. He had invited me frequently but I always found reasons not to go. It wasn't that I didn't believe in God. I just never felt the spirit like Pete or other people did.

I decided to attend this evening because I wanted to know what kind of preaching Pete had heard over the years. The messages apparently had no impact on him, for while he was professing his love for Jesus, he was sexually abusing one stepdaughter and cheating on his wife with another.

This Wednesday night sermon was about accepting God's plan, knowing one's purpose, and refraining from trying to understand why things happen, but instead, having faith things will work for the best. It was similar to the eulogy at Kanya's funeral. I went in knowing people could take the message of a sermon and make it applicable to them in some way, but it made the pastor's message no less effective. It grabbed me and demanded my attention.

Replaying the message in my head, I wondered about my purpose. If everyone had unique talents, what were mine?

Perhaps I was already using them. Maybe it wasn't a coincidence I was next on the rotation to grab Kanya's murder. Lourne once slipped up and admitted I was intelligent and tenacious, traits every good detective needed. Perhaps my strengths were the reason the case found itself on my desk. Or maybe it was a combination of my strengths plus my relationship with the family. Another investigator might not have gotten close enough to the family to discover their secret. He might have gone in another direction and never found the real reason behind Kanya's death. Maybe I was the only one to clear this.

Or maybe I was just blowing smoke up my ass. Someone else might've solved the case faster if a pre-existing relationship to the family hadn't thrown blinders on him. My turn in the rotation could've just been a coincidence.

I could never confirm it or get a direct answer, but I decided to believe God used me to find justice for Kanya and to make things right. I pictured her smiling down at me, content that I had been able to finally reveal the truth.

As for Pete, thinking of him made me feel like I crawled through a sewage pipe. He had abused my trust and friendship. I couldn't believe how well he had laid the guilt on me for nearly blowing the case with the release of the photos—he was probably smiling inside the entire time. I didn't want to think of the good times, encouraging words, and funny moments we had shared. Instead, I wanted to believe he was being punished eternally by the same sexual horrors he had put Kanya through.

I wasn't ready to attend a church regularly—one step at a time. But I did like picturing myself as an enforcer of the 6th commandment—the law declaring that people shalt not kill, a rule some Atlantans had trouble following. Maybe my purpose was making sure that those who violated that commandment faced the consequences.

The job of a homicide detective had a high burnout rate. Lourne loved telling struggling detectives that the job wasn't for everyone. While he seemed to delight in kicking poor performers off his team, his statement was true. It took smarts, a strong stomach, a macabre sense of humor, the ability to compartmentalize, and stubbornness to plod forward. That described me, for the most part. And after I almost died three times over, I had to add 'blessed' and 'lucky' to that list.

My cell phone buzzed. Dispatch had routed a call from Officer Bagley, the prepubescent rookie who first responded to Kanya's murder. He was presiding over a new murder for me—a deceased black male, found lying outside the Markham Homes project in South Atlanta.

I started the car, turned to a jazz station, and looked at the night sky. God was calling me to find the latest perp who had broken that 6th commandment.

It was time to kick ass.

Time to use my gifts to find and punish the guilty.

Time to start the cycle all over again.

Made in the USA
Monee, IL
17 January 2023

25517331R00197